"This book hooked me immediately with Wendy's voice and rage and longing... what Wise does with the Peter Pan mythos here is nothing short of astonishing"
    Sam J. Miller, Nebula Award-winning author of *Blackfish City*

"A dark and delightful retelling of Peter Pan. *Wendy, Darling* is a gorgeous achievement, and one you don't want to miss"
    Gwendolyn Kiste, Bram Stoker Award-winning author of *The Rust Maidens*

"*Wendy, Darling* is a daring, gothic re-envisioning of everything we think we know – and an important, vivid adventure"
    Fran Wilde, two-time Nebula award-winning, World Fantasy finalist author of *Updraft*

"Richly imagined, surprisingly dark, and heartbreakingly beautiful, this daring reimagining doesn't only revisit the myth, it brings it up to date"
    Marian Womack, author of *The Swimmers*

WENDY,
DARLING

WENDY DARLING

A. C. WISE

TITAN BOOKS

Wendy, Darling
Print edition ISBN: 9781789096811
E-book edition ISBN: 9781789096828

Published by Titan Books
A division of Titan Publishing Group Ltd.
144 Southwark Street, London SE1 0UP
www.titanbooks.com

First edition June 2021
10 9 8 7 6 5 4 3

A CIP catalogue record for this title is available from the British Library.

Printed and bound by CPI Group (UK) Ltd, Croydon CR0 4YY

For everyone who has ever dreamed of flying

DARLING

There is a boy outside her daughter's window.

Wendy feels it, like a trickle of starlight whispering in through a gap, a change in the very pressure and composition of the air. She knows, as sure as her own blood and bones, and the knowledge sends her running. Her hairbrush clatters to the floor in her wake; her bare feet fly over carpeted runners and slap wooden floorboards, past her husband's room and to her daughter's door.

It is not just any boy, it's *the* boy. Peter.

Every inch of her skin wakes and crawls; the fine hairs all along the back of her neck stand on end—the storm secreted between her bones for years finally breaking wide. Peter. Here. Now. After so long.

She wants to shout, but she doesn't know what words, and as Wendy skids to a halt, her teeth are bared. It isn't a grimace or a smile, but a kind of animal breathing, panicked and wild.

Jane's door stands open a crack. A sliver of moonlight— unnaturally bright, as if carried to London from Neverland— spills across the floor. It touches Wendy's toes as she peers through the gap, unable for a moment to step inside.

Even though she's still, her pulse runs rabbit-quick. Backlit against that too-bright light is the familiar silhouette: a slender boy with his fists planted on his hips, chest puffed out and chin tipped up, his hair wild. There is no mistaking Peter as he hovers just beyond the second-floor window. She blinks, and the image remains, not vanishing like every other dream stretched between now and then. Between the girl she was and the woman she's become.

Of course, Wendy thinks, because this may not be the house she grew up in, but it's still her home. Of course he would find her, and of course he would find her *now*. Bitterness chases the thought—here and now, after so long.

At the same time, she thinks *no, no, please no*, but too-long fingers already tap the glass. Without waiting for her say-so, the window swings wide. Peter enters, and Wendy's heart swoops first, then falls and falls and falls.

Once invited, always welcome—that's his way.

Peter doesn't notice Wendy as she pushes the hall door open all the way. He flies a circle around the ceiling, and she wills her daughter to stay asleep, wills her tongue to uncurl from the roof of her mouth. Her legs tremble, holding her on the threshold, wanting to fold and drop her to the floor. It's such an easy thing for him to enter, and yet her own body betrays her, refusing to take one step into her daughter's room, in her own house.

It's unfair. Everything about Peter always was, and it hasn't changed. After years of her wanting and waiting, lying and hoping, he's finally here.

And he isn't here for her.

Peter lands at the foot of Jane's bed. The covers barely dimple

10

under his weight, a boy in form, but hollow all the way through. Maybe it's the motion, or the light spearing in from the hall behind Wendy, but Jane half-wakes, rubbing at her eyes. A shout of warning locks in Wendy's throat.

"Wendy," Peter says.

Hearing him say her name, Wendy is a child again, toes lifting from the ground, taking flight, about to set off on a grand and delicious adventure. Except he's not looking at her, he's looking at Jane. Wendy bites the inside of her cheek, bites down in place of a scream. Does he have any idea how long it's been? Swallowing the red-salt taste of her blood finally unlocks her throat.

"Peter. I'm here." It isn't the shout she wishes, only a half-whispered and ragged thing.

Peter turns, his eyes bright as the moonlight behind him. They narrow. Suspicion first, then a frown.

"Liar," he says, bold and sure. "You're not Wendy."

He makes as if to point at Jane, evidence, but Wendy's answer stops him.

"I am." Does he hear the quaver, as much as she tries to hold her voice steady?

She should call Ned, her husband, downstairs in his study, either so absorbed in his books or asleep over them as to be oblivious to her flight down the hall. It is what a sensible person would do. There's an intruder in their home, in their daughter's room. Jane is in danger. Wendy swallows, facing Peter alone.

"It's me, Peter. I grew up."

Peter's expression turns into a sneer, Jane forgotten, all his attention on Wendy now. Jane looks in confusion between them. Wendy wants to tell her daughter to run. She wants to tell her to go back to sleep; it's only a dream. But the mocking edge in Peter's voice needles her, pulling her focus away.

"What'd you go do that for?"

Wendy's skin prickles again, hot and cold. The set of his mouth, arrogant as ever, the flicker-brightness of his eyes daring her to adventure, daring her to defy his word-as-law.

"It happens." Wendy's voice steadies, anger edging out fear. "To most of us, at least."

Peter. Here. Real. Not a wild dream held as armor against the world. The years unspool around her as Wendy finally manages to step fully into her daughter's room. And that armor, polished and patched and fastened tight over the years, cracks. For a terrible moment, Jane is forgotten. Wendy is a creature made all of want, aching for the cold expression to melt from Peter's face, aching for her friend to take her hand and ask her to fly away with him.

But his hand remains planted firmly on his hip, chin tilted so he can look down at her from his perch on the bed. Wendy takes a second step, and her armor is back in place. She takes a third step, and anger churns stronger than desire—dark water trapped beneath a thick layer of ice.

Wendy clamps her arms by her side, refusing to let one turn traitor and reach toward Peter. She is no longer the heartbroken girl left behind. She is what she has made of herself over the years. She held onto the truth, even when Michael and John forgot. She survived being put away for her delusions, survived the injections, calmatives, and water cures meant to save her from herself. She fought, never stopped fighting; she refused to let Neverland go.

12

It's been eleven years since St. Bernadette's, with its iron fences and high walls, full of frowning nurses and cruel attendants. A place meant to make her better, to cure her, though Wendy knows she was never sick at all. And here is the proof, standing before her, on the end of her daughter's bed.

Wendy straightens, hardening the line of her jaw, and meets Peter's eye. In the last eleven years she's built a life for herself, for her husband and her daughter. She is not that lost and aching girl, and Peter has no power over the Wendy she's become.

"Peter—" Wendy hears her own voice, stern, admonishing. The voice of a mother, but not the kind Peter ever wanted her to be.

Before she can get any farther, Peter shakes his head, a single sharp motion, dislodging her words like a buzzing gnat circling him. His expression is simultaneously bored and annoyed.

"You're no fun." He spins as he says it, a fluid, elegant motion. Peter blurs, and Wendy thinks he's about to leave, but instead he seizes Jane's hand. "Never mind. I'll take this Wendy instead."

Peter leaps, yanking Jane into the air. Jane lets out a startled cry, and Wendy echoes it—a truncated burst of sound. She isn't quick enough to close the space between them as Peter dives for the window, Jane in tow. Instead, Wendy falls forward, bashing her knee painfully and catching herself on the window sill.

Wendy's fingertips brush Jane's heel and close on empty air. Peter spirals into the night, a cock's crow trailing in his wake, so familiar, so terrible it overwhelms her. Wendy doesn't hear if her daughter calls for her; the only sound in the world is the ringing echo of Peter's call as two child-sized figures disappear against a field of stars.

"What is this place?" Wendy asks as the hired car comes to a halt outside a massive iron gate surrounded by a dense green hedge too tall to see over.

Visible through the gate, a long path of crushed stone leads to an imposing building, brick facade and blank-eyed windows glaring out at them. John sighs, his voice tight.

"This is St. Bernadette's, Wendy."

John doesn't wait for the driver. He opens his door and circles to open Wendy's as well, taking her arm either to help her or keep her from running away.

"We spoke about this, and Dr. Harrington, remember? He's going to help you get well."

Wendy bites the inside of her cheek; of course she remembers. Her brothers are the forgetful ones; all she can do is remember. But the bitter, petty part of her wants to make this as difficult as possible for John. She wants to make him explain it over and over again, how he plans to leave her here, wash his hands of his mad sister. What would their parents think? If Mama and Papa had never boarded that cursed ship, the one meant to be unsinkable until it met an iceberg, would they allow John and Michael to treat her this way? She's thrown that very question at him more than once, watching his face crumple and taking delight in it. Yet, through it all, her brother's resolve hasn't wavered.

Lines gather around John's mouth, the same expression he wore as a child, always trying to be so serious and grown up. Only in Neverland had Wendy ever seen him truly be a little boy. Playing follow the leader, chasing Peter through the treetops, flying. Why would he ever want to forget that and leave it behind?

She studies John in profile as they approach the gate, the way the sun highlights the proud line of his nose, the firm set of his jaw, catching in his glasses and erasing his eyes. His poor vision had kept him from the war, but so many other burdens—herself included—had fallen on him instead. He's still young, twenty-one, and just barely a man now, but already his shoulders stoop, carrying the weight of years of a man twice his age.

He must feel her watching, but he doesn't look her way. The ache in Wendy's chest is replaced by the first edging-in of panic. John truly means to go through with this; he means to have her committed.

She pushes the trapped-bird flutter down as the gate clanks open, guided by a man in a white uniform, his expression stoic. John looks briefly pained, and for a moment, Wendy considers relenting. At least he had the decency to see her imprisoned in person. Michael refused to accompany her. But why would he? The way she treated him was the final straw that forced John's hand. She screamed at her baby brother, she hurt him when he was already so fragile after coming home from the war, broken in body and broken in soul. John had no choice—he's sending her away for her own protection, and even more so for Michael's.

Wendy looks away from her brother, from the man in white, her throat suddenly thick. If she keeps looking at John she will break, and she's determined to be jailed with her head held high.

She focuses on the grounds to distract herself. Once upon a time, this place would have been a fine country estate, and it still looks the part. On either side of the path, emerald-bright lawns stretch away to the iron-laced hedges in front, and high stone walls on the three other sides. There are flower beds and shade-giving trees, croquet hoops staked into the grass, and small groupings of tables and chairs. It's almost idyllic. Here, she could forget the rest of the world is at war. She could—if she were to allow herself—forget that St. Bernadette's is a cage, but that's something she never intends to do.

Despite her best efforts, panic spreads, blood beneath the skin turning to a bruise. Should she try one more time to explain herself? If she lies convincingly enough, perhaps John will let her stay home and help with Michael. His leg still pains him, a lingering effect of the shrapnel that tore it apart, but the dreams are worse. Wendy and John have both woken to the sounds of Michael's troubled sleep, believing himself back in the trenches, or in the base hospital awaiting another surgery before finally being sent home. If she could encourage him in his therapy, and be there to soothe the memories and vision away, maybe Michael himself would even forgive her in time.

But, no, she's out of chances. John and Michael may not see it, but she *did* try. And she failed. After their parents' deaths, she tried to be a mother, keep everyone fed and clothed. A disinterested uncle had come to stay with them, a guardian in name only. Their mother's brother, a man Wendy had met only once as a very young child. He had done only the bare minimum required of him to look after their welfare; all else had fallen to Wendy, John, and Michael themselves. John, always so serious, had done his best to become the man of the house, taking all the responsibility onto his shoulders that he could, losing even more of his childhood in the process. If any bit of Neverland had remained in his mind, it vanished then. So young, and yet too old for silly stories and games, for make-believe.

None of them had taken time for grief. It hadn't been afforded to them. Their uncle certainly had no interest in giving space to their sorrow; any display of emotion at all was considered unseemly. Then Michael had gone to war and come home broken. And the silences that stretched between her and John, between all of them, had grown worse.

She should have kept to those silences, but the truth came bursting out. Watching her brothers suffer—John with the weight of the world on his shoulders, Michael with his eyes full of ghosts—Wendy couldn't hold her tongue. With John of age to truly become the man of the house, and their uncle finally gone, she'd wanted to remind them of happier times, or so she'd told herself. Only instead of speaking reasonably, she'd shouted. Lashing out, insisting they see the world her way, refusing to listen. The more they'd resisted her, the more she'd kept on shouting. Until she couldn't see her way clear to stopping, couldn't find her way back home to common ground.

Anger became her habit, Neverland her defense. The more they'd tried to draw her out, the further she'd retreated into their shared past, to save herself from their denial, to save Neverland itself, as determined to remember it as John and Michael were to forget. No, John might as well ask her to cut off a limb; she wouldn't be able to do that either. She cannot, and will not, deny Neverland. Even now.

Wendy stiffens as Dr. Harrington, impeccably dressed as always, walks down the path to join them. She keeps her gaze on his polished shoes, timing her breath to his steps. White stone crunches beneath his soles; his watch chain bounces, glittering

17

with his motion. Anything to avoid looking into his eyes, into the face of the man who will be her jailor for who knows how long.

Even when the footsteps stop, Wendy keeps her chin tucked down. The uniformed man who opened the gate lines his shoes up—far more scuffed and plain—just behind Dr. Harrington's bright ones. His place at Dr. Harrington's shoulder is a subtle threat, and despite herself, Wendy looks up. The uniformed man stands a good head taller than Dr. Harrington. There's a squareness to him, his shoulders broad, his hair cut neat and close. She wonders why he isn't overseas, fighting.

There's a name stitched over the man's breast pocket—*Jamieson*. He catches her looking and his mouth twists, the expression an ugly one. Wendy starts, a fresh thrill of fear going through her. She has done nothing to this man, and yet Jamieson looks at her as though he wants to do her harm. She knew boys like him in Neverland, bullies following at Peter's heels, but held in check by the brightness of his games. To Jamieson, she is a wild animal to be muzzled and chained at the slightest excuse. A yearling to be broken if she refuses the saddle.

"Mr. Darling." Dr. Harrington extends his hand to John, breaking Wendy from her dark thoughts.

Bitterness rises in her all over again, fear momentarily forgotten. Dr. Harrington and John shake hands, so civilized—neither of them looking at her—as though she were a mere business agreement, not a patient or a beloved sister. And all the while, John still has his other hand on her arm. She pulls away roughly.

"I am perfectly capable of walking on my own." The words snap, and she steps away from her brother; more pettiness. All three men watch her, as if she might turn into a bird and fly away.

Wendy lifts her chin, but does not look at any of them. She won't even say goodbye. Let that sit on John's conscience. Without leave, she walks past Dr. Harrington toward St. Bernadette's front doors. If this is to be her fate, she'll go to it on her own, not dragged or guided. Her boot heels strike hard against the crushed stone even though her legs tremble beneath her skirt, but she refuses to slow or give in.

"Wendy!" John's footsteps scuff the path behind her.

It puts even more resolve into her step, and Wendy quickens her pace. She doesn't turn, doesn't stop, and hears Dr. Harrington intercept her brother, his voice smooth and practiced, used to soothing patients.

"Perhaps it's better this way, Mr. Darling. Your sister is in good hands here. Once she's had a chance to settle, you can visit her, of course." Implied is that Wendy will be more docile then. There isn't a speck of doubt in Dr. Harrington's voice—he will see her cured.

Despite herself, Wendy's shoulders hunch. Dr. Harrington's words grate, his tone scraping at her, through flesh to bone. She wants to turn and pummel him, closed fists against his shoulders and chest, but she forces her arms to hang loose at her sides. She's broken more plates and cups in her rages at Michael and John than she cares to count. For once, she must keep her temper under control.

"Miss Darling." Dr. Harrington catches up to her, Jamieson still shadowing him. Wendy doesn't turn to see if John remains on the path, watching. "Allow me to show you to your room."

Dr. Harrington says the words as though she is a guest, free to leave whenever she wants.

"I think you will find it most amenable here. Our staff and facilities are excellent. The only thing we want in this world is to make you well."

Wendy's mouth opens, but no sound emerges. Somehow, they've reached the end of the path, climbed the steps. The door frames them. Dr. Harrington takes her arm. Jamieson stands behind him. Even if she were to pull free, there is nowhere to run.

"This way."

In her determination and pride, she's walked herself right into the trap, and now it's ready to snap closed behind her. It's too late. One more step, and Wendy crosses the threshold. The air changes immediately, heavy and dim. Wendy feels the loss of the sky overhead like a stolen breath. She hadn't realized how much comfort she'd been drawing from that perfect stretch of blue.

She glances to the ceiling, pressed tin, hung with a chandelier. Rich carpets in patterned jeweled tones cover the floor of the entryway, lovely but worn. A few steps in, and the ceiling gives way to a high, open space. Curved staircases at either end of the foyer sweep up to a balcony that overlooks the ground floor. A stained-glass window lets through light, but its quality tells Wendy it doesn't look onto the outside. Everything here is enclosed, safe, but false.

Dr. Harrington leads her past a reception desk without even a glance at the woman in a nurse's uniform seated there. The woman doesn't glance up either, and Wendy suppresses a shiver at the coldness of it all. She is merely a transaction, one of how many patients marched through the doors because they are inconvenient to their families, or worse, actually sick. Is there anything in this place to heal them?

Wendy tries to take in more of her surroundings, but Dr. Harrington speeds his pace, taking her past a common room with large windows overlooking the garden, and a smaller interior room where two nurses rest their feet. They turn a corner. The air changes again, and Wendy feels it immediately—a transition from the old country estate house to a newly constructed wing.

Fresh panic gnaws at her, and this time it refuses to be tamped down. The hallway stretched before her is plain, and there is nothing hospitable about it—all pretenses dropped. This is not a country estate, a place where people come to rest and get well. It is a place where people are locked away. Where patients scream and no one answers.

Doors line the hallway, set with small glass windows. More twists and turns carry her over gleaming checkerboard tiles. Wendy feels numb, dizzy. They pass larger doors spaced further apart. Medical facilities, treatment rooms. The size of the building eludes her; she can't hold a picture of the whole in her mind.

"Please, Dr. Harrington—" Wendy's voice emerges breathless, a weakness she would rather not admit but can't help. Something in this place presses down on her, and she gulps for air.

And then she stops, the full weight of her body holding her in place despite Dr. Harrington's hand on her arm. A girl with long, dark hair passes, going the opposite direction, head down so Wendy can't see her face properly. Even so, the sight of her strikes Wendy as a physical blow, and a name rises to her lips so swift she almost speaks it aloud—*Tiger Lily*.

She's sworn to herself to keep Neverland secret here, to guard it close to her chest. Whatever John has told Dr. Harrington can only be half of the truth at best. If Wendy were to tell him anything real, Dr. Harrington would only take to it with a microscope and a scalpel, turning it into something ugly. So she swallows down Tiger Lily's name, even though it burns, looking away as the girl walks past.

As much as she might wish it otherwise though, her mind rebels. She can't help recalling a bank of emerald grass beneath the silver drooping bows of a willow tree. Locked away from all the world, she and Tiger Lily wove crowns of reed, linked their hands together—brown and white—and set the crowns on each other's heads.

The memory aches. She can't stop herself from glancing up, but the girl has already moved down the hallway. The loss in her wake makes it hard for Wendy to breathe, but she forces herself to keep going. Dr. Harrington looks at her, a frown of disapproval that she has upset the natural order of things.

The girl isn't Tiger Lily. She knows that, and to distract herself, Wendy tries to reconstruct the girl's actual appearance from that brief glance, and after a moment, she convinces herself that the girl doesn't resemble Tiger Lily at all. It was only her mind playing tricks, wanting something familiar in this place of terror, something that felt like home.

"Here we are." Dr. Harrington's voice, falsely bright and sharp-edged, brings her back.

He opens a door, unlocking it swiftly and dropping the key into his pocket as though Wendy won't notice. The opened door reveals a spare, cell-like room, purpose-built with white-painted walls, a narrow bed, and a single chair. The window has no curtains, and on the outside there are bars.

"We have what we like to think of as patient uniforms here." Dr. Harrington smiles.

The expression is awkward, as though he's letting Wendy in on a joke.

"Everyone here is equal, no matter where they began. They are all here to get well."

He gestures to a plain cotton dress folded atop the bed, nearly the same pale gray as the blanket it lies upon. The girl they passed in the hall, the one who isn't Tiger Lily, wore the same.

With his next words, Dr. Harrington's tone shifts, all efficiency, dropping the welcoming pretense that Wendy is merely a guest. He speaks by rote, addressing a patient whose individual wants and concerns he means to dismiss, and leaves no space for Wendy to respond.

"A nurse will be along shortly to help you change, and your own clothing will be stored for safekeeping. Your door will be locked at night until you are acclimated. This is for your safety, of course. Meals are served in the dining hall, unless extenuating circumstances dictate otherwise. During your first few days you will be brought meals in your room, again, until you adjust."

Before she can question what extenuating circumstances might be, Dr. Harrington pats Wendy's hand, his expression warm and fatherly again. The gesture, she presumes, is meant to be reassuring. It is anything but.

She keeps her lips firmly over her teeth, hiding them. She wants to snarl. She wants to run. She wants to break and fold into herself—abandoned, doubted, disbelieved. She does none of these things, standing still with her hands clasped before her as Dr. Harrington withdraws. The door closes and she hears the tell-tale scrape of a key in the lock.

Silence fills up the corners of the room, a pressure against her skin. Wendy sits on the edge of the bed. Springs poke through the thinness of the mattress. There is a finality to the stillness.

She has no love for the particular dress she's wearing, but the thought that she'll have to give it up for the shapeless gray uniform beside her makes her want to scream. The fact that she will not even be trusted to change her own clothing, like an unruly child, is even worse. She fingers the cuffs of her sleeves, touches the rough woolen blanket, trying to let the simple feel of the fabric ground her. It does nothing.

She breathes, focusing on the movement of her ribs, the expansion of air in her lungs. All of this is only a test. Tomorrow, John and Michael will bring her home. She'll learn to behave. No more broken plates. No more tantrums.

Deep down, Wendy knows John and Michael aren't coming for her. At least not until she proves she can behave, until Dr. Harrington deems her well. And if that never occurs? If John decides it is more convenient to forget one more thing from his childhood, and leave her safely locked away? Through the bars on the window, the sky is brutalized, chopped into neat sections. No one is coming for her. No one at all. Not even…

The weight is too much. Wendy snatches the pillow from the bed and crushes it against her mouth. She gasps air in shallow breaths, each growing more ragged until her lungs threaten to burst.

Then into the terrible silence around her, pillow-muffled, full of fear and rage, Wendy Darling screams.

24

Wendy returns to Jane's window. The inspectors from Scotland Yard have come and gone. For hours her house has been filled with men's voices—their rough laughter when they were unaware of her listening, their questions that she can give no answers to, the stink of tobacco clinging to their uniforms and skin. She hates every last one of them. Now, only her father-in-law remains, and she hates him most of all.

Ned's father arrived with the inspectors, without Wendy or Ned having spoken to him about what occurred. Wendy can't help but believe that her father-in-law arranged with the chief inspector—a personal friend—that he would be contacted immediately should any emergency calls originate from their house. Anger simmers beneath her weariness, made worse by the fact that she can say none of this aloud. Silently, she curses her father-in-law, and curses Scotland Yard for spineless cowardice.

As if she and Ned are insufficient on their own to keep their household safe. The thought brings bitter laughter, but Wendy traps it behind her lips. Oh, but she *is* insufficient. The knowledge twists blade-sharp, stealing her breath. She lost Jane. She let Peter steal her daughter away.

Wendy knots her fingers, staring at the darkened streets beyond Jane's window. She is tired to the bone, and at the same time, sleep is the farthest thing from her mind. The inspectors and her father-in-law asked her dozens of questions, then asked them all over again to Ned. As if by virtue of his sex he must know more than she ever could. And all the while, questioning or silent, her father-in-law had glared at them both.

Untangling her fingers, Wendy wraps her arms around her upper body, holding onto her elbows to keep from flying apart.

She lied. To the men from Scotland Yard. To her father-in-law. Even to Ned. She told them she simply woke—a mother's instinct—and came to her daughter's room to find her gone. The aftertaste of dishonesty lies thick on her tongue. But what else could she say?

She's been lying to Ned for years, withholding this one vital piece of truth. For eleven years she's played at being a good wife, a good mother; there have been days she's even managed to convince herself. But now it's all falling apart, as much of a sham as her mothering of Peter and the boys in Neverland.

She chose this, she tried, and still she failed. It takes everything in Wendy not to shout, to hurl everything she can lay her hands on and scream the truth until her throat bleeds. She is not, and will not, ever be good enough for anything but lies and make-believe.

She leaves the window, pacing through Jane's room. Her fingers trail over butterflies carefully pinned under glass, over collections of rocks and seashells and leaves, all held in cases of their own. Jane's books. The globe atop her shelf, marked with pins for all the places her daughter wanted to visit. Of all those lands she dreamed of, Jane couldn't have pictured Neverland. Wendy should have warned her. She should have…

Wendy lifts a butterfly case. The label is written in Jane's neat hand—neater than Wendy's ever was at her age. Holly blue, *Celastrina argiolus*. Jane caught it on the holiday they took in Northumberland, so excited she'd clutched the jar like a treasure all the way home.

The memory tightens Wendy's throat, threatening her with tears. She wants to smash the case, smash everything in the room. Instead, she sets the glassed-in butterfly down as gently as she can.

"Come away, darling." Ned touches her shoulder.

Wendy jumps. She never heard him enter. How long has she been standing here, staring? His hand is warm and strong on her shoulder and she wants to shrug him away, but she forces herself to turn.

Tiny threads of crimson in Ned's eyes mark his own grief, and the tightness in his posture is unmistakable. Beneath his neatly trimmed moustache, his lips press a thin line. He's as afraid for Jane as she is, maybe more so, because he understands even less of what's going on. She should tell him. She should, but she won't.

"Where's Mary?" The words emerge sharp, in place of comfort.

Wendy hates herself, but even so she can't stop herself from looking past Ned's shoulder as if Mary might appear in the doorway carrying a tray laden with tea. Her pulse catches. Her father-in-law stands there instead, light from the hallway transforming him into an imposing blot of shadow.

"I sent *Cook* home." Ned stresses Mary's title, his tone matched to hers.

Wendy hears the brittleness under it, but she straightens, stepping back an inch as if too much closeness, even between husband and wife at a time like this, might be improper somehow. She cannot see her father-in-law's face for the light behind him, but she imagines his frown. Wendy knows his opinion of Mary, and she knows it isn't one Ned shares. Under normal circumstances, he never would have sent her home. He would call

27

her Mary, rather than Cook, and he might be the one to make tea for all three of them as they shared their worries over Jane. But as long as Ned's father is here, none of that matters.

To her father-in-law, Mary is that *girl*—always emphasizing the word. *A bad influence on your household*, and by that, Wendy knows he means a bad influence on her. *You know how their kind are*. And those are only the words he's spoken in her hearing. To Ned, Wendy knows he's said far worse, calling Mary *savage* and *heathen*, *dangerous* and *untrustworthy*. Only Ned's steady touch, his calm, has kept her from lashing out at her father-in-law and forbidding him from ever setting foot in her home again. Not that she could. Despite everything she has worked to build for herself in the past eleven years, so much of Wendy's life is by her father-in-law's grace alone.

In addition to being Ned's father, he is Ned's employer, and John's. She suspects, though her brother refuses to speak to her candidly on the matter, that John is indebted to him financially. There was a time, before he began working for Ned's father, when John put his trust in the wrong man, investing money their parents had left them in what appeared to be a promising business venture, thinking himself a grown man when he was still so young.

Most of this Wendy has gleaned from overheard snatches of conversation, snooping and sleuthing on her own. Any time she's asked directly, her brother always steers the conversation away, telling her business dealings are not a woman's concern.

It's more than that though. A delicate balance exists between Ned and his father, and thus between her and Ned's father, and even her and Ned—one she is still trying to understand.

Ned fears his father's disapproval, and he craves his respect, craving it all the more fiercely every time it is withheld. Despite everything, despite the man Wendy knows Ned to be deep down, part of her husband still longs to be his father's image of what a man should be. Thus his bluster before Scotland Yard, thus his acquiescence to every one of his father's rules. It is an irony Ned doesn't seem to realize. His father respects strength, yet Ned remains cowed. What would happen, she wonders, if he stood up for himself, if he demanded respect for who he is, and not who his father wants him to be?

"Of course," Wendy says. "Very proper."

She hears the frost in her voice, swallows around it like a lump of ice in her throat. Ned flinches, the slightest of motions. Is it from her, or from resisting glancing at his father? His eyes find Wendy's, begging her for patience, even now, when their daughter is missing.

He's hurting, as unhappy about his father's presence as Wendy, but they must keep up the facade. Wendy knows. She understands. But her daughter is missing. Peter stole Jane from her very bed, and every moment her father-in-law spends here, every moment they play pretend, is a moment she could be out there saving Jane.

Wendy almost lays a hand on Ned's chest. It would be a small gesture of appreciation, a bridge between them, a sharing and lightening of their burden, but she can't help the anger rising and rising in her like a tide. She lets her hand fall. It's her father-in-law she hates, but Ned is closer. And even if he was only bowing to his father's pressure, Ned is ultimately the one who sent Mary away.

She imagines Mary arguing, Ned insisting with hurt in his eyes, and now Mary sitting alone in her tiny rented room. Mary is the only person who might understand. Wendy can't speak to John or Michael, and even if she undid years of lies and told Ned where Jane is, would he believe her?

Her fingers curl into the fabric of her skirt, bunching it into a fist before she forces herself to let go. She won't lay a hand on Ned's chest to comfort him, but she won't lash out either. In this moment, it's all she can do.

Movement draws Wendy's eye, Ned's father shaking his head before he withdraws. Footsteps echo in the hall, pointed as he descends the stairs. Wendy bows her head, still keeping the space between herself and her husband. Ned's shoulders hunch. Each footfall is a frown, a harshly spoken word. Then eventually the front door opens, and closes, and they both slump without moving closer together.

When Wendy does look up, she finds Ned watching her as if she might shatter, the pieces of her embedding themselves in his skin. Wendy presses her lips into a close line. If she speaks, if she says anything at all, she might blurt out the truth. She knows the bluster Ned put on in front of the men from Scotland Yard was all for his father's benefit, acting the masterful head of his household with no time for the nonsense of women. She shouldn't resent him for it, but she can't quite forgive him either. It's unfair, expecting his trust and support when she hasn't given it in return. But she can't be that bridge. Not now. Not while her daughter is gone. The kindest thing she can do is withdraw.

"I'm tired," she murmurs, looking down.

If she looks up, she'll see the hurt in his eyes, all the truths she's failed to tell him. When he answers her, Ned's voice is strained, as though still performing for her father-in-law.

"Of course, darling. You should rest."

Wendy dips her head. She doesn't intend to look up as she steps past him, but Ned touches her arm.

"The inspectors are doing everything they can. They'll find Jane and bring her home."

Despite her better judgment, Wendy meets her husband's eyes. The loss in them is dizzying, threatening to break her all over again. The stutter—nearly vanished in the eleven years she's known him—betrays itself when he speaks, a sign of his exhaustion. She should say something kind, reassure him, but she's already wasted too much time. She needs to go after Jane, and she can't do that with Ned watching over her. Wendy pinches the inside of her arms to keep them crossed.

"Of course." Her jaw aches with holding back words. "You're right. The police will take care of everything. I'll go rest. You'll fetch me if you hear anything?"

She says it knowing there will be nothing to hear. Scotland Yard won't find Jane. Only Wendy herself can do that. By the time Ned comes looking for her, she'll be long gone.

"Yes, darling. Of course I will." Ned kisses her brow. Wendy stands perfectly still; his lips on her forehead burn.

Darling, darling, darling. She knows the word for fondness, knows Ned means nothing by it, but she can't help loathing it. The word has become a weapon, not in Ned's mouth, not on purpose, but over the years it's been a word to soothe, to dismiss, to hush. Her own name taken from her and turned against her—a gag, a chain. She would be happy never to hear it again.

With Ned still looking after her, and guilt dogging her steps, Wendy retreats to her room.

She allows herself a moment to sag, to feel the ache of Jane's loss. As she does, a memory drops from nowhere, jarring and sharp. She's running, her hand in Peter's hand, the ground shaking, the earth bellowing.

It's so real, so present, Wendy has to lean her weight against the post of her bed to remind herself she's a grown woman in London. She isn't a child, tagging along at Peter's heels. There's a lifetime of difference between who she was then and who she is now.

And yet over the years, in the quietest moments, she's allowed herself the indulgence of remembering what it felt like to fly, to play follow the leader, to chase Peter along the twisting paths of Neverland's forests. She wants that now, the purity, the simplicity, the freedom.

But this is something different. Not running for joy—running *from* something. Something terrible.

She can almost touch it. Her reaching fingers meet solid wood, a door, the memory locked away behind it. Something secret. Important.

She pushes it away. Now isn't the time to think about what she's lost. She needs to focus on what she has, how she will rescue Jane. Peter stole from her; she will steal from him in turn. She's learned a great many things since he last saw her, and she will use every one of them against him to bring her daughter home.

Peter told her once that girls couldn't go to war. Back then, she'd thought it terribly unfair, but he was right in a way. Wendy isn't a soldier. She stayed home while her little brother went off to face guns and trenches, gas and grenades—but that doesn't mean she isn't a fighter. More than a fighter, she's a survivor as well.

She survived St. Bernadette's using the first skill that ever made her useful to Peter. That must count for something. As a child, her sewing was clumsy, but thanks to Mary's patient instruction, she's so much better now. Three years under Mary's guidance with nothing else to do in that white-walled prison except practice making her stitches neat and tight.

Here, in the outside world, pockets are a convenience, a luxury; in the asylum, they were a necessity. Mary taught her to sew small, secret compartments into the hems and sleeves of her shapeless uniform, quick stitches strong enough to hold but easy enough to unpick so they wouldn't be discovered in the laundry; invisible from the outside, tucked close against her skin. Sometimes merely touching them, even if they were empty, just knowing they were there, was enough to keep Wendy steady, anchoring her.

John had believed a private institution would mean better care. But Dr. Harrington had been the only full-time doctor in residence, and with less oversight, it was easy for the attendants to practice casual cruelty. Jamieson especially.

If Dr. Harrington's attention was elsewhere, Jamieson would rally his fellow attendants against Wendy. They would trip her walking through the hallways, trying to loosen her temper, make her "hysterical," so Dr. Harrington would prescribe bromides or have her locked in her room. There, they might "forget" to feed her, or her food would arrive with splinters or bits of broken glass tucked inside. And there were other things, too. Punishments she didn't deserve. Torture.

But for every cruelty dealt to her, Wendy had retaliated. She stole unimportant things. Buttons. Shoelaces. Half a tin of loose tobacco leaf, a whole stack of rolling papers. Everything went into her secret pockets while she hid her smiles, watching the attendants grumble and search fruitlessly. Then she would return the stolen item days later, in a different place, making the attendants doubt their sanity the way they tried to make her doubt her own.

And never once was she caught. Those are the other skills St. Bernadette's gave her. Stealth, silence, the ability to slip beneath notice. All she had to do was pretend to take her medicine. Be good, be calm. Remember. Lie. Pretend to forget.

But of course, she couldn't forget. Peter had lodged beneath her skin like a splinter. Even at her lowest points—when she was tempted to give in and let go the way John and Michael did—she couldn't dig him out. Peter was and is a part of her; Neverland is a part of her. The angled planes of Peter's face, the fire of his hair, the gleam of his eyes—they are as familiar to her as her own features, as Ned's, as Jane's. She will use that to her advantage, too.

Even now Wendy can call to mind perfectly the innocence in Peter's eyes the first night she met him. The way he held his shadow draped over his arms like the skin of some animal, hope lighting the planes of his face, asking her to make him whole. She'd taken the proffered shadow, silky and cool in her hands like the finest of fabrics, as if it was the most natural thing in the world. Of course a boy might become separated from his shadow, and of course a girl might sew it back on again.

At the time, she hadn't thought it at all strange. Not even when, at the first touch of her needle, he'd shrieked as though she'd stuck him with a hot poker. Afterward, he'd gone around crowing and strutting as if he was the one who'd done something clever. As though Wendy had had no part in it at all, and she'd accepted that too.

By the time they'd arrived in Neverland, the shadow she'd stitched onto him had frayed and unraveled, withering like a rose cut from its vine. They'd landed on the beach in the harsh noonday sun and Peter had stood with his hands on his hips, the broken point at the center of a sundial. His Lost Boys had gathered in a circle around him to greet the Darling children, each trailing a shadow stark behind them on the white sand. Peter alone had cast none.

She should have known then, but all she'd seen was the promise of adventure, a boy who would teach her to fly.

Wendy kneels, retrieving her sewing box from beneath the bed. Needles, pins, spools of thread. Her little scissors, wicked and clever and bright. Sewing might not be a heroic skill, but it is hers. Simply carrying these things with her will calm and center her, a little piece of home in Neverland to remind her what she left behind, to remind her what it cost to visit there the first time.

Wendy closes her eyes, rests her hands on her thighs, and releases a breath. It's still there, the connection between her and Peter, buried deep beneath her skin whether she wants him there or not. She spent years trying to shed herself of him, only to fail. Now she clings to that bond like a physical thread, binding the two of them. He can't hide from her; she will follow that thread all the way back to Neverland.

Once invited, always welcome. Isn't that his way?

NEVER, NEVER

A hush of sound, like running water, or a rolling storm. She turns her head toward the sound and finds her eyelids stuck shut. Has she been asleep? Dreaming? She dreamt of falling. No. Flying.

There's a smell of growing things. It reminds her of Kensington Gardens. She used to walk there with her parents when she was very small, and now that she's older, her father still takes her sometimes, looking for leaves and flowers and insects for her collections. Her favorite bit is the pond with its big white and gold fish coming to the surface to nibble at breadcrumbs, tails flashing and mouths making little 'o's.

Her thoughts drift, simultaneously heavy—sticky as her eyes—and light. She was just in the gardens, wasn't she? Or she's in the gardens now, reaching to catch one of the gold and white fish with her chubby fingers. No, that isn't right. That happened years ago. She was four years old and she wanted to catch a fish to show her papa, but her mama snatched her hand away with a sharp "no!".

"You must never reach into the water like that, _____, or you might fall in. It's an important rule, just like you must never go

36

away with strangers, and you must always stay where your papa and I can see you. Do you understand?"

She isn't that small anymore, or foolish enough to need those lessons from her mother. Only she has gone away somewhere where her mama can't see and there's something wrong. There's a humming blank in her memory where her name should be. If she thinks hard enough, she can see her mother's lips move to shape the sound, but there's nothing there. Only _____! How could she possibly have forgotten her own name?

She must know it, somewhere, only there's something standing in the way. She tries to think it for herself, un-sticks her lips to shout it aloud, but what comes out instead is, "Mama!"

Her eyes fly open, painful, her lashes feeling like they're tearing as they part wide. There was a boy. He took her hand, and they fell into the sky. Her body jerks in panic as though she's falling again, but there's a length of rope lying across her chest and legs, pinning her down. It's heavy, damp, and smells of salt and the green weediness she mistook for fish ponds.

She tries to sit up, but her arms and legs are clumsy, flopping uselessly when she tries to push the rope away. Is she sick? Is that why she's so weak? Maybe the boy at her window was only a fever dream.

Calm. She must be calm and take things one item at a time. Analyze her surroundings. That's what a good scientist would do, and she does intend to be a scientist one day. That much she knows, even if she can't remember her own name. She breathes in, focusing on what information she can gather while lying still.

The ground beneath her is faintly damp and it gives strangely beneath her. This certainly isn't her bedroom. None of her things are here—the globe her papa gave her on her last birthday, the magnifying glass she uses to see the delicate scales of butterfly wings and the veins in her leaves.

Her mama warned her about going away with strangers, but she didn't. Not on purpose. Tightness rises in her chest, making it hard to breathe, threatening her with tears.

The sound of her involuntary, hitching breath makes her angry, and she pushes the fear down as hard as she can. Panic won't do. She must be rational. Assess her situation, look for clues.

She turns her attention straight up, easy enough since she's already on her back. Light filters through branches laid together haphazardly, making a shelter. They're balanced against something solid. She's able to tilt her head back just far enough to see the curving bulk of a wooden construction, but she isn't able to make out the whole.

The harsh laughter of gulls calling to each other clarifies the sound of water. It's the steady hush of waves. She must be on a beach. But how is that possible? Her parents would have told her if they were planning a holiday, and certainly they wouldn't have spirited her away in the middle of the night. She would have packed appropriately, bringing her nets and collecting jars. And there's still the boy, and her mother reaching after her. She certainly isn't on holiday, and something is very wrong.

Applying a burst of effort, she rolls onto her side, the coils of rope slithering free, not even tying her down, just piled haphazardly as if someone meant to bind her then forgot. She sits up, twisting around so she can see that the curve of wood holding up the branches is the hull of a ship. The sand beneath her is wet, the dampness soaking through her nightgown, leaving her cold.

"Wendy! You're awake!" The branches rustle and the boy from her window pokes his head through them, grinning.

Wendy. That's her mother's name. And she's... Jane. The name is suddenly there, like something emerging from the fog, still half obscured so she isn't certain it truly is familiar after all. Is it her? Her thoughts move slowly, like the long strings of almost-burnt sugar Cook pulls into caramel. She helps Cook in the kitchen sometimes. The precision of the measurements please her, and the way slight variations can produce different results is just like a scientific experiment. But even better, at the end, patient stirring is rewarded with a taste test.

She can almost feel the smoky sweetness on her tongue, the mass of candy clinging to her back teeth. She shakes her head, a sharp motion, bringing her thoughts back to the here and now. She isn't normally the flighty sort; she's a very sensible girl, her mother and father have often told her so. Right now, though, her head feels thick and muzzy, and it's hard to concentrate.

"Who are you?" She presses her back against the ship, drawing her knees up and wrapping her arms around them.

He looks like a boy, not much older than her, but if he brought her here, if he stole her from her room, he might be something far more dangerous.

"I'm Peter, silly." The boy crab-walks between the branches and into the shelter.

She remembers landing, panic gripping her, and the boy pressing something into her hands saying it would make her feel better. Was it medicine? She can't recall the details, her memory is incomplete, scattered. A broken shard of sky sliding free, the beach tilting beneath her feet, the hard rain of stars. Darkness.

It was night when they arrived, and it's morning now, or even afternoon. How long has she been gone? Her parents must be worried sick about her.

"I have to get—" She starts to demand he take her home, glaring at Peter as she does, but her tongue sticks to the roof of her mouth. Her throat is bone-dry and the words get lost between her tongue and her lips. They jumble in her mind, and she can't put them in the right order again, even in her head.

Frustrated, she snaps her mouth closed, staring at Peter. He's done something to her, bewitched her like in one of the fairy stories her mama used to tell. He might even be a creature out of one of those stories. There's a scent to him, wild and raw, like the green pond smell from earlier, but also like honey. They fell through the world, like a knight falling into faerie, and now she's here, wherever here might be. Sunlight peeks through the branches and glints in Peter's hair—a fire, consuming everything in its path.

He watches her in turn, tilting his head as if her stillness and silence puzzles him. As if she's the strange creature from another world, which here she might be for all she knows. His hands dangle loose between his knees, which stick up at odd angles from the way he crouches on the sand. Freckles spray his nose and cheeks like stars, but the color of rust. His teeth are too sharp. The thought chills her, and she looks away. It must be the branches casting shadows through his smile. She almost convinces herself, and risks another glance. He lowers his lashes, peeking at her almost shyly as if to show her she has no reason to be afraid. His eyes—they're a gray-blue like a storm, like the pigeons in Trafalgar Square.

"What is this place?" She finally manages to put words in order, and they're far gentler than what she meant to say. She wants to call him a rotten thief and shout at him until he tells her where her parents are.

"It's Neverland, of course. Where else would it be?" Peter says the words like she should know what he means, even though he's speaking complete nonsense. She's studied every single part of the globe her father gave her, and there's no such place as Neverland.

"How could you forget?" Peter says.

She shakes her head, too frightened now for words. There's a cold crawling feeling in her stomach, something important she's missing.

"I'm Peter." He points at himself, speaking slowly and loudly now. Then he points at her. "And you're Wendy."

"That's not my name." The fear spikes, scrabbling in her chest. "That's my mother's name. I'm—" But when she reaches for it, her name is gone again.

Her voice wobbles. She has a feeling like she's looking at a puzzle—pieces are there, only she can't fit them together. Peter's smile flickers, a candle guttered with darkness, but returns an instant later just as bright.

"Of course you're the Wendy. I found you and brought you back to Neverland so you can be our mother again. That's the way it works." He tilts his head again, making her think of a bird. Not pigeons this time, something sharper and cleverer, like a starling or a crow.

He's still smiling, but it's a hard smile. He isn't making any sense, but she's afraid to ask him to explain himself again, or tell him that he's wrong – there's no such place as Neverland, there can't be, and he needs to take her home. She looks closer. Peter isn't a starling at all, he's a different bird, one with a beak hooked for hunting. A hawk, maybe. Why does she think of birds every time she looks at him? The answer is almost there, she can feel it, but every time she concentrates on it, it slips away from her.

She doesn't want to think about what she doesn't know. It's too big and too frightening. If she tries hard enough, perhaps she can convince herself this is all a bad dream. Her mother and father will come for her soon and everything will go back to the way it's supposed to be. They'll wrap her up in a warm blanket and set her in front of the fire. Cook will make scones with clotted cream and jam for tea, and they will all listen, rapt, as she relates the story of her strange adventure.

Perhaps her mother will even bring out the special china, the set that belonged to the grandmother she never met. It will be a proper celebration, to show how happy they are that she's home. Her mama smiling, the light her papa gets in his eyes when he's listening to someone tell a particularly good tale. Her eyes prickle, but she forces a smile to show she isn't afraid, and lifts her chin.

"I brought you more to drink." Peter reaches outside the shelter to retrieve a tarnished silver cup stamped with a pattern. "It'll make you well again, so you remember Neverland."

He extends the cup toward her with an encouraging expression. Is this what he gave her before? It doesn't look like medicine, and it smells sweet. Despite Peter's claim it will make her better, she isn't certain she wants to drink it at all. How can it help her remember a place she's never been, a place that doesn't even exist?

She stalls, examining the cup, aware of Peter watching her with impatience growing in his eyes. She recognizes the insignia stamped upon the cup's side – His Majesty's Royal Navy. Her papa took her to see the ships in the harbor once, bright sails fluttering from their tall masts, so beautiful and proud. How is it she can remember that and not her own name?

"Drink." Peter nudges her fingers, and the cup is halfway to her lips without her even realizing she'd taken it from his hand.

He pushes at the bottom of the cup, tilting it so she has no choice but to swallow the liquid or choke on it. It's thick and sweet. It tastes good, and even as she's drinking it, it makes her thirsty for more. She drains the cup and Peter watches in approval. She knows it isn't wise to take things from people she doesn't know, especially not food or drink, but with the cup empty, she does feel better. Perhaps Peter isn't dangerous after all. Perhaps he really does want to help her. The crawling feeling inside her calms, fear receding. Even sitting on the cold, wet sand, she feels safe and warm, like floating in a hot bath. She yawns widely.

"You can sleep now, if you'd like," Peter says. "We'll play a game when you wake up. I bet you have all sorts of new things to teach us."

Before she can ask what he means, he's gone, quick as a flash, scuttling out through a gap in the branches. She wants to call after him, but her tongue feels even heavier than before. Maybe she will lie down after all. Her insides feel warm from the drink, even better than the tea Cook makes. It's like being wrapped in a blanket, tight like a cocoon. Maybe when she wakes, she'll be a butterfly. The thought makes her smile, already drifting. She is safe here. There's no reason to be afraid at all.

SECOND STAR TO THE RIGHT

Wendy pulls the pins from her hair one by one and sets them in a precise line on top of her dresser. That done, she twists her loosened curls into a simple braid. Strands of gray thread the coppery-brown. Even though she was barely more than a child at the time, the first ones appeared when her hair grew back after the nurse at St. Bernadette's shaved her head to stubble.

From the back of her wardrobe, Wendy retrieves the wide-legged trousers she sewed for herself last year. She promised Ned she wouldn't wear them outside of the house. Like their furniture, like her agreement to call Mary by the title *Cook* whenever anyone else is around, it's another concession to her father-in-law. Trousers are too modern, too mannish, not becoming of a proper lady. As if somehow the clothes Wendy chooses to wear might reflect on the tastes of her husband and his father, and not simply her own.

She pulls the trousers on, then slips her needles, her thread and her scissors into their deep pockets. She sewed them deeper than the pattern required, and she could fit several more items, but what else would she bring? What does one bring to the imaginary land of their childhood to rescue their daughter from a boy who refuses to grow old?

Wendy presses her lips together, trapping bitter laughter behind her teeth. There's an edge of panic to it; if she lets it out, she might never stop. Everything about this is absurd, and yet it's terrifyingly real. Her stomach twists around itself so she forces herself to focus on her wardrobe instead. She selects a blouse with long sleeves. It's inadequate, but it will have to do. She digs out an old pair of low-heeled boots, worn but in good condition, and last, a shawl. She's been freezing since Peter took her daughter away.

Wendy pushes opens the window then climbs onto the small sewing desk beneath it, bracing her hands on the sill and leaning into the night. Reflexively, she pats her pockets again, though she knows nothing will fall out. She crouches on the windowsill, gazing out at the London night. It's time to bring her daughter home.

LONDON 1917

Wendy sits by the window in the common room, exhausted and numb. True to his word, Dr. Harrington kept the door to her room locked all night long, but in no way did it make her feel safe. She spent the night jumping at every sound, every shuffled footstep in the hall. Now, despite the tension singing through her, she can barely keep her eyes open. Her chin dips toward her chest, and between one over-long blink and the next, the girl who isn't Tiger Lily drops into the chair beside her, an accusation on her lips.

"Why were you staring at me?" The violence of the girl's motion startles Wendy, and she scoots sideways in her chair involuntarily. The legs scrape, and one of the nurses glares at her.

"I wasn't." Wendy drops her head, staring at the floor, her answer barely a whisper.

The girl leans forward to peer into Wendy's face, her eyes narrowed.

"Not now, yesterday, in the hall."

Wendy risks a look at the girl. Instead of Tiger Lily's shining plaits, the girl's black hair hangs loose about her face. It isn't tangled, but it's un-brushed even though the distinctly clean smell of soap hangs about her. Her skin is darker than Wendy's, but now that she's inches from Wendy's face, it's clear the resemblance to Tiger Lily ends there. This girl's face is rounder, and there are scars pock-marking it, like the ghosts of some childhood illness. There's a gap between her teeth, which she bares in something that's closer to a challenge than a smile.

"You reminded me of someone, that's all." Recovering from her initial surprise, Wendy lifts her head farther, hardening the line of her jaw. Neither of them has any choice in being here; why should she let this girl intimidate her or chase her away?

"There's no one here who looks like me." The girl's chin juts out, defiant. "My people are part of the Kainai Nation, and now that my mother is dead, I'm the only one in London."

She speaks the words as if the sheer force of them could make them true. Wendy is taken aback, but there's hurt behind the anger the girl wears like a cloak, and that's something Wendy understands. Now it isn't so much Tiger Lily the girl reminds her of, but Peter's boys, so very far away from home, not daring to admit they miss their beds and mothers.

"I'm sorry. I don't know what you're talking about. What is the Kainai Nation?"

Wendy can't guess at this girl's age. In one instant, she looks younger than Wendy, the next much older.

"They're my people."

"Is that… I mean, you're an Indian, aren't you?"

"Kainai. The Blood Tribe. Part of the Blackfoot Confederacy. I don't know anything about India." She draws the last word out, glaring, and Wendy's cheeks flush hot.

"I'm sorry," Wendy says quickly.

To her relief, the girl doesn't leave. She settles back, arms crossed, but under her annoyance Wendy sees a glimmer of curiosity, and she seizes on it.

"I didn't mean to upset you, and I truly am sorry. How did you end up here if…" Wendy stumbles over the words, feeling as though she's stepping onto a frozen lake, uncertain whether the ice will hold.

The girl snorts, a sound almost like laughter.

"Do you mean here?" She gestures at the room. "Or London?"

"Both, I suppose."

Wendy fights the urge to smile, afraid it will cause the girl to turn sullen and angry. This girl may not be Tiger Lily, but in this place with its screams and its glaring nurses and attendants, she's the closest thing Wendy has found to a friendly face. The fact that the girl hasn't gotten up and stormed away makes Wendy think she might feel the same way. Under all the bluster and bravado, maybe she's lonely too.

The girl rolls her eyes as if telling Wendy her story is an imposition. But there's an edge to her voice that makes Wendy think it's been a long time since anyone listened to her.

"My father died when I was a baby. An Englishman married my mother when I was ten years old. He brought us to London from Canada. He didn't want to bring me, but my mother wouldn't leave me behind."

There's a fierceness to the girl's expression as she speaks of the man who married her mother. Wendy doesn't blame her. What sort of a man would ask a mother to leave her child behind?

"A year after we came to London, my mother died giving birth to my baby sister. The baby died too, before she even had a name. My mother's husband kept me with him for a while. I slept in a room with the maidservants where he could pretend I didn't exist. Then he met an Englishwoman he wanted to marry, and she didn't like being reminded that he'd been married before, so he sent me here. I was fifteen. That was four years ago."

Wendy's mouth drops open, a sick feeling in her stomach. She can't imagine anyone treating another person that way, let alone a child, but the girl shrugs when she's done speaking, as though the story doesn't cut at her anymore, at least not on the surface.

"That's terrible." Wendy reaches to touch the girl's arm, but the look of disdain the girl throws her stops her cold.

The ice on the imaginary lake shifts under her feet and she drops her hand into her lap, examining her nails as if that's all she meant to do. The nurse who helped her change her clothes yesterday also trimmed her nails painfully short, another measure for her supposed safety, just like her locked door.

"What about you? How did you end up here?" the girl asks.

Now it's Wendy's turn to make an unladylike sound that's almost a laugh.

"I make up stories. Lies. I can't tell what's real and what's make-believe." Wendy's lips twist; it's all so absurd when she says it aloud. "At least that's what my brother and Dr. Harrington tell me."

"What kind of stories?" The girl uncrosses her arms, her expression unguarded now, but Wendy can't stop the rage she felt on the girl's behalf hardening into a knot of fear. She promised herself to keep Neverland safe. What if this is a trap? What if the girl reports back to Dr. Harrington?

The girl surprises Wendy by touching her hand when Wendy was afraid to touch her before. Her eyes aren't what Wendy would call warm, but there's a sincerity in them. She looks young again, younger than her nineteen years, and somehow much older at the same time. Wendy can't imagine growing up in this place. It would be so easy for St. Bernadette's to make a person hard, spiteful, but Wendy doesn't see that in the eyes meeting hers. Resolve. Strength. Maybe a little bit of hurt and resentment. But not cruelty. Not a snitch or a spy.

"You don't have to tell me if you don't want to," the girl says.

The words loosen the fear in Wendy's chest. She wants to trust this girl. And more than that, she wants to show St. Bernadette's that it can't make her afraid either. She'll tell her story, but only when and to whom she chooses.

"There was—is—a boy called Peter. When I was younger, he took my brothers and me away to another land, far away. There were mermaids and pirates and Ind—"

Wendy catches herself. She tries to think back—did Tiger Lily ever say a name for her people? Or were she and the others simply Indians and nothing more because Peter named them so?

"Go on," the girl says, and Wendy finds a new kind of self-doubt blooming, suddenly shy. She wants this girl to like her; she might even dare let herself hope they could be friends.

"You won't laugh at me?"

"No. I want to hear. But here." The girl bends and takes something from a basket sitting on the floor next to her chair. She pushes an embroidery hoop, dangling with colored threads, into Wendy's hands. "The nurses and attendants usually won't bother us if we look like we're busy doing something they approve of. If we're just sitting around talking, they might get suspicious."

"I'll only make a mess of it." Wendy tries to push the circle back into the girl's hands, thinking of her mother's attempts to teach her sewing as a child. She knew it to be an essential skill for a young lady, but she'd always made a mess of it, too impatient, always eager to be doing other things like reading or making up stories of her own, corralling her brothers into performing little plays for an audience of toys in the nursery. As a result, Wendy's stitches had always come out crooked, her threads tangling and breaking. The only real success she'd ever had was sewing Peter's shadow back on, and even that had withered and faded as soon as they'd reached Neverland.

"I'll teach you," she says.

"I don't think the nurses will let me have a needle." Wendy glances at her clipped nails. The idea of them allowing her even a tiny sliver of metal sharp enough to draw blood is unthinkable.

The girl waves a hand, dismissing Wendy's concerns.

"The nurses bring their own embroidery and sewing to keep themselves occupied, but they're forever losing and misplacing things. It shouldn't be too hard to get you your own supplies. I'm very good at keeping secrets and hiding things." She flashes a grin. "I'm Mary, by the way, Mary White Dog. Mary is the name my mother gave me. My grandmother gave me the name White Dog, but they don't like me to use it, so on all the papers here I'm Mary Smith."

The torrent of words leaves Wendy feeling breathless, but giddy as well. She gathers herself, offering her own name in turn.

"I'm Wendy. Wendy Darling. I'm very pleased to meet you."

"Wendy." Mary grins full on now, a crooked and charming thing. "Tell me a story."

LONDON 1931

The night air catches at Wendy's hair, tugging strands loose from her braid and blowing them against her cheeks. She looks down. It isn't that far to the courtyard below her window, but it's far enough. If she fails, if she falls, she'll break a bone at least, probably more than one.

When she and John and Michael had first returned from Neverland all those years ago, Wendy had been dreadfully sick. She'd spent weeks in bed with a fever, as if something there had infected her and her body could no longer tolerate the London air. Her parents had been patient at first, bringing cold cloths for her forehead and warm broth to drink, holding her hand gently and asking her where they'd been. They'd been gone nearly two weeks, and then suddenly reappeared in the nursery again as though they'd never left.

She'd tried to explain, but it had sounded like a fairy tale, which is just what her mother and father had thought it was. They'd thought her confused, delirious with her fever. When the fever had faded and the story persisted, they'd grown frustrated, even angry. She remembers the way John and Michael had looked between her and their parents, doubtful and a little afraid, wanting her assurances but not knowing what to believe.

In the time she'd been sick in bed, their parents had already half convinced John and Michael that Neverland couldn't be real. Wherever they believed their children had actually been Wendy never did discover, only that in their minds, there was no doubt that the stories she told could not possibly be true. They had accused her of filling her brothers' heads with nonsense, confusing them. Already, Wendy could see the seeds of doubt taking root in Michael and John, and she'd been desperate to convince them, win them back to her side.

She'd been afraid, heartbroken, and still sick in ways she couldn't explain even though her fever had faded. How much easier it would be to hold onto Neverland if her brothers continued to believe in it too.

Wendy had climbed to the top of the tall wardrobe in the nursery, not even hesitating a moment before she jumped. She had been so certain she would fly around the ceiling, just like they did that first night with Peter, that she hadn't felt a moment of doubt or fear until she'd crashed to the floor and broken her arm.

Wendy rubs at her arm, as though she might feel the ghost of the old fracture there beneath her skin. She'd been a child then. If she tries the same thing again now, as a grown woman, how will she explain herself to Ned and her brothers if she fails?

Hysterical—the ghost of the word rings in her ears. John trusts her now, and even Michael. Would she undo all that? For a chance to save Jane, yes.

She could sneak down the back staircase, but what if her father-in-law left someone watching, one of the men from Scotland Yard lurking in the shadows?

No. The first time she traveled to Neverland, she left by the window. And Peter took Jane via the window, so she will go that way too. All her belief, held onto through the years—she must focus on that now, banish every single shred of doubt. Her mind and her truth are her own. No part of her belongs to Dr. Harrington or her brothers. She is alone, and she alone can save Jane.

Wendy fixes her gaze on the stars, pushing away thoughts of the hard, bruising, breaking stones below. Jane. She must think of Jane. Happy thoughts. She edges her foot forward. Happy.

Except her happiest thought is also her most terrible—the memory of holding Jane for the very first time. The sweet, blood-sticky weight of her, red-faced and crying, placed into Wendy's arms. Jane had Ned's hair then, just a few strands of it plastered dark against her still-soft skull. In that moment, love had cracked Wendy open wide, leaving room for fear to slip in. Loving something means having something to lose.

It's a truth Wendy has known since she lost Neverland, since Michael went to war and came home with ghosts in his eyes, since their parents boarded a ship doomed to sink. And oh, how much sharper that knowledge became when she first held Jane.

How did her own mother feel all those years ago, entering the nursery to find not one but all three of her children gone? If she'd survived, maybe Wendy could have found a way to ask her, and to find out whether she too had been terrified when Wendy was first born. But she'd had no one to ask about being a mother, no one to warn her of all the ways it could make and unmake her heart in a single breath—watching her daughter take her first steps, watching her trip and fall.

Had she and John and Michael even thought, as children, what their grand adventure would do to their parents? No, they'd been callous and cruel. They hadn't looked back even once as they'd flown in Peter's wake. And when they'd returned, Wendy's insistence on a grand adventure, her desire to return to that wonderful land that couldn't possibly exist. What must that have done to her parents' hearts, not knowing how their children might have been hurt, where they'd gone? Finding their daughter, even returned to them, suddenly transformed into a stranger.

Wendy herself had thought nothing of that then, how she made her parents and her brothers' lives more difficult. She had thought only of freedom as she leapt through the nursery window that night, of the chance to perhaps be something more than a second mother to her brothers, even for a little while.

Then they'd arrived in Neverland and she'd discovered a whole new set of rules, changing at Peter's whim, and he'd wanted her to be a mother to all of his boys, not just Michael and John. Even so, she'd still ached to return. Why? Was it that the good had outweighed the bad, or was it that she'd left a piece of herself behind? Something unfinished, undone?

Wendy peels her fingers from the window frame, takes a breath, empties her mind of everything but Jane, and lets go.

Air whistles shrill and sharp. Her clothing snaps like sails and flags on a long-ago pirate ship. Jane. Jane. Jane. Wendy thinks of her daughter fiercely, love and pain wrapped all in one. Happiness. Home. The thought slips in, unbidden. She's going home.

She shoots upward, toes nearly scraping the courtyard's stone as she rises sharply and soars over the gate, diving into the sky above London. Up, up, Wendy twists until the sky is beneath her and she's swimming down into it, flying through to the other side of night where Neverland lies waiting.

The rush of air is no longer a scream, but a triumphant yell. Her body remembers flight, the ache of muscles held taut against gravity, and the years fall away. Wendy stretches her arms, her shawl spread between them like wings, and embraces the glittering dark. She banks, rolls, then turns a loop, shedding fear with each motion. The map of London spread below her becomes mere points of light, blurred together as she gains speed.

Is that Westminster Abbey? Kew Gardens? She skims low again before rising once more—a shooting star in reverse. It is glorious. The pain inside her uncoils, and for just a moment, Wendy allows herself to laugh out loud. The wind snatches the sound from her and streams it out behind her.

Neverland. She marks the stars against the velvet sky. They're no longer the stars above London. She's already passed through that invisible barrier to where they're different, other and impossible. Too far to turn back now, not that she would. Wendy finds the second star from the right, knowing it like an anchor to her soul, and sets her course, flying straight on 'til morning.

LOST BOYS

Her mouth tastes of berries and the faintest hint of sandy grit. She's been helping Cook make jam to go with the scones, licking the spoon once all the stirring is done. It must be the sugar combined with the heat from the stove that's left her so lightheaded.

She shakes herself, as if clearing away a sound on the edge of hearing. No. Of course. She isn't in the kitchen. She isn't even at home. She's in N_____. The name is just there, on the other side of the sticky muzz filling her head. Oh, why can't she think straight? Jam and burnt-sugar caramel and the lingering sweetness in her mouth…

Neverland! She snatches the name from the air, like a butterfly caught in her net. She must hold the net closed tight so it doesn't flutter away again. But when she reaches for her own name, it remains gone. The boy, Peter, called her Wendy, and he called this place Neverland.

Wendy. Her mother's name. Does Peter know her mother somehow? She's never heard her mother speak of Peter or a place like this, and she would remember a story as strange as this one, wouldn't she? She must remember to ask Peter when he returns.

She sits up; it's easier than it was before. Was it earlier today that Peter gave her the sweet drink meant to make her feel better? Yesterday? She remembers lying on the sand. She remembers being afraid, and then not, all her thoughts and worries washed away like the tide.

The smells of saltwater and damp wood reach her. Outside her makeshift shelter, birds squabble. Her head aches, but her limbs feel stronger than they did before. She gets to her knees, crawling forward to peer out between the shelter's branches. The squabble of birds resolves into boy voices, then Peter calling her.

"Wendy! Wendy, wake up! I've brought everyone to meet you."

"I'm not Wendy, I'm…"

Panic scrabbles in her chest, then Peter's words sink in. Everyone? What does he mean? Who else is here? She crawls out between the branches, squinting against the light. Peter stands barefoot on the sand, hands planted on his hips, hair a copper flame. A half circle of boys stands arrayed behind him. The youngest looks no more than five, chewing on the ragged tail of his shirt. His eyes are wide, his cheeks dirty, and there are leaves caught in the nest of his hair. All the boys' clothing looks in need of mending, in fact, and none of them are wearing shoes.

Her mother and Cook have been helping her learn how to sew. Cook even said that she's a faster learner than her mother was at more than twice her age. Every time she practices, she does her best to make everything neat and even, thinking about her stitches like she's making scientific notations. She blinks. Why is she thinking about sewing? What is it about this place that makes it so hard to keep her thoughts straight for more than a moment at a time? It's endlessly frustrating. There was something she meant to ask Peter, wasn't there?

The boys all stare at her, some shy, some gaping in curiosity, others with eyes narrowed in suspicion. She glares right back at them; they have no right to look at her that way when she had no choice in coming here. The youngest boy, the one with his shirt in his mouth, moves closer to Peter, sheltering behind him, and her bravado fades.

In the bright midday sun, the boys' shadows trail away from them like spilled ink. All except Peter, who casts none. She knows for a certainty that all solid objects cast a shadow. Her eyes must be playing a trick, or...

"Say hello, Wendy. We're going to play a game, but first we must have introductions."

"I—" Before she can protest, Peter interrupts her, his voice sharp as a hand clapped over her mouth so that she finds she cannot say anything at all.

"We'll start with you. You're Wendy, and I'm Peter." His smile flashes bright as the light reflecting off the water, dazzling her just the same.

She wants to object, but looking at Peter's smile, it's as if the earth and sky suddenly switched places, leaving her dizzy and breathless. When the world rights itself, she blinks, wondering at the circle of boys around her.

She feels exposed with all of them peering down at her. She gets to her feet, brushing sand from her nightgown as best she can. Peter was speaking, wasn't he? What was it that he was saying?

She straightens, standing as tall as possible and putting her shoulders back for good measure. She remembers Cook, who is shorter than both her mother and her father, telling her that it's the best way to stand up to someone trying to intimidate you. Just like animals in nature that make themselves look bigger to scare predators away. She can't imagine anyone arguing with Cook when she gets that particular look in her eyes, not even her grandfather, though she'd like to see him try.

The thought almost makes her giggle, and with it, some of her fear vanishes. Now that she looks at them properly, she sees a good number of the boys, even the ones who look closer to her age or older, are shorter than her.

"I'm called Arthur, just like the king." The tallest of the boys steps forward, nearly knocking over the youngest one as he does. He says his name like a challenge, daring her to contradict him, his expression hard.

He's wearing the skin of some sort of animal—she can't tell what—draped over his shoulders. The cuff ends of his pants are ragged, the waist held up by a length of tied rope. He carries a stick, almost as tall as he is, knife cuts evident where branches and bark have been hacked away. He plants one end in the sand and leans on it as he peers down at her.

"Are you really called Wendy, then?"

A gull screams, its shadow falling on the boy, then the sand, as it circles overhead. The way Arthur and some of the other boys look at her, it's as if they know her, or think they do, though she's certain she's never seen a single one of them before.

"I'm—" She wants to say no, but Peter cuts her off once again, keeping her from answering.

"Of course she's called Wendy. She's here to be our mother." His mouth presses into a straight line. The expression makes him look far older than his slight body implies, but it's only a moment before it cracks again in a lopsided grin. "Isn't that right, Wendy? You're our mother, and you're going to cook for us, and tell us stories, and take care of us when we're sick."

"I don't know how to cook." She blurts the words, and they aren't entirely a lie.

She really is only at the beginning of her lessons with Cook, and she's never made anything on her own. Half the time when she's in the kitchen, she lets herself get distracted by Cook's stories about her home in Canada before she came to England. As long as her mother isn't around to keep an eye on them—and sometimes even when she is—it's easy to get Cook telling stories about Star Boy, and the Above People who live in the sky, or all the different birds and animals and plants in Canada that don't live in England.

And really, what does it matter whether she knows how to cook or not? Who is Peter to order her about and tell her what she is and what she'll do? She isn't interested in being anybody's mother, not now and maybe not ever, and besides, half these boys are older than she is anyway. She's about to open her mouth to say as much, but Peter talks over her once again.

"Don't be silly." He seizes her hand, putting an end to the argument before it's even begun.

He tugs at her, so she's forced to follow him or trip and find herself with a mouth full of sand. Then he's nearly running, and she's too stunned and breathless to object. The boys fall in behind them, talking and shoving as they follow along.

Peter leads them away from the brightness of the beach. She turns to glance over her shoulder, seeing the ship properly for the first time. It's only half a ship really, wrecked upon the shore like the bleached skeleton of an impossibly huge whale. One mast remains whole, the other cracked halfway down. A flag stirs at the top of the unbroken mast. Time and weather have faded it from black to gray, but as the wind snaps it straight, a skull and crossbones grins at her.

Pirates. Her father read Robert Louis Stevenson's *Treasure Island* with her after they went to see the ships in the harbor. She'd loved the story, and asked her mama to tell her a story about pirates too. Her mother's stories were always made up from her head instead of out of a book, but they felt just as real as anything written down, like they'd always existed and her mother was just remembering them.

She used to beg her mother to show her the book the stories came from, certain she must be hiding it somewhere, just knowing it would be full of the most wonderful and terrifying illustrations. All the stories fit together, all of them about the adventures of a Little White Bird and a Clever Tailor. Absolutely anything could happen in her mother's stories.

Once she understood there really was no book her mother pulled them from, she didn't see why the Little White Bird or Clever Tailor couldn't meet a band of dastardly pirates in their next story. As soon as she'd suggested it though, her mother's face had changed, a cloud coming down over her eyes, and she'd said that was enough stories for one night. She'd been afraid to ask for stories about pirates ever again.

There aren't quite as many bedtime stories now that she's older, but sometimes something she says will bring that same cloud-cover look into her mother's eyes. She never knows which things those will be though, and what not to ask about. It isn't that her mother yells, or even gets angry with her, but the silence that results is worse. It's like her mother goes away in those moments, to somewhere where she might not be able to find her way back again.

"Come on." Peter tugs her arm again, dragging her toward a line of trees.

High above them, a faint smudge like the palest of smoke hangs against the blue of the sky. Then the ground changes from sand to dirt, beaten flat by a thousand footsteps. It's like entering a completely different world, a clear line drawn between the beach and beneath the trees. She glances up into the thick canopy overhead, catching a brief flash of red and blue that might be a bird. She tries to identify the trees by their leaves and bark, but nothing looks familiar, and Peter moves too quickly for her to get a proper look.

"This is where we live." Peter stops so suddenly she crashes into him.

Her mouth drops open, and for a moment she forgets to be afraid, or even annoyed. A castle with turrets and ladders and defenses sprawls between the trees. Bridges and walkways and platforms tilt madly around branches and trunks, some looking ancient and some brand new. It's almost like something grown instead of built, except some of the wood is clearly salvaged from the ship on the beach. Other sections are carved right into living trees, or woven from branches still attached to the trunk.

The whole structure looks like it's been started, abandoned, and restarted many times over countless years, no one part of it matching another. The most uniform part she can see is a barricade of long pikes surrounding the trees on two sides, enclosing the camp. In the middle of the trees is a space that's been completely cleared. There's a fire with a cast-iron pot hanging over it, something else she guesses must have been salvaged from the ship.

"This is where you'll cook for us," Peter says.

He beams, as if at some clever trick he's pulled, and she finds herself dizzy again, but not in the lightheaded way. Her blood fizzes from the tip of her toes to the top of her head, making her cheeks hot.

"I told you, I don't know how to cook!" She yanks her arm free of his grip, stomping her foot.

He still hasn't explained where Neverland is, or why he keeps calling her by her mother's name, and he hasn't listened to a single thing she's said. He never asks, all he does is tell, as if his words are the law holding this place together and making things true, and she's utterly fed up with it.

All around the boys fall silent, eyes wide, watching to see what she'll do, what he'll do in return. Peter's eyes, full storm gray in the shadows, go even darker, flickering from hurt to anger. There's a dangerous thing there—she can just see the very edges of it—and she's glad she didn't shove him, even though she wanted to very much.

"Enough." Peter grabs her arm again, nails digging in, and she can't hold back a small, startled noise.

When he lets go, crescent moons of red linger, imprinted on her skin. As quick as his smile vanished, it returns, and it's the sweetest thing in the world, sugar melting in a copper pot. She finds her cheeks warming again, inexplicably wanting to forgive him just as badly as she wanted to push him a moment ago.

"Cooking is easy," Peter says, his tone gentle, coaxing, patient. "Look, I'll show you."

He looks at her from beneath his lashes, his smile curling at the edges and encouraging her. Curious despite herself, she moves closer. When she has lessons with Cook, there are precise rules to follow, but what Peter does now is the opposite of scientific precision; it is utter chaos. He snatches handfuls of leaves and throws them haphazardly into the pot. She tries to catalog them, giving herself an anchor to hold onto—oak, rowan, ash. Those are common enough, but there are also leaves that look like coral wood and Java plum, leaves she's never seen in person but has spent hours studying with her father from the books in his library. They aren't leaves that should be growing all together in one place.

Peter adds a handful of gooseberries. Her tongue sticks to the roof of her mouth. There are stones in his hand, too, smooth and salt-crusted from the sea. She wants to protest, but her voice has abandoned her again. Peter's movements are mesmerizing. Her stomach growls, and she realizes how long it's been since she's eaten. As Peter stirs the whole mess with a stick, a smell wafts from the pot, delicious and impossible.

"See?" Peter's eyes twinkle, sly and merry, but with a knapped-flint edge, daring her to contradict him. "I told you it was easy."

"But that's..." Her words trail off. Instead she nods, agreeing. The meal does smell nice. A little taste couldn't hurt, could it?

"Now, you serve supper, and afterward we'll all play a game."

Peter's words don't sound like a suggestion, even though it doesn't seem fair. She's more of a guest than any of them, and guests aren't meant to be put to work. But she nods again, collecting a stack of bowls from next to the cook fire. It's easier to go along. Her head hurts less when she does.

The bowls are hollowed coconut shells, and something about this strikes her as terribly funny. Everything about this place is absurd. She can't help laughing as she scoops bowls into the pot, filling them and handing one to each boy.

"See? Now we're having fun!" Peter's laugh echoes her own, light and delicate like a falling leaf brushing her skin. She shivers.

As she hands out the last bowl, the boy who takes it gives her a pained look. There's a bruise on his cheek just below his left eye, and the skin is tight and swollen. Before she can ask what happened, Peter slurps loudly, drinking down the contents of his bowl in one go, smacking his lips.

"Eat up, everyone. While we eat, Wendy will tell us a story."

"I don't know any stories."

"You must," Peter says. "All mothers know stories. Otherwise what's the good of them?"

Again, there's that glint of something dangerous in his eyes. She swallows around a lump in her throat and looks down.

"May I at least try some of my soup first? It smells so good." She wants to seem reasonable, like she's going along with him. Perhaps by the time she eats, Peter will forget about her telling a story.

She glances around at the others. The boys eat, some heartily, some looking afraid. She turns her attention to her own bowl, confused. It looks just like the mock turtle soup Cook makes at home, only she knows it's nothing more than leaves floating in water gone cloudy with mud. She watched Peter put everything into the pot, but somehow she can't hold the image in her mind.

There are two truths, one sliding over the other, like the moon in eclipse.

Her stomach growls again. She brings the bowl to her mouth and sips tentatively. To her surprise, the soup is rich and warm. Maybe that's the trick of it, believing that the soup *is* soup and not giving herself time to doubt.

She's about to take another sip when Peter touches her arm, stopping her from lifting the bowl. His eyes are bright as he peers at her face, intent in the way that makes her think of an animal—maybe a fox—watching from the underbrush. Even though he casts no shadow, the leaves do, carving his face up into sections of light and dark. She has the sudden impression that bits of his skin might lift away, like a mask hiding something terrible underneath.

"You can eat later. Now you must tell a story. That's the proper order of things." Peter's tone insists, even though his voice is soft. There's a soothing hum to it, like a note played on a flute, too low for her to properly hear. She feels it nonetheless, thrumming in her breastbone. It's like the wind blowing through cattails and dancing in the tops of the trees. It makes her want to go along with everything he says, though she has no idea why.

Perhaps she can remember one of her mother's stories about the Tailor and the Little White Bird. One story couldn't hurt, could it? She takes a breath, thinking how to begin, but all the tales she's heard over the years go tumbling out of her head. She knows the Little White Bird is always tricking people, from emperors and kings all the way down to stable boys and the other birds he claims are his friends. But beyond that, she can't think of a single specific detail—not one of his adventures or his tricks or anything at all.

She thinks about the Clever Tailor instead. Maybe she could start the story there. Sometimes the Tailor is the Little White Bird's friend, helping him with his traps and games, but in other stories, the Tailor is the one trying to stop the Bird from getting what he wants. Or is she remembering it wrong?

"I think…" She pauses. The idea of stories makes her sleepy, makes her think of her mother tucking her in, and now she wants to lay down. She yawns, her jaw cracking as her mouth stretches wide. Peter shakes her shoulder, and she sits bolt upright.

"Once upon a time," he prompts.

"Once upon a time." She repeats the words dutifully, even though her tongue feels thick and clumsy. "There was a Bird who wanted to go to the king's palace. So the Bird asked the Tailor to make him a suit of all the feathers he could find. The Bird couldn't fly anymore, so the Tailor helped the Bird build a kite."

She stops, shaking her head. She's getting the stories mixed up. Those things happened in two different tales. She wants to snuggle down into her blankets and listen to her mother tell the story right. It would be raining outside, and every now and again a big crash of thunder would make the story more delicious. All the angry scary things outside, like the storm, and her safe inside with her mother.

When she was very young, some of the stories about the Little White Bird would scare her. She could never work out exactly what sort of bird he was supposed to be. Sometimes he seemed fierce, like a hawk, and other times he would strut around proud like a peacock. Still other times, he was as small and gentle as a dove, and he seemed terribly sad. The way the Bird kept changing so she could never tell exactly what he was, so that at any given moment what he pretended to be might be a lie, frightened her most of all. Beside her, Peter taps his foot impatiently.

"You aren't telling it right." His voice is snappish.

Her shoulders hunch automatically, forgetting Cook's lesson and shrinking in on herself. How has she managed to get it all so wrong? There are other stories, aren't there? Stories where the Little White Bird is sweet, where he is the kindest, most gentle creature in the world.

She can almost see her mother's face, alight with a mix of wonder and melancholy, as though her heart was breaking with too much joy and too much sorrow all at once as she mimed cupping the Little White Bird in her hands as the Clever Tailor did in her story, rescuing the Bird from a nest of thorns. It's the story of how they met, how they became friends, when the Tailor saved the Bird's life. A happy story. Perhaps Peter would like that better.

"Come on." Peter taps his foot again, puffing out his cheeks and blowing out air.

His annoyance sharpens her focus, calling up annoyance of her own. How would Peter know her own stories better than she does, or whether she's telling it right or not? She straightens her shoulders, clears her throat and tries again. Even if she gets it muddled up, she knows one thing—right now she doesn't feel like telling a story where the Little White Bird is kind and nice at all.

"The Bird went to the market where all the other birds were selling pies they'd baked or wooden toys they'd made." Her voice grows clearer, stronger. "He went in disguise, rubbing ashes on himself, so he could steal a feather from every bird at the market and turn himself into the most beautiful and strongest and fastest bird of them all."

Around her, the boys set down their bowls, watching her intently. They look interested. Only Peter doesn't seem to approve at all. He scowls, brows lowering over his strange-colored eyes.

She thinks she remembers the next bit, where the Tailor goes in disguise too, sneaking around to all the other birds to tell them the Little White Bird's plan. They turn the Bird's trick around on him, and by the time he reaches the end of the market, it's all his feathers that have been plucked. He looks so foolish he can't possibly go to the king's palace, so he goes away to hide on an island in the middle of the ocean until his feathers grow back.

Except she can't remember exactly how the trick works, even though the stories where the Tailor gets the best of the Little White Bird were always her favorite. They feel important, like her mother was trying to teach her something, trusting her to be clever enough to puzzle it out. She wants to be clever, like the Tailor, but right now she doesn't feel clever at all. Especially not with Peter watching her, his eyes narrow and sparking with hard-edged bits of light.

"I don't like this story. It's boring." He jumps up. "We'll play a game instead."

The words fall like a blow. Her mother's stories aren't boring; they're the most wonderful things in the world. She opens her mouth to object, but something in Peter's expression stops her. It's like her mother's expression, when storm clouds roll in, closing down her face, but worse. A suggestion of hurt lingers in his eyes, but it's buried deep.

She glances around the fire for the boy with the bruise on his cheek, suspicion over how he got it filling her with fresh dread. Peter is exactly the kind of boy to lash out in his pain, like an animal cornered but still possessed of its teeth and claws.

"I want to hear the rest of the story." It's the youngest boy who speaks up, the one who sucked on the tail of his shirt on the beach and hid behind Peter.

His expression is open and guileless, eyes shining with hope as he looks between her and Peter. Peter rounds on the boy, but the boy who called himself Arthur reaches him first, cuffing the boy hard enough that he tumbles off the log he'd been sitting on to eat his supper.

Peter nods approvingly. Pride straightens Arthur's spine even as the fallen boy struggles against tears. His face is a picture of misery, but she can see that he doesn't want to cry in front of the others. She can only imagine what they would do to him if he dared. She wants to go to him, comfort him, but Peter brings his hands together in a sharp clap, drawing all attention his way.

"Everyone get up! No more sitting around. It's time for games."

He twists his head around, owl-like, to look at her. The boys get to their feet, even the one Arthur pushed. They mill around, full of nervous energy, the camp suddenly charged with the storm that is Peter. She's the only one left sitting. She looks to Peter, but his anger is gone, replaced by disappointment, as though she's gravely wounded him.

The considering frown on his lips now is like the sweet way he smiled at her before, only in reverse. It takes the air from her lungs, leaving her throat thick. She tastes salt, her frustration returning and threatening to overwhelm her. What does he expect of her, and why does it change from moment to moment? Why can't she remember her mother's stories right? What if she never sees her mother again? What if there are no more stories and she forgets more every day? What if one day she finds her mother is

70

gone completely, not just her stories, but everything about her, vanished like her own name?

She vows silently to tell the stories to herself every night until she finds her way home, as much as she can remember. She won't let Peter take them away from her, and with them, she'll hold onto her mother too. As she moves to stand, her foot nudges her abandoned soup bowl. She scoops it up, tipping the bowl back and swallowing it all in one go, wincing as she does.

It's gone cold, and worse, something catches and scrapes in her throat. She coughs, doubling over, and puts her hand to her mouth. Another violent cough expels a tiny stone into her palm. She stares at it, her eyes stinging and watering. Peter swoops to her side, thumping her back. She closes her fingers quickly, hiding the stone, and squints up at him. From this angle, he looks much taller, the shadows from the firelight carving into his face and changing its shape.

She blinks. Shadows and firelight. When did it get dark? She doesn't remember the sun going down.

"All better," he says. "Come along, Wendy. It's time to play." There's no trace of anger, no disappointment either. He spins on his heel, all innocent joy as he skips away.

"I'm not Wendy, I'm—" But her name sticks in her throat like the stone, raw and scraping, and she coughs again.

The boys follow Peter, some eager, some dragging their feet. As he steps among the trees Peter seems to flicker, solid and real one moment, slipping out of the world the next. She squeezes the stone in her hand. She must keep trying to remember. Nothing here is what it seems. Peter may look like a regular boy, but in truth, he's a dangerous thing. He may not be human at all.

STRAIGHT ON 'TIL MORNING

Wendy lands at dawn, both tired to the marrow of her bones and more awake and alive than she's been in years. Her body aches as though she truly did fly all through the night, even though she knows time moves differently in Neverland. The sun rises and sets according to Peter's whims; the weather changes with his moods. Days might pass with only the soft light of the moon and stars, or the sun might blaze high overhead for weeks at a time. And all the while, only an hour or two might go by in London.

How long has she been gone? Has Ned missed her yet? Has Mary? And what about Neverland? It's been twenty-seven years for her, but how much time has passed here?

She surveys the long stretch of beach. This is the first part of Neverland she ever saw, tumbling breathless to the sand with her brothers all those years ago. The terrain looks unchanged, and yet everything is subtly different. There's a loneliness, seeped into the very grains that make up the shore, hushing in the relentless tide.

On her first visit, a gaggle of boys waited to greet them, hailing Peter like a conquering hero come home. Hook's pirate ship loomed in the distance, a ragged black threat against the horizon. The beach, the woods, the tide—everything had been full of danger and adventure held in equal balance then. But now the beach is utterly empty. Wendy might be the only person left in all the world.

She pushes a lock of hair—sticky with salt and tangled with flight—behind her ear. Sunrise paints the waves a creamy orange-gold, too perfect to be real. The air is sweeter here, like ripened peaches warmed on a window sill, or hot, fragrant tea on a cold day. She breathes deep, the salt-tang invigorating her, carrying no hint of rotten fish and green weeds the way it would back at home.

Home. The word stops her. As she leapt from the window and into the sky, she had thought of herself as going home. But isn't home the life she's built with Jane and Ned? With Mary? There was a time she would have given anything to be back here, but she isn't the child Peter stole anymore. That time is long gone. Or it should be.

She knows the pride of seeing Jane take her first step, watching her grow and learn new things every day. She knows the warmth of Ned's hands in hers on their wedding day, and the feel of Mary's head resting against her shoulder. She knows what it is to have her brother look at her with respect instead of fear, not like she's a child about to break something, or a wild animal to be caged. She fought hard for the life she has now. How could this place ever be home?

Yet her blood hushes as the tide hushes, the rhythm of her pulse matched to the waves lapping the shore. She cannot deny part of her still belongs here, the part that raged against John,

Michael, St. Bernadette's, and Dr. Harrington. The part that refused to accept their truths in place of her own. Neverland is as much stitched to the fabric of her being as London. She cannot belong to one place or the other, but both together, a thread stretched between worlds.

Wendy feels it—a thrum along the length of her, the tension anchoring her both here and there. She's always been divided, since the moment she landed on this beach twenty-seven years ago, since the moment she arrived back into the nursery in her parents' home.

Is that why she was so sick when she first returned home? Her body rebelling, as if a piece of her had been cut away, a feverish infection come to rest in its place?

She can't help but wonder—what would it be like if she'd stayed? If, like Peter, she'd refused to grow up? She could have spent a lifetime breathing this air. Running and jumping and flying. She would never have known the horrors of St. Bernadette's. And she never would have known the new weight of Jane in her arms, rocking her to sleep and murmuring lullabies.

Her pulse falls out of time with the tide, beating a more complicated rhythm—half love, half fear. Wendy unlaces her boots, strips off her stockings, and steps gingerly onto the sand. It's cool against her soles, just the right firmness for building sandcastles. This is the place her heart belongs; this is the place that stole her daughter away.

The first time she was here, everything seemed uncomplicated. And now? Is this what growing up means, the thing that terrifies Peter so? As a child she only saw bright colors, pure sunlight, or utter dark. All of Neverland is built around those stark contrasts—the sun becoming the moon in the blink of an eye, the sharp demarcation between beach and forest, Hook and his pirates versus Peter and his boys.

A tremor passes through her, and for a moment Wendy wants that surety again, the world flattened to black and white, right and wrong. She has the urge to turn a cartwheel on the sand, pound her feet along the line of surf and let the years fall away as she runs. Instead, she wiggles her toes, burrowing them deep before spreading her arms wide and twirling. Her shawl flares, the trees and sky, the ocean and the shore, blurring into one.

When she stops, she's dizzy. The waves tumble smoothed stones and leave behind a delicate lace of sea foam. Nothing can ever be as simple as merely good and bad again.

She thinks back on the beach holiday she took with Ned and Jane in Brighton when Jane was six years old. Wendy pictures her daughter running along this shore instead of that one, chasing seabirds, her footprints tracking wildly across the sand. She pictures her pausing to dig for shells, trying to uncover the secret homes of tiny, scuttling crabs. She imagines Ned's fond smile, his cheeks coloring with a day of wind and sun, Jane's fingers sticky with melting ice cream as memory and imagination bleed into one. The ache is nearly too much. She should be sharing this moment with them. Her family. Or, she should have shared it with them long ago, the day she agreed to marry Ned, the day her daughter was born.

Even as the ache grows in her like a bruise, she knows Neverland is a lie. This is the ideal of a beach, the tide wild enough for adventure but never so rough as to be a threat; the water never too warm nor too cold. Every tree in Neverland is perfect for climbing, and the stars always make fantastic pictures in the night sky. It's a world built by a boy to satisfy his every whim. It isn't real.

Ned and Jane are her true home. She belonged here once upon a time, but they are the life she chose. Every day since leaving St. Bernadette's, she has chosen them, and she will choose them again now. As much as that long-lost part of her wants to run, to fly, to be utterly free of responsibility, the star she navigates by now is Jane.

Wendy tucks her rolled stockings into the toes of her boots. If she'd told Ned the truth long ago, they might have protected Jane together. Their lives may not be perfect under the ever-present shadow of her father-in-law, but it is a better life than Wendy ever could have hoped for on the day she first heard Ned's name.

There are husbands and wives, she knows, who barely speak, inhabiting separate realms in their households. She and Ned have learned to be partners. Friends. Her father-in-law would be scandalized to know that some of the ideas his son brings to him for their business originate with Wendy. He might drop dead on the spot if he knew Ned takes Mary's advice as well. If he could see them sitting down to meals all together, or the private jokes Ned and Mary share that even Wendy has no part of...

The thought makes Wendy's eyes sting, and she blinks rapidly. More secrets. It's emblematic of her life, it seems. Truths kept from her father-in-law—working side by side with Mary in the privacy of their home, calling her Cook and treating her as a servant under the eyes of anyone else. Teaching Jane to call her Cook as well lest she slip up, no matter how much it hurts Wendy to do so.

And what of Michael and John? Is her reconciliation with them as much of a half-truth as her life with Ned? The breeze blowing from the cream-colored ocean carries a chill suddenly, nipping at her, and Wendy pulls her shawl closer. If John and Michael could return here, would they be happy? Would things be different between the three of them, all the weight of the intervening years melting from their shoulders? Could Michael laugh again, the ghosts slipping from his eyes? Might his shattered leg even heal, letting him run again the way he had as a boy? Might John finally smile without lines of worry crinkling at the corner of his mouth and across his brow?

Wendy thinks of Elizabeth, John's young bride, impending motherhood just beginning to show in the slight curve of her belly and the glow of her skin. She's seen the adoration in her sister-in-law's eyes when she looks at John, but worry still shadows John's brow. What if he could bring his child here, hold his or her hands as they splashed together in the tide?

The impossible simplicity of it hurts. Neverland isn't what she once believed it to be, an escape, a cure for all ills. As children, they ran away here without even any troubles to escape from, and wasn't it Neverland itself that left her scarred? The memory she couldn't shake that caused the rift between herself and her brothers in the first place? And now it's put her daughter in danger.

Wendy shakes herself. She's been stalling, putting off her search. What if she can't find Jane? What if Neverland keeps her hidden? Or what if she finds her and it's too late? There's a pull to this place, an allure Wendy can't fully explain. It's why even when she chafed under Peter's rules, she longed to stay forever. Peter had made it easy to forget so many things—his unfair rules, the small cruelties she'd witnessed among the boys, even her home. There were times with Peter when London felt like a distant dream, when returning to her parents felt like the lie, and Neverland where she truly belonged. Even now, she feels the subtle pull, the way she'd wanted to run on the sand and forget everything else, even her mission to save Jane. What will Neverland do to her daughter? What if Jane forgets her, forgets Ned, forgets herself? What if when Wendy brings her home, Jane sickens the way Wendy herself did as a child, rages against London as her home, breaks her bones insisting she can fly?

Wendy should have spent every night arming her daughter against the day Neverland came for her instead of telling her half-truths couched as fairy tales.

She shades her eyes, peering down the curving length of beach. Just before the land dips out of sight, the prow of a ship juts up toward the sky, the angle of it all wrong. Behind her, a spire of rock rises from the trees, which are a scatter of deciduous, conifer, and tropical all mixed together. Above the trees, it seems for a moment that a ribbon of darkness drifts against the sky. Wendy squints, trying to see better. A murmuration of starlings? No. Smoke. Like something at the center of the island burning.

A faint memory of Peter promising to show her something, a secret, holding that promise like the sweet, crisp perfection of an apple, just beyond her reach. He would show her, as long as she followed his rules. Had he ever, or had the promise only been another of his lies?

Looking again, Wendy can no longer see whatever it was she thought she saw. Smoke, dissipated now, like a flock of birds moving on. Like something alive.

Wendy lets her hand fall to her side, pushing the unsettling thought from her mind and focusing on the trees again. If Jane were here beside her now, she would point out the difference in leaves and bark, sharing facts Wendy would never know if her daughter didn't tell her. She aches for Jane's explanations, her ordered world, and scrubs a hand over her face, trying to focus.

She should be able to cut through the woods here and come out at the sheltered lagoon on the other side of the island. Unless everything has changed since she's been gone, Peter erasing the map of Neverland and writing it over again.

Wendy retrieves the rolled stockings from the toes of her boots and pulls them on over the sand-grit clinging to her soles. She shoves her feet into her boots, and turns her back on the water. Birds chatter as she steps beneath the trees, their voices subdued. Do they recognize her? The Wendy come home. This *was* her home once. She cannot deny it, and in fact, doing so might put her daughter in even more danger. She needs to own her past, and use everything she learned here once upon a time to save Jane and bring her back safely.

LONDON 1918

Tears roll silently down Wendy's cheeks as the razor scrapes across her scalp. Shame fills her; it's a silly, vain thing to cry over, but she can't help feeling a fundamental part of her is being taken away. Her hair, her choice to wear it long or short, pinned up or spilling down her back—now she has no choice at all.

Locks scatter on the tiles, curled like question marks. Lice, the nurse who wields the razor claimed, but from the pinch of her lips Wendy knows it's a lie. If it were lice, the room would be filled with patients waiting to have their heads shaved, but it is just Wendy and the nurse alone. This isn't for her protection, or her health; it's punishment.

Jamieson accused her of stealing. Wendy never even saw what she was meant to have taken. All she saw was the expression on his face as he cupped his big hands and angled his body to hide the "proof" he showed Dr. Harrington.

"What about the other girl?" Dr. Harrington had asked. "You say she was involved too?"

It doesn't surprise her that Jamieson would try to implicate Mary. He hates them both—for their sex, for the color of Mary's skin, because they find ways to smile and laugh, speaking with their foreheads together, sharing stories and secrets. Although Wendy suspects that at the end of the day, Jamieson needs no reason to feel justified in his actions; cruelty is its own reward.

"Mary had nothing to do with it." Wendy had spoken quickly. "It was all me."

Doubt in Dr. Harrington's eyes, scorn in Jamieson's, but what did it matter? The whole accusation was built on a lie. In truth, Wendy stole all the time, but her thefts were never discovered. Whatever Jamieson had produced as evidence was something he'd planted himself, but which of them would be believed? Certainly not a girl who made up stories about an imaginary land.

So now Wendy is strapped to a chair, leather cuffs pulled tight around wrist and ankle, even though she hasn't once struggled. The last curl falls, a leaf dropped from a winter tree. Her scalp feels chilled in the empty, tiled room. A sudden memory— Peter touching her hair, calling her a wood sprite, promising to introduce her to the Queen of the Dryads. He never did, distracted by another one of his games.

Wendy laughs, a bitter sound she immediately cuts short so it turns to a cough. There's a click as the razor is set down. Wendy looks straight ahead as the nurse undoes the straps and leads her to the door. As they pass the common room, other patients flinch, looking away too quickly, or reflexively touching their own hair. Wendy scans the room, but Mary isn't there.

She hopes Mary is being smart, staying out of sight. Despite Wendy's protestations that she committed her supposed crime alone, she wouldn't put it past Jamieson to find some other way to torment Mary while Wendy was having her head shaved. There's strength in numbers, Wendy has learned that much, even if that number is only two. Jamieson rarely goes after either of them if they are together, and therefore he's always seeking ways to separate them.

Wendy has gotten good at interventions, creating distractions, and when necessary, redirecting Jamieson's attention to herself and away from Mary. Jamieson is not a particularly subtle man. If she's able to catch him whispering with the other attendants, or even simply glancing Mary's way, she knows it's time to go to work. Once, Wendy secreted a small amount of cleaning powder in one of the many temporary pockets sewn into her clothes. The smallest of pinches in Jamieson's tea—not enough to harm him, really, just enough to make him sick—saved Mary last time. Another time, one Wendy is particularly proud of, a well-aimed stone upset the wasp nest built into a crook of the tree Jamieson favored for smoking beneath, sending him screaming and running.

The thought brings a smile to Wendy's lips, but the sense of victory is short-lived. She'd paid for those transgressions even though Jamieson could never prove his sickness or wasp-stung flesh was her fault—bruises where Dr. Harrington would never see, pain inflicted but leaving no mark. She'd once spent nearly two days locked in a small supply cupboard until Mary had contrived to get her out. His suspicion was enough. Or perhaps, like all the other times he'd chosen to hurt her, he would have done it regardless of whether she took action against him or not.

Now, as the nurse marches her down the hall, it takes all of her will not to run her hands over her scalp, but she will not give the nurse the satisfaction. Another memory comes unbidden to her mind—sitting on a rock beside Neverland's lagoon, one of the mermaids braiding her hair, weaving in fragrant blossoms with thick white petals that shimmered in the sun. Wendy blinks, lifting her chin higher.

Only once she's alone in her room does she allow herself to run a hand over her head. The ghost of her hair bristles against her palm. Wendy sits in the center of her narrow bed and tucks her feet beneath her body. She closes her eyes, resting her hands on her knees, straightening her spine. It's been fourteen years, but she can still summon the feeling of wind streaming past her skin, whipping strands of her hair around her head like a wild nest of snakes as she flew. Hair that, like so many other things, has been taken from her now too.

A deep ache fills her, like a bruise close to the bone. She is worn thin, a piece of cloth washed so often the individual threads begin to show. She will not let Neverland go, she cannot let it go, but every day it seems farther away. If only she had some sign, something to hold onto, she could endure forever in this place without breaking.

When it had become clear to them that Wendy wouldn't change her story, their parents had sent John and Michael away to a boarding school, while keeping Wendy at home under their watchful eyes. It was as though they had believed that separating her from not only her brothers but all other children entirely would force her to give up what they had seen as a youthful fantasy. But it had only ingrained Neverland in her further.

Wendy had spent those nights in the too-empty nursery without the soft sounds of her brothers breathing beside her recounting to herself every detail of Neverland that she could—the precise way the bark felt under her palms as she climbed the trees while chasing Peter, the way the mermaids' scales flashed in the sun, the scent of smoke from Tiger Lily's camp fire, the way the deck had rolled under them when Hook's pirates had captured them, even the particular way the terrible pirate captain had smelled.

Being apart from her brothers for the first time since they had been born had taught Wendy her first lessons in silence and lying. She had learned to keep her truths to herself, telling her parents what they wanted to hear. But she had never stopped believing, and those memories, the way she learned to conjure Neverland into her room at night, will serve her well now.

If she concentrates, she can call to mind exactly how it felt, how the sky over Neverland tasted as she flew, and the exact color of the starlight... There was a time when the stars were so close all she had to do was stretch out her hand to catch one. Wendy stretches out her hand now, curling her fingers into a waiting space. She holds her breath, yearning, concentrating all her will on that invisible tether connecting her to Neverland. But her hand remains empty, no star filling her palm. She closes her hand into a fist, slamming it into the bed in frustration.

She's a fool. Did she really expect to capture a star in her palm? In this world, the one she's trapped in, such things aren't possible. Stars are distant and impossibly huge, not points of light to be gathered and held against the dark. She knows this, and still it hurts. More than she imagined possible. She's tired beyond belief. Angry. And she's beginning to feel hopeless.

For a year she's listened to Dr. Harrington telling her she's sick, and to Jamieson calling her a liar. She's seen John tire of arguing with her and turn away, his shoulders sloped in defeat. Michael refuses to even visit her most of the time.

There's a crack, a fissure running all the way through her and it widens every day. There are times she wants to give in to John and Dr. Harrington. Would it be so bad to play make-believe, pretend to be a girl who never flew, never left home?

But why *should* she be asked to forget, to pretend to be something she is not? She'd learned to lie to her parents, but she's grown up now, twenty-five years old. Shouldn't she be the one to make the rules? Why should she let others define her reality?

Wendy concentrates, willing her body to lift from the bed. *Fly*. It used to be so easy. Even a fraction of space between herself and the bed would be enough. It would lessen the ache; it would make all the rage, all the suffering, worthwhile. But even without her hair, she's too heavy. Everything in St. Bernadette's holds her down.

When she'd tried as a child, leaping from atop the wardrobe, she'd let doubt cloud her mind. She'd been sick, weak, finding herself disbelieved, seeing her brothers already forgetting. If she refuses to let that doubt in again now, fills up every space inside her with thoughts of Neverland, surely she cannot fail again.

Wendy bites her lip, digging her shortened nails into her palm. She reaches for the sensation of Peter taking her hand, for the moment her toes lifted from the nursery floor, the dizzy fall through the window and up into the sky, all elation and breathlessness. Everything was bright and wonderful, the stars shining in so many more colors than she'd ever imagined possible. She remembers laughing, the light catching in her teeth and tasting of plums and honey. And...

Smoke. Raw meat. Wet fur.

Wendy falls. Her stomach drops and even though the bed in St. Bernadette's still holds her, she plummets into endless dark. Peter's hand is still on hers, but his grip is unshakable. Rather than holding her up, he pulls her along faster and faster, running until her feet burn.

It's a secret, Wendy. The best secret I know. I've never told anyone before.

It's a feeling she imagines akin to being struck by lightning. Hollow, tingling, numb. A pain that isn't quite pain. There's a hole inside her. A place where something has been torn away.

Wendy slams a door over the empty space, a primal reaction. On the other side of the wood, something breathes. On the other side of the wood is a raw wound, and she draws away.

Her eyes fly open, her breath coming fast and hard. There's something there. Something in Neverland she's forgotten, something terrible. There's a bit of darkness lodged inside her like a splinter, digging and digging, infecting her blood.

Shaking, Wendy rises and creeps to the door. Despite the

nurse's punishment and her shorn head, it is unlocked. Perhaps the nurse forgot, or perhaps she expects Wendy to be broken and properly cowed, subdued without any need to lock her in. She eases the door open and peers down the hallway in either directions. No attendants or nurses in sight.

Wendy's pulse trips. Her back teeth ache, unspecified dread filling her. Whatever she saw… No. It must be a lie… Neverland was a beautiful adventure. Peter was and is her friend. Nothing terrible happened, and there are no monsters. If she could only taste the sweet air once more to remind herself, if she could just see Peter's smile one more time, then she could endure an entire lifetime in St. Bernadette's and never lose faith.

She hurries down the hall, almost running, her bare feet slapping lightly at the tile. She *can* fly. She just needs to see the sky; she just needs a little height to get her started.

As she approaches the common areas, Wendy lowers her head and slows her pace. Luck is on her side; three women emerge from the large common room as she passes. Wendy falls in behind them as they climb to the second floor where the rooms are nicer, larger, more elaborately furnished. It's where patients who have committed themselves voluntarily, or patients whose families have more money than sense, are housed.

Wendy snuck up there with Mary once. They'd spent hours exploring and spying on the "patients" there who had their own dedicated staff and were treated more like hotel guests. They were so sure they'd be caught, laughing behind their hands the whole time and sneaking tea cakes and sandwiches from an unattended tray left behind. They'd never been discovered, slipping in and out like ghosts. Wendy will be a ghost again now.

At the landing, she turns away from the women. There are windows overlooking the lawn at the opposite end of the hall, and she makes for those. Through the glass, Wendy can see false balconies just deep enough for a single person to stand. The windows are locked, but unlike the windows downstairs, they don't have bars.

From one of the many pockets secreted in her clothing, the ones Mary taught her to sew, Wendy pulls a set of hairpins stolen from one of the nurses. The lock is easily picked. She pushes the window open and climbs onto the tiny balcony. A fresh breeze greets her and she spreads her arms, almost weeping with relief. She's so close. Neverland is just on the other side of the painfully blue sky.

Wendy rests her hands on the stone railing, soaking in its sun-warmth for a moment before pulling herself up. The stone is just wide enough to allow her to balance on her bare feet. She crouches, peering over the edge. It's not that far down, yet the emerald lawn looks impossibly distant. She peels one hand off the railing, then the other, holding her arms out to either side as she straightens.

Just one quick trip, and then she'll come right back. Even if she doesn't see Peter, she needs to feel the wind against her skin, to fall through the sky and see the stars from the wrong side. Just a sip of Neverland's air, then she'll return and stay as long as John and Dr. Harrington want; she won't complain or misbehave ever again. She leans forward ever so slightly, waiting for the shift in balance, the sky to catch her weight, her feet to lift from the stone.

"Wendy." Mary's voice is low and tense.

It isn't a shout, and maybe that's what saves Wendy from wheeling around and losing her balance. Mary stares at her, eyes wide and dark. Wendy had been so intent on not being seen she hadn't noticed that she was being followed.

"What are you doing?" Accusation in Mary's expression, a hard edge under her level tone.

Leaving.

Wendy doesn't say the word aloud, swallowing against a sudden painful lump in her throat. Oh, she promised herself she'd return, but Wendy knows deep down that once her feet had touched the sands of Neverland's beach, she never would have looked back. How long would it have taken her to forget Mary? To forget her brothers? Forget everything? She would have run and kept running and never have thought of England again.

Because that's what Neverland is—running away, cowardly, without even saying goodbye. It's leaving behind everything you claim to love to embrace purely selfish joy. No responsibilities, no consequences, and nothing matters or ever changes.

Wendy chokes on the knowledge, a sound between a cough and a sob. The rift inside her widens. She feels exposed. Standing here with her shorn head, she's proving Dr. Harrington right. She's sick, a danger to herself; she needs help.

"I don't know." It's barely a whisper.

She can't make herself move, not to step down from the railing, not to let herself fall. Mary holds out a hand. A lifetime passes, but Wendy finally closes the distance, one that seems immense, and places palm against palm. The touch grounds her, and she winds their fingers together, clinging tight. Mary's skin is warm; there are calluses from her needlework, and from baking in St. Bernadette's kitchen.

"I'm sorry. I thought…" But she can't get farther. The words lodge in her throat like broken glass. What *was* she thinking? Mary holds her steady, and once Wendy climbs down, she folds Wendy in her arms.

"I thought if I could fly—"

"Fool," Mary whispers, and Wendy stiffens in her arms, but Mary doesn't let go. After a moment, her body softens against Wendy's, and Wendy finds herself relaxing too.

"Shh." Mary runs a hand over Wendy's bare scalp. "You don't have to prove anything to anyone. You *can* fly, but if you let them see, they'll only try to tie you down and break your wings."

Wendy pulls back, staring at her friend. Mary's eyes remain hard, defiant, but glittering with an edge of mischief.

"Do you think I don't know I'm better than this place? Every time the nurses speak more slowly, assuming I'm dull because I wasn't born on English soil, or with white skin, don't you think I want to scream at them and slap their terrible faces? I know better, and so should you."

Wendy catches her breath. Mary is right. The harder she fights, the tighter the bindings will grow. But that doesn't mean she can't resist—their small thefts, the temporary pockets sewn into their clothes, picking locks and slipping beyond sight, those are the ways they will fight back.

Wendy uses her sleeve to wipe her cheeks and nose. Mary knows her better than anyone, and she's right. Neverland is hers, it is precious; she will not give it to anyone to use as a weapon against her. It's enough that Wendy knows, deep in her heart, that if she'd jumped, the sky would never let her fall. And one day, she and Mary together will fly.

*

89

Wendy scans the canopy of trees for a glimpse of the brightly colored birds she remembers from when she was a child, the ones she heard chattering as she stood on the beach. They're eerily silent now, and she sees no sign of them, as if when she stepped beneath the trees they all fled. Wind sways in the treetops, a rippling hush. She catches a flicker of motion, but it isn't red or blue. It's a brownish-gray, vanishing through the branches too fast for her to track. By the time she focuses on the spot where it was, it's already gone.

She pulls her shawl closer, but the motion doesn't come again. The leaves cast shadow patterns on the forest floor. They shift with the breeze, but everything else is stillness. The air feels haunted, and Wendy feels watched. Even the trees seem paler, washed of their color somehow, the leaves almost translucent, like ghosts of themselves. She hurries her steps until she's out from under the trees, looking at the rocky caldera surrounding the lagoon. It's right where she expected it. At least this part of Neverland hasn't changed.

Tiny shells and fossils of starfish and insects stud the porous stone that surrounds the water and hides it from view. Wendy runs her fingers over the stone. Jane would love this. She would probably know the name of every species embedded in the rock. She pulls her hand back, and it's a moment before she can breathe again for the ache in her chest.

She removes her shawl and ties it around her waist, then unbuttons her cuffs and rolls her sleeves to her elbows. She checks her pockets; everything is secure. Wendy reaches, and as she does, the rock molds itself to her grip—just as she remembers. She pushes off with one foot, pulling herself up, and searches for a spot to wedge the toe of her boot. Her limbs aren't as flexible as they used to be, but her fingers still find holds in all the right places. Like Neverland's trees, the rocks here understand adventure, a desire to be higher than everything else. King of the hill. Or queen.

There's a pleasant burn to climbing, and Wendy revels in it—the stretch of her muscles, the sweat gathering beneath her clothes. She welcomes the way her breath comes harder. It's so unlike anything she would do at home in London. There her greatest exertion might be a stroll in the park or a game of croquet, but here, she is the Wendy again. The girl who flew.

Exhilaration fills her, and just as soon, dread comes on its heels, tripping down her spine. A memory nags her—climbing a rock to a secret place. Something Peter showed her, but what? Something that made her afraid.

At the top of the caldera, Wendy pauses. The breeze picks up a foul smell, one teetering on the edge of rot, carrying it to her from below. She should be able to hear the chatter of mermaid voices, the drifting melody of their song. There's only more silence, like there was on the beach. Light sparkles on the water below so that Wendy has to squint her eyes against it, but the water itself seems empty. Are the mermaids hiding from her? Or are they afraid and hiding from something else?

Instinct screams at her to turn back, but even if she wanted to, gravity takes the choice from her hands. Her grip falters, and she slides, tumbling down the incline toward the blue eye of the lagoon below.

The breath rushes from her, and all Wendy can do is shield her face and try to slow her descent. Her foot catches on something, pain jolting up her leg, and for a moment she's airborne—falling, not flying. Then she's crashing through the long grasses and wild sea roses bordering the lagoon, the bruising violence of her impact driving the rest of the breath from her body. She rolls to a stop just at the edge of the water.

A whine emerges and she sucks in a breath, coughing, and for a moment she's sure she'll suffocate, drowning on dry land. The blue sky mocks her from above, clear and perfect and bright, but every part of her body aches. It's a moment before she can roll over, planting her hand to lever herself up. Her palm slips in slick weed and foul mud, the source of the stench, plunging her arm into the water and bringing her eye to empty eye socket with the skull glaring up at her from the shore.

Wendy scrambles back, pain momentarily forgotten. The skeleton lies with one arm flung outward, the other tucked beneath its chin, head pillowed on sun-bleached bones. The lower half of the body trails into the water, which is still so painfully clear that below the torso she can see the bones of a powerful tail, stripped of its shimmering scales.

Wendy crawls forward, stopping just short of touching the skull. It's impossible. She can't be seeing what she's seeing, despite the evidence in front of her eyes. Nothing can die in Neverland. Peter told her so.

But here is the skull, incontrovertible, her own truth against Peter's, and she's done taking other people's word for how the world functions. Her fingers hover in the space above the pale curve of bone. There should be thick, shining tresses, bound with seashells, woven with coral and sea roses. She lets her hand fall. Who was this? Wendy struggles to call to mind each mermaid's face, almost human, but at the same time strangely *other*—their pointed chins, their cheekbones sharp and canted, and their eyes shimmering like mother of pearl.

The memories were so clear once, but now, when she needs them the most, she finds them dulled, slipping away the harder she tries to hold on. Voices raised in song ring in her head, paired with the musical tones of their names, sung to her from the water the first time she met them—Sea Bloom, Salt Rose, Coral Bramble.

In the lagoon's depths, there are more skeletons. Dozens of them, some entangled, some alone, some seeming as though they simply dropped through the current as they swam. A gull screams, and Wendy jumps. The cut-out shape of the bird's wings passes across the cloudless blue as she looks up, and she shudders to think what the curved tip of its beak has been feeding on.

Grief-fueled rage leaves her arms trembling, but she scoops up the first stone she can find and hurls it at the bird. The stone goes wide, arcing back into the water, breaking the still surface so wavelets lap the bones at her feet. A choked sob catches in Wendy's throat as the bird glides on, oblivious.

She closes her eyes, breathing against the tightness in her chest. And now, when she no longer wants it, memory comes flooding back, conjuring the feel of fingers combing through her hair, the susurrus of gossip passing as flashing tails fan the water. The mermaids knew every inch of the secret underground tunnels lacing through the water beneath the island. They could cross it in a flash, carrying news from one shore to the other. There was a time when the birds were their allies, bringing scraps of news in a language Wendy couldn't understand. Now Wendy imagines those tunnels clogged with more bones, death under her feet threaded through every part of the island.

It isn't just the mermaids' deaths; she selfishly mourns their knowledge, their news. She's certain they could have told her where to find Jane.

She opens her eyes. The memory of a song hangs over the lagoon, the last note on a wind instrument, unplayed. Wendy brushes at her trousers ineffectively, only succeeding in smearing more mud on the fabric. She remembers sitting with Mary in the parlor window, planning alterations to the pattern, stitching everything by hand as Mary told Wendy her grand ideas for the bakery she would open one day. Another choked sound, half laughter, tasting of salt, and Wendy scrubs at her eyes.

What could kill so many, so quickly? And why didn't Peter stop it?

She turns away from the water, irrationally angry at herself, at Peter, at the mermaids. She shouldn't have delayed so long on the beach, and now she's wasted more time. Neverland may not be big, but there are ever so many places for a clever boy to hide. On top of that, Peter could rearrange it all on a whim. Jane could be anywhere.

So, where next, then? The pirates or the Indians? Weariness and fear clamor inside her, and she pushes them both down. She'll go inland, cut across the island toward the shipwreck. If she'd been thinking more clearly, she would have started there—the beach is the first place Peter brought her. Why wouldn't he do the same for Jane?

She circles the lagoon, climbing up the other side of the caldera. There's less joy in it this time. The rock still shapes itself for her grip, but her body aches from her earlier exertion and from the fall. She feels bruises forming, and on top of that, she isn't a girl anymore. She's too old to play queen-of-the-castle.

At the peak, Wendy pauses to push sweat-stuck hair from her face, scanning for the strange smoke she saw earlier. From this side of the lagoon, she can see over the tree tops. She's about to start her descent, when all at once, a group of branches shiver with a violence that has nothing to do with the wind. The leaves ripple, marking the passage of something unseen. The motion jumps from tree to tree, bending them with an invisible weight.

Wendy's pulse stutters. Whatever it is, it's too big for a bird, or a squirrel, or even the little golden monkeys with white faces that Peter showed her how to look for on their hidden perches. It's moving away from her, but that doesn't stop the fear locking her in place.

Ghosts. The word comes unbidden. Neverland was never haunted before, but there was never death here either.

Another thought follows close on the first's heels, closing like a fist around her heart. *Not ghosts, monsters.*

Running, with her hand in Peter's hand, breathless and trying to keep up. *I'll show you a secret, Wendy, something I've never shown anyone.*

There's something terrible at the heart of the island. Something Peter showed her once. But when she reaches after it, it's like a door slamming shut in her mind, so abruptly she stubs her fingers against it, leaving her blinking and dazed.

The shaking in the trees stops just as suddenly as it started. She was… There was something…

Wendy shakes her head, letting several heartbeats pass.

95

Whatever it was can't have been important. She scans the trees, trying to see what caused the motion, but there's no sign of anything. The shaking doesn't reoccur, but there's no birdsong either. No gentle creak of branches in a regular wind.

Haunted. Neverland is haunted. The lagoon is full of skeletons in a place where nothing is supposed to die, and her daughter is out there somewhere. She has to find Jane. Wendy turns her back deliberately on the trees, and descends the rest of the way to the ground.

HIDE AND SEEK

All around her, boys sleep, their bellies full of more soup made from dirt and stones. This time, she didn't eat, and now her stomach growls, hollow and sick. How will she survive here? How do these boys live on nothing but dirt and bark and leaves? She pushes the thought away, unsettled in a way she can't name.

Didn't one of her mother's stories have the Clever Tailor traveling to a land filled with the ghosts of children? The boys around her seem solid enough, but maybe they're really ghosts. Maybe that's why they don't need to eat the way she does. She wishes she could remember how the Tailor in the story tried to set the children free. Then she could help the boys, send them home. Surely they ache for their own mothers and fathers as much as she misses hers.

Peter keeps telling her she's here to be their mother. That must mean there are no other mothers here, no sisters, or fathers, or aunts, or uncles either, she supposes. Only her and the boys. Which means there's no one here to help her, or tell her how to get home.

She surveys the camp. The last embers of the fire glow dark orange, threads of smoke whispering away from the ash. There was smoke earlier, wasn't there? She peers up, but sees nothing but a full moon shining over the trees, unnaturally bright. In fact, there's nothing natural about it at all. It's a smooth, silvery disc, like a coin hanging in the sky, or a hole cut in the paper-dark with a bright light shining through, nothing at all like the real moon.

The thought rips through her, and just like that, she's crying. She's furious with herself; it's such a silly thing, but she misses *her* moon, seen through *her* window.

Her grandfather took her on a trip to the Royal Observatory on her last birthday. She'd felt very special and very grown up, particularly when he'd arranged for one of his friends there—a proper scientist just like she'll be one day—to let her look through a telescope at the moon. She remembers how big and close and impossible it seemed—all the shadows and dips and craters not visible without the special lenses the telescope had.

How is it she can remember that moment so clearly, but her own name keeps slipping away from her? It's as though someone has pulled a curtain over part of her mind; she's aware there are things there, hidden from view, but they're gauzy and distorted. If she doesn't concentrate, they start to vanish. Worse than that, at times she's found herself not minding the forgetting at all.

After the meal Peter had declared supper, he had dragged them all down to the beach again for a complicated game with rules she never quite managed to grasp. She'd been cross at first, but then hours had slipped away as she ran and tromped with the boys, stamping their feet into the sand and calling to each other. The sun had reigned overhead the whole time, full and blazing and not moving once in the sky, despite the twilight that gathered while they ate. Only when Peter had grown bored with the game had she noticed her exhaustion, and how grubby she'd become, her nightgown stiff with salt and her hair tangled.

What would her grandfather say? The thought almost makes her giggle, but the sound turns into a hiccup instead, and she smudges the tears from her eyes. He's quick to praise her when she sits up straight, her knees together and her hands carefully folded in her lap. When she forgets and slouches or fidgets, or bounces excitedly, wanting to show him the latest samples from her collection, he turns silent and presses his lips together in a frown. He doesn't believe science is a proper pursuit for a young lady. But then he took her to the observatory, so maybe deep down in his heart there's some softness in him after all, despite what her mother believes.

Sometimes, if she's able to catch her mother in just the right mood, she'll do the perfect scowling impersonation of her grandfather. She knows her mama doesn't like her grandfather, even though she's never said as much aloud. With her father, she's less sure. Sometimes both her mother and her father look sad after her grandfather visits, but some instinct tells her it's one of those subjects she shouldn't ask about.

Thinking of her mother brings a fresh pang to her chest, so sharp it almost steals her breath. She wishes her mother were here now to brush the salt tangles from her hair, to tell her one of her stories properly. Maybe she's getting too old for fairy tales, but right now, it's the only thing she wants in the world. The thought makes her cry even harder.

She might never see her mama or her papa again, or Cook. Or her grandfather, who she would be happy to see even if he scolded her or sighed in disappointment at her for looking an unladylike mess. There are so many things she hasn't done or seen yet. What if she never gets the chance to go to a university and study to be a scientist, or travel around the world?

She scrubs the tears from her eyes and wipes her hands on her nightgown. To her relief, her eyes stay dry, even though they feel hot and achy. She's sick of feeling sorry for herself. So what if no one is coming to save her? She'll just have to save herself.

She stands, listening for any change in the breathing around her. At least the too-bright moon makes it easy to see, so she doesn't step on any of the boys lying scattered around the remains of the fire as she picks her way to the edge of the camp. Should she return to the shore? All ships have lifeboats, don't they? Perhaps there's a lifeboat near where she woke up. Could she row herself all the way home? Even though she doesn't know where Neverland is on a map, if Peter flew her here without stopping it can't be all that far from London, can it?

At the barricade, she pauses and glances over her shoulder. None of the boys have moved, dark shapes on the ground, draped in hammocks strung between trees, and curled up on platforms tucked among the branches. She squares her shoulders and steps over the invisible line separating Peter's camp from the woods. A thrill runs through her, making her feel brave and dangerous.

With luck, the boys won't notice she's gone right away. She hurries her step. The sun could come up at any time, as she's seen, but if she's quick, perhaps she can escape while darkness holds and before anyone has had too much of a chance to miss her.

A terrible shape drops onto the path in front of her, and her heart jumps into her mouth along with a startled shout.

She can't make sense of it. All she can think of is a massive spider or crab, angled limbs sticking up in wrong directions. It blocks the path completely; there's no way to get around it. Are there monsters in Neverland?

Should she run back to the camp? Wake Peter and the boys? At the moment, she can't do anything at all. It's like being stuck in one of those dreams where you want to run but your legs won't move. Eyes shine at her through the dark, a hint of a smile beneath them like the thinnest crescent moon.

All at once the shape resolves into Peter, but she feels no relief. There's a wrongness to him, the way he's crouched on the path, angled limbs like a marionette, like a wooden doll, all jumbled in a pile. He throws his head back, letting out a crowing call, a weird, warbling echo that makes the skin prickle all up and down her spine.

She takes a step back, and Peter leaps up, catching her wrist as the sound echoes across the camp, calling the boys awake. She has the sudden impression that they mean to tie her up, burn her like a witch. Perhaps they will eat her.

"Wendy has thought of an excellent new game!" Peter exclaims as sleepy-eyed boys join them, the menace vanished all at once, his expression pure delight.

Fear still hasn't loosened its grip on her. She feels unsteady, struggling to keep up.

"A game?" She repeats Peter's words dumbly.

"Moonlight hide and seek," Peter says, his expression sly. Is it possible he doesn't realize she meant to leave? Or does he know and he's already forgiven her?

He darts forward, tapping a boy of middling height with pudgy cheeks and large hands.

"Tag! You're it!" Peter dances away, spinning out of reach. "Everyone run and hide and Bertie will come find us."

Then he's gone, rabbiting away into the dark. A beat and the other boys scatter, leaving her and Bertie blinking at each other. Bertie rubs a hand over his face then shakes himself; she thinks of a bear waking from a long winter sleep.

Bertie's smile when it spreads across his face is slow, and nowhere near as wicked as Peter's, but there is a calculating gleam to it. They come to the same realization at the same moment—if he can tag her before she runs, she'll be it instead of him. He swipes at her, but the motion is clumsy and she twists away. His fingers just miss her. Part of her knows that being it would give her more chance to escape, but instinct—the ingrained rules of the game that tell her being it is bad—takes over, and she bolts. The terror of being caught—the idea of being forced to hunt through the dark for all the boys who must know this island far better than she does—sweeps everything else from her mind.

She darts among the trees, running a zig-zag pattern, hoping to throw Bertie off her trail. Unlike the boys, she may not know the best places to hide, but she's certain she can at least outrun him.

She hears boys crashing through leaves and branches, making no effort to be quiet. Sound distorts oddly among the trees, so she can't quite tell which direction it's coming from. She wishes Bertie would break off to pursue one of the others, but he remains focused on her, lumbering after her through the brush—a terrible, heavy sound. She doesn't dare look back, pushing herself into an extra burst of speed.

Finally, the sound of pursuit grows more distant. She doesn't slacken her pace yet, pulling even farther ahead. Instead of feeling tired, the longer she runs, the lighter, faster, and more agile she feels. It's like the beach all over again. She no longer cares where she's going. The air is sweet, almost like the tea Peter gave her to drink when she first arrived. Fear drops away, and she runs for the joy of it, forgetting about finding a place to hide as she leaps over fallen logs and dodges roots and stones.

Her blood sings, giddy, and she gives herself over to a wonderful sense of freedom. Being up past her bedtime. Being clever. And perhaps most importantly, not being it. Imagine Peter's face when he sees she's evaded being caught. Perhaps he'll even declare her the winner of his ridiculous game!

She must have run clear across the island by now, and she feels as though she could go on, running forever, but she slows. There's an ache in her legs, but in a pleasant way. She can't hear any of the others, which makes it the perfect time to look around on her own without Peter rushing her here and there.

Plants rise on either side of a faintly visible path, massive dark green leaves glossy in the moonlight. They remind her of elephant ear plants, but even larger, and with blooms nearly as big as her head. She pauses for a closer look. The petals are all coral and sunset at the edges, deepening to purple-red at the flowers' hearts.

There's nothing like it in England. It might be a whole new species, and she could be the first one to discover it. Excitement thrills though her, and she touches one of the delicate stamens. Her finger comes away dusty with bright yellow pollen, and she has the sudden impulse to lick it. She imagines it would taste like crystallized honey, like the sweet drink Peter gave her.

"Don't." The word startles her, a rustle among the leaves followed by a small, pale face, and she jumps back.

The youngest of the boys, the one who sucked at his shirttail, gazes up at her, eyes wide and frightened.

"The flowers are bad." One hand is clapped over his mouth and nose, as if he's trying to stay quiet, or trying not to breathe too deeply, and his words are muffled.

She looks down at her finger, smeared in pollen, and hastily wipes it on her nightgown. Was she really about to taste it? Whatever would make her do such a thing? She knows far better than to put strange plants in her mouth. It could be poison. But the heady scent of the flower, making her feel warm and safe and…

She lifts the collar of her nightgown over her mouth to stop from breathing the intoxicating smell. Where is she? She's never seen this part of the island before. She was in the camp and… and she ran. Peter on the path, and then the game. She stares at the boy, but he makes no move to tag her, or give her position away.

"Are you all right, Wendy?"

"That's not my name. I'm…"

Oh, she wants to shout in frustration, but if any of the other boys are near, she'll give them both away. She tucked the stone from her soup, the one that was almost in her throat, into her sleeve earlier, and she slips it free now, squeezing it until her hand hurts and her eyes sting.

"Did Peter make up a new name for you too?" Above his fingers covering his nose and mouth, the boy's eyes are wide with curiosity now instead of fear. "I used to be called something else, but I'm called Timothy now. Peter gave me a name, but I didn't like it so I chose a new one. We're allowed sometimes if…"

He darts a glance away down the path, body tense. She follows his gaze to a scrap of shadow shifting beneath one of the trees.

"What—" But Timothy is already gone, flying down the path and leaving her alone.

She squints, but she can no longer see the shadow. Maybe it was only her imagination. An insect chirrs, a sound like a cricket, but also like rubbing a finger around the rim of a dampened glass to make it sing. If only she had her collecting net and specimen jars. She takes a step forward. The sound cuts off abruptly and a sudden chill passes over her. Between one footfall and the next, the sense of someone watching her creeps over her, certain and unshakeable. She spins around, expecting to find Bertie, or even Peter, ready to leap out and tag her. But there's no one. It's like hearing someone call her name in an empty room, except worse, because she doesn't even know her name right now.

She puts her shoulders back and lifts her chin. She will not cry again, and she will not let the weight of what she doesn't know crush her. And she will certainly not let any of the boys play tricks to scare her just because she's a girl.

"Hello?" She makes her voice loud, stepping forward as she calls out. "Is someone there?"

A branch cracks. She turns toward the sound, but she can't make out anything in the dark. The path narrows ahead, trees leaning in to form a tunnel. There's something ominous in the way the trees bend unnaturally close. They make her think of a deep hole burrowing into the earth, or the mouth of a great beast waiting to swallow her, like Jonah and the whale. But what if the path leads to a way out?

She takes another step. Something strikes the top of her foot. She jumps back, and something else hits her shoulder, sharp as an insect sting. She whirls in a circle, but she still can't see anyone, and anger rises in her, making her shout.

"Peter, is that you? Stop it right now! You aren't being funn—" Her words are cut off as the next blow just misses her, the flying object skipping into the fallen leaves covering the path.

Her mouth hangs open, stunned. Then all at once the projectiles fly thick and fast, like hard, pelting rain, driving her back from the tunnel-like path.

She ducks, covering her head with her arms, managing to snatch up a few of the missiles without being hit. She raises an arm, meaning to throw them back into the trees and show that she isn't defenseless, but she can't even see her attackers to aim.

She backs along the path, and once she can no longer hear projectiles hitting the ground, she pauses to look at the objects in her hand. Stones, and among them is an arrowhead. She has one in her collection at home. Cook gave it to her. She had it sent specially from Canada. A long time ago, her people used to make them, and use them to hunt. Now they still make them, but they don't use them for hunting as much anymore.

The one in her hand isn't sharp, but still she feels lucky that none of them hit her with more than a glancing blow. Perhaps whoever threw them wasn't trying to hurt her, merely scare her away.

She drops the stones and turns the arrowhead in her hand, studying it more closely, wishing she knew more. Maybe then it would give her some kind of clue. She'd tried to ask Cook more about the arrowhead she'd given her, but unlike the stories Cook told—passed to her by her mother—talking about real history seemed to make her sad. She'd been surprised as well, as though she'd never expected anyone to ask. It was only when Cook hadn't been able to answer all of the questions, admitting she didn't know as much of her history as she should, that she'd left Canada so young and hadn't been back since, that she began to look troubled.

Her mother had come into the kitchen then and told her to stop pestering Cook, shooing her away despite Cook's protests she didn't mind. She'd peeked back in from the doorway and seen her mother and Cook with their heads leaned close together, whispering. They'd both looked sad then, in a way she didn't know grown-ups could be, and she'd hurried away.

"Ha! I found you." A hand closes around her arm, and she lets out a cry of surprise. "Now you have to help me find everyone else. Those are the rules."

"Bertie?" She covers the arrowhead quickly, holding it tight.

Sweat dampens Bertie's forehead, and he breathes heavily. That, and the way he avoids her eyes keeps her from correcting him to say that she's it now, and he has to run and hide. He's afraid; he doesn't want to hunt through the dark alone, though he would never admit it, especially not to a girl. A thought strikes her then—if the game of hide and seek is still going on, who threw the projectiles?

"Have you found anyone else yet?"

"No." Bertie looks a little bit relieved, but pushes his chest out, a bossy edge creeping into his voice. "You're the first. Now you have to help me."

His hand is still on her arm. There's a dampness to his fingers, clammy fear seeping from his skin to hers. She glances behind her, but there's no sign of whoever did the throwing. Maybe they weren't trying to hurt her or scare her; maybe they were trying to warn her. But about what? Could there be something dangerous at the end of the path? Or something that needs protection?

"Come on." Bertie tugs her arm insistently.

There'll be time to unravel the mystery later. Besides, having Bertie along would only bungle things up. He's too loud, and right now, too jumpy. His need to get away is palpable. She can feel his pulse in his fingertips, and it's almost infectious. It makes her want to run, too.

"Okay, let's go find the others."

She follows him, ignoring the shivery feeling like a hand brushing across the nape of her neck, telling herself it's for Bertie's sake they're leaving, not her own.

LET'S PLAY WAR

There's something terrible at the center of the island.

Wendy comes to with a violent jolt, the knowledge in her mind as sure as she knew there was a boy at her daughter's window. Her pulse beats too fast, and for a moment she's disoriented. She wants the whole thing to have been a terrible, beautiful dream, but no—she is still here in Neverland.

She didn't intend to sleep. She isn't safe here, and neither is Jane. She'd only meant to sit for a moment with her back against the smooth trunk of a tree and rest her aching eyes. But her traitor mind had lulled her with images of home, Jane and Ned and Mary, all of them safe and far away from Peter's grasp. Then she'd woken among tangled roots, her pulse racing, feeling some horrible thing, just out of reach.

Wendy puts a hand to her face, brushing at the imprint of leaves pressed into her skin. She tries to brush the dreams away, too, but they aren't dreams. More like a memory, but one dissipating like smoke, slipping beyond her reach.

She stands, stretching, and her joints pop. It's not just from lying on the ground with roots poking awkwardly into her back. She's aged. She's grown up. And Peter is still the same boy she left behind. She thinks of him standing at the foot of her daughter's bed—the wicked grin, the fire-bright hair.

The elusive memory returns, sharp as a knife slash—his hand in hers, running through the trees. *I'll show you a secret. A really good one. One I've never shown anyone before.* The sensation is so real, Wendy gasps aloud to catch her breath. But when she tries to grab hold, the place where the memory should be is a ragged hole, like fabric with a bit torn out. *Come on, Wendy. Keep up. It's the best secret you've ever seen, I promise.*

Wendy clenches her jaw, leaving her teeth aching. Whatever did or didn't happen last time she was here isn't important. What matters now is Jane.

The sky was flush with stars when she'd sat down to rest, but now the sun is up, steadily climbing the sky. There's no telling how much time she's lost. She moves at a quick clip until she emerges from the trees and back onto the beach. Wendy is surprised to find the ship much closer than she thought. Did the landscape shift as she slept, the coastline curling in upon itself at Peter's whim? Or did she walk farther than she realized?

The sand bears dimples in the places the tide doesn't reach, the memory of feet surrounding the ship without drawing too close. She remembers the welcome party of boys that greeted her, Michael and John when Peter finally brought them down from the sky. There are long branches scattered around the remains of the ship's hull as well, the kind that might be used as a shelter. Was Jane here? Did Peter bring the boys to meet her on the same spot where Wendy met them herself?

She almost bends to touch the footprints in the sand as though she could guess which ones belong to Jane. Her daughter, here in

Neverland. It still doesn't seem possible. The two worlds should never have touched. Jane is the life Wendy built to save herself from Peter. She should have told her daughter everything. Kept her safe.

Wendy takes a shuddering breath. Her clever, curious daughter. Will she be smarter than Wendy, less susceptible to Peter's charms? Wendy can only hope.

She draws closer to the wreck of the ship. Beached and snapped in two, the prow pointing up toward the sky. But the interior might be intact, and there might be weapons or something else she could use. If anything in Neverland ever gave Peter pause, it was Hook. She can very well imagine the boys looking on the ship, even destroyed, with superstition, refusing to step inside what was once the realm of their greatest enemy.

Once. She comes close enough to touch the hull and rests her fingers against the weathered boards. What could be powerful enough to tear a ship in half this way? Were the pirates on board when it happened, and if not, where did they go?

NEVERLAND – 27 YEARS AGO

"Why must I stay behind? It isn't fair."

"Because you're a girl. Girls don't go to war." Peter's fists rest on his hips, elbows jutting out like strange wings. His tone is imperious, as though everything he's saying should be perfectly obvious and Wendy is dull for not understanding.

"You have to heal the soldiers when they're wounded so they can rejoin the war. Those are the rules."

"What rules? Who made the rules?" Wendy is taller than

Peter; when she pokes him in the chest he takes a step back, and there's a moment of satisfaction as she looms over him. His scowl deepens, his bottom lip pushing out as he glares up at her, but Wendy ignores him. "If Michael and John get to go, I should get to go too."

"No. You stay here." Peter crosses his arms. He moves to the makeshift tent's doorway, and somehow his slight frame fills the space so Wendy can't see any way to slip past him.

"Fine." She crosses her own arms, turning her head and refusing to look at him. She hopes his expression is hurt, but she won't give him the satisfaction of looking to see for sure. She makes herself hold the pose, not turning around again until he's gone.

The sense of triumph is temporary. Almost as soon as the tent flap falls shut behind him, Peter is shouting orders, her presence and their argument just as likely forgotten.

"Everyone, it's time to choose our swords," Peter says.

Wendy sticks her tongue out at the tent wall, even though there's no one left to see her. Of course when Peter says *everyone* he doesn't mean her. His words never say what they ought to, and yet the way he says them is so certain. It infuriates her.

It doesn't matter that the swords are only long branches and sticks stripped of their leaves. To the boys they're real enough and the fact that she doesn't get one of her own still stings. Wendy keeps her eyes fixed on the tent wall, watching the sun cast the boys' flickering shadows against its skin as they gather their weapons. All except Peter's.

She thinks again of how he made such a fuss when she sewed the shadow he brought her back onto his body. And after all the squirming and pouting, after all the trouble she went to, it unraveled almost immediately. Wendy knows she isn't the best seamstress—and according to her mother, she might just be the worst—but her stitching isn't *that* bad. Shadows aren't meant to come apart like that, or, now that she thinks about it, even be separated from the people they belong to in the first place.

Why should it surprise her though—when none of Peter's other words mean what they should—that he might have lied to her about his shadow, too? It's clear enough that he managed to lose his somehow, but she's almost certain the one he brought to her to sew back on didn't belong to him.

As the boys drift away from the tent, Michael and John among them, Wendy's shoulders slump. She wonders if either of her brothers spoke up for her, or whether she was the only one to argue with Peter's ridiculous rules. She looks around the tent, restless and irritated. Peter hasn't even left her anything to do, other than clean up the boys' things and she's had quite enough of that already. Everything can just lie where it is and rot for all she cares.

With nothing else to occupy her, Wendy tries to count on her fingers the number of days they've been here, but she loses track immediately. Time is tricky in Neverland, just like everything else. Days and nights blur together, and there's so much to see and do, it's easy to become distracted.

Are their parents worried? At least they must know that she and Michael and John are together, and she'll take care of them, like she always does.

Shouts echo through the trees, layered over the sound of wooden sticks clacking together. She's tempted to peek her head out, maybe even find a tree where she can hide and watch the war. It *sounds* exciting at least, and she can imagine Peter leaping over the other boys' heads, laughing and quick. She's about to slip outside when a sheepish face pokes through the tent door. Roger, she remembers, is what the boy is called. There's a gap between his two front teeth, and his brown hair refuses to lie flat, sticking up every which way like a bird's nest. He holds his arm against his chest as he ducks inside.

"Peter says I've been kilt and I have to sit here 'til you fix me so I can go out and fight again."

Wendy wants to be cross with him, but it isn't Roger's fault.

"Oh, all right." She points. "Sit there."

Roger hangs his head as he obeys, and she finds a bit of cloth that they were using to play blind man's bluff last night.

"How were you killed?" Wendy asks, assessing Roger critically.

"Stab wound, right here." He taps his finger against his chest. "Peter ran me through with his sword."

"Let's see, then." Wendy carefully peels Roger's hand away from the bloodless wound. She wraps the strip of cloth around the spot he indicated, careful to be gentle, and ties a knot at Roger's shoulder.

"Do you like it here?" The question pops into her mouth as she works, surprising her. It feels daring.

"Yeah. It's brilliant!" Roger grins, the gap between his teeth looking even wider. "It's all games and no bedtime or vegetables."

Done with the knot, Wendy lets her hands fall to her sides.

"What about before? When you… When you were with your mother and father?"

"Didn't have any."

114

"No parents?"

"I don't think so." Roger shrugs, but a frown carves lines around the corners of his mouth like he's trying to remember something. She wants to ask who made him eat his vegetables or set his bedtime if he had no parents, but the line forming between his brows stops her. She imagines him like a cup, balanced on the edge of a table. If she tips him too far, he'll shatter.

"Am I all fixed up?" His voice is hopeful and troubled all at once. Mostly, Wendy thinks, he just wants to get away from her.

"Yes. All healed. Run along." She waves him toward the door, watching as he bounds off, back into the war.

Over the course of the war, she sees every boy at least once, all except Peter, because Peter always wins. Later, when the war is done and they've had supper, Peter sits beside her on one of the logs circled around the fire and nudges her with his shoulder.

"Are you terribly cross at me, Wendy?"

"I suppose." Wendy doesn't look at him.

Mostly, she's tired. She asked every boy who came into the tent some variation of the questions she asked Roger, and their answers were all the same. The only ones she didn't ask were John and Michael. What if she already found forgetting in their eyes? What if John and Michael couldn't remember their parents? She's already found that if she doesn't concentrate, she starts to forget home, or ever being any place other than here. So she didn't dare ask, afraid of what the answer would be.

"Come with me." Peter seizes her hand suddenly, startling her and pulling her to her feet. He grins at her, the glint in his eyes promising adventure, and just like that, she's forgiven him, wanting to follow him wherever he might go. "I promised you a secret and I'll show you now since you were so good about fixing all my soldiers up. It's a really good secret, too. I've never showed it to anyone before."

Wendy braces herself and crawls inside the torn ship. Despite knowing it to be grounded in sand, she half expects the deck to sway beneath her, timbers creaking as Hook leans over her, his posture designed to intimidate. She can't help straining after the sound of shouting voices, the lines groaning, and the sails snapping in the wind. The other half of her expects skeletons like the bones littering the lagoon, but the ship is eerily empty, eerily still.

The ship's interior is largely intact, only tilted askew. The mermaids in the lagoon, as horrible as their deaths are, at least those are deaths Wendy can understand. Here, it's as though she can feel the missing crew moving around her, as though at any moment one of Hook's pirates might brush against her sleeve hurrying from one end of the deck to the other. She doesn't believe in ghosts, not the kind that haunt houses and ships. Yet, as a girl she saw an impossible monster with dark mottled skin and slavering jaws rise from the waves to snap at Hook's remaining hand. She's met mermaids; she can fly. So why not ghosts, too?

If Hook were here, would he still seem a villain to her eyes? As a child, she'd failed to see the truth of Peter, or even consider there might be more to him than his games and bright smiles. Had she misjudged his greatest enemy as well? Might she see a flicker of desperation in Hook's eyes? Fear? Wendy can only imagine what his life in Neverland must have been, a grown man trapped by the whims of an impetuous child, as subject to Peter's quicksilver moods as the tides and the winds and the weather.

Wendy tests her footing on the canted deck. The boards complain, but her foot does not go plunging through. How many years has the ship lain baking in the sun, all the moisture sucked dry, as though it always belonged on the sand and never upon the sea? The last time she was here, she and John and Michael spent most of their time tied to the main mast, until Peter saved them. She never saw this part of the ship back then. She has no idea what a real pirate ship might look like, but now that she's here, she takes in Peter's idea of one. The remains of tangled sleeping nets hang from the ceiling in one narrow room. In what must have been the galley, she finds overturned crates and emptied barrels. And in every space she crawls through, the pervasive sense of haunting remains, of being watched and yet utterly alone.

Finally, at the ship's prow, she finds a large cabin that must have belonged to Hook. Shreds of rich brocade—dark like new blood—hang from the railing above a narrow bed. There's a writing desk, overturned and smashed against one wall. A sea chest thrown open, its contents scattered around the room. The frame of a full-length mirror still holds shards of silvered glass. They glint dully in light slanting in through a window that once looked out to sea and now points toward the sky.

The heavy, warped glass distorts the light, turning it a sick-yellow color, like weak tea. A shadow passes in front of the glass, flickering through the shard of mirror at her foot, catching her attention. An eye peers up at her from the broken glass. Wendy swallows a shout, clapping a hand over her mouth to hold in the sound. It's Hook's eye, dark and glittering.

She reels back, bracing herself against the wall, heart pounding. From this angle, the mirror only reflects the blank wood of the ceiling. She slides a foot forward, edging toward the broken glass. She makes herself look, holding her breath. Nothing. It is only a mirror, and nothing looks back at her save her own reflection.

Even so, her nerves remain strung tight, the haunted feeling clinging to her. She tries to imagine a storm terrible enough to cause this kind of destruction. Had Peter finally tired of endless battles against his old foe and dreamed up a wave big enough to pick up Hook's entire ship and smash it against the shore?

Wendy glances at the items thrown around the room—empty bottles, some broken, some whole; a glass bauble, cracked and smoky; a few coins. They're worn, but she can still see the images, stamped on one side with a leering skull, the other with some sort of bird. There's no mark identifying them as belonging to any country, but then there wouldn't be, would there? They're only Peter's idea of a pirate's treasure.

Wendy gets down on her hands and knees and peers under the bed. Something glints in the dark space, and Wendy's breath catches. It might be more mirror glass, and she's afraid of what she might find looking back at her, but she makes herself lie flat, stretching to pull it free. Captain Hook's sword.

Wendy rocks back onto her heels, staring at the blade for a moment. It's just as she remembers it—curved, the hilt wrapped in red leather. She stands, slipping her hand beneath the guard of tarnished, filigreed gold, and tests the grip. When she swings it experimentally, the blade sings a high, whistling note in the air. Wendy rests the pad of her thumb gently against the edge without pressing down. It's still sharp.

When she extends her arm, the sword balances naturally. It's like the treasure—not a sword a real pirate would use. It doesn't matter that she has no experience with weaponry. Any sword in Neverland would be able to be wielded by an untrained child as easily as by a seasoned warrior. Like the ship itself, like the pirates, the sword she holds is a plaything, a boy's fantasy of what a sword should be. A toy, but one sharp enough for killing, because that's the kind of boy Peter is.

There's no scabbard or belt that she can find, so Wendy tightens her shawl around her waist and tucks the sword into it. A moment of vanity seizes her and she glances regretfully at the broken mirror. It's a silly thing, but she wishes she could see herself. Does she look as fierce and formidable as the captain himself?

She pictures Hook's sneer, his red velvet coat—like blood, like poppies—flaring as he paced and turned, all wide lapels and gleaming buttons. Even in her terror, she'd wanted to rub that velvet between her thumb and her forefinger to see what it felt like. The air around her shivers, the timbers beneath her feet shaking with absent footsteps. The longer she stands in his cabin, the more it seems she can conjure Hook's ghost. She sees his regal figure striding the deck, shaking his fist and daring Peter to come claim his prize—Wendy and her brothers. She can even smell the oil worked into the long, heavy curls hanging down Hook's back, blacker than a raven's wing.

In the stories Wendy had told Jane of the Tailor and the Little White Bird, she'd turned Hook from a pirate into a prince, a wicked and cursed one. Petals scattered from the hem of his coat every time he turned, and poisoned blossoms sprang up beneath the heels of his polished boots. He'd used their petals to lure the

119

Little White Bird into a deadly sleep, until the Clever Tailor had woven a net out of every color of thread to trap the prince and save the Bird.

Wendy shakes her head. Her stories seem foolish now, and her actual time with the pirates almost seems like one of them. Were they ever truly in danger? At the time, the threat seemed real. She remembers the sour stink of fear, the way Michael had trembled, pressed against her side as Hook tied them to the mast. John, with his chin raised but his eyes owl-wide behind the gleam of his glasses. For all his bluster, though, Hook had never really been cruel to her or her brothers.

He'd lashed them to the mast, but the bonds hadn't been tight, and hadn't he made sure they had tea to drink, and biscuits from the ship's stores? She'd hated him, but only because she was meant to; he was Peter's enemy, therefore he was her enemy too. She hadn't seen it clearly then, but now Wendy can picture the slant of Hook's shoulders, the lackluster movement of his hand and his hook as he'd secured their bindings. They'd been merely bait, but even Hook must have known that when he came for them Peter would inevitably escape. He'd captured Wendy and her brothers knowing he had nothing to gain, only frightening them, fulfilling the one role Peter designed for him to play.

She wonders—is it that Hook *couldn't* hurt them, or he chose not to? How easy would it have been for him to turn his sneering posturing into true violence, taking his impotence against Peter out on them instead? They had been in Neverland, but not of it, not yet. Did its rules still apply, or could he truly have fed them to the monster beneath the waves, or even simply snapped their necks?

Wendy shivers at the thought, caught between horror and sympathy for the man she once hated and feared so much. That heady floral scent she'd always taken for the oil in Hook's hair, what if it had been something else? A drug, to ease the pain of being trapped here, forced into the role of a villain.

Wendy tries to picture the captain alone in his cabin, head heavy, breathing out smoke. The wavering light of a candle would make his shadow tremble as he tried to forget, tried to dream, tried to sleep. Wendy passes her gaze over the cabin walls again. The room seems smaller than when she entered, the air heavy, tainted and close. Redolent with ghosts. She can't stay here.

As Wendy climbs out of the captain's cabin, she moves with less caution. What if Hook never belonged here either, as much Peter's captive as Wendy and her brothers were his? Could he have been an actual sea captain once, a merchant, a soldier with a whole life beyond Neverland? If Hook had come from somewhere else, a place like her own England with real war and death, would this place have seemed like a paradise to him at first? Or would it have seemed a mockery of the real world with its violence and wars?

It had certainly felt like a paradise to Wendy's own young eyes even though she hadn't been escaping anything. She and John and Michael had been happy, with parents who loved them. The terrible things hadn't come until later—their parents' deaths, St. Bernadette's, the war. If Peter had given Jane a choice, rather than simply snatching her hand, would she have flown away as easily as Wendy, Michael, and John?

Even now, she remembers clearly—there wasn't a moment of hesitation. Peter held out his hand, and Wendy took it, Michael and John at her heels. She hadn't spared a thought for consequences, the way her mother would feel, whether her brothers might be in danger. It had all been a grand adventure, a game, just like Peter and his boys playing at war.

She remembers the day Michael, just after his eighteenth birthday, but still very much a boy, returned to the house, papers in hand, to tell Wendy and John he had enlisted and was going to war for real. There'd been a shine in his eyes, a kind of fever Wendy couldn't understand. Had the war too seemed like a grand adventure? It was how most people had spoken of it early on; a lark, an assured victory, and certain to be over by Christmas.

But the war had already been going on for almost a year by then, and still Michael had chosen to go. And then the reality had come for all of them, and boys like Michael most of all. While he lay in those mud-filled trenches, did he ever think of Peter's games, and how little they prepared him for the true horrors he'd find there? She'd heard Dr. Harrington remark to John once how lucky Michael had been to come home at all when so many didn't. But one look at her baby brother, even now, is enough to make Wendy question whether Michael himself felt the same. He'd come home broken in a way no bandages, medicine, or stitching could fix.

When he'd first returned home from war, Wendy had never understood why Michael had continued to deny Neverland so vehemently. Wouldn't he have wanted to cling to it as an escape, a shield, the way she used it later in the asylum? Now she understands perfectly well, a realization she should have come to far sooner. Why wouldn't Michael continue to deny Neverland? Nothing here ever meant anything. The boys run through with stick swords stood right back up again and rejoined the battle. All she had to do was tie make-believe bandages around bloodless, invisible wounds, and they were good as new. Holding that truth alongside the reality of real war would have been like rubbing salt into a wound. Not just a lie, but a mockery of everything Michael had seen.

Of course Neverland wouldn't have been a balm for Michael. He'd gone deeper into the real world than either she or John, and he'd seen all the evil it had to offer. The boys that would never grow up in his world weren't magic-touched, they were simply rotting in their graves.

Wendy lets the ship take her weight, unsteady in a way that has nothing to do with the canted deck. The memories drag at her, the heaviness making her feel as though she's been trapped in the ship for hours, always climbing and never emerging. Did Michael feel the same in the trenches, hiking miles in the mud and always waiting for enemy fire or bombs to fall?

She knows so little of what he suffered there, only the aftermath, only the pain, but none of the specific details. Ned and Michael speak of the war sometimes, making a show of playing at cards, but rarely glancing at their hands. She's glad her brother and husband have each other. It used to hurt her—selfishly— that Michael could not speak to her as well.

But then, what had she ever done to make him trust her enough to speak his pain? All those times she'd thrown his truth back in his face, demanding he remember Neverland? Why would he ever want to confide in her, after everything she put him through?

He'd surprised her recently though. John, his then-fiancée Elizabeth, and Michael had all come for tea, while Ned had been out with his father and Jane. Mary had taken the day off, though thankfully she'd left the kitchen well stocked with scones, which Wendy surely would have burned. Afterward, Michael had offered to help her do the washing up, taking her by surprise. She couldn't remember the last time they'd been alone together, and she'd been almost afraid, but she'd accepted Michael's offer.

Everything felt fragile and uneasy, despite the warmth of the kitchen. Wendy had been on edge, feeling like everything would shatter around her with the slightest wrong movement, remembering broken plates and cups of old, and screamed words. Then Michael had spoken, and his voice had caught her so off guard that Wendy had dropped the saucer she'd been holding. Soapy water sprayed the floor, and Michael flinched at the sound.

Wendy remembers holding her breath, feeling herself on the edge of tears. But Michael had looked at her, and offered a pained smile. Her brother, a stranger, both wrapped in one skin. She'd almost gone to her knees to take his hands in her wet and dripping ones to beg his forgiveness. But fear had locked her in place, and she'd remained still, letting her hands drip, letting the shards of the broken saucer lie.

"I want to remember," he'd said, making her heart stutter.

Her first irrational thought was that he meant Neverland. Even then, after everything, after St. Bernadette's, after the hurt she'd done to him that had sent her there, it was where her mind turned first. But he meant the war, his own scar, just as Neverland was hers.

"Some men, all they want is to forget, but I want to remember." His hands trembled, one gripping a dishrag, the other the head of the cane he still used.

His wounded leg shook too, a sign of fatigue, but she knew his pride would make him refuse if she offered him a chair. His lost expression implored her, a child again, waking from a bad dream in the nursery and asking her to make it better.

"I want to remember every bit of it," he'd told her. "But the harder I try to hold on, the more things slip away. I forget faces, names, and it's like I'm killing them all over again. They're dying, and there's nothing I can do to save them. Then there are other times when all I can do is remember and it's too much. I don't want it."

Michael raised the hand holding the dishrag, pressing it to his head, and Wendy could only imagine what horrors unfurled within the private theater of his mind. The world gone orange and black and red in an explosion, shrapnel and flame blooming like some great, terrible flower, men screaming and bleeding and dying.

"I survived. It's my duty to remember. I owe it to the men who died, but they run through my hands and I can't hold on."

He'd lowered his hand; tears stood out in his eyes, hovering on his lashes without falling. Wendy had never seen him look so old and so young all at the same time.

"How do you remember, Wendy? How do you hold on?" It was the closest he'd ever come to asking her about Neverland, the only hint she'd ever seen that part of him might remember. He'd looked at her, heartbroken, breaking her heart in turn; he'd been her brother again, reaching out to her, and she'd had no answers. All she could do was put her arms around him, resting her hands against his back and leaving damp patches on his shirt.

He'd shuddered in her embrace, then gone stiff. When they

stepped apart, it was as though they were strangers again. He'd retreated, closing himself off, and they'd gone back to silently washing dishes. Only Wendy had done it with tears running down to the point of her chin.

Wendy pushes herself away from the wall, feeling worn-through and thin, even more wrung out than before. She wants to be done with the onslaught of memories. They're of all the wrong things, not the thing putting her, putting Jane, in danger here and now.

The sword bumps at her hip as she climbs back into the sunlight. The bowl of the sky is pale blue, like the shell of a robin's egg. She imagines Hook and his pirates falling upward into that infinite blue. Soaring. Vanishing.

A new fear grips her. At her bedroom window, she was able to hold off doubt, but now with all the grief weighing her down, she feels utterly rooted in Neverland's soil. There isn't even a sliver of room for happy thoughts in her mind. If she tried now, could she fly? And if not, when she finds Jane, how on earth will she get them home?

THE HUNT

She turns the arrowhead over and over, trying to puzzle out its meaning and coming up with nothing. Something about it nags at her, familiar yet wrong. Like the moon shining over Neverland, the arrowhead is a little too perfect to be real. The flint shines against her palm, each chip knocked from its edge precise, and every one exactly the same shape and size.

A sound reaches her, soft and regular, and it's a moment before she picks it out as crying, and not just another insect or a night bird. She tucks the arrowhead into the sleeve of her nightgown, warm between the fabric and her skin, and creeps to the edge of the platform, looking for the source of the crying. It isn't quite dawn. The world is pearly gray and all around her, boys sleep. Like this—some curled on the ground, some draped in trees like big jungle cats—they look younger than they did in the harsh shadows cast by the moonlight. Even Arthur. Peter is the only one she can't see. She pictures him roosted in the top of a tree like a wild bird.

The scene in the camp reminds her of pictures in her father's books, black-and-white drawings of ancient ruins in far-off places. She'd hoped to visit those places someday, but now that she's farther from home than she's ever been, home is the only place she wants to be. The ache of missing it reaches for her, a palpable thing. The familiar scent of tobacco from the pipe her papa indulges in on special occasions. The smells of baking from the kitchen. Her mother, humming softly, unaware that anyone is listening. Even the ragged meow of the cat who comes to the kitchen door begging for scraps, the one who bites as often as she purrs, but still bumps into everyone's legs asking to have her head scratched.

She recites the details to herself, trying to fix them in her mind. If she doesn't, they'll become like a story someone else told her, distant and far away. Peter hasn't given her any more of the sweet tea to drink, but there's still something standing in the way of her name, like a door she can't see beyond. It's this place, the details of Neverland writing over the details of her home. Earlier, when she tried to think of them, she couldn't remember the color of her mother's eyes. She can see her mother's face, but it's blurred, out of focus, the eyes a muddy blue-brown-green, and it terrifies her.

In the pre-dawn dark beneath the leaves, she can just make out a hunched shape on the next platform over. Easing onto the thick branch that supports both of their platforms, she scrambles across, quietly enough that the boy doesn't even look up. It's the boy who was hidden among the leaves where the sweet-smelling flowers were—Timothy. The one who asked to hear the end of her story.

She's relieved to see he made it back to the camp, but her relief doesn't last long. His small body shudders, trying to hold in a grief so much bigger than him. She edges closer and sits beside him, touching his shoulder, and putting a finger to her lips when he looks up, startled.

"What's wrong?" she whispers.

His tear-stained face is blotched red and pale, his eyes made bigger by the saltwater. He stares at her, and after a moment she lifts her arm, feeling awkward. He dives against her, burrowing into her side so she can feel his shuddering breath.

"Bad dream." His voice is muffled.

She pats his hair. It's gritty with sand.

"You can tell me, if you'd like."

"I was in another place, and I had a bed so big it was like an ocean. There was a window, and two people standing in front of it, but they didn't have faces and I couldn't remember who they were."

"Did they hurt you?"

He shakes his head. She feels it against her ribs.

"They just stood there, looking at me. One of them sang, and the other one reached out to touch my head, then I woke up."

He pulls away from her so she can see his face. The tears no longer flow, but his eyes remain wide.

"Do you know who they are?" His expression pleads with her, and something catches in her throat.

Her heartbeat is an ache, the feeling of loss. Her mother's blurred face hangs in her mind, the tune of her humming muffled so she can't quite hear it anymore. For a moment, she can't speak, and she swallows hard.

Parents. Parents singing a lullaby and tucking him in for the night. And for Timothy, it is a bad dream. He can scarcely remember what he lost, but the terrible sense of something fundamental missing from his life remains. Looking at him, the bewildered fear on his face, she hurts. The pain isn't just for him, but for herself as well.

The longer she stays here, the more parts of herself she'll lose. She's certain of it now; it's already begun. She'll wake up one day and it won't be just her mother's features that are blurred. She might not remember that she ever had parents at all.

Timothy continues looking at her, hopeful, expectant, waiting for her answer. Would it be crueler to tell him? If Timothy knows the people in his dreams are his parents, will it be like opening a floodgate, reminding him of everything he's lost? Maybe it's better to only know he lost something, and not exactly what. How awful or careless must Peter be to take a mother and father away from a child so young?

"I think…" Anger, directed at Peter, cracks her voice. She swallows, trying again. "I think the people in your dream are people who love you very much. You don't have to be afraid."

Relief washes over Timothy's face, immediate and pure. She envies him, and hates him, and wants to protect him all at once as he nestles against her again. All she can do is not pull away, putting her arm around him and feeling the tension run from his body.

"Will you tell a story? Like you did before?" He murmurs the request softly, barely audible. The sound makes her think of warm milk, but she tenses all the same, her muscles going rigid so he flinches away from her.

Fear spikes. What if she can't remember any stories? What if she gets them all wrong again?

She forces herself to relax, pulling him close again, trying to ignore the speeding of her pulse. Timothy tilts his head to look up at her. He isn't like Peter. He's a little boy, so far away from his family that he doesn't even remember what a family is anymore.

She's never thought all that much about the fact she doesn't have brothers or sisters. Now that's she's about to have a little cousin—if she ever makes it home, that is—she's started wondering what it will be like to teach someone the things she knows. If she had siblings, she likes to think she would be a good big sister, helping to keep them safe, loving them, just like her mother with Uncle Michael and Uncle John.

"I could try," she says. She remembers her family, at least for now, even if she doesn't remember her name. She hasn't lost everything, so she can give Timothy this little bit of comfort.

"What sort of stories do you like?"

"Adventures." His voice is already sleepy, lulled by the words she hasn't even spoken yet.

"All right, an adventure story."

Timothy nods, a motion against her ribs as she takes a deep breath. Off amongst the leaves, in the deep shadowed places where the air is thick black and purple, fireflies blink in a lazy rhythm. Neverland is paused in the space before morning, stars still twinkling overhead, brighter than the ones she knows at home. Insects chirr, and a night bird she can't identify trills a strange song.

"Once upon a time, there was a Clever Tailor..." Nerves grip her.

But before doubt can fully take hold, inspiration strikes her. She doesn't need to recite her mother's stories; she can make up her own. That's what her mother does, after all. She finds herself grinning as the next words leave her mouth.

"And the Tailor had a daughter who was very clever too, but instead of sewing and doing magic, she was a scientist."

She swells with the thought of the words, pride filling her. Timothy pulls away from her side to peer up at her.

"What's a scientist?"

"Oh. Well, it's someone who studies books and learns things about the way plants and animals grow, and the way planets move, and how to make people better when they're sick." She struggles to find terms that might be familiar to him.

Timothy frowns. His hair sticks up on one side of his head where he's been pressed against her, and she reaches automatically to smooth it down. He tolerates the touch, but his frown lingers.

"Looking at books doesn't sound like an adventure," he says. His voice holds no judgment, not the way Peter's would, only the beginnings of disappointment. But there's doubt, too, as though Timothy is merely waiting to be convinced. She thinks quickly, then launches back into the story.

"Well, the Tailor's daughter was a different kind of scientist. All her instruments were also magic. She had a telescope that could see every star in the sky, no matter how far away. And… it could transport her to those stars to visit the people living on them and other planets too."

Timothy's expression brightens.

"That's all right, then. I like magic." He leans against her again. Is that where they are, she wonders, on another star? There's a catch in her voice when she speaks again, but Timothy doesn't seem to notice.

"The Tailor's daughter also had a magical compass that could point north like any other compass, but also point to where the best adventures were…"

Timothy stays pressed against her side as the words unspool.

It's almost like her mother is telling the story through her, but even better, like they're telling the story together. It makes her a little less afraid; it makes her feel a little less alone. Even though she can't see or feel her mother, she knows with absolute certainty they'll find their way back to each other soon.

When the sun comes up, it's a surprise—a glitter of light breaking all at once through the leaves. Was she truly lost in the story, or did daylight simply pounce like a tiger, sudden and rude, like everything else in Neverland? The camp's stillness shatters with a sound that is half cock's crow and half war cry; Timothy bolts upright, going from half-sleep to alert fear in an instant. She looks down from the platform into the camp.

Peter stands beside the ashes of last night's fire, as if dropped out of the sky and landing just there as the sun rose. Even from here she can see his cheeks are flushed, his eyes bright and his hair wild. Unlike the mess of Timothy's hair though, there's something sharp-edged and dangerous about Peter's locks. It makes her think of a broken crown resting upon his head, and the leaves caught there might almost grow from his scalp.

His hands rest on his hips, elbows jutting sideways, and his expression is impatient as the camp wakes and gathers around him.

"We have to go." Timothy nudges her. It's not a suggestion. Without waiting, he scrambles down, and she follows, her pulse going harder in a way that has nothing to do with the climb.

"We're going hunting." Peter casts his voice like a net, snagging everyone as she and Timothy join the circle. "We must have a proper feast to welcome our new Wendy."

Peter's gaze skims over the boys and stops on her. It feels like a pin driven though the center of her body, holding her down the

133

way she mounts her butterflies at home. She opens her mouth, feeling as though something is expected of her, but the moment she does, her mind goes blank.

It's more than the sticky sweet drink; it's Peter himself who makes her forget, who turns her strange. She has only a moment to think it then she finds herself blinking, a step or two closer to where Peter stands, as though a moment of time has slipped away without her marking it.

She closes her mouth. When did she open it? Did someone ask her a question? Peter's expression digs at her, simultaneously seeking approval and daring her to contradict him. She fights the urge to squirm, even though everything in her wants to crawl away. Like every game Peter has proposed since she got here, she doesn't understand the rules to this one either; she only knows she can't be the first to look away.

She keeps her head up, keeps looking at Peter. Confusion passes through his eyes like a cloud across the sun, then his lips form a slow smile and he nods, as though she gave him her approval even though she did no such thing. She wants to stamp her foot and shout at him, but there's no time. Peter whirls away from her to address the expectant circle of boys, all watching him eagerly. Except for Timothy, who remains pressed against her side.

"Hunters, gather your weapons. We are going to catch a boar."

Boys scatter in every direction, like an anthill broken open. It looks like chaos, but in no time they're assembled again into tense, eager lines, each holding a weapon. It makes her think of the pictures she's seen of her Uncle Michael and her father dressed in their soldier's uniforms, lined up with other men, ready to fight a war. Some of the men in those pictures scarcely look older than the oldest of the boys around her now. She's allowed to look at the pictures, and even hold them, but she's not allowed to ask Uncle Michael about the war.

Her papa looks handsome in his uniform, but Uncle Michael looks lost, afraid. She thinks her father might tell her about the war if she asked, but she also thinks her mother wouldn't like it very much if he did. Besides, if she can't ask her Uncle Michael, maybe it isn't right to ask her father either.

Peter's boys aren't wearing uniforms. They're as ragged as ever, and she wonders if they even have other clothes besides the ones they're wearing. How long have they been here? Did Peter steal them all away like he stole her? Instead of guns, the boys hold spears, bows and arrows, slingshots, knives, and swords. Some of the weapons look as though the boys made them themselves, but others look stolen from the ruin of the ship, like the cup Peter made her drink from, and the hammocks.

It doesn't matter what weapons the boys use, or what they're wearing. Even though she isn't allowed to ask about the war, she understands enough about what it means. War is where men go to kill each other. These boys—even though some of them are younger than she is—hold death in their eyes.

As she looks around at the assembled line, some of the boys refuse to meet her gaze. Others, like Arthur, glare back at her, defiant. For those who will look at her, she tries to convey without words that they don't have to do this. She doesn't want a welcome feast; she doesn't want to be here at all.

Desperation gnaws at her. How can she make them understand? Peter strides down the line, and all eyes turn to him, his chest puffed up like a general inspecting his troops.

Only then does she notice that Timothy is missing. She scans the camp, relief filling her as she catches sight of him crouched near the pile of weapons.

She tries to signal to him without drawing Peter's attention. Timothy doesn't look up, staring at the sad offering of broken spears and unstrung bows. She glances back at Peter. He seems distracted enough that she risks hurrying to Timothy's side, touching his shoulder. His head snaps up, cheeks blotchy with tears that he scrubs at furiously.

"What's wrong?" She whispers it, glancing over her shoulder, but Peter is focused on giving orders.

"I don't want to go." Timothy wipes his nose with the back of his hand.

He looks at the ground between his feet, his shoulders hunched up toward his ears. She has to strain to hear him.

"Last time we went hunting, the boar got away. I stepped on a stick by accident and it made such a loud noise the boar knew we were coming and it ran. Rufus said it was his fault, to protect me, and Peter boxed him so hard he cried." Timothy looks up at her, his expression miserable.

She thinks of the boy on the beach, the one with the bruise on his cheek. Just then, a slight hand touches her shoulder, and she jumps.

"Here you go, Wendy." Peter grins, thrusting a long stick smoothed of its bark and sharpened at one end into her hand. "You can use my spear."

She's too stunned to do anything but take the spear. Peter doesn't even look at Timothy. His eyes are fixed on her, bright and hard. The spear is half again as tall as she is, and she can't imagine why Peter would give it to her. Why would he want her along on the hunt? Unless he's testing her, or he thinks she'll escape if he leaves her alone. And what happens if she refuses?

"I don't—" she begins, but Peter cuts her off, bouncing on his toes.

"Everybody has to hunt the boar. Nobody stays behind."

He's looking straight at her, but she understands that Peter is really talking to Timothy. Even though he's smiling, there's something dangerous in his eyes.

"Everyone follow me now."

He spins away, skipping a few steps before plunging into the trees, a whooping call trailing behind him. Arthur is next, right on Peter's heels, then Bertie and the others, flowing after him. She and Timothy are alone, and she reaches for his hand.

"We don't have to go," she says, but even as she does, she knows it's a lie.

It's colossally unfair. Why should Peter make the rules and no one else gets a say? But she feels it in her bones, an unassailable truth of this place. Everyone hunts the boar; no one stays behind. She looks at Timothy. His eyes are wide and trusting but bright with fear. It hurts, looking at him. She takes a deep breath to prove she can, even though her chest feels tight and funny.

"It'll be okay," she says. "I'll protect you. I won't let anything bad happen, I promise."

A call echoes between the trees. A kind of chant, only she can't make out the words.

"We'd probably better go," she says, moving toward the sound.

It's only a moment before she and Timothy catch up with the

rest. All together, their feet make a rhythm on the forest floor, like drums. A flash of bristled fur appears, just to her left, between the trees. If she hadn't hung back, she might not have seen it at all. Her voice sticks, then she shouts.

"Over there! I see the boar!"

The words surprise her. What is she doing? And more importantly, why? Her blood fizzes, pride and terror flooding her belly. She doesn't want to hunt anything. But she does. Her grip tightens on the spear; she can't help imagining what it might feel like to drive it into something living. Powerful. Strong.

It would be so easy, like pushing a pin into a butterfly with the pad of her thumb. The thought makes her smile. Something about the drumming of their feet, the chanting caught between the rustling trees, makes it seem all right. This is good. Everyone hunts the boar. No one stays behind.

She turns and runs and the boys stream behind her just as they followed Peter a moment ago. She swells the way Peter did. She is important, worth listening to. She isn't holding Timothy's hand anymore, and she doesn't care. He's just a baby anyway.

The thought, in her own voice, cruel and sneering, smacks into her, stealing her breath. Guilt brings her crashing back into herself. Her palm is slick against the wood, and she wants to let go of the spear, but she finds herself gripping it tighter. Sweat stings her eyes. She licks her lips and tastes salt. The air buzzes. No, it's her head buzzing, like it's full of bees. She wants to hunt. She wants to do things she never would, or could, back home. Who cares about rotten old London with its rules anyway?

She lets out a joyous whoop, cut off as Peter rushes past her, knocking into her so hard she goes down on one knee. It snaps her out of her desire to kill, and she stares at Peter, dazed.

"It's this way. I found the boar, it's over here!" he shouts, pointing in the opposite direction.

She can see the boar clearly, but Peter ignores it willfully, smashing through the greenery and breaking the rhythm. The boys wheel around, disoriented, uncertain. But Peter's reality asserts itself over hers, and they all turn to follow him. He bounds across the path, laughing, the movement itself a game, the boar temporarily forgotten. The tail of boys becomes a snake, whipping back and forth.

She climbs to her feet, breathing open-mouthed. The spear is still in her hand and she throws it away from her, as far as she can, shaking. Neverland is changing her; she can't let it.

A shout draws her attention as Bertie knocks into a boy called William. Or perhaps it's the other way around. They tumble into the bush, grappling at each other. The other boys gather around, cheering them on. They aren't soldiers anymore, just silly boys playing with sticks and toy swords. Until Arthur hits a boy whose name she doesn't know, the blow deliberate and hard. Blood, shockingly bright, spurts from the boy's nose, coating his lips and chin and scattering onto the leaves.

Her heart leaps into her throat. She looks to Peter to stop it, and her heart lodges there. Peter grins approvingly as the boys fight. He looks so strange, not a boy anymore, not a person who can be reasoned with at all. He's something else. He's…

Timothy reappears, and she remembers her promise to keep him safe.

"Don't look," she murmurs, turning his face against her side.

The rolling tumble of Bertie and William crashes into Arthur. Arthur abandons the boy with the bloodied nose and grabs Bertie instead, hauling him to his feet.

"Oy! Watch it!"

Arthur drives a fist into Bertie's stomach. Bertie doubles over, and the boys fall silent. Her own stomach clenches in sympathy. Someone whistles; feet stamp and applause echoes through the trees.

"Bravo, Arthur! Bravo!" She doesn't know who says it, but as the cheers fade the boys fall back into line as though nothing happened. Even the boy with the bloody nose. Even Bertie, though he moves slower than the rest, hunched and trying to catch his breath.

She keeps a tight hold on Timothy's hand this time as she hurries to catch up to Bertie.

"Are you all right?" She falls into step beside him.

"Fine." He tries to make the word hard and clipped, but it comes out strained, his breathing still not entirely back in control.

"But—"

Bertie whirls on her, his face scrunched, and for a moment she thinks he'll hit her the way Arthur hit him. And then she sees the water in his eyes, and how hard he's trying not to let it turn into a proper cry.

"I said I'm fine. Leave me alone!"

He bellows the words then trots away from her, not looking back. Up ahead, Peter gives a triumphant shout.

"The boar! Everyone gather round."

There's laughter now, boys falling over each other, elbowing and jostling and getting in each other's way. She isn't certain how the boar got in front of them again when Peter was clearly leading them the wrong way, but there it is—bristled hide, wickedly curving tusk, beady, evil-looking eyes. She's never seen a boar up close before, and it looks so much bigger than she ever imagined. How, with all the shouting and chaos, have they not frightened it away? Any animal with an ounce of sense would flee rather than stand and be killed.

The mass of boys, running and shouting, spills into a clearing. Even then the boar doesn't move. Curious despite herself, she joins the crowd, standing on her toes to see over the heads of the boys in front of her. The earth is pounded flat in a near-perfect round, closed in on all sides by trees. The boys spread to the edges, forming a perimeter with their bodies, leaving Peter and the boar facing each other in the middle.

It feels deliberate, like she's sitting in the audience at a play. Only instead of a stage there's only the ground, and Peter in the center, the sun beaming on him like a spotlight.

Her skin flushes hot and cold as Peter circles the boar. It's almost a dance. She strains to get a better view and at the same time, she doesn't want to see what will happen next.

Dread fills her. Peter waves the short sword he's been carrying, like it's a baton and he's conducting an orchestra. The way the blade catches the light, glinting, makes her realize for the first time that it's a real sword, not a makeshift thing carved from wood. Peter leaps forward, feinting, yelling as if he expects the boar to challenge him. But the boar remains utterly still, haunches up, head down, almost like it's bowing.

"Run." She turns to Timothy, teeth clenched around the word.

He gapes up at her. Something terrible is coming, like a storm waiting to break.

"Hide. I'll come find you, I promise."

Timothy turns, pelting away. She watches him go before dragging her gaze back to Peter. The circle of earth, the way the boar remains perfectly still, all of it is unnatural. It's not just the boar though, it's everything—the silent boys, their expressions solemn and watching. It's not war she thinks of now, but something like being in church with her grandfather—a ritual, solemn and terrible and centuries old.

Malevolence rolls from the boar's bristled stance, hatred in its eyes, but even still, it doesn't move. There's intelligence there, not animal intelligence but something akin to human. The boar knows what is about to happen, and it loathes Peter for it, but there's absolutely nothing it can do. It waits. The cruel sweep of its tusks could tear Peter apart, but it remains transfixed as Peter hops around it, jeering and taunting. Then all at once, Peter lunges. His blade goes in and a hot spray of blood splashes his skin.

The animal doesn't bellow or make any sound at all, and that only makes it worse. It simply collapses under Peter as he falls on top of it, stabbing and stabbing again.

Her eyes sting. *Leave.* She has to leave and it has to be tonight. She'll take Timothy and Rufus and even Bertie. She'll take everyone she can and they'll go somewhere far away where Peter can never find them.

The boar's sides finally stop heaving, and Peter looks up, his eyes finding hers. The freckles scattered across his skin are joined with blood now, and his grin is as wide and wicked as ever, pure delight. Like the boar, she's hypnotized. She can't look away as

Peter rises, wiping the short blade of his sword on his blood-spattered clothing. He gestures to the boys around him, and they dutifully come forward. Two of them hold a long pole, a third carries a coil of rope. They go to work in utter silence.

Peter approaches her, his eyes still shining. She wants to ask him why, but the breath in her throat merely wheezes and no words emerge. His hand lands on her shoulder. Rinds of crimson darken the ends of his nails. He leaves a smudge of red on the fabric of her nightgown.

"There," he says. "Now you're one of us properly. Wendy and Peter and the Lost Boys."

THE FROZEN GIRL

Colored threads trail from the embroidery hoop and lie across the drab gray of Wendy's skirt—a tangle of roots, fresh-pulled from the ground. She moves her needle and the hoop just often enough to make it look like she's stitching, but her attention is on the two attendants monitoring the room. It was a great deal of work to convince the nurses she could be trusted with a needle, even under supervision, acting the model patient for weeks on end. The attendants are always there, watching, and she, in turn, has been watching them. She knows their patterns as well as her stitching by now; she knows when they will grow bored and let their attention lapse. Any moment Jamieson will reach for his tobacco tin and rolling papers, prop the door to the garden open and step halfway outside to smoke.

When his hand goes to his side, patting at his pocket, Wendy bites the inside of her cheek. The papers he's looking for are tucked into the hem of her skirt, a space sewn to be invisible from the outside. Wendy drops her gaze, taps the side of her embroidery hoop twice, then stands once Jamieson's back is turned. She doesn't dare look at Mary for fear of giving them away. Instead,

Wendy moves swiftly toward the hall as Jamieson recruits the other attendant, Evans, to help him search. They're tearing apart the cabinet where the nurses keep their tins of biscuits and tea and the occasional nip of brandy, Jamieson cursing as he does.

In the hallway, Mary falls into step behind her. Farther down the hall is another door the attendants and nurses often prop open in nice weather so they can enjoy the sunshine while they smoke. Mary was the one who came up with the idea of using a small bit of cloth wedged into the lock to keep it from catching properly. Since then, they've learned how to hit the door just right to pop it open again, using it regularly to sneak into the garden to pick wild strawberries in the summer, and once in the winter to stage an elaborate snowball fight.

Wendy throws her shoulder against the door now while the hallways are clear and they tumble outside, laughing and covering their mouths against the noise. Wendy grabs Mary's hand and they sprint across the lawn.

"Strawberries?" Mary asks, her voice breathless.

"Better." Wendy turns to grin at Mary over her shoulder. "You know the old tree growing right up against the wall in the far west corner?"

"Sure." Mary almost stumbles, and Wendy slows, steadying her.

"I heard a rumor that a group of patients used it to escape years ago. We're going to go see if it's true."

"We're going to run away?" Mary stops and Wendy stops beside her, still holding her hand.

A frown curves Mary's lips, something almost like fear briefly in her eyes. Mary is never frightened, and Wendy opens her mouth when understanding strikes her. Mary hasn't been outside

St. Bernadette's walls in years. She was a child when she entered, and she scarcely knows anything of London besides the house of her mother's husband. Mary has told her that even before her mother died, her mother's husband rarely brought her along on outings. Her mother was lovely enough that her husband was proud to show her off, but Mary, with her rounder face, her gapped teeth, her darker skin, he preferred to keep hidden.

"Maybe not run," Wendy says carefully. "Maybe just climb and look over the wall."

"If you go, so will I." Mary lifts her chin, defiant, her eyes dark and hard again.

Is she thinking of the day when Wendy stood on the narrow balcony on St. Bernadette's second floor, when she'd meant to fly, meant to leave everything behind? Wendy squeezes Mary's hand. A thrill runs through her, half exhilaration, half fear. Until this moment, she hadn't fully thought what they might do.

Could they really climb over the wall, run and never look back? How would they live without money, two lone women on London's streets? Could they disguise themselves as men and stow away on a ship back to Mary's home in Canada? Or somewhere else? Perhaps join a traveling fair?

Wendy considers as they resume walking, then all at once they're at the tree. Wendy stops, gaping up at it. Mary presses against her side, as if the tree itself embodies everything she might fear about the world beyond the wall. Wendy's certain Mary isn't even aware she's doing it, and she doesn't intend to point it out, even welcoming the sun-warmed length of her.

The tree is gray with age, seeming almost to melt into the stone wall, both running riot with vines. Other sections of the property are guarded with iron fences, buried in thick hedges, but here there's only the wall, tall enough Wendy can't see over it. The sky feels tantalizingly close, the tree's branches scraping against the blue so that Wendy almost imagines that if she did climb, she too could scrape her fingers against it like thick paint.

Boldness seizes her, and Wendy can't help but grin.

"Race you."

At the challenge, Mary's expression turns sly and bright and mischievous, all hints of doubt and fear gone. She answers Wendy with a grin of her own, showing the gap between her front teeth.

"You're a proper Englishwoman; I bet you don't even know how to climb a tree."

Even though there's nothing at all alike in their voices, Mary's words bring Peter's taunting to Wendy's mind. She pictures him impossibly balanced on a branch that should be too slender to hold him, sticking out his tongue at her and wiggling his fingers by his ears like absurd horns or antlers gone awry. *You can't catch me, Wendy. Girls can't even climb trees. Everyone knows that.*

"I'll show you." Wendy answers Peter and Mary at once, gathering the rough fabric of her skirt. "I bet I can climb better than you."

Wendy sticks out her tongue, then grasps one of the thick vines wound about the tree. She's in Neverland again, scrambling barefoot up a trunk, Peter darting through the air above her like a nagging fly, half delighted, half enraged. She remembers how the branches shaped themselves to her hand, knots rising for her to grip with her toes. She didn't hesitate a moment, not even the first time. It never even occurred to her to doubt the tree would hold her. It held Peter after all, and the only thing in her mind had been showing him girls could so climb trees, every bit as well as boys.

Wendy sizes up a knot near the base of the tree. It bulges outward like melted candle wax, almost as good as the trees in Neverland. She plants her foot on it, meaning to haul herself upward until a meaty hand lands on her shoulder, yanking her back down. Her foot slips, and she bangs her knee painfully against the rough bark.

Jamieson. Wendy twists in his grip. She'd been so intent on climbing, on Peter, she hadn't even heard the attendant come up behind them. Evans is there too, holding Mary, one hand over her mouth to keep her from shouting a warning.

Jamieson hauls Wendy upright just as Mary bites down on Evans' hand. Evans shouts, shaking the hand, then raising it to strike Mary, but she doesn't even flinch. He's nowhere near as tall as Jamieson, but taller than Mary certainly, though that doesn't stop her from glaring up at him.

Wendy's heart surges toward Mary, and a cry—so much like Peter's cock-crow of victory—is almost at her lips before she tamps it down. Evans hesitates, glancing at Jamieson. Wendy takes satisfaction in seeing the skin of his raised hand turn red, looking painful where Mary bit it.

Before either attendant can act, Wendy throws herself against Jamieson's grip. He tightens it, keeping her from getting between Evans and Mary.

"It was all my idea." Wendy ignores Jamieson, his pull on her arm, and addresses Evans. "I forced her to come along."

Mary turns her glare on Wendy now, and Wendy glares right

back, willing Mary to stay silent. Even with their escapades, Mary has earned the trust of many of the attendants and nurses. She's allowed to work in the gardens and in the kitchen, harvesting vegetables and learning to bake, while Wendy is banished to scrubbing and laundry duties. She'd scrub till her knuckles bleed raw though if it means Mary keeping her privileges. She's seen the joy Mary takes in baking, even simple things. If she could, Wendy imagines Mary would even improve on the dull recipes given to her to prepare.

Jamieson snorts, a sound that isn't quite a laugh.

"You're always the leader when there's trouble, aren't you, Darling?" He wrenches her arm until she has no choice but to face him.

At the corner of her eye, Evans lowers his hand, looking sullen. Jamieson digs his fingers into the muscle of her arm, and Wendy bites back a yelp. She will not give him the satisfaction.

"Look at me when I'm talking to you." Jamieson leans closer, showing teeth stained yellow-brown by tobacco.

Everything about his expression is unpleasant. It leaves Wendy feeling vaguely sick, but she raises her chin, keeping her lips pressed together. Jamieson's stance makes her think of Hook, leaning over her on the bridge of his ship. If Jamieson thinks he can frighten her, he has no idea.

"Yes," she says, voice even. "Always the leader. Just like last time, and the time before."

It doesn't matter whether or not he believes her. It's as though he can smell Peter on her skin, his wildness, his magic, and it's enough to make him want to break her. She holds Jamieson's gaze even as his expression hardens, malice glittering.

His smile, already sickening, shifts to something entirely predatory. It's only then Wendy realizes her mistake. Dr. Harrington is in Switzerland at a medical conference. There is no one to rein Jamieson in. Her pulse turns erratic, beating madly against her skin. She opens her mouth, but it's too late. Jamieson shoves her hard enough to make her stumble. He still has a grip on her arm, so the motion wrenches her shoulder painfully, and now she does let out a sound of pain despite herself.

"Leave her alone," Mary bellows, squirming like lightning in Evans' grip.

"Get her out of here." Jamieson's tone is dangerously close to a snarl, but Evans looks almost as frightened of Mary as he does of his fellow attendant.

"What should I do with her?"

"I don't care. Lock her in her room." Jamieson turns away, turning his attention back to Wendy.

"Get up." He kicks at her legs even as he hauls her upright. Wendy grits her teeth, breathing fast, determined not to make another sound.

She staggers upright, lurching toward Mary again as Evans drags her away. Jamieson kicks her legs out from beneath her again, only his painful grip holding her partly upright. Wendy's hair hangs in her face, not grown back to its full length but enough to get in her eyes. She glares at Jamieson through the locks, breathing hard until he pulls her up again and she grits her teeth against another cry.

He grabs her chin with his free hand, turning her head as if looking for some mark on her skin. Behind the anger, there's almost bafflement in his eyes, as if even he is seeking to understand why he hates her so.

She knows she is treading on dangerous ground. She knows there are any number of things he could do to her without repercussions, because she would never be believed. She's heard things, she's seen bruises, and patients curled in on themselves in miserable fear.

"I could leave you in the sick ward, and say you snuck in there on your own. It would be just like you, going where you're not wanted. I'll wager even Dr. Harrington would think it would serve you right if you fell ill from your own foolishness and died. Or perhaps I should give you to Old Nettie?" At his voice, thick and sweet as treacle, Wendy goes cold. He leans in, like he really wants to know her opinion.

She knows the woman Jamieson means—not old, but her hair gray nonetheless, her arms wiry and threaded with scars caused by her own hands. It isn't fear that curdles Wendy's stomach but anger and heartache. Nettie is sick; she cannot help the way she lashes out against herself and others. She needs help, help Dr. Harrington cannot give, and Jamieson would use her as a weapon, set her off and turn her against other patients.

"Or maybe I should give her your little friend and make you watch."

Loathing fills her, so pure it overwhelms her. Starlight bursts behind her eyes and her ears ring. Everything in Wendy longs to fight, to fall on Jamieson and scratch at his eyes, bite at his throat, but if she does, he'll hurt Mary.

"Do whatever you want with me." Wendy bows her head.

"What's that? I didn't hear you."

"I said—" Wendy raises her voice, goaded despite herself, but before she can get the words out Jamieson strikes her hard across the mouth.

Her head snaps back and she tastes blood. Wendy glares, showing her teeth, showing them stained red. She understands now—she can't be too docile, too beaten, not yet. He wants to see her fight, then he wants to see her broken.

He pulls her roughly toward the asylum door and drags her inside. Wendy resists just enough. Jamieson's stiff shoes make echoing footsteps over the wooden floors and tiles. Passing the common rooms, heads lower, nurses and patients looking away and pretending not to see as Jamieson drags Wendy down the hall toward the treatment rooms.

She focuses on keeping her breath under control. She's doing this for Mary. If Wendy can keep his attention on her, he'll forget all about hurting Mary.

Jamieson kicks open one of the doors, shoving Wendy inside. It isn't until she sees the cast-iron tub full of water and ice that true panic takes hold. Jamieson planned this all along. Perhaps he even planted the rumor of the tree in the first place, knowing she wouldn't be able to resist. How could she have been so foolish, playing right into his hands?

"Let me go!" Wendy thrashes, all decorum and control forgotten.

He will hurt her for real this time; he may not even care if he gets caught. He might even kill her. Accidents happen, and who would ever know? Wendy stomps her heel down as hard as she can, trying to catch Jamieson's foot. But he's wearing hard-soled shoes, and she only slippers. He doesn't even slow, dragging her inexorably toward the ice-filled bath.

Wendy throws her weight backward, but it's nothing against Jamieson's bulk.

She wants to be brave, to tell herself it's only water. Dr. Harrington prescribes warm water baths to help her sleep, and once an icy spray to calm her blood. This is different. Her parents drowned in icy water. Now Jamieson means to drown her too.

"Get the blindfold," Jamieson speaks over her head.

Wendy twists around to see Evans closing the door. She imagines Mary locked in her room, pounding against the door while the other attendants and nurses pretend not to hear. At least she's safe. Wendy clings to the thought as hard as she can.

Evans approaches, and while Jamieson is distracted, Wendy jerks her head backward as hard as she can. Pain blooms at the back of her skull, but it's worth it for the feeling of connecting with Jamieson's nose. Instead of letting go, he punches her in the side of the head. Stars the color of ash burst behind her eyes, and her ears ring again. Her legs buckle, but Jamieson holds her upright. Evans slips a blindfold over her eyes, pulling tight, and Wendy bites her lip against a cry as it tightens over the spot Jamieson struck.

Jamieson lifts her, as easily as he might a child, keeping her arms pinned to her side. She kicks wildly, but none of her blows land.

He drops her into the ice.

Water sloshes over the sides of the tub. Her head goes under. Wendy comes up gasping and choking. The cold burns, like her skin has been stripped from her bones. She scrabbles at the sides of the tub, more water splashing, but Jamieson holds her down. He dunks her under, and time stops.

Blood rushes in her head, magnified by her panic and the water, louder than anything she's ever heard. Her lungs scream with the need to expand; she won't be able to stop herself from breathing in a mouthful of water. Pressure throbs behind her eyes, aching as she fights to keep her mouth closed. She can't, she can't let him win.

Jamieson hauls her up, dripping and spluttering. Wendy coughs, her body shaking, her jaw clenched against the cold. She braces herself, but Jamieson doesn't push her under again. He holds her—his hands on her shoulders, showing her how easily he can keep her in place. It's almost worse, the tension of his arms, the tension of her body, waiting for him to shove her down. She kicks out, but her heels only slip, finding no purchase on the bottom of the tub. She can't stand up, she can't escape. She can't do anything. And just like that, Jamieson has won.

Wendy stops fighting. She wishes she could stop shaking too, but that's beyond her control. Tears stream beneath the blindfold, and she hates herself. Their heat does nothing to warm her; she barely feels them. Slowly, she pulls her legs up, wrapping her arms around them, trying to preserve heat, make herself small.

She isn't certain when the pressure lifts from her shoulders, or how long it's gone before she realizes it's no longer there. She grips the sides of the tub, her fingers numb and clumsy. She expects Jamieson to smack them down; they might even shatter, brittle with the cold. But the blow doesn't come.

It takes multiple tries to work her shaking fingers and get the blindfold undone. Water has tightened the fabric, making the knot even more stubborn. When she finally pulls it off, ripping out several strands of hair as she does, she's alone. Her knee is already tender from hitting the tree, and she strikes it against the side of the tub, slipping as she climbs out. Her legs betray her and she falls, hitting the tiled floor hard. Her breath leaves her in a whine and she curls onto her side, letting misery wash through her for several moment before she even tries to move again.

The drab gray cloth of her dress clings to her skin, weighing her down. Wendy crawls to the door, gets her fingers around the handle. Locked. She rattles it. Pounds on the wood with hands still aching with the cold. Blood stands out beneath her chilled-white skin. She screams, but plenty of people scream in St. Bernadette's. No one will come for her. She's trapped until Jamieson chooses to unlock the door. All around her is tile and metal and unforgiving blank walls. There's nowhere to escape the cold.

Wendy lies on her side, body pulled in tight around itself, eyes closed. *Peter.* There isn't even a window here to show her the sky or the time of day. She can't fly away from here, from this. Maybe she never could. *Peter, where are you? Why don't you save me?*

MAKE BELIEVE

The crowing call goes out across the island, echoing through the trees, seeming to come from every direction at once. A flare like lightning, like ice-cold water, runs the length of Wendy's spine—joy and fear all wrapped into one.

His call. Not quite human, not animal either, and for a moment, it undoes her completely. The sound is home; she knows it as well as she knows her husband's eyes, her daughter's smile. It's written in her bones. It means adventure. It means something terrible and wonderful is about to happen and she aches to rush headlong toward that call with all its promise and threat.

Even now. Even after everything. Peter. She wants to run with him. To stand at his side and conquer the world.

And in the same heartbeat, she wants to put her hands around his throat and squeeze until the light leaves his eyes. He took Jane away from her. He stole her daughter, and Wendy has crossed worlds to get her back.

Her boots sink into the sand. The call comes again and she turns, trying to pinpoint it. The boys are close enough for her to hear them shouting to each other, though she can't make out the words.

The wild riot of sound bounces deceptively, first in front of her, then behind. Among the trees, then further up the beach. She runs a few steps, then stops. She backtracks, frustrated, and loops over her own path, erasing her footprints with new ones. The next time she hears Peter's call, it's faint, far distant, and she can't hear the boys anymore at all. Neverland twists around her, confounding her and keeping Peter out of her reach.

Behind her lies jungle. Up ahead, birch trees, their bark peeling away in papery strips to reveal curls of pink as soft as sunrise. To her right, a massive willow trails long, silvery leaves into the clear waters of a pond.

As a child, she'd delighted in the way Neverland constantly changed around her. She would follow Peter up the beach only to end up in the skirts of a snow-covered mountain. Or they would trace the path of a secret river through pine trees to find the smoking peak of a volcano. Now, the fractured puzzle pieces of the island infuriate her.

Before she can decide which way to go, movement among the trees catches her eye. It's the same flickering she saw as she looked out over the trees from the lagoon, leaves rattling, branches swaying without any wind, and her breath catches. A shape darts from one slender trunk to the next. Fear presses a hand to her chest, but in the next instant, anger overwhelms it.

"It's no use skulking about. I can see you." It's a lie, but miraculously her voice doesn't shake.

Between two of the trunks, a shadowy figure resolves. Human, or at least she thinks so. Suddenly, the trees don't allow enough light. Wendy squints. The shape resembles a woman, but her skin is like a wasp's nest, papery grayish-brown. She's like a dead thing, lain ages in the ground, and yet there's something

157

familiar, like Hook's ship, like the lagoon. The thought fills her with revulsion, familiar yet utterly wrong, the Neverland she knew perverted, unraveled and poorly stitched together again. She knows the woman; she can't possibly know her.

"Are you…?" Her voice breaks. She takes a step, then stops.

She isn't a child to be frightened by ghosts. She's a grown woman, and she's faced real monsters, the kind who wear uniforms and wield needles and restraints. She drops her hand to the hilt of Hook's sword, ready to draw.

Leaves crunch under a light step as the woman moves closer. Wendy gasps. This close, she can't pretend. If the laws of Neverland hold true, the woman before her should be a girl still, just as Wendy last saw her. She isn't though, she's older, but not as old as Wendy, not as old as she should be if Neverland were a rational place. Not a girl, not quite a woman either. Perhaps not even living, but something else, something caught in between.

"Tiger Lily." The name cracks in Wendy's throat and lodges there.

The woman flinches, as if the name were a blow. Thin, her skin like dried mud, baked and cracking. Her hair, which should be dark, framing her face in thick, glossy braids, hangs lank, wispy and brittle. Her eyes are worst of all, sunken above cheeks that protrude like blades, and full of pain.

Wendy knows those eyes like she knows Peter's call. Tiger Lily, trapped inside the husk standing before her, swaying slightly as if the next breeze might knock her down. Tiger Lily, a ghost haunting herself.

"No." The word is a husk too, a dried, blown leaf scraping across the ground.

Is it a denial of the name, or Wendy herself? Both, or neither? But Wendy knows for the ache inside, heavy and bruised. This is her friend.

"Tiger Lily." Wendy repeats the name, more firmly, reaching out her hand.

Tiger Lily's shoulders curl in upon themselves, and she looks down, away. Scraps of cloth and leather cling to her narrow frame. Wendy remembers elaborate beads and beautiful stitching, more precise and perfect than anything she could ever produce, even with Mary's patient tutelage. Behind Tiger Lily, other forms emerge to stand between the trees, but draw no closer, giving the two of them space.

Peter's Indians. Like Tiger Lily, they are drained and dry. Hunched. Mere echoes of what they once were.

"Please," Wendy says.

Tiger Lily drags her gaze back to Wendy's. Her eyes go wide, but her posture straightens, even though the motion looks painful.

It's all the sign Wendy needs. She closes the distance, throwing her arms around her friend. Tiger Lily feels hollow, and she's afraid to hold her too hard, as if she might snap in two if Wendy holds her too tight.

Wendy forces herself to let go, step back, look her friend in the eye.

"What has he done to you?"

LONDON 1920

Wendy keeps her head bowed, sliding one foot in front of the other. All she has to do is make it to the door at the end of the hall. John is waiting for her in the garden; Dr. Harrington told her he sent ahead to say he had big news. Perhaps she is being released. His visits have been few and far between and all of them brief. It's clear this place frightens him, leaves him feeling guilty for what he's done. That he's here again now, and made it clear he means to stay more than a few moments, must mean his news is big indeed. Perhaps John and Michael have finally come to their senses and remembered Neverland.

Three more steps. Two. Hope flutters in her chest, a fragile and terrible thing. She shouldn't allow it, but she can't help herself, even now. One more step and she's outside. The sunlight makes her squint, and the smell of fresh grass tickles her nose. Wendy raises her head. John sits at a small table beneath one of the massive oak trees dotting the lawn. There's even tea.

It's so civilized, the picture of familial bliss. Wendy wrestles down the thing clawing at her throat—a scream, laughter, a shout. She makes herself cross the lawn at a steady pace. Flowers spill from neat beds all around her, wild bursts of color, like bright jewels scattered on the lawn. If she doesn't look too closely, she can almost forget there's a fence with thick iron bars hidden within the dense greenery on either side of the gate. If she doesn't look behind her, she can pretend there's no wall that she tried and failed to scale.

Wendy allows herself a moment to tilt her head back and look at the perfect, cloudless sky. The blue is dazzling. She could fall into it, fall and keep falling. At the end she'd find herself on the other side of the world, listening to the mermaids singing in the lagoon. She smooths her hands over her sleeves and her skirt, feeling the hidden pockets secreted away there. It keeps her hands from shaking.

She stops just short of the table and John rises to meet her. His expression is practiced, a veneer of calm plastered over nerves. In reality, there is nothing easy about him at all. Wendy makes a quick inventory of all the things hidden inside her clothes— buttons, a length of thread, a single page from a newspaper, folded and folded again into a long strip running around her hem. The litany calms her, but she doesn't return John's smile.

He kisses her cheek, motioning for her to sit. He's spent years accusing her of playing make-believe, but here he is acting as though this is an ordinary social visit, as though he's simply a brother visiting his sister at home.

Wendy keeps her back stiff as she sits. Let John be the one to break the silence. She can see the words piled up behind his pained smile. It gives her a small amount of pleasure, but it's a scant comfort. The terrible truth of it is, she could walk out the gate with him. All she has to do is lie. Tell John and Dr. Harrington what they want to hear. That Neverland doesn't exist, that it's all a story she made up. All she has to do is say she's sorry and promise never to speak of it again.

"Tea?" John lifts the pot, holding it poised over her cup.

"Please."

"Two lumps. I remember." His expression softens.

She wants to be angry with him, but his smile disarms her. Light slants through the leaves, catching his hair, burnishing his glasses, and he is only her brother again, not one of her captors. Buried deep behind his eyes is the ghost of the boy who flew with her, who whooped and hollered at Peter's side, who played at war and follow the leader.

Wendy opens her mouth and closes it again, searching her mind for something safe to say. If she asks where that little boy went, if any part of him remembers, it will only cause disappointment to crowd his expression.

Behind the shine of his glasses, faint crow's feet line his skin, and the sight of them takes her by surprise. When did he grow up? When did she? She was so determined to hold onto the boy John was—the one who flew with her through the stars—that she utterly missed it.

This John simply appeared before her one day, not a boy but a man, full of demands about her behavior. It strikes Wendy—even though he's her brother, she barely knows anything about him. There's nothing she can ask him about without looking like a fool. Who are his friends? Does he have a sweetheart? Does he hope to marry one day?

He has mentioned important meetings in the past, usually as his excuse for not staying long. The first time he visited her, months after leaving her here, he mentioned a business opportunity, something to do with importing goods from all around the world to sell in England, but he'd never mentioned it again. When she'd asked, his face had grown pinched, drawn with shadows, and in a clipped tone he'd told her that matters of business were not a woman's concern. She wonders now, did the investment he made go badly for him? Is it money that troubles him, worrying about paying for her care here, and keeping the house they grew up in?

Guilt and fear needle her. Lost for what to say, Wendy chooses silence. She folds her hands in her lap and watches John pour tea, add sugar, stir, and precisely set the spoon aside. His movements are careful, as though the entire world around him is breakable, not just her. There's a touch of gray in his hair, just above his ears to go with the lines at the corner of his eyes. She thinks of his arms around her, holding her back as she screamed, clawing and trying to get her hands on another plate to smash. There'd been no gray in his hair then, but she can't miss it now that she's seen it, even though he's younger than her.

All at once she sees it, how he aged so quickly and she never noticed. Her heart turns over in her chest. She hasn't been a big sister to him since they came home from Neverland, not the way she should have been. The weight of their parents' deaths fell upon him more squarely than it did on her. The weight of *her*, resting on John's shoulders on top of it. He had to grow up and put Neverland aside. He had no choice.

And what of her? She'd had no business concerns to occupy herself with like John. Unlike Michael, she could not go to war. As a woman, what could she choose? Only marriage, only motherhood, and she'd had enough of playing mother in Neverland. The thought of being a wife—it had frightened her in a way she couldn't say. John had hinted at it, more than once, before St. Bernadette's. He had even tried to engineer a chance meeting, inviting a young man to the house as if he had no idea Wendy would be there, and inviting them both to sit down for tea.

He'd meant well, she knows that much. It hadn't only been wanting to get his troublesome sister off his hands; she's certain he genuinely expected her to be happy at the prospect. What woman wouldn't want to marry, after all? But Wendy had found herself stunned to silence by the very idea, terrified and angry at once. She'd barely spoken a single word to the man, stretching awkward silences through the room until the young man had taken on the look of a frightened animal, desperate to flee, and John had finally admitted defeat.

If growing up meant marrying, then of course she would cling to Neverland all the harder, refusing to let go.

She sees the weight of all that on John's shoulders now, and more. She's been cruel, thoughtless, digging into John's wounds again and again, demanding he look at the blood. She opens her mouth, an apology crowding her throat. But John speaks first.

"I have good news." John hands her the cup. It rattles in its saucer. "I've found someone—that is, Michael and I have found someone who's willing to…" He clears his throat. "I mean, there's been an offer for your hand, Wendy."

The words land like a blow, and all thoughts of apology fly from her mind. Wendy's fingers go numb around the eggshell thinness of the saucer. The cup slips, crashing to the table. Shards fly and hot liquid splashes. John leaps up, knocking over his chair as he does. His cheeks are ruddy above his moustache. He's flustered, but he recovers quickly, waving away the attendant standing at a discreet distance as he looks their way.

"Oh dear. Well, never mind, darling."

He cleans the mess, and Wendy watches him, stunned. She is a creature made of skin wrapped around a core of ice, solid and immovable. She is a girl in a bathtub. She never climbed out. She is frozen through and through.

"I know it's rather a lot to take in." John doesn't look at her; the color never disappears from his cheeks. "But Ned is a good man. His father is… His father has been rather a lot of help to me, in business. They are a good family. Ned will be a good match for you."

Ned. The name echoes, a dull thud against the bones of her skull. Does John realize how many times he's said the word "good"? Is he trying to convince himself or her? How good can Ned possibly be, to offer marriage to a woman he's never met? And has John forgotten his last disastrous attempt to matchmake? But nothing has changed since then. As a woman, she is expected to marry, to find a husband to take care of her, and at twenty-seven, she is already nearly too old.

She pictures a towering man with Jamieson's face, neck thick, smile the thin edge of a knife—the kind of man grown from a boy who delights in pulling the wings off flies. She pictures a man like Dr. Harrington, one with a kindly face but a keen eye bent on studying her. A man who might mean well, but who is all the same set on picking her apart.

And what does John mean by mentioning Ned's father? The way her brother refuses to meet her eyes, the flush of his cheeks makes her wonder. Does John owe this man money? Is she to be sold to pay back his debt?

How could John do this to her? Just when she thought she understood him, just when she thought the broken thing between them might finally heal.

"I thought you would be happy. Even if… Even if you think you don't want to marry, surely it would be better than being in this place, wouldn't it?" John's hands finally still, and he looks at her, his expression pleading. "Say something, won't you, Wendy?"

"What should I say?" She meets his gaze, steady and unblinking. Buried within the ice at her core, Wendy Darling, the girl who remembers how to fly, screams.

"Say you're happy. Or at least that you'll consider it." John pulls his chair closer, sitting and taking her hands. The cuff of his shirt is stained with tea.

"Michael and I only want to take care of you, the way you always took care of us. All those stories in the nursery, the games. The way you sat with us when we were sick. You stayed awake with me when I had bad dreams. You sang lullabies."

He means every word, Wendy can see it. The rift inside her widens; she wants to forgive him, and she can never do so.

"You know," John smiles, a fond thing, "Michael told me when he was over there, on the continent, it wasn't Mother or Father he thought of. It was you. That was what got him through when the bombs were falling. When men were dying around him."

Wendy wants to strike him. How can he sit here and tell her this like it's a kindness? Has he never looked into Michael's eyes? Does he think to make her feel better, giving her the burden of their little brother, alone and lost in the mud, whispering her name?

John lets go of her hands, straightening the cuffs of his jacket to hide the stain from the tea. His gaze is restless, uncertain where to land.

"You'll be safe and cared for, Wendy. Please let us do this for you."

John and Michael could take her out of this place any time. Being married is not a condition of her release, except that John is making it so. She should be furious with him. She is, but she's tired as well. Wendy looks up at the sky again, the blue of it going through her like a blade. Accepting this proposal means she could walk through the gates, never look back. She could put all this, Dr. Harrington and Jamieson, behind her. She could finally lay the burden of Neverland aside and build a life for herself.

Perhaps she could even bring Mary with her. A new life. A new Wendy Darling.

She lowers her gaze to look at John again. The fracture running through him is clear, the weight of Michael and her and everything else, the strain of trying to hold them all together wearing him down over the years. Whatever other reasons he may have, he genuinely believes that this should make her happy. There's an earnestness to his expression—isn't marriage and motherhood what every woman wants? He believes he's giving her a gift, not delivering her to a new kind of imprisonment. Wendy takes a deep breath. Just this once, at last, she will choose kindness. Her brothers should not have to bear the burden of caring for her for the rest of her life. She will do this thing for John. For Michael.

"Yes," she says.

The word passes her lips, and it seems to come from somewhere beyond her. She looks past John, to the hedge, as if she could see the horizon beyond it. Perhaps a fresh start would be the best thing after all, a new life that protects her brothers from her, protects her from herself.

"Oh, Wendy. I'm so glad. I'll speak to Dr. Harrington straight away and arrange everything for your release." John catches her hands, pulls her to her feet and kisses her cheek. "And Ned, of course. You'll have the opportunity to meet Ned, but I'm certain you'll be very happy with him."

Does John intend to bring him here, to let him see her caged in this place? What sort of man would be willing to marry her not only knowing the truth of her, but seeing it with his own eyes?

Ned. That name again. It doesn't ring like a clear bell, signaling the morning, a bird trilling up the dawn. It falls flat, like a stone. *Ned.* The sound of a window shuttered against the sky.

She knows without asking that he doesn't have hair the color of copper and flame. That he doesn't know how to crow like a rooster. That he cannot fly. John's words flow over her, and Wendy fails to listen. Then John leaves, promises to return soon trailing behind him. She's left alone beneath the tree with one shattered cup only half cleaned up, and the other full of liquid gone cold.

She picks up one of the shards, lifting it to see the sunlight stream through it. How easy would it be to bury the shard in her skin? In Dr. Harrington's skin? Could she do it?

She lets it fall. That is the way the old Wendy Darling would think, but she is going to be a new Wendy. Shouldn't the thought make her happy? Then why is her chest so tight? Why is it so hard to breathe? She hurries across the lawn to where she'd promised to meet Mary after her brother left. Mary rises as Wendy approaches, leaving the embroidery spread across her lap to fall to the ground.

"What happened?"

"I… I'm getting married." Wendy's shoulders hitch. She puts her face in her hands. Her cheeks are dry, but she shakes her head in disbelief.

Mary touches her shoulder, a simple, comforting thing. She doesn't ask what's so terrible about the idea of marriage, and for that, Wendy is grateful.

"It means leaving this place." Wendy speaks between muffling fingers. "But…" She shrugs. Her shoulder blades feel like wings stripped of their feathers.

"If you had your choice in leaving," Mary asks, "where would you go? Would you go back to Neverland?"

The question startles Wendy. She lowers her hands. Once upon a time, the answer was simple, so that it was barely even a question. The word *yes* is on her tongue, quick as a heartbeat, but she falters. Mary waits patiently on her answer; her eyes make Wendy think of pine bark after a hard rain.

Neverland isn't her home, but is London really her home either? She doesn't belong with Michael and John, and besides, they ought to have lives of their own. Where then? She wants to say *with you*—after all, Mary is the only other home Wendy has known—but it seems unfair to need another person so much. Could she be a home for Mary too? Could they need each other enough to make a life away from this place? And even if they could, who would let them? The world is full of men granting and withholding permission, leaving women like Mary and herself to exist by their sufferance alone.

Suddenly, it all feels so hopeless. Wendy shakes her head, letting out something like a laugh.

"Neverland." She leans her head against the tree and closes her eyes. The harder Dr. Harrington and John worked to take it away from her, the more fiercely she held on, until Neverland became something else entirely. But it isn't perfect, and it isn't a home. Because home means family and consequence, and taking the good with the bad. Neverland is simply a place to run away and hide.

Wendy feels around the edges of the hole left inside her, the thing behind the locked door. She's tired of it. Weary to the core.

"Neverland is a lie." She opens her eyes and looks at Mary. "I don't mean it isn't real, because it is. I mean things there aren't what they should be. Neverland is a story, a little boy's idea of pirates and Indians and mermaids. Except Peter isn't really a boy. He's something else. I don't know what he is, but I think he made himself into the idea of what a boy should be, and sometimes that's a very dangerous thing."

Wendy takes Mary's hand, lacing their fingers together and looking at them joined, light and dark.

"What about you," Wendy asks. She is half afraid of the answer, but she doesn't know what answer to give to Mary's question, and so turns it back on her instead. "What would you do if you could leave tomorrow? Where would you go?"

Mary looks startled in her own right, and Wendy's breath catches a bit, her pulse wanting to go faster. This feels different than the stories they've told each other over the years, of what they would do if they ever escaped. Those were mere fantasy, a way to survive. This is frighteningly close to real. Not running away from something, but running *to* something, a real life, a new home, a different kind of family.

"Would you..." Wendy hesitates. The thought of Mary going back to Canada, an ocean between them, is too much to contemplate, so she asks a different question instead.

"Would you look for the man who married your mother?"

Revenge. She doesn't say the word aloud. Would she strike back at Jamieson if she could? And Peter? If Mary was given the chance, would she lash out at the man who put her here?

"No." Mary snaps her answer. The wet-pine of her eyes looks darker still, the black at their center going almost all the way to the edges to swallow up the ring of brown.

"I don't want anything from him, and I don't owe him anything either. We were never family. He isn't anything to me, and he isn't worth even a moment of my time."

Mary's grip tightens, matching the vehemence of her words. It's a different kind of anger than she's seen in Mary before, and it makes her wonder whether Mary is trying to convince herself with her words. The man who married her mother means nothing to her, and yet he is a wound that hasn't entirely healed.

"I wouldn't go back to Canada either." Mary answers Wendy's unspoken question, and relief stings her eyes. She swallows hard as Mary goes on. "I don't... My people are there, but I don't know them, not really. I was so young when I left. I don't know where I belong."

Wendy almost shouts *here, with me*, but she holds her tongue. It isn't her place to presume, no matter how much she aches at the thought of leaving Mary behind, going out into the world to marry a man she doesn't even know.

"I'd like to travel," Mary continues, "but it isn't easy."

Mary lifts their clasped hands; the sun dapples through the tree overhead and hits the contrast in their skin, speaking for her. Mary lowers her head, as if afraid her hope will betray her if she speaks too loud.

"Ever since I've been working in the kitchens here I've started to think that I would like to have a little bakery, my own shop, but..."

Mary raises their clasped hands again, the same answer, and it strikes Wendy that Mary doesn't expect to ever leave; she expects to grow old and die without ever seeing the world outside the walls of St. Bernadette's again. Wendy's pulse snags on hurt, a vicious anger rising through her. The world of men and their rules, forever saying what women—especially women who look like Mary—can and cannot do.

The unfairness presses on Wendy's skin, and her body feels too small to contain all the injustice.

"Are you really going to do it?" Mary asks after a moment of silence.

"Get married? I suppose." With her free hand, Wendy plucks at her sleeve, trying to imagine herself clad in a wedding gown. "Play pretend. Play wife and mother." Wendy tries to smile, and it hurts, a deep ache that goes all the way through her. "It wouldn't be the first time, after all."

*

"Wendy." Tiger Lily touches her own throat when she speaks, as if speaking physically pains her. Her voice is a cold wind blowing from a lonely place. It hurts to hear it, and Wendy's name in her mouth is a terrible thing.

For a moment, Wendy can only stare, wanting to undo everything done to Tiger Lily and bring her back to the girl she remembers. Tiger Lily's twig-hard fingers brush Wendy's cheek. They're almost bone, and Wendy has to fight not to flinch away from the touch. The wonder in Tiger Lily's eyes— that is real, that is human, despite the ruin of her flesh, and Wendy keeps her gaze there as if she could forget the rest of what Tiger Lily has become.

"I started to think I dreamed you." The words scratch, and Wendy touches her own throat reflexively. "The girl from the other side of the stars."

Tiger Lily's lips crack when she smiles, but there's no blood. A lump rises in Wendy's throat, and she can't swallow it down. Tiger Lily, trapped here while Wendy was locked behind St. Bernadette's walls; had the rest of Neverland forgotten so that Tiger Lily been doubted and disbelieved too, told Wendy was only a story or a dream?

"But you're here now," Tiger Lily says.

"I'm here." Wendy makes herself fold her arms around Tiger Lily again, feeling her hollowness. She is skin wrapped around bone, with nothing else inside.

"What happened?" Wendy draws back, wiping at her cheeks.

"Peter." Tiger Lily spreads her arms, a dry, rustling sound, and her lips crack again, her expression grim this time.

Peter, of course, Peter. Wendy knew before she asked. Anger and guilt war inside her. If she'd stayed, she could have stopped this. She could have saved Tiger Lily and the mermaids.

"Don't," Tiger Lily says, as if reading Wendy's thoughts. "Don't blame yourself for him."

Wendy lets out a breath, and a small measure of the tension inside her unwinds. She wants to believe what Tiger Lily says is right, and yet blaming herself feels like the only useful thing she can do. Peter is a breaking storm, too vast a target for her rage, leaving only herself in his stead.

"Come," Tiger Lily says, jostling Wendy from her thoughts. "We'll talk."

Tiger Lily tilts her head, a gesture for Wendy to follow. As she does, Wendy glances at the trees, wondering suddenly whether there are eyes and ears listening. The birds could be spies for Peter, even the leaves themselves, for all she knows. The creeping

173

feeling of being haunted returns, even though the source is different this time.

Tiger Lily leads her between narrow-trunked trees, ducking beneath branches and looped vines like massive snakes. Her footsteps barely make a sound. When she first saw the trees shake their branches, Wendy had thought of ghosts. Looking at Tiger Lily now, she wonders whether she was truly wrong.

Tiger Lily bends to lift a heavy section of ropy vines, revealing the entrance to a cave. Just one of the many cracks and fissures and secret tunnels riddling Neverland. Wendy remembers Tiger Lily telling her once it was possible to travel all the way across the island and never see the sun, like a whole second Neverland buried underground.

Wendy ducks through the entrance, and as she does, the ground shudders, a distant rumble of thunder. Glancing over her shoulder, she sees a faint smudge rising above the trees, a claw mark in smoke dragged across the sky at the center of the island.

It's clearer than when she first glimpsed it from the beach, and darker too. Now, it makes her think less of a flock of birds and more of a living shadow streaming across the sky.

Wendy's muscles lock up, her legs refusing to carry her inside. Peter holding her hand, leading her into the dark. *In here, Wendy, it's the best secret ever.* A struck-match smell, but so much bigger. Rain-drenched fur, meat left out to spoil.

There's something there. Something she should remember.

Her fingers skim the wood of the door in her mind and it trembles, like a vast breath rattling it from the other side. Splinters catch at the pads of her fingers. Cracks craze the door's surface. Panic tells her to run, run, run, and never stop.

Tiger Lily touches her hand, and Wendy starts, biting back a cry of surprise. She pushes the fear away, willing the tightness clenching at her to let go, and steps into the cave.

The struck-match smell recedes. The only scent in this cave is the memory of smoke, ghost-faint, but nothing more. No blood and heat and iron.

Wendy's eyes adjust, showing her a circle of smoothed logs surrounding a cold fire pit. Above them, a natural chimney leads up through the rock, letting in a shaft of pale, rain-washed light—the color of the sky right after a storm. Soot from old fires darkens the cave walls, but there are deliberate markings too, made in red and black paint.

Wendy moves closer, studying them. She thinks of the days she and Mary had spent hidden away in forgotten corners of St. Bernadette's halls, Mary trading Wendy story for story. Wendy had told stories of Neverland, and in exchange, Mary had told Wendy the Kainai legends her mother passed on to her as a child.

She remembers Jane, standing at the counter in their kitchen, barely tall enough to see its surface, watching Mary knead bread. Mary had told Jane those same stories, sketching pictures in the flour scattering the countertop. Blood Clot Boy, and Napi, the Old Man who first made people, and who tried to steal the Sun's pants.

A sob catches in Wendy's throat. The memory is so close, she can feel the heat of the kitchen, smell the baking bread. She'd told her own stories to Jane, stories of the Little White Bird and the Clever Tailor, but she should have told them truer.

She'd told the stories to protect herself, not Jane, reclaiming fragments of Neverland and stitching them into toothless fairy tales to help her daughter sleep at night. The Tailor had sewn stolen feathers into a fabulous coat for the Little White Bird to help him fly faster and higher than all the other birds and win a race. And all the while in Wendy's mind, she'd held a picture of herself as a child, sewing Peter's shadow back onto his body.

Wendy breathes out, forcing the ache from her lungs. She blinks back tears, resting her fingers on the painted images on the wall. A ship with full, billowing sails, the mermaids in their lagoon, a boy surrounded by a group of other boys—the only one not casting a shadow. She moves her hand back to the pirate ship, and turns to look at Tiger Lily over her shoulder.

"What happened to them?" Wendy asks.

"They left." Tiger Lily moves closer.

"What?" The answer startles her, driving all other thoughts from her mind. "How? Where did they go?"

Tiger Lily lifts her shoulders; her body makes a dry cracking sound like logs settling in a fire.

"There was a storm and a tear in the sky. Hook and his ship sailed through."

"But I saw the shipwreck on the beach. I climbed inside." Wendy touches the sword at her hip.

The hilt seems almost to shiver beneath her touch. She felt it herself, the haunted air of the ship, the sense of the pirates still there, and yet gone. Hadn't she even pictured them falling into the sky?

She tries to remember what happened to Hook when Peter rescued them. The memory is there in fragments, like two contradictory truths overlapping each other. That monstrous beast with its terrible teeth and snapping jaws—she'd seen Hook devoured by it, torn apart, hadn't she? She'd been horrified. He'd been a villain, but surely he didn't deserve to be eaten alive? Did she beg Peter to help him? She can't remember anything but Peter's trilling laughter ringing in her head, his voice innocent and dismissive, almost cruel.

No one ever dies in Neverland, silly.

Had she seen him devoured, only to have him resurrected again, brought back from seeming-death to continue to serve as Peter's eternal enemy? And even if Hook couldn't die, surely he would still feel pain? The thought leaves Wendy chilled. Does Peter really have that kind of power over life and death?

She thinks of the mermaids in the lagoon. She looks at Tiger Lily, her corpse-like face, her sunken eyes, and she knows the answer.

Tiger Lily shakes her head.

"I hid and watched from the trees. I can only tell you what I saw, not what it means. There were two ships, and they were the same ship. One fell, and one flew through the sky. There was a hole, and through it I could see different stars."

Wendy's breath catches, fear momentarily forgotten. Different stars. Her stars? London? Tiger Lily continues.

"Some of the pirates fell screaming out of the sky and they drowned. Not Hook though. Hook survived."

"How do you know?"

Tiger Lily's lips finally shape a smile. Her voice still rasps, but for a moment it sounds less pained.

"Stubborn. He would never accept defeat or let Peter beat him one last time. So he must have lived somehow."

Despite herself, Wendy finds herself smiling too. The expression feels strange, and she calls to mind again the picture of

Hook she built for herself on the ship—a broken man, a trapped man, a sad man.

How much worse would it be if he were not only trapped in Peter's endless games, but caught in a cycle of being killed and brought back to life again, all at a young boy's whim?

Tiger Lily moves to sit on one of the logs surrounding the dead fire. She draws her legs up, wrapping her arms around them, melancholy taking over her expression. Tiger Lily's hunched shoulders, the thinness of her body, all of it makes Wendy think of bundled sticks, ready to burn. Tiger Lily rests her cheek on her knees and looks at Wendy.

"I wish I understood how he did it so I could leave too."

Wendy moves away from the wall to sit at Tiger Lily's side. After a moment, she puts her arm around her friend's shoulders and draws her close. It's easier to touch her now without feeling that shudder of fear. Tiger Lily rests her head against Wendy; it weighs almost nothing.

"Before the pirates, I used to think nothing could ever die in Neverland, but…" Tiger Lily holds her arms out in front of her, letting her cracked skin speak for her.

"You're not…" Wendy starts, but she swallows the words, a painful lump in her throat. Whatever she could say would be a lie. Tiger Lily isn't dead, but she isn't alive either. They were the same age when Wendy first came here. Tiger Lily isn't the girl Wendy left behind, but she isn't a full-grown woman either. She's something else.

"What about the mermaids?" Wendy asks instead.

"Peter."

Tiger Lily tenses, and Wendy hears the shift in her already

pained voice, as if Peter's name hurts her more than other words. What were he and Tiger Lily to each other before Wendy arrived? After she left? For Peter to wound Tiger Lily like this, he must have cared for her once very much.

"Peter forgot the mermaids, so they wasted away," Tiger Lily says, lifting her head from Wendy's shoulder.

"He forgot?" Wendy can't fathom it, but at the same time, she can.

It wasn't even malice, just simple neglect. A boy leaving his toys out in the rain, not caring if they rot or spoil. Callous too, changing so any gust of the wind might carry him off in another direction, never once looking back at what he left behind.

Despite Tiger Lily's words, Wendy's mind circles back to guilt. If she'd stayed, could she have kept Peter from getting wrathful and bored? Could she have gathered the fraying threads of Neverland and kept them together, their colors bright? And even if she could have, should Peter's whims be her burden? He'd wanted her to be his mother, abdicating responsibility so he didn't have to care, trusting her to catch him if he ever fell.

Mothers are meant to keep their children safe, but also to prepare for life. Help them grow. What can a mother be to a boy determined to remain perpetually young? Only a shadow, forever chained to him and trailing in his wake, bearing all his hurts so he doesn't have to.

Wendy draws her legs up too, mirroring Tiger Lily's posture. She rests her cheek on her knees, and all at once, she feels every moment of her journey here, the years separating her from when she was last in Neverland. She feels her age, the little injuries of time and the big ones. The fine lines at the corners of her eyes, the

179

strands of gray in her hair, the extra weight on her bones. They're all earned. Since she was here last, she survived an asylum, her body bore a child. But Peter hasn't changed at all.

He's earned nothing, so he takes what isn't given.

She thinks of him standing at the foot of Jane's bed, his hands on his hips, his cocksure smile. He hadn't even seen her—a grown woman, a mother in truth now. She imagines in his mind it had been mere moments since he left her, as though he'd only put her aside briefly, rather than forgetting about her for years. He had assumed Jane was her; he hadn't aged, so why should she? And when she hadn't fit Peter's story anymore, he simply refused to see her at all. In a whole world built to fit his whims, Wendy is the fractured piece slipped out of place.

"What about you?" Wendy asks.

She glances at Tiger Lily again. The question hurts. Tiger Lily's eyes change, dark and light at once. They make Wendy think of guttering candles.

"He got angry," Tiger Lily says. Her voice raw and distant at once in a way that makes Wendy think of Mary in the asylum, talking about the man who married her mother.

"When the pirates left. He punished us. He made us burn, but we didn't die. He changed us. He made me into the worst thing he could imagine, someone grown up. He wanted to prove—" Tiger Lily's voice breaks, and when it comes back, it's softer, diminished somehow. Embers, logs cracking into the last of the fire and going out.

"He wanted to prove that we belonged to him. That he could make us and unmake us just like the mermaids, and we could never leave him."

"No. You're not…"

Wendy's throat is too full to speak. Tiger Lily's words echo in her head—*He made me into the worst thing he could imagine, someone grown up.* Wendy brushes at her cheeks, furious with herself. She should be focused on Tiger Lily, but all she can picture is Peter's face as he stood at the end of Jane's bed, seeing her daughter and not her. No wonder Peter couldn't see her. She has become everything he hates.

She looks at Tiger Lily again. Is this what Peter thinks growing up means? Becoming a shell with the ghost of the child you once were trapped inside?

Despair shines in Tiger Lily's eyes. Her expression begs Wendy to disprove her, tell her that her words are wrong. They *are* wrong. Anger sweeps through Wendy, sudden and bright, and it clarifies her thinking.

"You don't belong to Peter. Some of the pirates left, and that proves it. As much as he wants to, he can't control everything in Neverland. Trees and plants are one thing, but people are something different.

"Tell me…" Wendy stops, remembering Mary's reaction the first time Wendy asked if she was an Indian. "Your people must have a name for themselves. Not what Peter calls you, but something that's all your own."

There's a breathlessness to her words, leaving Wendy feeling dizzy and giddy all at once. Tiger Lily glances at her, puzzlement in her sunken eyes replacing the despair. Wendy pushes on.

"There must be stories you tell to each other. Not these," Wendy indicates the painted walls, "but stories that are just your own."

A dangerous scrap of hope flutters in Wendy's chest. Her stories. Mary's stories. They're all ways of trying to make the world true, to reshape it in an attempt to control and understand it. Even Peter's stories, or maybe his most of all, tried to do that, but what if Neverland has its own stories? Older, truer stories.

"Most of the time we were just Peter's injuns." Pain cracks Tiger Lily's voice, a different quality than before. "But…"

Tiger Lily straightens slightly, and something changes in her eyes, a spark that wasn't there before. Hope blooms in Wendy too, and she leans toward her friend. Tiger Lily's gaze shifts, looking to a middle distance Wendy can't see.

"There are times when I remember stories told around a fire. Not like Peter's stories." Tiger Lily gestures to the walls.

Her voice is hesitant, but in Wendy's mind it conjures a fire built high, stars overhead, tall pines surrounding everything. An owl hoots softly. Tiger Lily and the others gathered together, shoulders touching, a circle excluding Peter and keeping those around the fire safe. The mermaids must have had their own stories, too. Maybe even Hook and his pirates. She wants to believe it, desperately. More importantly, she wants Tiger Lily to believe it, too.

"You were never just Peter's injuns." Wendy's voice quavers. She fights to keep it from becoming petulant, a child arguing with Peter over his arbitrary and unfair rules.

For Tiger Lily's sake, she would have stayed, *should* have stayed. Being Peter's mother wouldn't just have been about protecting him from the world, but protecting the world from him.

Tiger Lily's shadow sprawls across the cave floor, sharper and darker than the pale light coming through the smoke hole should warrant. It's twisted, a shackle, rooting Tiger Lily to the ground. When Wendy blinks, the image is gone.

"I remember what it feels like to burn," Tiger Lily says.

Despite the softness of her voice, the words startle Wendy, sending a chill down her spine. Tiger Lily holds her arms out again, and for a moment, Wendy almost thinks she can see fire running underneath Tiger Lily's skin.

"If Peter wanted to, he could snuff me out any time."

"No." The word is stronger, more adamant now.

Wendy thinks of moments she and Tiger Lily spent together years ago—without Peter, without the Lost Boys, just the two of them lying belly-down on sun-warmed and flattened grass along the banks of one of Neverland's many ever-shifting rivers. She thinks of her fingers and Tiger Lily's trailing in the crystal-clear water, fish with scales of silver and gold coming to nibble curiously, then dart away. Those moments were real. Tiger Lily is real, not just a Peter-created shadow.

There is so much she wants to tell Tiger Lily, about St. Bernadette's, everything she suffered, and everything she learned. She wants to ask about Tiger Lily as well, how things have been for her in Neverland since Wendy saw her last. And she wants to tell Tiger Lily how much she ached for Peter in that time, how she never let go, how part of her aches still, and how she's ashamed.

"Tell me one of your stories," Wendy says instead, meeting Tiger Lily's eyes. "One of the stories you remember from around the fire."

She wants to conjure for Tiger Lily the picture she saw of safety and family, a place Peter can't touch. She wants to root

Tiger Lily in herself, remind her she is real, that she won't burn or vanish in a puff of smoke just because Peter wills it.

"All right." There's uncertainty in Tiger Lily's voice, echoed by the doubt in her expression, and dread pricks at Wendy's skin. "But I can't remember any happy ones, only the ones about monsters."

THE FORBIDDEN PATH

The scent of cooking meat fills the air, charred, on the edge of burnt; she's never smelled anything so good. Fat drips from the spitted boar, crackling and popping where it hits the fire. Her stomach growls, and she feels sick at the same time. She watched Peter slaughter the boar, saw the hate in its eyes, and saw it rooted to the spot by Peter's will. She watched the boar being butchered. She shouldn't want to eat it with the remembered stink of its offal still in her nose, but she hasn't eaten anything since Peter's awful soup. And this is real—meat browning, sizzling and rich.

She squeezes the stone in her hand, trying to hold onto the memory of nearly choking on it. Nothing here is what it seems. Nothing is safe. If she eats the boar, what will happen? Will she forget more of herself? There are all sorts of myths and fairy stories about cursed food and what happens to those who eat it, like Persephone and her pomegranate seeds. Her mouth waters, a sour taste, and she hates herself for it.

Across the dancing fire, Peter watches her. There's a brightness to his eyes, an intensity. The flames make his features sharp, wicked.

"Wendy?" He says the name softly, and it lands like a hook

in her flesh, pulling at her. It's so familiar, settling around her like warmth, like home. It must belong to her with the way it fits against her skin, even though she can't remember clearly.

"Yes, Peter?" She hears her voice as if from very far away.

Peter's lips curve into a smile, his eyes sparking delight.

"You're our guest of honor, you should have the first bite."

He holds a broad leaf out toward her, piled high with meat. She never saw him cut it, but it's there, steaming into the night, and her stomach growls again.

"Go on. Take it."

She stands, circling the fire, even though everything in her screams to turn around and run. Peter's smile is gentle, encouraging. She takes the leaf, heat from the roasted boar soaking through and into her palms.

"That isn't fair." Arthur speaks up, standing to glare between her and Peter. "She didn't help to kill the boar at all. Why should she get the first bite?"

A fresh skin lies draped over Arthur's shoulders, cut from the boar.

"You didn't help either," Bertie pipes up. "It was all Peter."

Peter turns to beam at Bertie, who puffs up at the attention while Arthur scowls.

"That's right," Peter says. "I killed the boar, so I choose who eats first, and I say it's Wendy."

She wants to refuse. Her eyes sting, and the hollow ache gnaws at her. She's so hungry it hurts, and the way Peter looks at her, the bright pinpoints of his eyes—she can't refuse.

All at once she falls on the meat, stuffing it into her mouth with her bare hands. It burns her lips and her fingers and she doesn't care. She chews and swallows and it only makes her want more.

"You see?" Peter claps his hands, delighted. "Everyone dig in!"

The boys follow her lead, falling on the meat like ravening wolves, like carrion birds. She finds herself jostling with them, fighting to get more. She claws at a reaching arm, Bertie's she thinks, shoving him away. All around her is the sound of chewing, chewing, chewing.

Only Peter doesn't eat, smiling serenely at the frenzy. When she finally slows enough to take a breath and properly look around, she sees Peter isn't the only one not eating after all. Timothy is nowhere to be seen, and Rufus sits miserably at the edge of the fire's light, arms wrapped around himself. He's bare-chested and his ribs press against his skin. There's a hollowness to him, and the way he holds himself makes her think he's fighting his own hunger, fighting with himself not to join the feast.

As if her attention draws his, Peter turns to look at Rufus as well. His expression goes through a rapid, flickering change that has nothing to do with the shifting, tricky light of the fire—mischievous, then calculating.

"What's the matter, Rufus? Why aren't you eating?" Peter's voice is sickly-sweet, coaxing, as if he genuinely cares about Rufus and his well-being.

"Not hungry." Rufus shakes his head, a violent motion. He rocks his body, arms still wrapped around himself, refusing to look up at Peter.

The meat in her stomach turns, fear unsettling her, and she's afraid she'll bring it all up again.

"That can't be true," Peter says. His smile, like his voice, is honey, but the light in his eyes is dangerous. "It smells so good."

He tears a piece of meat free, straight from the boar in a way that should burn his skin but doesn't. He steps closer to Rufus, waving the meat under his nose. Rufus turns his head away, and the firelight catches tears welling in his eyes that he struggles not to let fall.

"I think Rufus feels bad for the boar!" Peter crows the words, turning to flash a grin at the gathered circle of boys, who now shuffle uncertainly around him.

Tension strings the air. She feels it. A storm about to break, something terrible about to happen. Even though she swallowed it all, the meat feels as though it's sitting in her throat, a lump making it impossible to speak, making it hard to breathe.

"I think Rufus likes boars so much that perhaps he'd rather be one than be a boy. What do you think?"

Peter's smile is triumphant. His eyes glitter, waiting for a response from his crowd.

"I think..." Arthur hesitates. For all his bluster earlier, she sees uncertainty in him now. This game has rules none of them but Peter understand, and all the boys feel themselves on dangerous ground.

"I think." Arthur clears his throat, making his voice louder, borrowing confidence from Peter's encouraging gaze on him and standing straighter. "I think that Rufus should be a boar, and we should hunt him."

Arthur darts a tentative look at Peter, waiting for approval.

"Yes!" Peter claps his hands again. "Excellent idea."

Lightning quick, he darts forward, grabbing Rufus by the

arm and hauling him to his feet. He spins Rufus around, pushing him, so that he strikes the ground hard on hands and knees, tears spilling free—no longer just miserable, but terrified.

A shout lodges in her throat. She wants to run to Rufus and help him, but she's rooted in place, rooted like the boar in front of Peter, no choice but to go along. She looks desperately to the circle of boys, similarly frozen around him. Someone ought to go to Rufus and help him, but no one moves. They are all like toys, she thinks, like puppets, and Peter holds all the strings.

"Snort like a boar, Rufus. Run, and we'll try to catch you!" Peter dances in place, hopping from foot to foot in his delight.

On the next hop, Peter darts forth, slapping Rufus on the flank so he lets out a frightened squeal, a remarkably animal sound. Rufus tries to scramble away, still on his hands and knees, but feet and legs block his way. The boys move, tentative at first, none of them striking Rufus, only keeping him from escaping. But they grow bolder, aiming kicks, trying to grab him. He crawls frantically, trapped between them, begging them to let him go.

His words slur, clumsy, and she can't tell whether it's the tears making them thick or something else. Like the shape of his jaw or tongue might be wrong, like he might suddenly have tusks instead of teeth. Tears start in her own eyes as well, but she can't move to help him. It is as though a physical force holds her back, a wall keeping her out with the circle of boys on the other side.

She can just see him between their legs, flashes of hair and skin. Rufus' spine arches terribly as one of the boys grabs his head, wrenching it back, and for a moment her heart refuses to beat. She is certain this is where it will happen, a blade driven home, a knife slit across his throat. She cannot see for crying now,

189

can scarcely catch her breath between choking, hiccupping sobs. This time, there is no mistaking the tortured sound that comes from Rufus over the chaos of the boys. It's all animal. A scream. It is all fear.

She cannot run toward him, but she can run away, and she does, hating herself as she flees. She fully believes that Peter could compel Rufus, or any of them, to do anything. He could make Rufus believe he *is* a boar, completely and utterly, make him believe it so strongly that he would become one.

A root catches her foot and sends her sprawling. She skids on the path, her breath cutting out, pain shocking through her as she tries and fails to catch herself. For a moment, all she wants to do is lie there, curl in on herself and sob. Let Peter find her. What does she care anymore?

In the next breath though, the thought fills her with dread. She cannot stay. She cannot let Peter take her away from herself. She doesn't belong in Neverland. She isn't a lost girl. She has a home. She has parents. She has a name, and it isn't Wendy… She's—*Jane!*

The name is suddenly there, wrested from behind the curtain in her mind. Jane slaps a bruised and dirt-smudged hand over her mouth, muffling a sound between a shout and a sob. Everything comes rushing back to her—the stricken look on her mother's face as she was pulled through the window and all the stars went plummeting by, the cold as they flew, Peter's hand wrapped around her wrist and how the whole time she was afraid of falling.

She remembers the moment they passed *through*. There's no better word she can think of for it. The sky around her changed in ways that shouldn't even be possible, and yet it happened. It was like passing through water, surfacing through a puddle and suddenly being on the other side of everything she'd ever known. After that, the stars whirling past weren't the same ones visible from her window at home. She isn't even certain how she could tell, only that she knew, felt it deep inside, the sense of being somewhere else, somewhere wrong.

She remembers shouting for her mother. Then shouting for Peter to let her go, even though she didn't know his name then. As soon as she'd made the demand, she'd become terrified that he would comply and she'd plummet out of the sky. She'd swallowed her voice, squeezing her eyes tight shut so it had been a surprise when they finally landed, thumping down hard on the sand.

When she'd opened her eyes, she'd been dazed by bright sunlight, another impossibility, for a moment ago they'd been flying through the dark. She'd felt bruised from striking the ground, but she'd scrambled up as fast as she could, kicking at Peter, scratching, trying to bite him, trying to throw sand in his eyes. She'd called him names, screaming at him, unladylike things that would horrify her grandfather if he could see her, but which might, just might, make her mother proud though she would never admit it.

All the while Peter had only laughed at her, as if it were all part of a game. Every time Jane had lunged at him, he'd dodged neatly, or leapt into the air, flying a circle around her, swooping and cawing. She remembers being humiliated, tears of frustration burning in her eyes, feeling powerless and small. When at last she'd exhausted herself, sitting down to catch her breath, Peter had landed and crouched beside her. Even though they were the same height when she'd been trying to fight him, he'd seemed so much bigger then, looming over her in a way she couldn't understand.

"There now, Wendy. Why are you so upset? You should be pleased. You're back home in Neverland where you belong."

"I'm not Wendy. I'm Jane!" She'd shoved him then, as hard as she could, bursting upward and trying to kick him again even though she was tired, hurt, and frightened.

The grin he'd worn as he looked down at her vanished, his face closing up like storm clouds rolling over the sun. He'd gripped her chin with one hand, his face inches from hers, holding her so there was no way to look anywhere but at him. She couldn't even close her eyes, though she tried; it was as though they had been stitched open.

"No more fighting. It isn't fun anymore. You're Wendy and you're here to have fun, but only so long as you follow my rules."

He'd been angry, but at the same time, his voice had been strangely soothing. Jane remembers that, the contradiction. Even shouting, he'd been whispering, and he sounded reasonable, even nice. Despite everything, she wanted to keep listening to him. She wanted to do as he said, and at the same time, her heart kicked against her ribs.

She tried to squirm in his grip, spit in his face, scream at him, but every part of her felt heavy. For all the thrashing in her mind, she hadn't been able to move at all. Peter's eyes, fixed on hers, turned a color she'd never seen eyes go before. It was like staring into a fire, or looking directly at the sun. Light had flowed across his irises, like a ring of flame crawling across a log.

"Be good," he said, then he'd let go of her so suddenly she'd stumbled back to a sitting position.

She remembers the bruising jolt of her tailbone hitting the ground, biting her tongue as her teeth snapped together. There'd been a moment, incandescent as a flash, when she could no longer remember her name. It was as though Peter had cut it out of her, so swiftly she hadn't even felt the pain, hadn't even thought to miss it until later. Then there'd been the ship, and the heavy coil of rope, and the sweet, sticky tea that had only made it harder to remember. And then everything else. Hide and seek and the boar. The weight of it crashes into her like a wave, smashing into her first, then trying to pull her out to sea with its undertow.

Peter took her name away from her.

Her stomach hurts, simultaneously hollow and full. Peter took her name. He tried to make her forget herself. Jane clenches her jaw so hard her teeth ache. He made her want to hunt. He even made her want to devour what they killed.

She crawls to the edge of the path, bringing up all the hot, crackling meat she devoured moments ago. The chaos of boys fighting each other and frightening Rufus continues behind her. She pulls herself up, gingerly testing her weight. Nothing broken, only bruised. She limps away, moving as fast as she can, welcoming the pain. It helps her focus, helps her remember herself, and she will not forget again.

She is Jane. Jane. Jane. Jane.

Her name is a rhythm, matched to her heart, matched to her ragged breath. A stitch laces up her side, hot and fast, and brings her to a halt.

"Are you alright?" Timothy's voice comes out of the dark, soft and frightened, and Jane looks up, startled. Tree shadows dapple his skin as he emerges from beneath them. In the moonlight, he looks like a ghost.

She shakes her head, then nods, wiping at her tears and smearing them all over her face. She laughs, a huffing, uncontrolled sound that makes her stomach ache all over again, and it's a moment before she can get herself under control.

"No, but I will be." She straightens, makes herself smile for Timothy's benefit, and some of the doubt and fear unwinds from him, his shoulders relaxing.

She looks around, realizing where she is. She'd found a hammock in a pile of salvage from the ship and strung it up outside the camp so she could sleep away from the scatter of boys. She sinks into it now, exhausted, and after a moment, Timothy sits beside her. She's glad he's here and not with the shouting mess of boys.

They should return for Rufus, try to help him. But even the thought makes her pulse seize, her eyes burn. What can she and Timothy do against all of Peter's hunters? Better to let them grow bored, forget. They're bound to sooner or later. She has to believe it's true.

Timothy's added weight—slight as he is—makes the hammock sway. His feet don't even come close to touching the ground as he dangles them over the side.

Tiny lines crease the skin between Timothy's brows. He looks like he's trying hard to remember something as they sit in silence, Jane gathering herself, thinking what to do next. She can't run off and leave him to look for a way home. She has to help him, and Rufus too, and any of the others she can convince of Peter's wicked ways.

194

"Why were you running?" Timothy asks after a moment, his expression clearing from troubled to wide-eyed curiosity. "Is it because you saw a monster?"

The question catches her off guard, and she almost laughs, but Timothy's expression is so serious she swallows the sound down.

"No, I wasn't running from a monster." Except, she thinks, she was, just not the kind Timothy means. "There are no monsters here."

She makes her voice firm as she says it, as if will alone could make her words true.

"Is that because you're here to be our mother? That's what Peter said." Timothy looks up at her.

"I'm not…" Surprise at his words turns into something else as she sees the hope in Timothy's eyes.

"Peter says that's what mothers are for," Timothy goes on. He says the word "mother" like it's a strange creature out of a fairy tale, one he's only heard stories about but doesn't really understand. "Mothers cook and tell stories, but the best thing is that mothers scare monsters away."

"I…" Jane hesitates. The way Timothy looks at her makes her think for a moment that it could be true, she *could* be big and safe enough to protect him. Not a mother, but a big sister. At the same time, she feels terribly small. She misses her own mother, and she only wants to go home.

"No." She lets out a breath, and it hurts; maybe she should have lied. "I don't think so. I'm sorry."

"Oh." The disappointment in Timothy's voice is clear, but like before, there's a quicksilver mood change and he looks up again, grinning. "That's okay. We can still be friends."

"I don't belong here." She didn't mean to say it out loud, but the truth rings in her and she can't keep it quiet. "I need to go home."

Timothy looks like he might cry.

"You could come with me," Jane says quickly. The words expand inside her, feeling wild and dangerous, and she finds that she absolutely means them. "And Bertie, and Rufus, too. We can all go somewhere safe."

Peter stole her, he stole *from* her; she will steal from him in turn.

"Bertie and Rufus won't go with you." Timothy picks at the edge of the hammock, deflating some of the hope growing inside her.

"Why not?" Jane can't imagine Rufus would want to stay, not after what he's been through.

"They never remember." Timothy's weary expression suddenly makes him seem like the older one between the two of them. "I tried to tell Rufus how it was good of him to stand up for me against Peter, and how I was sorry Peter hit him, but he didn't even remember that."

"How could he forget being hit?" Jane thinks of the bruise on his cheek. She glances back in the direction of the camp, thinking of Rufus on his knees, squealing. Will he forget that too?

Perhaps, for his sake, it would be better if he did.

"It's the tea Peter makes. We all have to drink it, but if no one is looking, I spit mine out. I think Rufus does sometimes, too, but sooner or later he always drinks it again. I don't think he likes remembering."

Jane thinks of Rufus hunched and miserable by the fire, warring against himself, wanting to hold on and wanting to forget himself all at once. She's seen what happens to people who resist

Peter. And part of her understands—forgetting is so much safer, so much easier.

Timothy's frown deepens, his bottom lip sticking out. Jane sees the moment the troubled expression in his eyes becomes something else, fear, like the edge of the moon peeking out behind the clouds.

"When I don't drink the tea, sometimes I remember scary and bad things." Timothy's voice is a hush, barely a whisper, so Jane has to strain to hear him.

"But no one else remembers the things I remember, so maybe they're just a story I made up in my head." Timothy looks to her, his eyes wide in the moonlight. And for a moment, they aren't eyes at all, just darkness, and Jane thinks of ghosts again and her heart lurches terribly.

He blinks, and his eyes look normal again. Just a little boy.

"Tell me," Jane says. She makes herself touch Timothy's wrist, to reassure him, and to prove to herself she isn't afraid.

"Once upon a time," Timothy starts, as if he really does mean to tell her a fairy tale, "there were other boys here who aren't here anymore."

Jane's pulse trips, unease settling around her like a cloak, but she holds her tongue and lets Timothy continue.

"One boy was called Edmund. He would stick up for me sometimes, like Rufus does. Except since Peter gives us different names sometimes, maybe Edmund is still here and I just forgot, but I don't think so."

Timothy looks down at his hands, knotting his fingers together, then unknotting them, digging his nails into the rope of the hammock as though to pull the whole thing apart. Jane watches him. Should she put an arm around him? What would a good big sister do? He seems so fragile that she fears he might break.

"A long time ago, when Edmund was here, he said that Peter shouldn't get to be leader because he isn't even a real boy. He doesn't have a shadow, and that proves it, that's what Edmund said.

"They got into a fight about it, a really big one, but Peter never got tired or hurt, and Edmund did. Peter would jump up in the air where Edmund couldn't reach him and fly in a circle, sticking his tongue out, laughing, and calling Edmund all sorts of names. Nobody even tried to help Edmund."

Timothy blinks, rubbing at his nose with the back of his hand.

"Then all of a sudden Peter clapped Edmund on the back like they were good friends again and he said he wasn't cross anymore. I was still scared though, because Peter had the look he has when he thinks of a really good game. He said he and Edmund were going to go someplace secret and no one else was allowed to follow."

"What happened?" Jane whispers.

Distress is clear in Timothy's expression, like he's holding something big and terrible inside him and it's pressing out against his skin.

She's afraid he will wail, and draw the attention of the others. Once Peter grows bored with tormenting Rufus, he might come looking for her.

"It's okay," she says, trying to make her voice soothing, trying to sound like she believes her words, and there is nothing to be afraid of at all.

"I did a really bad thing." Timothy's eyes fill, tears overwhelming them and hovering on his lashes. "I followed even though Peter said not to, because I wanted to see the secret, and I wanted to make sure Edmund was okay. I tried to be really brave and really quiet and…"

Timothy's lower lip quivers. Jane hugs him close, presses her nose to the top of his head, feeling his body tremble against her. But the cry she fears never comes and Timothy takes a deep breath, squirming away so he can look up at her. There is determination in his eyes now, and she can see that he's trying to be very brave and very quiet all over again, and her heart aches for him.

"Peter took Edmund to a place where there's a little stream running out of a cave and into the sea. I climbed up a tree to watch. Peter made Edmund wait outside, then he went into the cave and came out holding a thing that was maybe a stone, or maybe a knife. I don't know." Timothy picks at the hammock's ropes again. "I didn't like looking at it. It made me feel bad, like there was something wrong inside my chest. Peter kept looking at Edmund, right in the face, and I think he was talking to him, but it was so quiet I couldn't hear them…" Timothy falters.

Jane imagines the worst, seeing Peter falling on the boar, blood joining his freckles like constellations traced between stars.

"Did he… Did he kill Edmund, like he killed the boar?"

Timothy shakes his head, tears spilling, and now his expression is one of frustration as well as fear. It's like there's so much he wants to say, but it's too big to explain. It's the same expression he wore when Jane asked him about his mother and father, like he's trying to remember something, and the remembering hurts.

"Peter touched Edmund with the stone, the knife, and then Edmund wasn't there anymore." Timothy's brow scrunches, fingers clenched and twisting between the rope so it cuts into his skin.

"I mean, he was still here, but he was all empty inside. He wasn't Edmund anymore. Peter pulled something out of him. It was dark and shiny like smoke and water, but like something alive and—" Timothy's voice rises in pitch, and Jane pulls him close, cutting off his words before he gives them away.

"Shh. It's okay."

After a moment, when she's certain he isn't going to shout, she relaxes her hold.

"I ran away. I didn't help Edmund even when he helped me." Timothy's words are muffled, the side of Jane's nightgown wet with his tears.

"There's nothing you could have done," she says. "It's not your fault."

Timothy pulls back. She sees in his eyes how much he wants to believe her, but there's misery there too, telling her he cannot. How long has Timothy been here? He looks like a little boy, but he might be older than her mother and father, or her grandfather even if what he's saying is true, and all this happened a long time ago.

"After, Peter came back to the camp and Edmund wasn't with him," Timothy says. "He was carrying a sack and I just knew somehow that the dark thing Peter took from Edmund was inside it." Timothy leans back, putting space between them again. He looks emptied out himself now, like the telling has drained him. "Peter looked very proud of himself and he told everyone he was going to go away and bring us back a mother, and she would make it so he had a shadow again and no one could say he wasn't real."

Jane rubs at her arms. Her skin feels too tight, wrong on her bones, and she wants to brush the sensation away but she can't. Timothy's eyes make her think of an owl, too round and too bright, taking up so much of his face.

"Nobody else even seemed to notice Edmund was gone, and after a while, it was like he wasn't ever here. There are other boys who went away too, like Roger and Tootles, and I don't know what happened to any of them. Sometimes I'm afraid Peter will make me go away too."

Timothy's shoulders curl inward so he looks even smaller, simultaneously old and young.

"I won't let that happen," Jane says, taking a breath. "We can look out for each other, you and me. That's what friends do, they protect each other."

"You won't tell, will you?" Timothy says. "About the tea, or Edmund, or Roger, or any of it?"

"Of course not." Jane feels her heartbeat, the rhythm of it, uneven and rapid in her chest. There's a feeling like she can't get enough air, and she can't decide whether she wants to run or laugh or cry, or all three.

"How long have you been here, Timothy?" Jane hates to ask it, but she feels like she needs to know. There are all these puzzle pieces in her head, but she can't quite line them up. She can't see the picture they make, just bits of it, all broken and scattered around.

"Always, I guess." Timothy shrugs, an air of defeat hanging on him.

Jane can understand why Rufus would want to forget, why all the other boys would want to forget, too. It's so much easier, so much safer for them to go along with Peter and live in a land of endless games and fun. But she is determined to remember. Peter stole her name. He stole her. He hurt people. She will not let that truth go.

"Do you remember…" Jane hesitates. There's another piece of the puzzle she can almost see but she's afraid to look at. Peter keeps calling her by her mother's name. Timothy's answer might mean she doesn't know her mother at all. "Did Peter bring back a mother like he said he would?"

"Oh! Yes!" Timothy nods, beaming, as though he'd forgotten until the moment Jane asked, a happy memory to replace the bad ones.

"Do you—" Her voice breaks, and Jane swallows, her throat suddenly thick. "What was she like?"

Timothy screws up his face again, thinking, and then his expression clears, and he looks younger than ever, smiling in a way that breaks Jane's heart.

"Pretty. She was nice. She told stories, like you, but better."

Timothy's eyes go wide, as if realizing what he's said might hurt her. He opens his mouth, but Jane shakes her head, wiping at her cheeks with the back of her hand and letting out a breath.

"It doesn't matter," she says. "Listen. If Peter went away and brought… a mother back from somewhere else, then there must be somewhere else to go to, a way off the island."

Timothy's face scrunches with incomprehension, like he can't grasp there being more to the world than just Neverland. Jane ignores his confusion, jumping up. She can't sit here a moment longer thinking of the possibility of her mother and Peter, her mother *here*, and never breathing a word of it to Jane. She can't think about Timothy knowing her mother before she ever did, Timothy being older than her, no matter how young he looks. The hammock rocks so violently Timothy almost falls out, but he scrambles after her.

"I'll help you look."

"But—" Even though she already suggested Timothy come home with her, being responsible for herself is one thing; being responsible for Timothy is something else entirely.

"I'm not scared." Timothy interrupts her, pushing his chest out and raising his chin.

It's so brave and ridiculous and wonderful that Jane can't help but laugh. She wipes at her cheeks again. Maybe a good big sister would insist Timothy stay behind, but would he really be any safer with Peter than with her? Deep down, she's glad to have Timothy with her; she'd rather not do this alone.

"Well, we'd best leave now then, before the others find us."

Another giddy thrill runs through her, and Jane suppresses a burst of nervous laughter. Is she really doing this? Is she really running away from Peter and taking Timothy with her? How will they get home, and what will she do with Timothy once they're there? She can't think about that now. There'll be time to figure it out later. Right now, they need to escape.

She gestures for Timothy to follow her, moving as swiftly as she can without making any noise. At the border of the trees, Timothy pauses. His expression is serious, his eyes wide in the drenching moonlight, and Jane is struck with the sudden fear that he means to turn back.

"This does mean we're friends, doesn't it?" The question catches her off guard; a sound rises in her throat that might be a laugh or a sob, but she turns it into a cough to excuse her watering eyes. If Timothy can be brave and fierce and sweet then so can she. Whatever they do to leave this place, they'll do it together.

"Of course we are." Jane thinks for a moment then draws herself up and extends her hand for a formal and proper shake, which seems to her a very grown-up thing to do. "I'm Jane, and it's a great pleasure to have your friendship."

Timothy beams, pumping her hand enthusiastically.

"Hullo, Jane," he says. "It's very good to know you and be your friend."

LONDON 1920

Wendy stands on the steps of St. Bernadette's trying not to fidget. After years in plain clothing designed to erase her shape, the skirt she wears is too heavy, her waist too pinched, the heels on her boots too high. They're her own clothes, but they don't feel like her anymore. They might as well belong to a stranger.

She has to consciously still her hands and not pluck at her sleeves or smooth her skirt to surreptitiously touch the reassuring pockets that are no longer there. The first thing she'll do once she's free of this place is sew herself a whole new set of clothing, ones with proper, deep pockets everywhere she can fit them.

The thought calms her, but only for a moment. Michael and John are bringing her home today. She's spent three years yearning for freedom, and now that it's within her grasp, she isn't ready. What will she do without Mary? What will she do with this man, Ned, whom her brothers have chosen as her keeper?

John has made it clear she must become the very model of a

marriageable woman. This is not only a chance at a normal life for her but for him as well. Wendy knows she's been a burden, but before she goes off to her new life, she wishes they could speak honestly as brother and sister. It's been such a rush since John delivered his news. She still doesn't know for certain why John chose Ned for her rather than some other man. Or perhaps he is the only choice, and her brother is that desperate to unload her.

And what of Michael? Does he like Ned? Consider him a friend? She trusts John to speak to Ned's breeding, but Michael might tell her honestly whether Ned is a kind man, whether he laughs easily or is serious all the time. Or at least he might have once upon a time. Now she isn't certain whether Michael is willing to speak to her at all. John informed her they were both coming to collect her, but does Michael want to be here, or is John dragging him along?

Wendy thinks back to the last time she saw her youngest brother outside St. Bernadette's. She'd broken him with her insistence that he remember Neverland, reducing him to tears. Had she sought to help him or herself? She still isn't sure. At the time she'd thought, perhaps, that remembering something good might help him, and she'd begged him to see the world from her perspective, but she'd never once tried to see it from his.

How much he must have forced himself to forget just to survive, how much the war had taken from him. But back then, she'd refused to let up. She'd pushed, even when his hands shook, when his eyes grew wild, when he sobbed. He'd shouted at her to stop, and she'd shouted right back at him.

If she'd relented, perhaps John never would have brought her to this place. The image is burned in her mind even now—John standing between Michael and herself, light reflecting in his glasses and erasing his eyes. Even so, she'd seen his expression—stricken. He'd been afraid—of her, for her—and she'd left him no choice. He'd needed to put her away to protect their baby brother, something she should have done herself, but she'd been so stubborn and certain she was right.

Wendy looks toward the iron gates. The path leading to them is a pale scar against the green. When she first arrived at St. Bernadette's she would have blamed Peter for the way she treated her brothers. If he hadn't abandoned her, if he hadn't stolen them all in the first place... But no. It is time to take responsibility for herself, to protect her brothers the way she always should have.

"Mary has come to bid you one last goodbye." Dr. Harrington's voice jolts Wendy from her thoughts.

He'd agreed to her release easily, happy to be rid of her, Wendy is certain. She doesn't miss the disapproval in the doctor's eyes, but to his credit he steps aside to give them at least the illusion of privacy. This is the moment she's been dreading most of all, and when she turns, Wendy's pulse lurches. Mary looks small framed against the hallway leading back into the asylum. In all the time Wendy has known her, Mary has never looked small. She's big enough to contain worlds, courage and love Wendy can't even fathom. Panic rabbits through her. She can't do this. She almost grabs Dr. Harrington by the lapels of his immaculate suit, telling him she's changed her mind, she doesn't want to go home at all.

Mary steadies her with an unforgiving look, almost a glare. *Don't you dare*, it says. *You are not allowed to be a coward.*

Wendy almost laughs, a sound dangerously close to breaking

her. She keeps it trapped behind her teeth and takes Mary's hands, leaning their foreheads together.

"I'll find a way to get you out too, I promise." Wendy shifts, placing her body between Mary and Dr. Harrington, so she can pretend they're alone. "Even if it can't be right away, I won't leave you here."

"Don't go making promises you can't keep." Mary's eyes shine bright. It isn't doubt in her voice, more a threat, mockingly delivered. Wendy can't help smiling, tasting salt as she does. She's never had a friend before, not one like Mary. How will she live while they're apart?

"I'll keep it. I swear." Wendy smudges the tears on her cheeks.

"Here." Quick enough that Dr. Harrington won't see, Wendy slips a precious stolen needle from the sleeve of her blouse where she threaded it earlier, tucking it into Mary's hand. Mary's mouth opens, but no words emerge. Their whole history together in a tiny sliver of metal; Wendy folds Mary's fingers over it. Mary taught her to survive, how not to give up hope. The only thing Wendy wants in the world right now is to do the same for her.

"Something to remember me by." She brushes her lips against Mary's cheek, soaking in the warmth of her skin. "This isn't goodbye."

Wendy steps back and already the needle is nowhere to be seen. Wendy schools her features, tucking the urge to smile into her cheek and biting down on it.

"Come now, let's not keep your brothers waiting." Dr. Harrington takes Wendy's arm, his grip insistent and firm.

For a moment, Wendy thinks she will strike him, but Mary's gaze pins her. She has a promise to keep. Wendy inclines her head, the barest of motions, and even that hurts. She should say more, but what can she say? There's too much between them, and words are not enough for what Mary means to her. Wendy can only hope, trust, that Mary knows.

Wendy turns, swallowing against an aching throat. She allows Dr. Harrington to walk her down the path, his fingers wrapped tight about her arm, as though even now she might flee. She has the absurd image of herself as a bride, Dr. Harrington walking her down the aisle to give her away. Wendy glances back at Mary one last time. If she looks for any longer, her courage will break and she'll sprint back into the dark. She knows she isn't safe in St. Bernadette's, but at least she understands the rules.

When she turns back, she sees John and Michael at the bottom of the path, waiting just inside the gate. They look terribly small, only boys in the nursery. Then the space between them folds, and Wendy is front of them and they are both taller than her, not boys at all but fully grown men. John with his fine moustache, Michael with his hair faded to a sandy paleness, leaning on his cane, a collection of ghosts keeping residence in his blue-gray eyes. John kisses her cheek. Michael hugs her with one arm, but the movement is stiff and formal as though they are strangers.

Wendy aches to say something to him, but John steps between them.

"Come now, darling." John takes her arm, his fingers taking the place of Dr. Harrington's. Wendy can't help flinching at the gesture and his words. "There's a car waiting."

There's a strained note in his voice, tension in his eyes as John glances toward her then away again just as quickly. He bundles her into the back seat, scarcely giving her a moment to collect herself, as if he too is afraid she'll fly away. His voice, his expression, something is wrong, and Wendy braces herself, but nothing could prepare her for John's words as he climbs in beside her and shuts the door.

"I hope you don't mind terribly much, but we have reservations for lunch at the club. Ned's father has arranged it all. He's very anxious to meet you."

"Ned?" Wendy turns cold, her ears ringing with the name as the car pulls away. She's to meet her future husband *now*? Without even a chance to reacclimatize to life outside St. Bernadette's walls?

John at least has the decency to look abashed, his cheeks reddening. Michael doesn't look at her at all.

"Please, Wendy. You must try." John's voice is that of a child, begging for a sweet, smoothed over with a veneer of concern.

Wendy's hands want to fly to the door handle, to pound against the car's window. She wants to throw herself into the street, anything but this. She thinks of Mary, her promise, and the future. She thinks of John and Michael and their past. She makes herself look her brother in the eye, seeing him truly. John cares for her. He wants what's best for her. She can't blame him for failing to understand her when she made herself impossible to comprehend.

"I am trying." Wendy keeps her voice as even as she can. "I will try, but I need time. It's too soon."

John's teeth worry at his lip beneath his moustache, an old habit resurfacing.

"Your future father-in-law was rather insistent. He can be… an impatient man." John coughs, looking away.

"There's something you're not telling me." Wendy almost grabs John by the ear, as if he were a boy again and she her mother's surrogate, trying to catch him in a fib. Instead, she curls her hands in her lap, proving she can control herself, proving she's changed.

"It isn't a matter for…" John shakes his head. "It's nothing for you to worry about." His voice is sharp, but underneath, Wendy thinks he might be embarrassed. She looks to Michael, pleading, but he ignores her, looking through the window as the city rolls past. Wendy feels her corset constricting her. More than heavy now, more than weighing her down. Her skin burns under her clothing until she wants to claw her dress free. Now she knows why John was so insistent over how she should be dressed, how her hair should be done. How could he do this to her? How could he be so unfair?

All too soon, the car comes to a halt, filling Wendy with fresh panic. She scans the street, wondering if she could run. How far could she get before they hunted her down? John catches her arm as she reaches for the door, as if sensing her thoughts. But there's more to it than that—the look in his eyes is something else altogether.

"Ned and his father know you've been… sick, but nothing more." A frown works at John's mouth, but his expression is sincere. "You might tell them it was the Spanish flu, or whatever you like. What you choose to disclose is up to you."

Choose. The word stops her. She hasn't had a choice in so long—not of where to go, or what to say, and now John is giving Wendy the chance to reinvent herself whole. The thought is dizzying, and she meets her brother's eyes, sees everything in them that he is trying to convey without speaking out loud. He

210

wants to be kind. He's offering her control of her life from this moment on, as narrow as the channel may be. Above all, with a fierceness that takes Wendy by surprise, he wants her to be happy.

All at once, the thought of so much choice panics her. *Could* she say it was the flu? St. Bernadette's had been lucky in that way, with few enough soldiers sent to the men's wards after coming home from the continent that they had largely escaped the sickness that had engulfed other places whole. Will Ned and his father press her, ask her for proof, and what will she say if they do? After so many years of lying, the thought of one more, a lie of her choosing that—if John is correct—her future husband will be eager to believe, nearly stops her breath.

John holds her arm for a moment longer, then lets her go. Trust. A gift, and she takes strength from it, forcing herself to breathe. She can do this thing. Moving stiffly, she climbs from the car. Her body feels numb, miles away and nothing to do with her. The real Wendy Darling flies far above the woman ascending the steps to the club preparing to meet her future husband.

By habit, Wendy brushes down the front of her skirt and straightens her sleeves. There are no hidden pockets, but running her hands over the fabric calms her regardless. Given the situation, she can allow herself this small comfort.

"I'm ready." Wendy lifts her chin.

John favors her with a smile—relief, and perhaps a little bit of affection. There's even a note of apology in his eyes as he holds open the door. As Wendy steps through, Michael finally catches her eye. The expression is flicker-brief, but Wendy sees a glimpse of the boy she knew in the nursery. He touches her arm, the barest pressure of his fingers resting on her sleeve.

"Don't worry, Windy." A crooked smile, and Michael's old nickname for her almost undoes her. "You'll like Ned."

Those words, brief as they are, give Wendy the courage to keep walking. She will do this for Michael, for John. For Mary.

As Wendy's eyes adjust to the transition from outdoor to indoor light, a tall, angular man steps forward. His hair is neatly parted, his moustache dark and carefully trimmed. The man's suit is impeccable—dark gray, the coat long, with a cravat of rose-colored silk stuck with a perfectly placed diamond pin. She's been out of the world long enough that she has no idea whether this is the current fashion, but nonetheless, she feels shabby. She stops where she is, and the man stops as well, a nervous air about him, making her think of a horse, easily spooked.

Just behind the man who must be Ned is a man she assumes to be her future father-in-law. The resemblance is uncanny. She might be looking at the same man twice, only one with several extra years of age. The iron gray of her father in-law's hair and moustache is the only thing that sets their appearances apart.

Ned holds out his hand, but his father steps forward, almost bumping Ned out of the way as he grasps John's hand and shakes it firmly. He greets Michael next, and only then looks to Wendy. His gaze reminds her of Dr. Harrington, examining her like a specimen, a particularly unpleasant one. John puts a hand on the small of her back, steadying her, drawing her forward.

"May I present my sister, Miss Wendy Darling."

Should she curtsey? No, that would be absurd. She inclines her head, does her best to smile. She's so focused on what to do with her hands, where to look, that she misses Ned and his father's last name. Did John tell her already? She can't remember.

212

It's to be her name too; shouldn't it be something she knows? She wants to laugh, feels the hysterical sound trapped in her throat, and tamps it down.

Without intending to, she ends up meeting Ned's eye. His cheeks immediately color. The reaction catches her off guard, making her want to laugh in a wholly different way. It's oddly charming that he should be afraid of her. Of all the things she might have expected, that wasn't one of them.

"There's a table waiting for us." Ned's father's voice is brusque, and Wendy sees what her brother meant about him being an impatient man. It strikes Wendy that he's treating the whole thing as a business transaction, one that he would rather have over and done.

As Ned's father leads the way to the dining room, Wendy tries to catch Ned's eye again, but he studiously looks everywhere but at her. She contents herself with watching him instead, as unobtrusively she can, while still remembering the important things—which fork to use, to sit up straight, to nod and smile as though she's listening. It's easy enough. Once they're seated, Ned's father dominates the conversation. John occasionally contributes when he's allowed. Michael doesn't speak at all, and neither does Ned. Wendy isn't even invited, as though she's merely a piece of furniture or decoration at a table meant for men.

It gives her time to observe, building herself a picture of the new world she's meant to inhabit. She sees now why John was insistent and ashamed all at once. Her future father-in-law is a force of nature, a bully—a man like Jamieson, though his methods are far subtler. He's a man used to the world giving way to him. Despite the similarity in their appearances, Ned seems to be his father's opposite, quiet, and almost afraid. Wendy feels a surge of pity for him. The parts of the conversation she absorbs center on Ned's brother, Allan. Not once does she hear her future father-in-law even mention Ned's name. He is as much a fixture, a piece of furniture at the table as she, both to be moved around at will.

While he doesn't look at his son, her future father-in-law looks at Wendy more than once, appraising, seeming pleased when she takes small bites of her food, keeps her hands folded in her lap otherwise, and maintains silence. She hates him, instantly and completely, but Ned, almost despite herself, she finds intriguing.

"Will you join me for brandy and a cigar, Mr. Darling? We have details to discuss." Ned's father turns to John as the plates are cleared, and Wendy starts, her stomach knotting with tension. She'd almost allowed herself to forget the reason for this luncheon.

"Of course." John stands, nervous and flustered. She's never known John to smoke a cigar in his life.

"Might we step outside for some air while you talk?" After so long in silence, Wendy's voice sounds small in the room, lost among the gentle clink of fine china, polished silverware and delicately cut crystal glasses.

The four men turn to look at her. Ned's father frowns. She imagines him making a mark on the debit side of a mental ledger. Rather than shrinking, she focuses her attention on Ned, smiling in a way she hopes will not intimidate him.

"I'd be pleased to volunteer my services as chaperone," Michael says.

Wendy turns, surprised, just in time to catch the faintest hint of mischief in his eyes. There's amusement in his voice as well, and it fills Wendy with hope.

"Of course, the garden is quite lovely." In his haste to stand and accommodate her request, Ned almost knocks his chair over. His father catches it before it hits the ground, righting it with a scowl.

If she were bolder, Wendy might loop her arm through Ned's, if only to spite his father, but she restrains herself. After all, this man is a part of her life now; she doesn't have to make an effort to like him, but she must at least try to get along.

As he and John retreat to another room, Wendy follows Ned and Michael through a set of double glass doors leading onto a stone terrace overlooking an enclosed garden. Crossing the threshold, Wendy takes a moment to appreciate the novelty of stepping outside of her own free will, of not being under the watchful eye of Dr. Harrington, or Jamieson, or any of the nurses. She draws in a deep breath, and not even the pinch of her corset is enough to dampen her joy.

Michael moves to one of the benches at the terrace's far end. Wendy surprises herself with disappointment; he intends to chaperone them in name only. It isn't that she fears being alone with Ned. A glance at his face is enough to tell her that he is still far more frightened of her than she is of him. Rather it's the fresh loss of her brother that saddens her. For a moment, she caught a glimpse of the old Michael, when he called her Windy, when he smiled as he offered to chaperone.

Perhaps it's terribly rude of her, but she watches her brother for a moment longer, ignoring Ned. It's been so long, surely he can't begrudge her. A bright slant of sunlight picks out golden highlights in the wheat of Michael's hair. It's thinner than Wendy remembers. Everything about him is thinner. The suit jacket she's certain John picked out for him hangs from his shoulders as if from a scarecrow. She can practically see Michael standing in a field, surrounded by high stalks of corn, staring endlessly at the horizon. A cloud of black birds might descend on him, and he would never move. Wendy's heart aches for him.

Michael leans his cane against the bench beside him and reaches into his pocket, pulling out a tin of tobacco and a paper. She doesn't miss the way his hands shake as he rolls the cigarette. He turns slightly, and her pulse snags, but he barely seems to register her. His face is lost in a wash of sunlight, ghosted out as he raises the tin toward Ned in a silent question. Ned shakes his head, and Michael turns away, his shoulders rising in an effective wall, shutting Wendy and Ned out.

The loss goes through Wendy again, like a bolt shot from a crossbow. Will she ever get her baby brother back? If she'd never shouted at him, if she'd found a way to be kind, would they be able to speak and laugh now as they did in the old days? Or would the war always be an un-healing wound inside him, regardless of her actions?

Wendy steels herself and turns her attention to Ned even as Michael remains an ache like a bruise at the back of her mind. "I hope you aren't holding back on my account." Wendy indicates Michael's cigarette. She tries to make her tone light, breezy, agreeable. Isn't that what women should be? Now that they are as alone as they are going to be, a rill of nerves courses through her. Sooner or later, despite her best intentions, she's bound to say the wrong thing.

"I haven't touched a cigarette since the war."

She shouldn't be surprised, given Ned's age, but somehow

she is. He appears the complete opposite of her brother. Shy, yes. Frightened, but not by his past, rather by what stands right in front of him. She can't imagine him holding a gun, or crawling through mud. Perhaps he was an officer, commanding from well behind the lines? Resentment bubbles up, thinking of Michael in danger and Ned safe in some bunker or camp.

"I thought all soldiers smoked." The words tumble out of her mouth before she can stop them, desperate to fill the silence.

Surprise shows in Ned's expression, but to Wendy's relief, he doesn't seem to take offense at her words. It was unfair of her to judge him, even in her mind, without knowing anything about him.

"I take a pipe very occasionally, but never cigarettes. It reminds me of too much."

Now it is Wendy's turn for surprise. She looks to her brother again. Michael remains lost in his own thoughts, showing no interest in them. A cloud of smoke hangs around him, so she sees him through a haze, both older and younger than his actual age.

"Then why would..." she lets the words trail.

Ned's reply is soft, compassion in his voice that startles her all over again.

"Perhaps that is precisely why your brother favors cigarettes. Many men don't want to forget."

Wendy turns to stare at him, this man who will be her husband. Her mouth opens slightly, but she's at a loss for words. Under her attention, Ned's cheeks color. He looks down, coughing slightly. Has she overstepped her bounds, or has he? Or are they both equally foolish and awkward? Silence stretches until it's almost painful. Wendy reaches for something to say, anything to put them back on safe footing, but Ned saves her, falling back on bland formality.

"I must say, it is a pleasure to finally meet you, Miss Darling. Michael and John have told me a great deal about you."

A faint stutter breaks into his words, and the blood rises to his cheeks again as he fights against it. That and the way he keeps a careful space between them makes Wendy swallow the response leaping to her tongue, too sharp for the situation: *And they have told me nothing about you.*

"John in particular has been a good friend to me ever since he came to work for my father." Ned looks out over the garden as he speaks, not at her.

"If you don't mind my asking." Wendy tries to be careful with her words, not wanting to frighten Ned, not wanting to sound ignorant. Ned knows she's been sick, but not where she's been. Why does he think John and Michael have kept her a secret all these years? "How do you know my brothers? Were you with Michael in…"

She lets her words trail again, afraid of upsetting him. For all she knows, Ned bears scars every bit as deep as Michael's and just as invisible to the naked eye. Ned's mouth twitches beneath his moustache, but he schools his expression quickly.

Ned glances over his shoulder and Wendy follows his gaze to Michael.

"I was in the European theater at the same time as Michael, though we didn't meet until after I'd returned home. John introduced us."

"I'm glad Michael has someone to speak to, then. Someone who understands." This much is true. She's certain John and

Michael don't talk, not about the war at least, and she fears Michael may not have very many friends otherwise.

They lapse into silence again, but this time more comfortable. Wendy almost allows herself to relax, until she remembers John and Ned's father are currently negotiating her future. Their future. After a moment, Ned gathers himself, his words emerging in a rush. His stutter returns, more pronounced now, and Wendy can't help glancing back toward the dining room, half expecting to find Ned's father looming in the doorway, a shadow against the curtains, a shadow over Ned's whole life.

"I know this is all rather sudden, Miss Darling, and I wouldn't blame you for any trepidations." Ned hesitates, fidgeting with the cuffs of his jacket. "To be perfectly honest, I never expected to be married myself. I might have preferred… that is, I had assumed I would remain a bachelor."

Ned looks down, and Wendy senses he's trying to tell her something. There are words between his words, ones he's afraid to speak, but for the life of her, she can't guess at them. She bites back frustration. Why are people so fond of riddles, making others guess what they mean? Why is no one able to simply speak plainly?

Ned's eyes, a warm, dark brown, meet her own. It is the first time he's looked at her directly since their luncheon began. They are kind eyes; in that, at least, Ned is completely unlike his father.

"Miss Darling, I should like to be honest with you." Ned lifts his chin. She sees the moment he wants to look away, but does not. Even so, the way he stands tells her he would much rather slouch, curl his shoulders inward as though to slip beneath notice, not just hers, but that of the world.

"It seems neither of us is to be given much choice in the

matter of our nuptials. My father is rather eager for me to be married, quickly, and I fear that as your brother's employer, and with your own health difficulties, he settled on you as a suitable match, feeling that you would be… pliable, lacking in other prospects."

Ned coughs, a short, embarrassed sound, the color in his cheeks even higher. Wendy can only stare at him, at a loss for what to say in the face of his candor.

"Given that neither of us chose this situation for ourselves, I am content to be your husband in name only, if that is your wish. I will ask nothing of you, however I do hope that we might at least be friends."

Earnestness shines in his eyes. There is a fragility there too, and even though they have only just met, she thinks that an answer in the negative might crush him. She has had so few friends in her lifetime, and she senses that in that regard, she and Ned may be the same.

"I…" Wendy opens her mouth, dazed by Ned's vulnerability, dazed by his offer.

She has no idea what to think of the man in front of her, and that alone is enough to intrigue her. There is a gentleness to him, setting him apart from his father, setting him apart from Peter, her first real friend. She glances briefly to Michael. He assured her she would like Ned; perhaps this is what he meant.

"I shall endeavor to be honest with you as well." Wendy smooths the front of her skirt, gathering herself and burying her nerves in the folds of the fabric. "I have not had many friends in my life. I am not the easiest person to be friends with, in fact, but if you are willing to try, then I am as well."

The words feel reckless, dangerous, but in the instant, Wendy means them. It's like the first time she flew, holding Peter's hand, the way they stepped from the window and fell into the night. Only they didn't fall. They soared.

She hasn't decided what she will tell Ned of her life, and she doesn't know what he may be willing to share of his. All she knows is that she would like to learn more about him. She would like to have someone else in the world besides Mary that she can rightfully call her friend.

Wendy allows herself a smile, a small one, and hope creeps into her chest. For the first time since walking out of St. Bernadette's gate mere hours ago, she feels as though she can breathe properly.

"Thank you, Miss Darling." Ned returns her smile, relief in it, and also genuine pleasure.

"Please," Wendy says, "if we are to be friends, you must call me Wendy."

*

Jane leads Timothy back to the spot where arrowheads and stones pelted her, keeping alert for more unseen assailants. She peers into the blue–blackness under the trees. Where the path splits and the trees bow inward, forming a natural tunnel and blocking most of the moonlight, the air looks almost solid there.

The very thought of walking beneath those trees repulses her, so that she can almost feel hands on her shoulders, turning her around, turning her away, pushing her back. It's like Peter's voice in her head, his eyes fixed on hers. *Wouldn't it be so much nicer to go back to the camp?* There's more meat to fill her belly, and more games to play. They can sit by the fire and be warm; no need to wander off into the dark where anything might happen, where monsters might eat them.

She can almost feel her name trying to slip away from her again as the thoughts roll through her mind, and Jane clenches her teeth so hard her jaw aches. The pain focuses her. She's known since she was Timothy's age that there's nothing to be afraid of in the dark. It's just like shadows, something blocking the light, but the light and the daytime always return. But she's frightened nonetheless.

At home all that might be true, but here… Unreasoning fear grips her, a fear she can't explain, like the crooked-tailed cat brushing unexpectedly against the back of her legs and making her jump. And just like that, she's certain. As much as she doesn't want to go—*because* she doesn't want to go—the path through the trees is the one they need to take.

She touches the arrowhead still tucked into her sleeve. It feels like a token for good luck somehow. She can't say why, but more than ever now she's sure someone, or something, meant to warn her away, to keep her safe, not merely to frighten her. She offers a silent apology to that unseen guardian for ignoring their unconventionally delivered advice.

Beside her, Timothy stares into the space beneath the trees, his posture rigid, an eerie emptiness to his eyes.

"Do you know where that goes?" Jane asks. She keeps her voice low, but Timothy still startles.

"Peter said we're never to go that way." He worries at his bottom lip, and Jane is afraid for a moment he might cry. His terror is real, and after all, she reminds herself, he's just a little boy.

"But do you know where it leads, why it's forbidden?"

Timothy shrinks, pulling his shoulders inward. Jane hates to press him, but she needs to know.

Timothy frowns, and once again his brow furrows as though he's trying to remember something. His hand inches toward the hem of his shirt, but he catches himself before bringing it to his mouth.

"It's a bad place."

He points, and Jane follows the line of his pointing, up above the trees, where a faint smudge like rising smoke hangs against the stars. She shivers, but forces herself to put her shoulders back and be brave.

"I'm sorry, but I think that's the way we need to go. It's okay," Jane adds quickly. "I'll keep us safe. I promise."

She wants to believe it. If her mother were here, what would she do? Jane remembers when she was just about Timothy's age and another girl knocked her down in the park. She'd been making fun of Jane for looking at bugs, calling her dirty, and when she'd said she was not the girl had pushed her. She'd landed face down in the dirt, cutting her lip on her teeth and making it bleed.

Fighting back tears, she'd demanded the other girl apologize, but the girl had merely smiled sweetly, claiming Jane must have tripped. Jane had run to her mother, calling the girl a liar and a monster, but rather than hugging her close as Jane had expected, her mother had taken Jane by the shoulders and looked her in the eyes.

"She isn't a monster, Jane."

"But, Mama—"

"No, Jane. She may have acted like a monster to you, and that's different. But do you know why she acted like one?"

Jane had shaken her head, not understanding the distinction, or what her mother wanted from her. She'd only wanted to be held and comforted. But there was that look in her mother's eyes, the one she got when Jane asked a wrong question. It made Jane think, even then, as young as she was, that they were having two different conversations. Jane was seeing the girl who pushed her, and the park, and her mother was seeing another world entirely. But her tone had been so serious Jane hadn't dared argue. It was the tone her mother used when she wanted Jane to learn an important lesson.

"It's because she's afraid." She had pulled Jane closer, but not into the hug Jane wanted. Her mother had turned her, holding Jane against her side so Jane could see the other girl, who didn't look afraid at all. Jane's mother had smoothed her hair, but the gesture didn't feel comforting, and she'd put her face right next to Jane's like she was telling her a secret.

"She can see how brave and strong you are, and it frightens her. It's like the Little White Bird in our stories. When he plays mean tricks on people, it's because deep down inside he feels small. Do you understand?"

Jane hadn't understood then, but now she thinks she might know what her mother was trying to say. Later that same night, she'd asked her mother if there was such a thing as monsters for real.

"I'm afraid so." Her mother had said it without hesitation and Jane had startled at the answer; it hadn't been the one she'd been expecting at all. She'd tried to twist around in her mother's lap in the big rocking chair beside the window, but she couldn't quite get to a place where she could see her mother's face properly to see if she was teasing. Her mother had stroked her hair again, rocking them gently, and Jane had felt warm and safe, the way she'd wanted to before.

"What happens if I meet a real monster?" Jane asked.

"Well." Her mother kissed the top of Jane's head. "You have to stand up, even when you're scared, because if you let the monsters frighten you and take away the things you love, then they win."

Jane had felt her mother turn her head, looking out the window at the starry sky as she continued talking.

"And the problem with monsters winning, Jane, is once they do, they want to win all the time. They want to win more and more, because they're greedy, and we can't have that, can we?"

"No, Mama."

Then her mother had tickled her, and Jane had forgotten all about monsters, laughing and begging her mother for a story before she went to bed.

Thinking back on it now, Jane wonders if her mother was talking about the girl who knocked Jane down, or the kind of monster that hides under beds, or maybe even the kind of monster her Uncle Michael and her father fought in the war. Maybe her mother had been talking about all three of them. Or something else entirely.

What she does know is that her mother was right—she has to stand up even though she's scared. Because otherwise the monsters win.

"Come on." Jane takes Timothy's hand, glancing down at him. The trust in his eyes frightens her even more than what lies at the end of the path, but he's counting on her. She cannot let him down. "Let's show the monsters we aren't afraid."

Wendy takes a deep breath, smoothing her hands over the front of her dress, then clenching them together across her midsection, the fingers of each hand gripping the wrist of the other. All she has to do is put one foot in front of the other and walk. She made the same journey in reverse almost a year ago. Step. Breathe. Step. She walked out of St. Bernadette's, surely she can walk back in. It can't be that hard. This time she is a guest, a visitor. No one can hold her or keep her here.

And yet her body itches, prickling with sweat all over. Sweat that doesn't quite emerge but remains secret, like a bruise, tucked onto the wrong side of her skin. The brick facade of St. Bernadette's leans out toward her, and it seems only the blink of an eye since she was here last. She never left, and now the door is a mouth, tongue lolling out to swallow her whole.

She shakes her head, dislodging the thoughts, and takes a determined step forward. White stone crunches under her boot heels. She's heard Jamieson doesn't even work here anymore. Some illness, leaving the left side of his body weak, perhaps the same hidden illness that kept him out of the war. She wants to feel spitefully, vindictively glad, but she can't summon either hate or pity, only apathy. Jamieson is nothing to do with her now; this isn't her life anymore.

The sun beats down, turning the scar of the path blindingly white. Leaf-stripped branches stir overhead in a gust of wind, and puffs of condensation frost from her lips as Wendy walks toward the door. She doesn't belong in this place; there's nothing to be afraid of here anymore.

Her footsteps sound extremely loud as she crosses the threshold. The sudden transition from bright sunlight to the relative darkness inside throws her for a moment. She's disoriented, and reaches a hand to steady herself.

"Miss?" A voice at her elbow, and Wendy jumps.

A nurse. A young one. No one Wendy recognizes.

"It's Mrs." The words come from her in automatic response. She's said them so many times to herself, trying to convince herself or convince the world, and they still don't feel like they belong to her.

"I'm here to see Mary—" Wendy's voice breaks, and she hates that it does, wishing it were stronger. "Mary White Dog."

She takes pleasure in saying Mary's full name, her true name, not the one given to her here. The nurse frowns before turning away, leaving Wendy alone in the entryway, and Wendy smiles to herself. She makes herself look up, at the railing running along the second floor where the private rooms are. She and Mary snuck up there so many times. She could almost close her eyes, trace her steps through this place and not get lost. She keeps her eyes open, forces her hands down at her side.

"If you'll follow me, please." The nurse returns and gestures, and Wendy obeys.

Her gait feels oddly stiff, as though all at once she's forgotten what walking means. Even though she knows he isn't here, she just can't stop herself expecting Jamieson to loom out of one of the doorways and catch her in a meaty hand. Ned had offered to come with her, for support, but she insisted on coming alone.

"If I don't face this now," she'd told him, "I never will. It's important."

He'd looked concerned, but let her go, hiring a car to take her. Wendy had almost told the driver to turn around several times, and again at the gates she'd almost panicked and fled. Now, as she follows the nurse, Wendy's fear shifts to something else. There's a sense of dislocation, as if she's floating. She isn't afraid; she feels almost giddy, and that seems wrong.

She glances at the faces of the patients they pass. Most keep their heads lowered, not even looking up as she goes by. She remembers doing the same, ignoring the outside world as a matter of survival. If they did look up, would any of them recognize her? And would it make their lives better or worse? Would her being here give them hope they might leave one day, too, or would they simply resent her for having freedom they do not?

Lucky, she tries to remind herself how lucky she is, how little separates her from the patients around her. After everything, John didn't give up on her. How many of these patients have brothers, sisters, husbands, wives, still hoping for their cure?

The nurse opens the door to one of the small sitting rooms, and Wendy's heart takes a moment to forget how to beat. The room is empty save for Mary sitting in one of two chairs by the window, silhouetted against the bright winter sky. How should Wendy act? What will she say? All the ease between them has fled from her mind, as though they're meeting again for the first time. Will Mary resent her? What will they talk about, now that they no longer know every single detail of each other's lives day to day?

At that moment, Mary looks up from the embroidery hoop in her lap, and her face splits into a smile—sun breaking through the clouds—showing the gap between her teeth, and Wendy's fear drops away. She forgets the nurse standing in the doorway, forgets everything and runs to Mary. They collide halfway across the room, crushing each other in a hug, breathless and laughing, both trying to talk at once.

"I'm so glad you—"

"I didn't know if—"

They stop, staring at each other in wonder, and laugh again. When Wendy looks around, the nurse is gone, and they're alone. She squeezes Mary's hands, the calluses and warm skin familiar under her fingertips, and leads Mary back to the chairs. They sit, knees almost touching, and Wendy keeps hold of Mary's hands. Now that she is here, she never wants to let go again.

"Tell me everything. How are they treating you? Are you all right?" The words rush out; she can't stop staring at Mary, scarcely able to believe she's real.

"Nothing ever changes." Wendy's heart drops, but Mary's lips shape a mischievous expression, and there's a glint in her eye. Wendy's heart turns again, a complicated feeling. She thinks of Mary sneaking through the corridors, pulling off little thefts, all the trouble she might be getting into while avoiding getting caught. She should be here by Mary's side.

"But look at you, a married woman now." Mary's words break into Wendy's thoughts, and something catches in her chest. She blinks rapidly, and Mary shifts their hands so now she is the one holding Wendy, the pressure of her thumbs steadying Wendy so she lets out a shaky breath.

Mary leans forward, their foreheads touch, and the world rights itself. Wendy lets her weight rest there for a moment. She closes her eyes, feeling the solidity of Mary. She opens her eyes, breathes out and sits back, only slightly dizzy now.

A married woman. The past few months have been a blur. Wendy is scarcely used to it herself. She feared it at first, then began to think it could be something she wants—a family, not like Michael and John, but one all of her own, chosen and not formed by blood. But even as she and Ned learn more of each other, she cannot shake the sense of something missing in her life, something she could not name. Until here, now.

This. Mary's hands in hers. The thought frightens her, too big to fully contemplate. She wants, but she isn't certain exactly what it is she wants, and so she pushes the feeling down as it tries to rise up in her like an all-consuming tide.

"Tell me how it is with you," Mary says. "Are *you* all right? How does your husband treat you? Do you love him?"

"I scarcely know him." Wendy pulls her hands back, folds them in her lap. The weight of all her doubt and uncertainty, lifted a moment before, returns. Words pile up behind her teeth, but Wendy can't think of how to speak them. This is Mary, they've never had secrets before, but not all of the secrets she carries now are hers to share.

Husband and wife. Of one flesh. Is this what it means to be joined in marriage, truly? From now on, she must carry Ned's burdens too, as well as her own. If Mary were truly part of their family, perhaps… No, she pushes the thoughts down again. It is too much, too soon.

She focuses instead on Mary's question, thinking how to answer it. Ned. Wendy conjures up his face, his kind eyes, his blushing stammer. At times, it barely makes itself known in his speech. Other times, usually when his father is around or a visit is imminent, he can scarcely get out his words.

Wendy thinks of the day they met, how he could barely look at her. And she herself, newly walked out of this place, practically new to the world. Can it really be less than a year? It seems like a lifetime ago.

Wendy looks up and finds Mary watching her patiently. She aches, the urge to speak and remain silent warring in her. If she could simply communicate with a look and have Mary understand everything that she is, everything she and Ned are together, it would be so much simpler.

"I... I think I might come to love him in time, but it's..." Wendy hesitates; the words refuse to come easily. She understands Ned, at least in part. It is her own piece of the puzzle Wendy now struggles to understand.

On their wedding night, instead of coming to her as a husband, Ned had silently handed Wendy a bundle of letters. The edges of some had been burned, the paper frail and flaking and smelling of ash.

"I barely managed to save them," he'd told her. She'd looked at him, questioning, but he'd only said, "You should know, and understand who it is you've married."

He'd moved toward the window, leaving her to sit on their marriage bed with the letters in her lap. She'd felt a moment of relief, uncertain how things would be between them once they were wed, uncertain she wanted him as a husband when she'd barely begun to know him as a friend. Her own emotions had been a complicated knot settled in her stomach, where Ned's had been stark on his face—sorrow and pain, hope and the willingness to trust braided together into one.

She lifted the first letter, unfolding it with care. She'd read, and Ned had watched her, pacing occasionally, and occasionally still, restless fear shivering beneath his skin. The letters were written by Ned, from the trenches in Verdun, addressed to someone named Henry. As the letters named shared memories, Wendy came to understand Henry had been a school friend of Ned's. And reading on, in wonder, she had learned how time had transformed Henry and Ned into something else, something far more than friends.

Periodically, Wendy had looked up to see Ned almost mouthing silently, as if reading along with her words etched on his heart.

"My father tried to burn them," Ned said as she set the last letter down.

The reading had left Wendy feeling wrung out. It had already been late when they'd entered the bedroom and now, beyond the windows, dawn had already begun to blush the edges of the sky. She'd read the whole night through.

"Were they never sent?" Wendy's heart had ached, thinking of Ned—a man she barely knew then—so lost in love. She could scarcely imagine how it must have been for him, love twisted into a source of shame, forced to bury his secret, never allowed to simply be.

"They were sent. Henry wrote letters in return." Ned's voice had broken then, not his accustomed stutter, but something more raw and wounded. He hadn't looked at her but out at the rising sun. "Those letters, his letters, I burned myself. To keep them safe. Henry… passed away recently. Complications from pneumonia. His sister returned these letters to me. I don't know if she ever read them, but my father found the package and…"

Ned shrugged, an inelegant and pained motion, bringing his

shoulders up in bony defense against the world. But when he'd spoken Henry's name, when he'd told Wendy the truth of him, Ned hadn't stuttered at all.

In that moment, Wendy had understood his father's desperation for Ned to marry, why Ned had agreed to marry a woman like her, sight unseen. She'd thanked him for his secret, and promised to keep it. In return, over the next several days, she'd given him St. Bernadette's, and everything that had happened to her there. While she'd maintained the fiction of the Spanish flu with Ned's father, she had given Ned as much of the truth as she could—Jamieson and Dr. Harrington, the tub of ice water and her shaved scalp. She'd given him everything except what had sent her there in the first place. She'd given him everything except Neverland, and Peter, saying only that there had been a time in her life when she couldn't tell truth from made-up stories, but all of that was behind her now.

In the days following, they'd spoken, shyly at first, and then more boldly. Over breakfast, over tea, Ned had confessed to wanting a child of his own someday, and Wendy had felt a fluttering response between her belly and her chest. She'd never truly thought on the possibility before of being a mother for real, but in that moment, she'd felt a blooming of hope. Since their wedding day, they'd kept the promise made to each other on the day they met; they'd become friends. They are husband and wife as well, but not in a way the rest of the world might understand.

"Would you be happier with a wife of your own instead?" Mary's voice is guileless, simple, un-judging curiosity in the tilt of her head and her watching eyes as Wendy's head snaps up at the question.

The question is so close to her thoughts, and yet miles distant. Love, family, like the words husband and wife, they are so fraught. The ache, the sense of something missing Wendy felt in the months between her wedding and this moment here, tell Wendy what she wants, but it isn't a want she can put into words.

Her hand makes an involuntary movement, knocking into the little table between their two chairs so it totters without quite falling, the sound overloud in the silence. There are women, Wendy knows, in St. Bernadette's who are here for no other reason than loving each other as Henry and Ned loved. It sickens her that the world could be so cruel, and yet she knows many of those same women, in secret, found their freedom here, making wives of each other in their hearts, in their minds, in every way that matters, away from the world's watchful eyes.

Wendy looks for hope in Mary's expression—holding equal parts hope and dread of her own—but finds no weight of expectation there. Relief floods her, and it feels like the same fluttering she felt when Ned spoke of wanting a child. She loves Mary, of this much she is certain. And she is growing to love Ned. But as for being a wife, to anyone, it is not something she can do in more than name only.

The realization falls into place with a dull thud. If Wendy speaks her heart aloud, will she lose Mary? Will she lose Ned? At the same time, she cannot imagine keeping silent. She can't share Ned's secret with Mary, but she can give her own.

"I don't think…" Wendy hesitates again.

She has no words for what she wants to say. She knows there are many men like Ned, many women like those in St. Bernadette's, called sick and sinful, mad and wrong. But out in the world, all she sees are men and women, happy husbands and wives, or at least husbands and wives giving the illusion of happiness. Families. Children. Like her own family—mother, father, herself, Michael, and John.

Only her mother and father are long gone now, and Michael is gone as much as he is here—his body returned from war but as a home for ghosts. She wants what they had before all that, a family, a house full of joy and laughter, people who care for each other. If Mary can accept the possibility that Wendy might want a wife, if Ned's heart can belong to another but he can still feel a kind of love for her, then perhaps this is possible too.

Wendy closes her eyes. She is a child again, standing on the window sill, her hand in Peter's hand. The sky stretches before her, and she is about to take a step, to fly or fall. Her heart is overfull, ready to burst. Every instinct in her screams at her to be silent, but if she doesn't speak, she will never know anything even close to happiness again.

"I don't think I'm made for that sort of love." Wendy opens her eyes, swallows. Her throat aches. It's hard, saying the words aloud. "Not the sort of love most people think of when they think of a marriage."

The words tangle in her throat, and Wendy swallows again.

"But." The words still remain halting and unsure, but she forces herself to go on. "I believe... that is... I think there are more kinds of love in the world than most people speak about out loud. I love you." She meets Mary's eyes, hoping desperately she will understand. "And I could love Ned in time. I want... I want us to be all together, like a family."

She searches Mary's expression frantically for any sense of

what her friend is thinking. The world is no longer beneath her feet. Wendy is free-falling, and she no longer remembers how to fly.

"I want you with us, but more than that, I want you to be happy. I want you to have whatever it is you want, even if that's a life apart from me." Wendy finally runs out of words.

She feels on the verge of tears, and at the same time, wrung out, hollow. Perhaps she does belong here after all. Perhaps she is mad, but not for the reasons John and Dr. Harrington thought. It's strange, perhaps not what she was raised to believe, but she can understand men loving men and women loving women. But not loving anyone at all? At least not being in love with anyone? Not feeling that desperate flutter, the skip and beat in the pulse so many poets speak of?

She's afraid to look at Mary now, and turns her attention to the window instead. With the chill in the air, no one is outside, but if she allows her eyes to lose their focus, she can easily conjure herself and Mary, running across the lawn. In her mind, she wills the wall and the hedge and the fence to vanish so the two figures can run forever, dwindling to black smudges against an endless horizon.

"You've told your husband about me?" Mary asks.

Wendy risks a glance back at her.

"Some. Not…" She waves her hand vaguely. "Not everything I said just now. I suppose I hadn't realized until just this moment exactly what it is I want. I'm still not entirely sure I do know."

Warmth colors Wendy's cheeks and she resists the urge to put her hands against them to cover the blush. Why is this so difficult?

"I still want to open a shop," Mary says. Her words are

careful, considered. Wendy glances at her again and sees the light gleaming in her eyes. It reminds Wendy so much of the expression Mary would get when they planned their escapades of old that it almost undoes her. Only now they aren't planning a theft, or an impossible escape, but their futures, real ones.

"Do you think you and Ned might help me?"

"I…" Wendy opens her mouth, but no words follow the first.

The question catches her off guard, almost as though Mary hasn't heard a word she's said. But of course Mary has heard her, and she's taken it all in stride, finding nothing strange in Wendy's desires at all.

"The rest we can figure out in time." Mary grins, showing the gap between her teeth, and Wendy's heart turns over.

Tears threaten again, hot and full behind her eyes, making them itch. This time it isn't fear though, but hope that they might all be together after all. A family. She blinks rapidly to bring them under control.

"I can speak to Ned. I'm certain he would agree to help, though we'll have to find a way to hide it from his father. Perhaps my brothers might help as well—"

Mary holds up a hand, cutting Wendy off. Surprised, Wendy falls silent.

"I won't take charity."

Wendy's cheeks flush, stung, as though Mary has struck her. Mary continues, light glinting in her eyes again and one corner of her mouth going up.

"But," she says, "I will come work for you, if you'll hire me at a fair wage."

Wendy stares, stunned all over again. Of all the things she

might have expected Mary to say, this was not one of them. The way Mary's eyes glint, it almost seems as though she's laughing at Wendy, but there's no malice in it.

"If your cooking is as bad as your sewing when we first met, I imagine you'll need someone helping you with every single meal, someone living with you and not just coming in to cook every now and then." Mary's smirk turns into a full grin, and Wendy can't help it, she finds herself smiling in return.

"If room and board is part of the wage, I can save up, and one day I'll have money to open the shop all on my own."

Wendy seizes Mary's hands again, squeezing them hard.

"I'm certain Ned will agree to those terms. I can't wait for you to meet him."

"I look forward to it." Mary pauses a moment, considering Wendy. "Am I right?"

"About what?"

"Your cooking?"

Relief bubbles through Wendy and comes out as laughter. Tears finally stream from her eyes, and she wipes them away.

"Absolutely. I'm a dreadful cook."

"Lucky for you I'm brilliant, and an excellent teacher, too."

PETER'S SECRET

Tiger Lily stands and beckons Wendy back to the cave wall with its black and red paintings. She runs her fingers over them—Pirate, Mermaid, Ship, Boy—crouching as the ceiling slopes down, crab-walking. Wendy follows, unease growing into a physical pressure against her skin as the pictures grow more abstract. Tiger Lily stops, her fingers resting against the wall.

"Here," Tiger Lily says, but she's angled in such a way that Wendy can't see the image her fingers rest against.

Tiger Lily glances over her shoulder, then shifts, letting Wendy see. Wendy has to get on her knees, shuffling closer. Tiger Lily draws her hand away, and it's as though the cave floor drops out beneath Wendy, sending her stomach into free-fall.

I'll show you a secret, Wendy. A really good one.

She can't make sense of what she's seeing. Horns. Claws. A jagged shape that makes the skin at the base of Wendy's spine crawl. Even without firelight, the drawing seems to ripple, warm to the touch.

"What is this?" Wendy hears her own voice, breathless and strangled.

Tiger Lily shakes her head. Their shoulders touch in the cramped space.

"An old story. A very old one."

"Tell me." Wendy grasps Tiger Lily's wrist, her grip tight enough that her friend flinches. "Please."

Wendy tries to gentle her tone, but her voice is barely under her control. This... whatever it is, she's seen it before. She knows. Or she almost knows. There's a hole where her memory should be, a door in her mind slammed over it long ago. Now, the door rattles, assaulted by a violent wind. No, not a wind. A breath.

"It's a story of the monster at Neverland's heart," Tiger Lily says.

Wendy relinquishes her grip, as though all at once Tiger Lily's skin burns. She looks down, expecting to see the seams of fire beneath Tiger Lily's flesh again, but there's only her ash-colored skin in the dark.

"The monster." Wendy repeats the words; they taste of heat, charcoal still smoldering and laced with smoke.

Tiger Lily shifts, so she's sitting. Wendy sits beside her, but even seated the space is claustrophobic, and her breath sounds over-loud in her ears. Tiger Lily draws her legs up against her chest, and wraps her arms around them, resting one cheek against the bony points of her knees. Her face is cast in shadow, but even so, her eyes are unnaturally bright, shining with a hint of the fire Wendy saw beneath her skin, from when Peter made her burn. Her voice is quiet, sorrowful almost, and her gaze focuses on nothing in particular. Wendy draws her legs up too, and listens.

"There are many stories about the monster, but all of them start a very long time ago, before there was a Neverland. None of the stories are clear on exactly what kind of creature the monster was to start off with—not an animal, or a man, or a raging fire, but all of those things mixed together, with blunt teeth and sharp horns, hooves and wicked claws. Or maybe it only became those things afterward. Stories that old tend to change over time.

"One thing all the stories agree upon is that it was already ancient when Neverland was born. Some claim the monster is the seed from which Neverland grew, and others that it was simply the first creature to step foot on the island, calling it into being.

"The way it came to the island, or created the island, is that it committed an unspeakable act, and it was sent into exile. Because of the act, the creature was split in two. Part of it was buried deep underground, and part of it lived on the surface in the light. The two halves were never meant to know the other existed."

Tiger Lily shifts her gaze slightly to look at Wendy, her eyes gleaming in the dark. Wendy's breath catches; she can almost feel the monster in the cave with them, hot breath rolling over her, claws and horns scraping the stone over their head, drawing sparks. It is too big for the space, and it makes the cave feel even smaller, the sloping stone bearing down as if to crush them. Wendy fights back a moment of panic, forcing herself to breathe as Tiger Lily goes on.

"Sometimes the story is different entirely. Sometimes the creature wasn't a monster, but a sadness, cursed with the ability to see the future. The creature saw that one day it would do a terrible thing, an unforgiveable thing, so it tore itself in two to prevent this fate from ever happening. It buried all the dark parts of itself deep underground and hid the rest of itself in a body it stole. It hid so well, it didn't even know itself anymore, and it forgot it had ever been anything other than what it chose to become."

Tiger Lily shivers slightly, like a cold breeze passing over her skin. Wendy feels it too, but at the same time she still feels a strange heat on her skin, like something breathing against her, and sweat prickles her skin. The light dims in Tiger Lily's eyes, leaving them pained. Wendy has seen the same expression in Michael's eyes, a simultaneous longing to remember and to forget.

"I don't remember anything else." Tiger Lily lifts her head and meets Wendy's gaze.

"It's all r—" Wendy starts, and her words lodge in her throat, thorn-like and tearing. *She* remembers. She shouldn't remember, can't possibly remember, but she does. A terrible creature, separated from itself, locking away all its darkness, like a skin shed. No, not a skin—a shadow.

Wendy puts her hands to her head, digging trimmed-short nails into her scalp beneath the weight of her hair as if she could pull the information out by force. The door in her mind rattles. The wood creaks, a weight leaning on it from the other side. She listens. Something breathes, a terrible wheezing sound like bellows.

Wendy draws a ragged breath, doubling over at the waist. Her head aches, a simultaneous weight at the door, demanding to be released, and her own fear pressed heavy against it from the opposite side, holding it shut. Tiger Lily touches Wendy's shoulder, concern in her voice lost in the roar of blood filling Wendy's ears. Wendy shakes her head, the barest of motions, and even that sends pain spiking through her skull. There's more pain waiting for her if she opens the door, but she can't keep it closed.

Whatever lies on the other side might be the missing piece

that helps her protect Jane, that lets her stop Peter once and for all. She straightens, as much as the sloped ceiling allows, and offers Tiger Lily a strained smile.

"It's all right." But her voice is as husked as Tiger Lily's.

Inside St. Bernadette's, there was no lock she and Mary couldn't open, no space barred to them within the walls. There were consequences for their sneaking and stealing, but they never let those consequences stop them. They never let fear stop them. And they never let something as simple as a door stand in their way.

The truth has been hidden from Wendy for years, but suddenly it seems so simple. This lock, this door, is like any other. With everything that's been taken away from her, everything she's fought to reclaim, she will not be denied her own memories. She will steal this piece of herself back. Peter has held it for too long.

She feels Tiger Lily watching her, but Wendy focuses her attention on the drawing on the cave wall, the creature of horns and claws. This time, when the door rises to block her, when instinct tells her to draw back, she throws her weight against it instead. She isn't the child who left Neverland, or the frightened girl waiting for Peter to save her. She's grown; she's faced terrors Peter could never imagine. She is strong enough to face this too.

Wendy throws the full force of her will against the door. The wood shudders. It cracks. It splinters, unable to hold her back, and Wendy tumbles through.

NEVERLAND – 27 YEARS AGO

"Come on, Wendy, keep up!" Peter pulls her so fast along the forest path it's like flying.

"Why won't you tell me where we're going?" Wendy's voice is breathless as she struggles to keep from falling. She wants to be annoyed with Peter, but her excitement betrays her. He's taking her somewhere special, somewhere just for her, where John and Michael don't get to go. It almost makes up for not being able to join in the war.

"I told you. It's a secret." Peter glances over his shoulder, flashing a grin.

Shadows flicker over his skin as they run. Feathers, falling leaves. They change the shape of his face, making it into the muzzle of a fox, the beak of a bird. Wendy's breath catches on wonder, then the underbrush grows denser, and she has to concentrate on her feet again so she doesn't trip.

"Up here." Peter lets go of her hand, jumping to grab a twist of root protruding from the side of a cliff there before them so suddenly it may well have dropped out of the sky.

He looks back at her once, then without waiting, he leaps again—nimble as a mountain goat—catching stunted trees and hidden handholds. Wendy watches him climb. The cliff face looks very high.

"Come on!" Instead of flying, Peter shows off a new skill, his feet always landing exactly where he means them to, his hands never failing to find a hold.

"Wait for me." Wendy reaches for a thick, jutting branch, testing it against her weight.

Climbing trees is one thing, but this is something else altogether. She cranes her neck, but she can't see Peter anymore. She focuses on the cliff, pulling herself up and finding the first foothold. Barely a foot off the ground, she's dizzy, giddy with a sense of adventure, her nerves tingling with fear. What if Peter is taking her somewhere dangerous, somewhere they shouldn't be?

She has to stretch for the next handhold, groping with her fingers while keeping her eyes on the rock ahead of her. Sweat gathers, sticking a strand of hair to her forehead. Peter makes it look so easy, Neverland always there to help him every step of the way. Branches scratch at her skin and her muscles tremble, but she's determined not to be left behind.

"Hurry up, Wendy!" Peter's voice trills with laughter. Wendy has the impulse to say something very unladylike, but she needs to save her breath for climbing. Loose dirt and pebbles slide under her feet. When she reaches for the next handhold, Peter catches her wrist, startling her. Her feet slip, leaving her hanging over empty air, but Peter hauls her up as easily as though she were a rag doll.

She lands in an ungainly heap, gasping like a caught fish. When she's able to sit up, she sees they're on an outcropping of rock. Peering over the edge, she's amazed to see how high she's climbed. Neverland spreads like a patchwork quilt below them, the lagoon glittering, the beach curling pale around the borders of the island.

"In here." Peter lays a finger to his lips, then points, his expression mischievous.

If he hadn't shown her right where to look, Wendy would have missed the crack in the rock entirely. In fact, if she turns her head even a bit, it vanishes. It's only a shadow, surely not big enough for a boy to fit through, but Peter turns sideways, slipping in as easily as water. Wendy hesitates, but she knows without having to be told that it's like flying—she has to believe. As narrow as the gap is, there's no room for both a girl and her doubt to fit through. Taking a deep breath, Wendy plunges into the dark on Peter's heels.

The moment she does, she regrets it. Pitch-black air clogs her chest, rock walls hemming her in. Wendy can't see two inches in front of her face. She wants to let her breath out, but she's afraid if she does she'll become wedged. What if she's trapped here forever without John and Michael ever knowing what happened to her?

But there's no space to turn around, and she isn't certain she can back out either. Besides, she can already hear Peter's taunts if she even tried. She forces herself to keep going. All at once, the tunnel widens. Wendy stumbles forward, a cork shot from a bottle.

The first thing she notices is it's strangely warmer inside the cave. It's as though there's a fireplace burning somewhere, just out of sight. Wendy's eyes adjust slowly. The ground slopes away, smooth and uneven at once, like cooled, melted wax. It's like standing in a cathedral, or a forest made of stone. Pillars of rock divide the space, dripping from the ceiling and growing up from the floor. She can't see every part of the space, and in fact, Wendy has the dizzying sense she's only looking at a fraction of the cave. It might extend forever in every direction, another impossibility, larger than it seemed from the outside. She turns to look at the narrow entrance behind her, but she can't make it out anymore.

"Come on." Peter grabs her hand again, making her jump. His palm is sweat-slick against hers, and she feels his pulse rabbiting through his skin. What kind of secret could be worth all this?

Peter tugs at her, but Wendy drags her feet. She wants to slow down and see everything, but Peter is a force of nature, unstoppable. He continues to pull at her, and reluctantly, she follows him.

As they move deeper, a ruddy light colors the rock pillars burnt orange, like a sunrise. It's as though the un-trees around them are on fire. Crystals glimmer, embedded everywhere, winking as stars in the dark. Wendy catches glimpses of niches and alcoves scattered about in unlikely places, making her think even more of a church, though she can't imagine Peter or any of the Lost Boys ever gathering to pray.

Off to one side, she catches a glimpse of a chamber, and in its center, a pyramid of pale-colored, rounded stones.

"Keep up, slowpoke!" Peter tries to hurry her on, but Wendy digs her heels in, her breath catching. And all at once she sees they aren't stones at all, they're skulls—human skulls, a whole pile of them, and when she looks closer, she sees other bones stacked in niches in the walls.

"Peter!" She yanks her hand from his, and he turns to frown at her. When he follows her gaze, his expression doesn't change—impatience, not fear or shock.

"You're too slow." Peter stamps his foot.

"But…" Wendy points, her arm a disconnected and ghostly thing floating in the dark. "Those are bones. They must belong to someone. You said no one can die in Neverland."

Peter's face scrunches, folding into lines around the constellations of his freckles.

"They aren't *someone*, silly. They're just skeletons. Come on!"

He grabs her arm so roughly Wendy has to move her feet or fall. She twists around, trying to keep the bones in sight. Does Peter really not know that people have skeletons inside? Or is he lying to her, keeping secrets? Does he even know what it means to die? She thinks of the boys playing war, their swords harmless, the bloodless wounds she spent the day binding.

She tries to think of the exact number of boys she saw in the tent that day, or before on the beach when they first landed. Are they the same? The numbers and names and faces shift and blur in her mind, making it hard to keep track. She's certain of herself, and Peter, Michael, and John, but aside from that, she couldn't say exactly how many children are on the island.

The opposite sensation of what she felt squeezed between the rocks as she wiggled her way into the cavern seizes her now. It's as though she's standing on the edge of something vast; at any moment, she might fall. Ahead of her, Peter's silhouette is ragged, wavering as the light grows brighter around him.

"We're here." He stops, and Wendy teeters to a halt behind him.

"What—" But she doesn't get any farther, forgetting the bones and everything else.

The cave floor slopes sharply, becoming a bowl. In the center of the bowl, there's a monster.

"It's my secret." Peter beams.

The orange light cuts harsh shadows into his face, making him utterly inhuman. Wendy's gaze slides to the thing crouched below them. It's like night, but darker. The orange glow doesn't illuminate the creature the way it illuminates her and Peter. There are no details, only a solid blot like spilled ink forming the impression of a hunched spine, bones pressed against skin, legs bending the wrong way, wicked, curving horns.

"No." Wendy shakes her head. She doesn't want to look at it, and she can't look away. She takes a step backward.

The monster turns toward the sound of her voice. It has no eyes, but somehow it's still looking at her. It huffs a breath, scenting for her, or showing displeasure, she can't say. The air smells of struck matches, like Wendy's old sheepdog when she comes in from the rain.

Wendy takes another step back and her heel catches on the uneven stone. She trips, hitting the ground hard, pain jarring all the way up her spine and making her teeth click together. The monster—it's still looking at her, and she is looking at it. The shape of it. She knows it. It's impossible. It...

Wendy feels a needle between her fingers, dragging thread through darkness and skin as Peter writhes and screams. That shadow, the one she sewed back onto him, withered and died. And the thing in the pit is...

"Wendy, what's wrong?" Peter stands over her, blocking her view.

Her gaze snaps back to him, momentarily free of the creature so she can think again. She breathes, mouth open, shallow breaths on the edge of panic. The angle and the light make Peter look taller, his head scraping the cavern ceiling. He's too big. Too terrible. A sliver of orange light has gotten trapped in his eyes, shivering like a flame.

"Monster." Wendy's voice breaks; she covers her face with her hands.

Neverland is so beautiful—the mermaids with their scales

shining in the sun, their voices like flutes made of glass; Tiger Lily's brown fingers next to hers, showing her how to weave reeds into crowns. Flying. Wendy has never had such adventures, never felt so free. This can't be the truth of it.

"Look at it." Peter crouches, pulling her hands away from her face and gripping her wrists. There's a seriousness to his expression she's never seen before. All at once, he looks like a totally different boy from the one who flew through their nursery window, who led them in games of follow the leader. He looks much older than his slight frame implies, like being here, now, next to the monster, has made him into another person entirely. "Look at me, Wendy. My secret."

His face is inches from hers, his breath harsh. Behind Peter, the shadow-monster snorts again, its sides heaving like bellows.

"No." Wendy shakes her head. Tears slide hot against her skin.

She wants Peter to be the boy who swooped in through her window. She wants the stars and the rushing dark, the velvety sky never letting her fall.

Behind Peter, his shadow moves. It doesn't come closer, but Wendy feels the weight of it nonetheless, as if its long fingers— tipped in wicked nails—hold her wrists instead of Peter's.

"Wendy!" Peter shakes her hard enough that she sees stars. Not flying. Falling.

"You're hurting me." She tries to pull away, but his grip tightens.

"You have to look at it, Wendy."

"It's horrible." She doesn't mean to, but she turns her head so she can see boy and monster both.

One crouched in front of her, one crouched in the bowl

of stone; they're the same. Until this moment, did Peter even remember what he was, how terrible the secret was he planned to show her? Outside of this cave, will he forget again? Darkness blots Peter's skin, not like the leaf-shadows in the forest, but underneath and inside him. The monster—it's that same jagged darkness writ large, outside Peter's body as though he could cast away all the terrible parts of himself and be only one thing, all boy and nothing more.

"No!" Peter bellows the word, and the thing in the hollow roars back, the walls shaking.

"Mothers are supposed to love their children. If you love me, you have to love him, too." His voice cracks.

Wendy yanks her arms away, hard enough that she smashes her elbow against the stone. She hisses in pain, trying to scramble back, but Peter catches her ankle. She kicks with her other foot. The rock scrapes her skin as Peter wrestles with her.

"No. No. No!" Peter is a child, throwing a tantrum.

He screws up his face, blotchy in the orange light. Tear tracks glitter and Wendy stills for a moment, pity stealing her breath. The moment leaves Peter enough room to seize her face between his hands. It hurts, as though his fingertips have burrowed straight to her bones beneath her skin.

"You have to love me." It's simultaneously a whisper and a shout. The boy whispering, the monster howling, or the other way around.

With the words, sharp as any scissor cut, Wendy feels the knowledge of the shadow snipped from her mind. Only the hole torn is jagged, cut by an inexpert hand. Threads trail, and the pain is the worst she's ever felt. She howls too, and the monster shrieks back at her before she slams a door over the space, over the sound, blocking it all out.

She can see the monster, then she can't. Peter crouches over her, a frightened little boy. Wendy blinks. Her head buzzes, dull, simultaneously empty and full. Something has happened; she's never seen Peter so afraid. There's something terrible behind him, and he needs Wendy to protect him.

Wendy scrambles up, ignoring the throb in her arm, the bruised feeling of her skull. She grabs Peter's hand.

They run. She's falling, then they're flying, then everything goes black. The ground trembles; the sky rages like the world splitting open.

"Peter!" She shouts the name, but the wind snatches it from her, leaving her breathless.

The air refuses her for the first time since she stepped out of the nursery window, too shaken, too frightened to believe in anything as pure and good as flying. She plunges through the dark, pine branches and needles whipping at her and snapping beneath her weight. She strikes the forest floor, and somehow nothing breaks, but the breath is knocked out of her. Silence. Her ears ring. From very far away and very close by, Peter calls her name.

NEVERLAND – NOW

Wendy doubles over again, shuddering. There's a taste in her mouth like bitter medicine and salt, like ash and wet leaves and smoke and meat served too raw. Her stomach clenches, but there's nothing to bring up. She's there in the cave with the shadow. She's back in St. Bernadette's being dropped into a tub full of ice. She's clawing and fighting to get away from both.

"Wendy." Tiger Lily speaks her name as though she's saying it for the third or fourth time. She catches Wendy's wrists, and only then does Wendy realize she's raking at the sleeves of her blouse, nearly tearing the fabric.

"The monster…" Wendy falters; her voice breaks. "I've been there. I've seen it. I know what it is and where to find it. Him." Her voice is steadier now, but Wendy still feels sick, dizzy.

Peter. His shadow. His first words to her in the nursery were a lie. *I lost my shadow. Will you help me? Will you sew it back on?*

Wendy touches her pockets. She touches the hilt of Hook's sword. Her hands shake. Ever since she returned from Neverland, people have been calling her a liar, telling her she doesn't know her own mind. The only consolation she had was her own steadfast knowledge of the truth—Neverland, solid and real all the way through. But Peter twisted that, he took it away from her. He made her forget.

"Peter showed me. He was proud. He… It was terrible. But he ripped it out of my mind. Like he tore a piece of me away, so I couldn't know to be afraid of him, and I couldn't remember for so long."

Wendy takes a shuddering breath. She feels small again. Hurt. Betrayed. Peter turned her own mind against her. He made her memories into a lie. Tiger Lily's arms go around her, and a tremor passes between them. Wendy can't tell where it begins or ends. He hurt them both. A boy. A monster.

"Come." Tiger Lily helps Wendy stand, leads her back to the ashes of the fire and the circle of light spilling through the rock above.

Wendy sits, and the tightness in her chest eases. The dark corner of the cave, the painting of the monster on the wall, wants to tug at her attention, but she refuses to look its way.

Peter. Should she have guessed the truth? Not a boy but an ancient creature, a wicked thing. Wendy tries to hold the words from Tiger Lily's story in her mind—of a creature unfathomably old—but even now her thoughts shy away from the truth. She wants to slam the door again, to forget.

Dreaming of Peter, dreaming of Neverland—those thoughts saved her from St. Bernadette's. And those thoughts put her there in the first place. She hurt her brothers for the sake of them. She kept them secret from Jane, from Ned, and for what? They were all lies.

Wendy feels herself crumbling and it's a fight not to dig her nails into her flesh instead of her clothing now, clawing down as if she could shed every horrible thing she's done with her skin. Like a shadow.

The thought goes through her, sharp as a needle, and she gasps aloud. She must tear the door in her mind from its hinges and never allow herself to forget again.

Which version of Tiger Lily's story is true? The one where Peter took responsibility for his actions, or the one where he had it forced upon him? Is his forgetting a mercy he gave himself, or a deliberate lie? Or is the truth somewhere in-between? No wonder he hates age—it's a reminder of what he once was, or a reminder of what he might one day be.

"Tell me," Tiger Lily says softly. "You saw something, in here." She touches a fingertip to Wendy's forehead, peering at her.

Wendy opens her mouth, but she can't find the words to

answer. She sees Peter looming over her, the angles of his face sharp, his eyes raging and heartbroken. *You have to love me*.

A little boy. A monster. Both and neither. Peter wanted desperately for Wendy to see all of him, like looking at two sides of a coin at the same time. John and Michael had only ever seen the boy, the adventures. But he'd shown Wendy all the darkness along with the light, and he'd expected her to be infinitely vast enough to contain it all. A mother, strong enough to scare the monsters away, strong enough to love the monster even when it cannot love itself.

"Peter showed me the truth, then he took the memory away." Wendy shakes her head. "The monster from your stories, that's what he really is."

Tiger Lily's expression mirrors what Wendy imagines must be her own. They both failed. Somehow they should have known what Peter was, and kept others safe from him. Even as the thought crosses Wendy's mind, anger rises in her. She wants to shout at Tiger Lily—how dare she think she bears even the tiniest bit of blame for Peter's actions? And she wants to laugh at herself, a bitter, hollow sound.

There's no sense in telling Tiger Lily that the fault is all Peter's. Wendy can't forgive herself, even with what she knows rationally to be true, so how could Tiger Lily?

"We'll stop him now," she says instead, squeezing Tiger Lily's hand.

Tiger Lily flinches, so brief that Wendy might have imagined it. Is she lost in her own thoughts of Peter, or something else? The way time passes in Neverland, Tiger Lily and Peter may have known each other for a hundred years, or a thousand. For all Wendy knows, those years could have been an endless cycle of knowing and forgetting. *It's the best secret, Wendy. One I've never told anyone before.* But can she trust his words? Would Peter himself even know if they were a lie?

She wishes she had words of comfort for Tiger Lily. She wishes they could anchor each other. Tiger Lily shakes herself, her eyes hard as they meet Wendy's. There is something remorseless in them, something hungry.

Movement at the mouth of the cave draws Wendy's attention and she tenses. One of the Indians enters, his posture remaining stooped even after passing through the cave entrance, as though Peter's curse has permanently given his bones a new form. Wendy imagines his face was once lean and strong, but now it's sunken into a starved sharpness.

"The girl is on the path again," he says. His voice, like Tiger Lily's, is strained, and at first, Wendy can barely make out the words.

"But…" Tiger Lily's eyes widen, going to Wendy. "Then it wasn't you."

Wendy looks from Tiger Lily to the man in the cave entrance. His words finally sink in, and for a moment, she forgets how to breathe. *The girl.* Jane.

"Where is she?" Wendy jumps to her feet, looking around wildly as though perhaps the man might have brought Jane with him.

Tiger Lily stands as well, her expression mixing confusion and alarm.

"You know who she is? She looks so much like you, I thought it must be you," Tiger Lily says. "Or that Peter was playing some kind of trick on us."

256

"We saw her on the path a few nights ago," the man in the doorway says. "We threw stones and arrowheads to frighten her away so she wouldn't go toward the center of the island. She's headed that way again now."

Wendy is dizzy with relief, dizzy with fear, the ground tilting beneath her.

"She's my daughter. Jane. I have to go to her."

The path and the cave and the monster at the heart of the island. Of course, where else would her brave, curious daughter go? Her heart trips, hard, but there's a kind of excitement in Wendy as well. If she goes to the cave, Peter will find her there. She thinks of the way the ground shivered, and the black smoke over the center of the island. Some part of him must already know she's here.

The hunger Wendy saw in Tiger Lily's eyes is inside her too, a gnawing ache replacing the hollow where Peter once took the memory of the truth from her. She wants him to find her, she wants to face him. For everything Peter took from her, from Tiger Lily, for everything he might try to take from Jane, Wendy wants to take something from him too. No. Everything. She wants to take everything.

"Tell me where the path is," Wendy says. The words come out more harshly than she intended.

"I'm going with you." Tiger Lily touches Wendy's wrist, startling her.

"But…" Wendy hesitates. She wants her friend with her, but she can't help thinking of the mermaids in the lagoon, turned to bone because Peter looked away too long. She can't help seeing the ghost of the girl Tiger Lily used to be, tucked inside what Peter has made of her.

"It's my risk to take." There's an edge to Tiger Lily's voice, and a hardness in her eyes.

Wendy looks down, away, heat flushing her cheeks. She has no right to presume to be Tiger Lily's protector, or tell her where she can and cannot go. Tiger Lily doesn't belong to Peter, and she doesn't belong to Wendy either. Wendy raises her head, an apology on her lips, but instead of anger, she finds hope shining in Tiger Lily's eyes, as fragile as a broken-winged bird.

"I want Peter to pay," Tiger Lily says. "And I want to prove to him and myself that I'm more than just a shadow creature he dreamed into life."

"Of course you are." Wendy catches Tiger Lily's hands, squeezing her fingers.

The hope in Tiger Lily's eyes catches like a spark, roaring in Wendy's chest. Flame steals her breath, and leaves her eyes stinging and hot. Through a blur of tears, Wendy sees Tiger Lily as she used to be—shadow-dappled, laughing as she showed Wendy how to catch the silvery fish leaping in Neverland's streams. Those moments apart from Peter that were just their own— Wendy should have seen then how Peter's idea of friendship was nothing like the real thing.

Yet even now, even after all this time, when she first heard Peter's call it cracked her wide, and she almost forgot everything to run to him once more. When it comes down to it, what if she crumbles? What if she isn't strong enough? What if she proves herself not the mother Jane needs, or even the mother Peter wanted, but simply the girl he left behind?

"I don't know exactly what we'll be facing," Wendy says, "but I don't think Peter will let Jane go easily. If I... If I falter, will you finish it, finish him, and make sure my daughter is safe?"

"I will." Tiger Lily doesn't hesitate.

Reduced as she is from her former self, the resolve in every line of Tiger Lily's being is clear. Peter hurt her. He stole from her. She is every bit as determined as Wendy to steal herself back from him.

Wendy lets go of Tiger Lily's hands, and Tiger Lily moves to exchange low words with the man who came to tell them he'd seen Jane on the path. Is she leaving instruction for what to do if she doesn't return? Tiger Lily touches the man's arm briefly, a familiar gesture. Wendy tries to think—did she meet him last time she was in Neverland? Did Tiger Lily have brothers?

Fresh guilt swarms Wendy. She can't remember. When she was first here, any brothers Tiger Lily had would only have been more boys to Wendy, and she'd already been surrounded by more than enough.

Looking at the man beside Tiger Lily, Wendy finds herself suddenly thinking of John. Perhaps she should have gone to him before leaving, and told him what she'd planned. Perhaps she should have given him instructions for what to do if she didn't come back.

In the eleven years since Wendy left St. Bernadette's they've found their way slowly back to trusting each other. If she'd asked him, would he have trusted her one last time, as mad as her words might sound, if she'd told him she was going to Neverland to look for Jane? There was a moment, not too long ago, when Wendy thinks they finally saw each other clearly—not trying to bury the past, but recognizing the scars it left on each of them.

John had come to her shyly, and told her of his intention to ask Elizabeth to be his wife. The words had surprised Wendy, but she hadn't been able to resist teasing him, delighted that she could do so again.

"Shouldn't you be speaking to her then? What have I to do with it?"

John's face had deepened in its red hue, not quite embarrassment or pain but some complicated thing in-between. All at once she saw laid bare the ways he'd been trying to find his way back to her since her release from the asylum and recognized the missing pieces in herself as she'd been trying to do the same.

"I want you to approve, Wendy." He'd said the words softly, and she'd been glad, because suddenly her heart had been close to breaking with a new weight it had never known before. "Without Mother and Father… I mean, it's just you and me and Michael. We're the only Darlings."

Her name. Their name. Despite Wendy's marriage, John had still called her Darling, giving her back to herself in a way she'd never expected. The idea had overwhelmed her, and she'd nearly missed that John had continued speaking.

"…it does matter to me what you think, Wendy."

"Of course! Of course I approve, and of course I'm happy for you." She'd got the words out somehow, and after a moment, she'd thrown her arms around him, holding her brother tight. She willed every terrible thing between them to fall away, to never have been, even knowing they never could have come to this moment without them.

When she drew back, she had truly looked at John—the hope in his eyes, the pink in his cheeks speaking more to his love for Elizabeth and his relief at Wendy's approval than anything else.

"Wait here a moment."

She'd left John, baffled, in her parlor, and run to her bedroom. There she'd rooted among the contents of her jewelry box and at last found the small, round case scarcely bigger than the ring it contained. The box's top, blue enamel, was painted with gold roses, and all around the sides of the box were printed with the same pattern. She'd nearly tripped running down the stairs so John had caught her as she stumbled into the parlor, looking at her like she was a mad woman as she grinned up at him.

She pressed the box into his hands and he stared at her in bewilderment.

"You don't remember it? Go on, open it."

Wendy had bounced on her toes slightly in her eagerness. John had opened the box, gazing at the ring that had been their mother's, a gift from their father when Wendy was born, and gifted to Wendy in turn on her tenth birthday. A plain silver band, gleaming like moonlight, and set with a single, tiny stone such a pale blue as to almost be white.

Once it had been a star to set her sights by, to wish on. After their parents' deaths, she had seen it as a chip of ice, a daily reminder of their loss. She had stopped wearing it, and tucked it away safe for some future she couldn't imagine yet, until the moment she'd handed it to John. As she watched John lift the ring from the box, she could suddenly see the ring without grief, thinking on the small stone as a piece of the future again, a gift she could give her brother as he began his new life.

"It belonged to Mother," Wendy said, and almost before the words were out of her mouth, John said, "I remember now," his voice rough.

"I couldn't, Wendy…" He'd tried to press the box back into her hands, but she'd refused to take it.

John's lower lashes had been damp with the threat of tears. She'd felt her own eyes grow hot, all the more at John's struggle to hold back.

"Jane should have it," he'd said. "Shouldn't you give it to her?"

Wendy had thought of gifting the ring to her daughter, but despite the way Jane looked at the night sky, it was always this world she seemed most rooted in. A stone on her finger should be deep green, like growing leaves, or perhaps the blue of beetle shells. Wendy had shaken her head.

"It should be with you. Mother would want you to have it."

John had stopped trying to hold back his tears then, sweeping her into a hug. They'd stood together for a long time, crushed against each other, and when John spoke again, Wendy had lost the first part of his words into her hair.

"…such children back then." He'd straightened, pulling away from her to meet her eyes again. "And look at us now. Did you ever think we'd be this grown up?"

"Never." The word had cracked in Wendy's throat, but she'd smiled through the last of her tears. "But now we're *the* grownups, setting the rules, running after our children so they don't hurt themselves."

John's cheeks had reddened again in a pleasing way.

"Don't you think you're rather getting ahead of yourself? I haven't even asked Elizabeth yet."

He'd folded the ring box into his pocket, his fingers straying to it again to touch it through the fabric as if to assure himself it hadn't vanished. It made Wendy think of her own habit in St. Bernadette's of touching her pockets and counting the items she'd stolen, and she almost laughed.

"I'm glad you've found someone, John. Elizabeth loves you, that much is plain, and I know you'll be very happy together. You'll be a good husband, and a good father someday too."

They'd embraced again as they'd parted, but as John stepped into the courtyard, she'd called him back. He'd turned to look at her, quizzical, and she'd spoken her next words in a rush, afraid she wouldn't get them out otherwise.

"Thank you, John, for all you tried to do for me. I can't pretend St. Bernadette's was easy, or that I was happy there, but I know you had my best interests at heart."

He'd stood there, utterly at a loss for words, until she'd shooed him away.

"Go to Elizabeth, and when she's said yes, you must both come around to celebrate. Jane will be so pleased. She adores Elizabeth and she'll be delighted to have an aunt."

The moment stands like a shining beacon in Wendy's heart. She has never felt quite as close to John as in that moment, not before or since, even when she stood by his side on his wedding day, even during all those years in the nursery when she took care of him and Michael. His words come back to her, about being grown up. She wonders precisely when it happened. Was it when their parents' ship went down, when word arrived that they would never be coming home? Was it when she married Ned, or when Jane was born? Or is it now, as she prepares to do the most grown-up thing she's ever done—face Peter, face her childhood, and let it go for good?

Tiger Lily moves back to her side. As she does, Wendy feels a bruising edge of guilt spreading beneath her skin. Her words before were honest—she doesn't know exactly what they will face, only that it will be dangerous. And deep down, she knows that if it means saving Jane, at the end of the day—at the end of any day—she will choose her daughter over Tiger Lily, over Peter, over herself.

"All right," Wendy says. She adjusts Hook's sword at her side. "I'm ready."

HERE BE MONSTERS

A sudden gust of wind rattles the canopy of trees and Timothy simultaneously flinches upward and scrunches down, trying to escape from and hide inside his skin at the same time. Jane can't help flinching too, but turns the motion into squeezing Timothy's hand, an attempt at comforting him and herself both. In the dark of the canopy tunnel, Timothy looks terribly small, but Jane is glad to have him here.

As frightening as it is being responsible for someone smaller and more vulnerable than she is, she'd much rather focus on keeping him safe than think about anything else. That way she doesn't have to worry about herself so much. She doesn't have to worry about what lies at the end of the path they aren't supposed to be on, or what will happen if Peter finds them, or how they'll get home.

"I don't like this place," Timothy whispers.

"This is definitely the way I came before," Jane says. "It feels…"

She stops; *right* isn't the word she needs. Nothing feels right here. There's a scent in the air like a hot iron, a feeling like a fever coming on. Even with the wind lowing in the branches, sweat prickles Jane's skin. A rumble comes from underneath them, shivering in the soles of her feet. It's darker here than she remembers it being in Neverland since she arrived. There's a moon beyond the clouds, but even so it feels like the island is aware of them, trying to obscure the path and scare them into turning back. But if Neverland doesn't want them here then it must be important, and she will find out why.

"This feels like the place we need to be," Jane says, more loudly than necessary, because her throat wants to tighten around the words and keep her silent. "It's just a little farther."

She says it with confidence, even though she has no idea where they're going. For once, the land seems to cooperate, and almost as soon as she says it, the tunnel of trees ends. And a cliff rises above them. Jane's heart sinks. It's almost like coming up against a sheer wall. Except here and there she sees roots and handholds. She's never climbed a rock like this before, but it looks like something she can do.

Jane tilts her head back. The cliff is so tall she can't see the top, and the smudgy darkness isn't helping. Everything around them is cast in shades of brown, gray and dark blue. If she knows Peter at all, though, there wouldn't be a cliff in Neverland if there wasn't also some way to scale it, so there must be a way up. The only way to find out is to try.

"Stay close to me." Jane doesn't give herself time to doubt. She digs her fingers into a crack in the stone and hauls herself upward. She sweeps her foot across the rock face until she finds a foot hold, then she pushes herself up again, reaching for the next branch.

There isn't enough space to twist around to see Timothy following her, but she hears him huffing and scrambling at her heels. She reaches again, and a gust of wind sweeps past her, making the branch she's holding sway precariously. She isn't that high up yet, but she can't afford to think about the ground at all.

*

Wendy ducks out of the cave, and Tiger Lily follows. No smoke darkness in the sky now, and the ground is still beneath their feet, but rather than comforting her, the stillness, the emptiness, is ominous. It's as though everything is waiting to see what she will do. The center of the island tugs at her, the heart of Neverland tied to her own heart. Even without Tiger Lily at her side, she's certain she could find her way there.

The path is barely visible, but Tiger Lily's steps are sure and unerring. Leaves hush under Wendy's feet, slick things dropped from the trees, while Tiger Lily makes no sound, a ghost indeed.

They walk in silence until they come to a place where one branch of the path veers off between trees that bend inward to form a tunnel. The shadows swallow everything there. Wendy ran this way with Peter, oh so long ago, the ground blurring beneath their feet. And Wendy knows in her heart that Jane came this way too.

Wendy turns a slow circle, as if she could pluck some trace of her daughter from the air. She crouches, brushing her hands over the fallen leaves. Her fingers close on a stone arrowhead and she lifts it, straightening and slipping it into her pocket. She imagines Jane standing in the same spot. She wouldn't be able to let a mystery like this lie; she would go to the end of the path.

Come on, Wendy, keep up. The heat, the breath of the shadow-creature. All of its rage echoed and packed small into Peter's trembling frame.

Wendy's hand falls to the hilt of Hook's sword again, and she suddenly feels foolish carrying it. Will she lop off Peter's head and stand over him crowing with her hands on her hips, like a cock at dawn? She slips the sword from the shawl at her waist, and holds it out hilt first toward Tiger Lily.

"You should be the one to carry this." Wendy tries to smile, but her eyes sting. "I'm not a warrior."

Tiger Lily accepts the sword, testing its weight. Wendy feels lighter without it, but the knot of fear remains. She smooths her palms over her pockets. Through all the running and climbing, she's managed to keep her sharp little scissors, her needle, her thread. She prepared herself with everything she needed as she left London, even before she knew what she meant to do.

The bending trees swallow all outside sound. There is only Wendy's breath, so loud and ragged in her ears she can't tell if Tiger Lily breathes at all. When they emerge at the tunnel's far end, the cliff is there all at once, looming over them. It sharpens Wendy's memory—craggy rock with tangled roots and twisted, stunted trees and bushes growing out of it at odd angles. She can see a few narrow ledges and plateaus from this vantage point, but the top of the cliff is hidden from view.

*

Jane keeps her mind on finding the next place to put her feet and hands. Her breath comes hard, and she's sweating. Even though she can't look down, she knows she's making progress. She takes a moment to be proud even though her fingers ache, wanting to cramp. She has to keep climbing.

For a while, the pride is enough to allow her to trick herself into forgetting what she's doing, how dangerous it is, and how far away the ground is. Then a terrible roar splits the air. Timothy whimpers, and Jane presses flat against the rock, waiting for the world to stop shaking. Dirt and stones bounce down around her. She squeezes her eyes shut, but she feels the grit settle, clinging to her hair and her skin. She's never been much fussed about baths one way or the other, but now, the first thing she wants to do when they do finally get home is soak in the tub for so long her skin prunes.

When the trembling finally stops, she risks shifting her weight, trying to get a better look at how far she's climbed. To Jane's surprise, her feet find a small lip of stone, just deep enough to hold her. She almost laughs, able to lower her arms and ease the burning ache in her muscles. But the moment doesn't last. Timothy needs her, and there's still more cliff above her.

A small tree juts out almost perpendicular from the rock above her head. Her arms protest, like someone has poured hot lead beneath her skin, but she makes herself stretch up on her toes as tall as she can. Her ribs ache, her toes barely keeping contact with the rock, but she's just able to grab the branch on her second try. Trusting it to hold her weight, Jane leans out from the cliff face until she can see Timothy.

He's a bare smudge in the dark, miserably pressed against the stone. At least the wind has stopped for a moment, and the ground is no longer shaking.

"Climb up beside me," she shouts. "There's room for both of us and we can rest a bit."

Jane isn't certain it's true, but she knows the worst thing would be to let Timothy stop, to let tiredness and fear overtake him. Timothy shakes his head, a motion she can just see in the dark. A surge of frustration almost brings a sharp reply to her lips until she realizes how stupid she's been. His legs and arms are shorter than hers. He can't reach all the places she can; she should have thought of it sooner.

"You can do it." Her voice cracks, afraid of a lie. "Just stretch as tall as you can."

The ground shakes again, and Jane tightens her grip. Beneath her nightgown, her sweat feels like ants marching across her skin. Timothy's shoulders hitch, but otherwise he doesn't move.

"Hang on!" Jane shouts.

The handholds that let her climb to this point are suddenly nowhere to be found. She can't figure a way back to him, and now her frustration is at herself. She should have been more careful, paid more attention. Her arms tremble with the strain of holding on. If she doesn't move soon, she's going to fall.

"I'm sorry, Timothy. There's nothing I can do. You have to climb." Her stomach sinks, heavy with a feeling of failure. She promised to take care of him, and she's already let him down.

Timothy raises a tear-stained face. The moon is cruel choosing this moment to show itself, needling Jane's heart with all the planes of fear it reveals.

She remembers the first time she went on holiday to Brighton with her family, and how her mama taught her to swim. At first the memory seems incongruous, but there's something there, something she can use. She remembers light sparking off the water, and her mother standing waist-deep, holding her arms out and saying, "I'll stand right here, Jane, all you have to do is swim to me."

"You promise you won't move?" The water had been clear, enough that Jane could see the bottom, but still that didn't ease her fear. It would be so easy to slip beneath the surface and get stuck there where her feet couldn't touch to push herself back into the air again.

"I promise I won't move an inch."

Jane had dutifully kicked and paddled like her mother had shown her, frantically slapping the water, gasping, and feeling like she was going to go under at any moment. The distance had already seemed impossibly far, the water so much colder and deeper than when the lesson began. But she was doing it. Somehow, against all odds, she was almost there, her fingers almost close enough to reach her mother's outstretched ones. Then her mother had taken a step back, and another, and Jane had had to keep swimming to reach her, furious when her mother finally stopped and gathered her laughing into her arms.

"You did it, Jane. You swam."

"You lied! You said you wouldn't move!" Jane remembers how her skin felt hot all over despite the water, her body fairly trembling with rage. She'd trusted her mother, and her mother had betrayed her. She'd wanted to strike her mother, and felt she would have been justified in doing so. But her mother had only beamed, delight and pride in her eyes so that Jane's anger had drained, and she'd been able to be a little proud of herself too, though she didn't dare admit it until the next day.

"I can see the top," Jane says. "All you have to do is climb up to me." She feels rotten and mean saying it, but she can see no other way. Timothy has to climb, and they have to keep going.

With painful slowness, Timothy reaches up toward her.

"That's it. Put your right foot just there."

She tries to point, and in that moment, Timothy slips. Rocks skitter beneath his small feet. Jane's heart flies into her mouth. She doesn't wait to see if gravity catches him; she lunges without thinking, even though he's too far away for her to ever reach. There's a terrible sound as the branch she's holding cracks. All at once, the ground goes out from beneath her, the earth and the sky switching places.

*

There's nothing to do but climb.

Wendy reaches for one of the thick, woody roots, protruding just above head height. The bark flakes against her palm, but when she tests her weight, the root holds. As she plants a foot on the uneven rock, a wind springs up, shoving against her. She falls back a step to keep her balance, and as she does, the ground shudders, like an animal trying to dislodge a fly from its skin. Wendy feels it in her bones, the shadow roaring at the heart of the mountain.

Peter knows, or some part of him knows where they are, and he doesn't want them here.

She lets go of the root, stepping back to see if she can get a better view. Movement catches her eye, and at first she thinks it must be a bird, then her heart lurches and her breath nearly stops. The figure is human. Even at this distance, Wendy would know her anywhere. Jane.

She swallows a shout, afraid of startling her daughter and

causing her to fall. But oh, holding back her daughter's name bruises her throat, and Wendy gasps for breath. She almost launches herself into the air, flying for her daughter, but Tiger Lily touches Wendy's shoulder. Wendy lays her hand on top of Tiger Lily's, and for a moment, all she can do is watch her daughter climb.

While they were in the cave, or the beneath the trees, night fell. Now Neverland's too-bright moon slips out from behind clouds, and the sharp silver light outlines a second figure, smaller than Jane, climbing behind her.

"Hang on!" Jane calls out, shifting her weight. Wendy's heart is in her mouth, but Jane's grip remains firm.

There are more words, but the wind steals them, and after a moment, the figure below Jane begins to climb. Or tries to, only the climber slips, and Wendy sees the moment her daughter— her brave, beautiful daughter—lunges to help the figure below her. And that is when Jane's grip falters.

Time doesn't slow or come to a halt. The ground isn't done with its shaking, nor the wind and trees and everything else shouting. But now, Wendy shouts back. A wordless yell tears through her. And as Jane falls, Wendy shakes off Tiger Lily's hand on her shoulder and launches herself into the sky.

*

She falls.

And just as suddenly, arms wrap around her. The breath she'd been gathering to scream goes out of her in a startled huff, and she looks up, impossibly, into her mother's face. Her mother's arms are around her, holding her tight, and they're flying. It's nothing like flying with Peter. Jane is safe, held, and it is the deepest truth in all the world that her mother will never let anything bad happen to her. She will not fall.

They rise, landing on a wide rock ledge. Jane gulps at the air, trying to catch her breath, and all the while, all she can do is gape at her mother. She feels like a landed fish, snatched from one place and dropped into another where nothing makes sense anymore.

How can her mother be here? Is she dreaming? Did she fall and hit her head on the ground? Worse, is she dead?

A tremor passes through Jane, and it has nothing to do with the shaking ground. She wants to bury her face in her mother's side, but her mother looks so fierce and wild with the wind howling around them and the cliff side trying to shake them off that Jane doesn't dare. The woman before her is her mother and a stranger both.

In an instant, her mother's face changes. She makes a sound between laughter and a sob, closing the space between them, and touches Jane's face. Her mother's eyes are wet, and her expression says she cannot believe the reality of Jane either. Then her mother throws her arms around Jane, hugging her so tightly Jane can barely breathe.

When her mother finally lets go, Jane has so many questions she wants to ask, but the words that tumble from her mouth are, "You flew."

She wants to ask how her mother can be here, and how she found her. She wants assurance that her mother really *is* here, despite the seeming solidity of her arms, and to be certain this isn't another of Peter's tricks. But she can't get past those first words. Her mother—teller of stories, healer of wounds, setter of bedtimes and rules—can also fly.

And of all the responses her mother might make, the one she chooses surprises Jane. Her mother throws her head back and laughs.

"Yes, I suppose I did."

Strands of her mother's hair escape the braid trailing down her back. Her cheeks are flushed, her clothing smudged with dirt, and the lines at the corners of her eyes crinkle.

"Jane!" Timothy's voice rises from below, sharpened by panic, and fear rushes back in, kicking Jane in the ribs. She looks to her mother.

"That's Timothy! We have to help him." Jane takes a step toward the cliff edge, but her mother catches her, holding her back.

"Stay here. I'll get him." Without a moment's hesitation, her mother steps off the stone ledge. Jane squeaks, but her mother doesn't fall. She soars like a bird, swooping down to gather Timothy in her arms and carry him to where Jane stands. Timothy immediately plasters himself to Jane's side. She touches his head to reassure him and herself both and feels the sweat-dampness of his hair.

"Are you all right?" Jane asks. "You're not hurt?"

Timothy nods, then shakes his head in rapid succession, remaining buried against her side. Jane feels his muscles quiver as if they were her own.

"One more," her mother says with a wink, and she spreads her arms, jumping into the wind once again.

It's no less frightening this time, but Jane watches more closely now, allowing herself to be amazed as her mother's clothes ripple around her. She's studied the way birds' and bats' wings work, and this is nothing like that at all. It isn't even like a kite, gliding on the breeze. It's like nothing Jane has ever seen before. Her mother skims almost to the ground before she swoops back to the ledge with someone else wrapped in her arms.

Jane thinks it's a woman, but she can't make her out properly until her mother lets go and steps away. When she does, Jane can't help the startled kick of fear against her heart that makes her back up a step. The woman looks like the pictures of preserved mummies she's seen in books. Yet she's clearly alive, even though her skin is the color of bark, dried and clinging close to the bone. She looks fragile, as though she might crumble at any moment. Instinct makes Jane put a protective arm around Timothy, and she almost tells him not to look.

Even as she makes the motion, shame floods her. Her mother would never deliberately put her in danger. She specifically went back to bring the woman here. The feeling of shame turns to embarrassment as her mother gives Jane a pointed look. Jane makes herself let go of Timothy and move closer again, looking at the woman to show she isn't afraid, while also trying not to stare.

Fresh questions flood Jane's mind, but she holds her tongue. She's seen so many impossible things in Neverland. Maybe the woman really is a mummy. She wants to ask how it felt having her organs removed, and whether her brains were really pulled out with a hook through her nose, but every single question that pops into her mind seems terribly rude.

"This is Tiger Lily," Jane's mother says. "My friend."

Her mother emphasizes the last words, making Jane glad she did hold her tongue. She hopes the dark is enough to hide her blush. She isn't quite certain what to do next, and ends up with a clumsy curtsey, then holding out her hand.

"I'm very pleased to meet you, Miss Tiger Lily." Jane uses her most grown-up voice, hoping she doesn't sound too foolish, hoping she's made her mother proud.

Tiger Lily's eyes shine with amusement, making her appearance even more unsettling. She inclines her head, a stiff movement, as she takes Jane's hand. Despite Jane's fears, Tiger Lily's skin is smooth, if dry. The fingers don't crumble beneath Jane's touch, but there is a lightness to her bones as Jane shakes her hand, her grip nothing at all.

"Hello, Wendy's daughter." The faintest of smiles touches the woman's dry lips.

"I'm called Jane." She nudges Timothy, until he peeks at Tiger Lily shyly. "And this is Timothy."

"It's a pleasure to meet you, Jane." Tiger Lily releases Jane's hand. "And Timothy."

Jane looks to Timothy, fearing his reaction, but his attention has already drifted to her mother. The way he looks at her makes Jane's heart skip. There's something like awe, and something like fear as well. Jane also sees a hint of the expression Timothy wears when he's trying to remember something he's forgotten.

"I know you, I think. Do I?" Timothy asks.

Jane tenses, and some primal instinct she can't place makes her want to shout a denial. Timothy can't possibly know her mother, and his words open up a space inside Jane that feels like sinking and falling and flying all at once. Peter called her by her mother's name. Her mother knew where to find her, and how to get to Neverland, and Jane is afraid all over again of what it all means.

Her mother turns from examining the rocks around them and faces Timothy. Jane holds her breath, waiting to see what her mother will say. Wind buffets them, fluttering her mother's clothing. She looks at Timothy more closely, and once again Jane feels the creeping edge of fear that has nothing to do with immediate danger. There is something big and frightening that she can't quite see. She can only grasp at the edge of it, like a shadow vanishing around a corner. Her mother touches the top of Timothy's head, a troubled frown tugging at her lips, and she shakes her head almost imperceptibly.

"Maybe once," she says. "But not anymore."

Before Jane can ask what her mother means, her mother turns to point at the rock face above them.

"There. That's where we need to go. Take my hand. Everyone hold on tight as you can." Without looking back, she reaches for Jane's hand.

Jane hesitates only a moment, just long enough for her mother to look back with an expression that sets Jane's pulse going in a new and complicated rhythm. There's a fierceness to her mother's expression, one that seems to bristle at her orders being questioned. There's also tenderness, reassuring Jane, and beneath it all, a hint of fear.

Jane takes a deep breath and puts her hand in her mother's. She's already gripping Timothy's hand, and Tiger Lily takes her mother's other hand.

"Think of something happy," her mother says. But her expression is grim, and there's a twist to her mouth as she says it, which makes Jane wonder what happiness has to do with flying. She certainly wasn't happy the first time she flew here with Peter.

Maybe it's just about filling up all the spaces where doubt and fear might creep in and make you fall.

Just to be sure, Jane thinks of walking in the park, not just with her mother or her father, but both of them together, her hands in theirs and sunshine bright over all of them. She thinks of her mother making up stories, and her father pulling books from shelves to help Jane answer her latest round of questions. It's an ordinary thing, a safe thing. Right now, rather than adventures or wonders, it's what she wants more than anything in the world. The very ordinariness fills her with a happiness so big it makes her chest ache.

Her feet are no longer on the ground. Jane fights the instinct to panic and kick her legs. She grips Timothy's hand as hard as she can as wind rushes past them. Jane doesn't look down. Then their feet are on the ground again, and it's over too soon.

The wind still howls violently. Leaves kick up from trees that are far below them now, swirling in eddies. Her mother lets go and puts a hand on Jane's head instead, absently running her fingers through Jane's hair and picking out the tangles. After a moment, she begins separating sections, loosely braiding it in a way that makes Jane think her mother isn't even aware she's doing it.

"You've been very brave, Jane. Thank you." Her mother uses her grown-up voice, the one for important and serious conversations with Jane's father, and Uncle John and Uncle Michael. There's a weariness in her tone, one Jane doesn't miss. "I wish there was time to take you and Timothy somewhere safer, but there isn't, so I need you to be brave for a little while longer. Can you do that?"

Jane nods, a different kind of too-big feeling filling her. Her mother's hands still. Jane's hair is so stiff with salt and wind and her time in Neverland that the braid holds without even the benefit of a ribbon to tie it in place. Her mother meets her eyes briefly, then smiles, though Jane sees the hollowness behind it. Her mother is afraid.

Even so, she bends to kiss the top of Jane's head, and Jane allows herself to take comfort in it for the moment, and not think about what might come next.

"Everyone follow me inside."

Jane startles at her mother's words as much as her tone, brusque and commanding. Where is there to go? But as her mother leads them forward, she sees it—a narrow crack in the stone. And even as she notices it, she doesn't want to notice it. It resists her eye, making her want to look away, to unsee it, so that trying to hold it in her mind hurts physically. Her chest tightens, verging on panic. She's certain they'll smash against the rock when they try to enter, and everything in her wants to dig in her heels and refuse to go. Can't her mother see what a terrible idea this is?

But her mother has a hold of her hand again, and Jane has no choice but to follow as her mother slides through the too-narrow gap as easily as water. Before she has time to properly think about it, Jane is in the dark too, crammed between two bits of rock. It's warmer almost at once, and it's more than just being out of the wind. Sweat trickles down Jane's spine, and she fights not to wheeze, not to fully give into fear and let her breath go at a wild, ragged gallop.

Her back and stomach both scrape the stone, but if she stops inching sideways like a crab, she'll become wedged. She continues until the passage widens, gasping aloud in relief as she finds herself within a cave, lit by some source she can't see that produces a deep orange glow. The relief lasts only a moment. Deeper inside the cave, something rumbles.

She can't tell precisely where the sound comes from; it seems to come from everywhere, vibrating the stone underfoot and the ceiling overhead. Jane glances up, sure the cavern will collapse on them at any moment, but it remains solid. Comforted that they aren't in immediate danger, Jane allows herself to study the cave—stalagmites and stalactites like melted wax, rising from the floor, dripping from overhead. There are veins of what look like quartz running through the stone, but just like everything else she's seen in Neverland so far, the cave is a patchwork that makes no sense. Igneous and sedimentary and metamorphic rock all mixed together like pieces of a quilt.

Jane wishes she had time to study the cave properly, but her mother leads them on, peering into the darkened spaces between stone columns as if searching for something. She shakes her head and murmurs something to Tiger Lily, words too low for Jane to hear.

Jane glances at Timothy to make sure he isn't too afraid. His hand is still in hers, holding tight, and his eyes are wide in a mix of wonder and fear. There is something awe-inspiring about the cave, equal parts built and grown. She can't imagine anyone putting it here; it looks like the kind of place that's always existed. At the same time, the niches and shelves of rock seem too regular in places to be natural formations. Her mother points to a wide stone ledge.

"You and Timothy climb up there and stay out of sight." The spot is half hidden beneath an underhang, cloaked in shadows.

Jane opens her mouth to protest, but the set of her mother's jaw stops her. By now, Jane is certain her mother being here isn't one of Peter's tricks, but at the same time, Jane barely recognizes her. She looks and sounds the same as always, but there's something wild about her, something strange, as though the person she is in Neverland isn't the same as the one she is back home.

And her mother's expression reminds Jane more of Uncle Michael—haunted. But underneath that is anger. Maybe even rage. It leaves Jane afraid to speak, and paradoxically, it is what convinces her that this is her mother in truth. Nothing Peter could conjure up would ever be this fierce and so beautiful at the same time. Her mother looks like a warrior, a queen, something out of one of her own stories about the Clever Tailor and the Little White Bird.

Jane swallows her argument, and boosts Timothy ahead of her onto the rock. Once he has a hold, she scrambles up after him. As she pulls herself onto the flat ledge, a thought strikes her. What if, all this time, her mother's stories really were about her, the Clever Tailor, and the time she spent in a magical land?

The thought frightens her, and Jane pushes it away, turning so she's facing outward again. At least they can still see most of the cave from here. The faint orange glow seems to come from a place where the ground slopes downward. Whatever the source, it's in the part of the cave that's hidden.

"Wendy!" Peter's shout comes from the direction of the cave entrance. Jane tenses, pressing herself flat against the stone. She should have known Peter would find them here, but is he calling her, or her mother?

"It's—" Timothy starts, his voice too loud. Jane slaps a hand over his mouth, pulling him back into the shadows of the rock overhang.

Timothy squirms, and Jane hisses in his ear.

"Hush."

When he stills, Jane lets go. His breathing remains fast, his eyes wide in the dark. Peter must know by now that she stole Timothy, and now he's come looking for them both.

"I wish we had a weapon." Jane tries not to move her lips as she speaks.

"I have this." Timothy pulls a slingshot from the pocket of his ragged trousers, holding it out to her.

"You're brilliant." Jane would hug him, but the movement would be awkward on their platform. She settles for patting his shoulder. She still has the arrowhead she picked up from the path tucked into her sleeve. It fits perfectly into the leather sling, and she draws the weapon taut, sighting along her arm. She's never fired a slingshot before, but how hard can it be? Peter's boys surely aren't trained hunters, and yet she saw them take down a wild boar. The rules in Neverland are different, and so it stands to reason that Jane can be a marksman too, if she tries.

There's just enough light from the orange glow to allow Jane to see her mother standing with her hands on her hips, facing the entrance to the cave. She can't see Tiger Lily anymore, but Jane is certain she must be nearby. Shouts echo, bouncing around the stone, then Peter bursts through the crack in the wall followed by Arthur, and a boy whose name Jane can't remember. All three boys are armed with swords, but all three draw up short at the sight of her mother. Peter recovers first, jabbing an accusing finger in her direction.

"What are you doing here? You're not allowed."

"Yes, I am." Her mother's voice is steady. Jane edges forward, bracing Timothy's slingshot against the rock. "You invited me."

"You're a liar." Peter glares at her mother, his face scrunching up.

Jane's breath catches, a soft sound in the dark, but enough to make Timothy look at her. She shakes her head. Even if she could speak without being heard, what would she say? Her mother *was* here, in Neverland, and never told Jane a single word about it. Her mind whirls, but there isn't time to process everything and still pay attention to what's going on.

"Peter." Her mother doesn't raise her voice, and in fact it's quieter as she says Peter's name. Her tone makes Jane shiver.

"No!" Peter stamps his foot. "You're not my Wendy."

Jane isn't certain, but she thinks she sees her mother flinch ever so slightly. Peter's tone is petulant and harsh all at once, but he still has to tip his head back to look her mother in the eye. If they weren't in danger, Jane might almost find it funny.

Next to her mother, Peter looks like a spoiled and rotten little boy. But threat bristles in his posture, and she remembers how he stilled the boar and what he did to Rufus.

"I am Wendy, Peter. I told you before, I grew up."

"You're not supposed to do that. It's against the rules!"

"You wanted a mother." Jane's mother spreads her arms. Behind Peter, Arthur and the other boy shift nervously. "That's what I am. I'm a mother, and you took my daughter away."

The words swell inside Jane and her fingers cramp around the slingshot. She wants to make herself known. She wants to run to her mother and throw herself between her and Peter, but she doesn't dare interfere.

"She isn't armed," Arthur calls out, his voice going from

uncertain to bold in the space of a sentence. Jane hates him, more than she ever did before. Can't he see how wonderful and formidable her mother is? Can't he see she's someone to be feared? "And she's all alone."

Jane bites her tongue, keeping herself from calling out. She nudges Timothy beside her, cutting her eyes to him and trying to convey without words that they must be ready even as they keep themselves hidden.

"You're not going to hurt me, Peter." Her mother ignores Arthur, keeping her attention fixed on Peter.

Her mother steps toward Peter. Jane holds her breath. Then everything happens all at once.

Peter darts forward. Her mother lunges, just missing Peter as he twists away, laughing. Arthur and the other boy shout, brandishing their swords. They look silly—boys playing with toys—but at the same time, those toys are sharp. Sharp enough to kill and skin and hack apart a boar. Jane feels like a coiled spring. Movement catches her eye—Tiger Lily, circling around behind the boys—and she clamps down on a cheer.

Tiger Lily's sword touches the throat of the boy who isn't Arthur. He lets out a strangled cry as Tiger Lily grabs his shirt, yanking him backward. Beside Jane, Timothy fairly quivers with excitement, and Jane flashes him a grin.

"Peter! They got injuns!" Arthur shouts.

"That's not fair." Peter scowls. "You're cheating!"

The boy who isn't Arthur squirms in Tiger Lily's grasp. Keeping her own sword pressed against his throat, she releases his shirt long enough to take his sword and kick it away before moving him over to one of the rock pillars, holding him tightly.

Peter waves his own blade erratically, turning and turning, trying to face them both at once. When he turns their way, Jane can't help shrinking back into the shadows. His face is sharp and furious, but he also looks as though he might burst into frustrated tears at any moment.

"You're not playing the game right!" Under the spoiled, whining tone there's a dangerous edge.

While Peter is distracted, Jane watches her mother draw closer. But before she reaches Peter, Arthur barrels into her. Jane can't hold herself back. She lets out a shout, scrambling from the rock shelf and charging toward Arthur. Timothy slides down after her, and there's no time to tell him to go back.

"Leave my mother alone!" Jane pelts across the cavern floor and as soon as she's within range, she lets the arrowhead fly.

It strikes Arthur's shoulder. He turns, slapping at the spot as though insect-stung. It's enough distraction for her mother to twist herself around and throw him off.

"Jane!" Fear lights her mother's eyes. She holds out an arm and Jane runs to her. She meant to rescue her mother and be a hero, but it's gone all wrong.

"I tried to be brave," Jane whispers, hugging her mother tight.

"I know." Her mother buries her face in Jane's hair. "You were very brave."

"Ah ha!" Arthur is on his feet again, running.

At first Jane can't see what he's running toward, then she remembers—Timothy.

"Jane, help!" Timothy tries to get away, but Arthur's legs are longer.

Jane pulls away from her mother, ignoring the hands trying

286

to hold her back. She has to get Timothy; she promised to keep him safe.

"Leave him alone!" Jane wishes she had another arrowhead to shoot.

All she has left tucked in her sleeve is the tiny stone from Peter's soup, and that isn't enough to hurt a boy like Arthur. She considers using it anyway. But she's too late.

Arthur lunges forward with the point of his sword. All the breath goes out of her body, and Jane skids to a halt. The blood drains from Timothy's face. He stands perfectly still, eyes wide.

"Hooray. That's it, Arthur, you got 'im!" Peter claps, bouncing up and down.

Jane ignores Arthur and Peter both, ignores everything but Timothy as she rushes to him and grabs him by the shoulders. He presses his hands against his mid-section, but Jane can't see any blood. Arthur towers over him, grinning. Jane whirls around, hitting him as hard as she can. Caught off balance, he staggers, tripping over his heels and letting out a stunned grunt as he hits the ground. Blood spots Arthur's chin, and his hands fly to his nose. Jane turns her attention back to Timothy.

"Let me see. What happened?"

"I got kilt." Timothy's voice is a breathy whisper, his face so pale he looks like a ghost.

Jane's hands tremble, but she makes herself kneel to loosen Timothy's grip on his midsection as gently as she can. There's no blood. Timothy's shirt is whole even though she could swear she saw Arthur's sword go right through him. Relief floods her, and Jane laughs, the sound bubbling up through her like water from an underground stream.

"There's nothing. You're all right!" Jane throws her arms around Timothy, hugging him as tight as she can.

Timothy doesn't move, doesn't put his arms around her in return. When she draws back, his face is solemn.

"Arthur got me. I'm kilt now. I can't move. Those are the rules." There are tears in Timothy's eyes.

Jane stares at him, uncomprehending.

"But that doesn't make any sense. You aren't hurt. See?" She plucks at his shirt, showing it whole.

"Those are the rules," Arthur says behind her. His voice sounds funny and muffled.

He's still cupping his nose. When he draws one hand away it's smeared red, and Jane feels a nasty surge of satisfaction.

With Jane's arms no longer around him, Timothy sinks to the ground, drawing his knees up against his chest and hugging them.

"Get up." Jane is unable to keep the frustration from her voice. "There's nothing wrong with you!"

Timothy presses his lips together, his face a picture of misery. Jane wants to shake him. It's only a silly game. Why must boys be so infuriating?

"You. This is your fault." Jane lunges at Arthur with a clumsy swipe, ready to hit him again and break his nose for real. Even though he's still armed, he jumps back.

"Jane!"

At her mother's shout, Jane spins around. Her mother takes a step toward her, then freezes as Jane feels herself yanked backward, her feet going out from under her. Peter! She forgot about him. She kicks her heels, scrambling for purchase on the stone, but Peter's grip is unshakable.

"Let her go." Her mother's voice is hard, but Jane hears the tremor inside it.

"Stay where you are." Peter hauls Jane upright, flourishing his sword; there's glee in his voice.

Jane considers stomping on Peter's foot, but she's afraid he'll do something to her mother if she does.

"Let her go, Peter." Her mother's voice is firmer this time. Jane feels Peter tense.

"Leave her, and you can have me," her mother says.

"I don't want you anymore, you're... old!" Peter hurls the word like it's the worst thing he can think of, but there's uncertainty in his voice.

"I'm the only Wendy." Her mother takes another step. Jane tries to keep very still, but her heart betrays her, beating wildly.

"Mama, don't." Jane barely manages a whisper. Her mother can't really mean to give herself up to Peter, can she? Jane takes a shuddering breath, tears slipping free as fear and exhaustion catch up with her. All of this is her fault. If she hadn't gotten stolen in the first place, her mother wouldn't be here, and none of them would be in danger.

"Peter." Her mother's voice shifts again.

Jane stills, done feeling sorry for herself. She knows that tone; it is a tone that is not to be questioned or disobeyed. She's seen it work on her father, even her uncles, and certainly more than once Jane has felt its power for herself.

The look in her mother's eyes matches the tone, but it's so much worse. It's a look Jane has never seen on her mother before. Burning and dangerous and stealing the breath from Jane's lungs. It reminds her of the look Peter used to hypnotize the boar, to hypnotize her and make her take its meat.

"Let. Her. Go." Her mother separates each word, dropping it like a stone. Jane's legs tremble.

Peter's grip slackens, and she almost collapses as he lets go. Her knees want to buckle, but her mother is there to catch her. Instead of folding Jane in her arms, she holds her by the shoulders and looks her in the eye. It reminds Jane of the day in the park, and the girl who knocked her down.

"I need you to stay with Timothy," her mother says. "I need you to be brave one more time."

Jane wants to shake her head, but there's that look again, and she swallows her words. Everything is happening too fast. She only just found her mother, and now she's losing her all over again. Jane curls her fingers around the empty slingshot in her hand, needing something to hold. She's dangerously close to flying apart, her whole body vibrating even as she forces herself to remain still.

Her mother gives her one last assessing look. She wonders, suddenly, whether she looks different in Neverland too. Not as fierce as her mother, but changed. Her mother's hands slide from Jane's shoulders, and she steps away. Tiger Lily moves to stand beside her mother, dragging the boy who isn't Arthur with her.

"What now?" Tiger Lily asks.

Jane's mother doesn't answer. Jane wants to shout, tell her mother to stay here, because if her mother does whatever it is she plans to do, something terrible will happen. But she promised her mother she would be brave, and be good, and she promised Timothy she would protect him, and she intends to keep her promises no matter how much it hurts. She holds her tongue, watching with stinging eyes as her mother straightens and holds out her hand.

Jane is amazed when Peter approaches. He drops his head, looking very much like a dog that knows it's been naughty. She can't see if there's a sly expression on his face, but she suspects not. For this moment at least, he's just a little boy. Something big and complicated turns over inside Jane's chest. Her mother is *her* mother; she can't be Peter's mother, too.

Peter lets his sword fall. The sound of it clattering against the stone is the loudest thing Jane has ever heard. Peter reaches for her mother's hand. Their fingertips brush. Her mother's expression is set, steady, and at the same time there's a sadness just below the surface, so vast Jane can't begin to understand. A sob wants to break free inside her, but then so fast she barely has time to register it, her mother grabs Peter's ear, twisting it hard.

"Ow! You cheated! That isn't fair." Peter flails, clawing, but her mother ignores him.

She drags Peter close, her voice dropping to something low and ugly, almost unrecognizable.

"Life isn't fair. You learn that when you grow up."

Peter's cheeks color like he's about to cry. Jane's mother turns to Arthur, who stands slack-jawed and staring. Her mother gestures to the boy by Tiger Lily's side.

"Take him and get out of here." When Arthur doesn't move, Jane's mother lunges forward, her teeth bared. "Now!"

Arthur scrambles to obey, grabbing the other boy's arm when Tiger Lily lets go. They run, not even looking back at Peter. They're cowards, Jane thinks. She knows Peter has been beastly to them, but Arthur and the other boy are meant to be his friends. Shouldn't they have at least some loyalty to him? Or maybe that's the problem. Peter doesn't have friends, only people he orders around.

Timothy told her that Arthur and the others never remember the horrible things Peter does. If they did, would they be happy here? Maybe some part of them does remember, and that's why they run.

"Jane." Her mother speaking her name draws her attention. "Take those swords. I need you to guard the entrance."

"Yes, Mama." Jane bends to pick up Arthur's dropped sword. Something about Peter's blade makes her uneasy, and she doesn't want to touch it. She can't see where Tiger Lily kicked the other boy's sword, but it doesn't matter. Even if she handed one of the weapons to Timothy, he wouldn't take it, determined that he's been "kilt" by Arthur's sword all because of Peter and his ridiculous rules.

She wants to ask her mother what she means to do, tell her that this all feels wrong, but surely her mother knows. Surely after coming so far to find her, her mother would never do anything to put them in more danger. Moving on stiff legs, Jane crosses to stand next to Timothy. The sword feels strange in her hand, lighter than she expected, but still awkward. What if Arthur comes back and brings the others? What if she has to use the blade?

"No matter what you hear, don't come any deeper into the cave. Do you understand me?" Her mother's expression is the same she used to summon Peter to her side. Still caught in her mother's grip, Peter looks stricken, miserable. Jane swallows hard.

She nods, not trusting herself to speak; the look in her mother's eyes frightens her. What's deeper in the cave? What does her mother mean to do? Peter's eyes widen, his body ever so slightly trembling. He glances at Jane, and for a moment, his expression turns imploring, as though she might stand with him against her mother. Jane quickly looks away.

"Let's go." Tiger Lily tilts her head, indicating the direction of the orange glow.

A look of fear passes over her mother's face, lightning-brief, then she nods at Tiger Lily. Jane bristles. Why should this stranger go with her mother, while she must wait here? Jane glances down at Timothy. He's a small, pale shape in the dark. Her mother can take care of herself, but Timothy cannot. It isn't that Jane is abandoning her mother, or even the other way around. Jane lifts her chin, putting her shoulders back. She is choosing this. She will stay behind for Timothy.

She sits, putting her arm around him. Timothy's expression is grateful, but even so, Jane's heart sinks as she watches her mother and Tiger Lily drag Peter deeper into the cave.

"What do you think will happen now?" Timothy's voice is small, but Jane still startles. Even with his weight pressed against her, she'd nearly forgotten he was there, her mind so taken up with worry for her mother.

She resists the urge to ask him how he can talk if he's been killed, pointing out the illogic of Peter's rules once more. In truth, she's glad for Timothy's voice. It's something to listen to other than the sound of their breathing, the sound of her mother and Tiger Lily's footsteps fading into the dark. Jane shifts, trying to get more comfortable on the stone, but there's no comfort to be had.

"I don't know." It's the only answer she can give. She wishes she had even some idea of what her mother had planned, but she's at a loss. And she still can't shake the feeling something terrible is about to happen.

"Jane?" Timothy's voice is even softer than before.

She turns to look at him. He isn't looking her way but staring straight ahead. Something in his fixed expression makes his eyes look sunken, the shadows around them deeper. Even his body leaned against hers seems rigid and cold, and she has to force herself not to shudder.

"What is it?"

"I think I remember."

The way Timothy says the words makes Jane's heart flutter, like it's a live creature, jumping around in her chest and wanting to escape.

"Remember what?"

"Before I was here." His words are halting, and he continues to stare straight ahead. She doesn't want him to go on, but it would be unfair to tell him to stop just because she's afraid.

"You can tell me, if you want. If it would help."

Timothy's breath comes more rapidly, his shoulders hitching beneath the pressure of her arm. His expression is fearful, but at the same time, the words seem too big for him, too much to hold back.

"There was a little wooden boat someone made for me. We went to sail it in the pond at the bottom of the big field. The grass grew up so tall we couldn't see the house anymore."

Jane holds her breath, dread filling her. She wants even more now for Timothy to stop, but her tongue sticks to the roof of her mouth; she can't get it to work at all.

"The boat got caught. I thought I could reach it with a stick, but I slipped." Timothy trembles harder now. There's a glassiness to his eyes, as though he isn't seeing the cave, but a pond, surrounded by high grasses and weeds, and a little boat, trapped and struggling to get free.

Jane sees it too. She sees the moment Timothy slips on the slick mud and goes under. A hand reaches for his, only slightly bigger than his own, maybe an older brother, or even a sister. His arms churn at the surface, but his head keeps going under. Then doesn't come up again.

Jane's lungs squeeze tight, as though she too is drowning. Bubbles rise from Timothy's lips, already blushed the color of dark plums. There are weeds all around in the murky green, wrapped around his leg, holding him tighter than the hand that tries to grab his wrist and pull him free. She feels the scrabbling panic in her own chest, the cold closing in, the feeling of being terribly and utterly alone.

Then suddenly not alone anymore. Not a weed wrapped around his ankle, but a hand, pulling him down to the other side of the world.

Jane shoves the thought away with such violence it's almost a physical thing. That cannot be what happened. She refuses to believe. She's let her own imagination run wild. Timothy has a loving family back in England waiting for him, and they'll be ever so glad when she brings him home.

Jane wills her pulse to slow, letting out a shaky breath. She pulls Timothy closer, fitting his body against hers, even as it remains rigid. In this moment, Jane decides she would like to be a big sister after all. Not just any big sister, but Timothy's.

If they can't find his family then he'll come live with them, as simple as that.

"It's all right," she says, finally unsticking her tongue. She squeezes his arm to punctuate her words. "I've got you now, and you're safe. I won't let you fall ever again."

SHADOW PLAY

"You can't do this. Let me go." Peter is back to fighting and squirming in Wendy's grasp as she drags him deeper into the cave, even as his shouts fade to a whine.

Everything inside her is held in a delicate balance. She keeps putting one foot in front of the other, not looking at Peter. If she does, that balance will collapse.

There's a scent to Peter, above the struck-match-and-ash scent of this place—fear. A boy smell, like any other lost child. She must be the girl made of ice, the one who survived St. Bernadette's. She must be the mother who came all this way to find her daughter. Nothing else. She cannot be the girl who flew the skies of Neverland. And she certainly can't be Peter's friend.

"What are you going to do?" Tiger Lily asks. Her voice is soft, and Wendy glances her way. Tiger Lily holds herself alert, as if sensing the thing that awaits them without knowing precisely what it is.

"I'm going to put him back together," Wendy says.

Somewhere in the back of her mind, she's known ever since she stood at her window and looked out at the night. The part of her mind standing behind a locked door was still hers, and she knew, even though Peter tried to rip the knowledge away. She filled her pockets with everything she needs—needle and scissors and thread. It's the first thing that ever made her useful to Peter, and now she will finally stitch him whole.

Peter shivers in her grasp. Wendy lets go of his ear, taking his shoulders and turning him so she can see his face. He isn't crying, but his eyes are wide.

"You can't," he says again.

"I can, and I will. Look." They've arrived; she turns him again, making him face the thing in the sloping bowl of stone.

And she makes herself look as well.

The shadow creature is smaller than Wendy remembers. Still, when it snorts the ground shivers, and she has to force herself not to flinch away. The air around the monster shimmers with heat. Its edges are ragged and tattered, hard to see.

Wendy looks to Tiger Lily. Her friend's expression is difficult to read. The cavern's ruddy glow traces the seams of Tiger Lily's face, threading her skin with fire. If she's afraid, it doesn't show in her eyes.

Wendy keeps her hands on Peter's shoulders, holding him still, not allowing him to look away. He stares at the creature, and Wendy tries to guess what he's thinking. How long has it been? Does he still recognize his shadow? Does it recognize him?

"You don't have to stay." Wendy speaks to Tiger Lily without looking away from the creature, mesmerized.

Is she being cowardly? If she's wrong, if this kills Peter, or makes him into a monster entire, will Tiger Lily go with him? What about Neverland? Wendy's stomach tightens, fear and guilt knotting inside her. In Tiger Lily's cave, she swore she would

298

choose Jane if it came to it, and she will not back down. But now, with Tiger Lily at her side, staring down Peter's shadow, something cracks inside her.

Wendy sees them as girls again, alone among a sea of boys. Running, splashing each other in the stream, climbing, staging their own private wars and proving themselves every bit as fierce and adventurous as Peter and his small army. Telling Tiger Lily stories of London. Lying together in the grass and naming the stars.

She's seen Peter glance at Tiger Lily more than once, his expression puzzled, like he's trying to remember something lost. Does he even recognize her, who she used to be, and what he's done? Wendy thinks of the last time they were in the cave, claiming the bones she'd seen didn't belong to anyone. Is he really callous enough to hurt without memory, to not see the people he causes pain? If all his darkness is in the shadow then maybe it's true. Except she's seen the light in his eyes, the way it changes like liquid fire. Peter was always monster and boy both, she just never saw it clearly before.

Tiger Lily straightens. The fire-colored light surrounding the creature outlines her. She faces Wendy, and even in shadows, her eyes are bright. Wendy sees the woman Tiger Lily might have become, should have become, if she'd been allowed to grow up properly and not into this wasted thing. All at once, her guilt and fear are irrelevant. It isn't her choice to make. It's Tiger Lily's.

"Peter is my fight as much as yours. Maybe more." Tiger Lily's voice is no longer a wounded thing, wind soughing through trees. It is flint, striking sparks. "You left. I stayed."

A different kind of guilt knifes through Wendy. She left;

Tiger Lily stayed. But back then, what else could either of them have done? What choice did they have?

"All right, then." Wendy takes a deep breath. "It's far past time."

She loosens her grip, but not enough to let Peter escape, guiding him down the slope ahead of her. Tiger Lily follows, and Wendy tries to ignore the way her legs tremble. The creature turns its head to track their progress, looking at them in its eyeless way. It makes no other move, and Wendy thinks perhaps it can't, rooted in the very stone.

As they near the bottom of the slope, Peter stumbles. Instinct makes Wendy reach to catch him before she can think whether it's deliberate or accidental. The movement puts her off balance, and Peter uses it, rolling forward and letting his weight pull them both down. Wendy loses her grip as she tumbles. When she stops, she finds herself resting up against Peter's shadow. It is solid and insubstantial at once. Hot and cold. The absence of light and unbearably bright; she can scarcely look at it.

"Catch him!" she shouts to Tiger Lily, scrambling to right herself.

As Peter tries to crawl away from her, Wendy grabs his foot, hauling him backward. He screams, lashing at her with his other leg. Wendy dodges, barely avoiding getting kicked in the jaw. Peter's eyes shine wild, sweat streaking his face.

Time surges backwards as Wendy tightens her grip. Peter hasn't aged a day; he hasn't changed. She thinks of their positions reversed, Peter looming over her and bellowing in her face, demanding she look at him and look at his shadow. Demanding she love all of him, or not at all. Her fear then turns to anger now.

Keeping one hand on Peter's ankle, Wendy gets her other hand on the back of his neck. She lets go of his foot, hauling him up like a mother cat would a kitten. Her nails dig into his skin, and she ignores the noise Peter makes as they do. He squirms, but she turns him toward his shadow and thrusts him forward at arm's length.

"Look at it, Peter. Look at yourself. All of it. You can't hide from what you are anymore."

He tries to back away, but Wendy keeps her elbow locked, her fingers at the base of his skull to keep him from turning his head.

"It's your shadow, Peter. Look at him."

"You're lying." Peter's voice is small. He tries to pull away, and the piteousness of him almost breaks her, but Wendy keeps her grip firm. "You sewed my shadow back on. Remember, Wendy?"

His voice is a little boy's. She can almost believe it. For a moment, it is *all* she believes. She is the monster, not Peter.

"No." Wendy's voice quavers, doubting what she knows to be true. Tiger Lily's stories. The bones in this very cave. Peter himself had called the creature his secret. "He's yours, Peter. He's you."

Her palm slicks with Peter's sweat, and the sound he makes now is altogether more broken, a panicked hitching of breath, like he can't catch enough air. Petty triumph fills her. Wendy imagines her own head scraping the cavern ceiling, as obscenely tall and monstrous as Peter seemed to her all those years ago. Instead of snatching memory from him as he did to her, she wants to cram the truth down his throat, fill him with it until he's bursting.

Wendy yanks him backward, so roughly Peter falls, and she leans over him again, glaring into his face.

"You see?" Her lips pull back from her teeth; it is not a smile. "Do you see now what you are?"

She has no need to hold him anymore. Peter curls in on himself, so much smaller than her, transfixed and still. He is a wounded animal, but even so, Wendy's anger remains. She pulls it around herself like a cloak, allows herself to feel all of it. Despite the fear in Peter's eyes, or perhaps because of it, she wants to hurt him.

She is bigger than him, stronger, and she pins him with ease. By the cave's light, Wendy sees the silhouette of her hand fall across Peter's face before she even realizes her arm is raised to strike. Peter blanches, freckles standing out like spots of rust, spots of blood. He looks so young. He looks afraid.

Before he ever stole her daughter, he stole her. He stole years of her life. All that time she spent locked away, believing in him, refusing to give up, he never came for her. He ordered her to love him, but did he ever even think of her once when she was out of his sight? He'd wanted not a mother in truth, but the idea of a mother, like his idea of pirates and Indians, soldiers and war. Someone to tell stories and keep the monsters away. Someone to save him from himself.

He'd demanded love like a shield, without understanding that love can be a blade as well, cutting far sharper than any pirate's sword. Loving something means having something to lose, something that Wendy understands all too well and Peter never will.

All at once, the rage drains from her. Wendy lowers her hand. Peter breathes hard. What has he made of her? What has she become?

"Help me hold him." Wendy's voice shakes and she doesn't dare look at Tiger Lily.

Tiger Lily made no move to stop her when she raised her hand, but still Wendy is ashamed. She has to be better than this, better than Peter and his temper-born cruelty.

She forces herself to look at Peter, really look at him. The boy who wanted to show her wonders, who taught her how to fly. Tiger Lily kneels, bracing Peter's shoulders. Peter's eyes are so wide that in the blackness of his pupils, Wendy is certain she sees stars. She thinks of the mermaids, dead in their lagoon. She thinks of Peter laughing and holding her hand. There is good and bad in him, just like anyone else, only more extreme.

"Hush, now." Wendy brushes the hair back from Peter's forehead. She almost leans to kiss his brow, a mother soothing a child awoken from a bad dream, but stops herself. A small kindness is enough.

She takes the needle and the thread from her pocket. Her hands are remarkably steady. Tiger Lily watches her silently, and it only takes Wendy one try to slip the thread through the needle's eye. She leaves the rest trailing from the spool. How much will it take to join boy to monster, to make an ancient creature whole again?

The thought is idle. Wendy's mind doesn't rebel as much as it should. Here, now, at the end of all things, she is calm, filled with purpose. Peter stiffens, his breath quickening, but neither he nor the shadow resist her when she reaches for it. Touching it is like plunging her hand into icy water. The cold burns, but she's felt worse. She will survive this too.

Wendy tugs the shadow closer. The weight of a beast so huge should overwhelm her, but it flows over her hands and arms, rippling yet remaining solid. It is everything, and it is nothing at all. A lifetime ago, in the nursery, Wendy remembers how Peter shrieked when the needle first touched his skin. She remembers the moments before she made her first tentative stitch, matching up the ragged ends of the shadow with Peter's foot, and how it hadn't seemed to fit at all.

She'd only been a child, and it seemed so natural then, tugging at the strange un-substance, stretching it to fit while Peter waited impatiently. She'd even teased him, asking how a boy could lose a shadow in the first place.

"Oh, lots of ways," he'd replied. The response she'd taken for airy at the time is unnerving now, and she sees it edged with a smile less coy and more sinister. She thinks, too, of the bones in the cave, and Peter's dismissal of them being *someone*. Could he have stolen a shadow from another boy? And if he had, what would that theft do? She imagines a Lost Boy being lost in more than just name, separated from himself and wasting away, unraveling as the shadow Peter had first demanded she sew to his feet did as soon as they arrived in Neverland. How many boys over how many years?

"You'll be our mother when it's all done?" Peter had asked, once she'd gotten the shadow to behave, once he'd stopped his whining and begun to watch her work with interest.

Though her stitches were clumsy and uneven, at least it grew easier without his squirming around so, though she'd still had to chide him for fidgeting.

"I suppose." She'd barely paid attention to the question; it had all seemed a game—a boy who could fly, who appeared at the window in the middle of the night, promising adventure.

"Could you love a boy without a shadow?" The question

strikes Wendy now as it didn't then—again the slyness, the way Peter lowered his lids, his lashes almost touching his cheeks, and looked at her from beneath them.

"I suppose," she'd answered again, tongue between her teeth, concentrating.

"Because it might come undone again, but if you were our mother you'd have to love me anyway, wouldn't you? Even if I was bad?"

Had she looked up then, met his eyes? And if she had, what would she have seen? Something like the Peter before her now, frightened but defiant?

"Well, I shall just have to sew it extra tight so that doesn't happen, won't I?" Wendy remembers impatience, barely even listening to the words Peter had said, wanting the promised adventures, and not the work of stitching her mother had tried to teach her. If only she'd paid more attention. But how could she have known?

Peter watches her now, wide-eyed. She touches the needle to his skin, and unlike all those years ago, he does nothing but whimper.

Wendy steels herself, then pushes the needle through. As a child, she was innocent of horror, and there was no revulsion at pushing a needle through flesh. It hadn't seemed strange that a boy and his shadow might become un-joined, and it was the most natural thing in the world to put them back together again. Now, knowing better, she expects her hands to betray her, but they do not. The shadow doesn't resist her, yearning for the thread, yearning to be whole, its hunger guiding her steady touch.

With the second stitch, she feels the needle in her own skin— Dr. Harrington with his drugs to make her calm, to make her sleep. Trying to convince her Neverland was only a dream. With the third stitch, at last, Peter screams, whipping his head from side to side. Without Wendy having to ask, Tiger Lily bears down, holding him as still as she can.

Tiger Lily's jaw is set and hard. But Peter. Peter... Tears wet his cheeks, and his trembling is such it's impossible to keep her stitches straight and even.

Softly, so softly Wendy isn't even certain Peter will hear, she sings a lullaby. He wanted a mother. At last, she can give him this, if nothing more. What emerges is more breath than song, hitching and broken. She used to sing it to Jane when she woke from bad dreams. She used to sing it to Michael and John once upon a time too.

The rhythm of her stitching picks up. The stars in Peter's eyes wheel, silver fire. He makes no sound, but his lips shape her name. Wendy falters.

She could show him mercy. She believed him to be her friend once, after all. But the world already makes too much room for boys like Peter, boys who under normal circumstances grow up to be men like Ned's father, who start wars and send boys like Michael home broken. Boys who never face consequences. She can't be his mother, or protect him from what he is any longer.

Wendy pushes the needle in again. Neat little stitches join boy to shadow, monster to flesh. And as they do, she watches the memory rush back in, as violently as her own returned. It's like black ink swirling through Peter's veins, a visible thing. He bucks, shuddering, and the ground shudders with him. Stones bounce and rattle into the pit.

"Keep going," Tiger Lily says.

The strain in her voice makes Wendy look up, and she almost drops her needle. The seams in Tiger Lily's skin have split and widened. Light the same color as the bloody light filling the cave burns from within, and flakes of ash rise around her body. Wendy reaches for her, but Tiger Lily jerks back.

"No. Finish it." Tiger Lily grits her teeth. Her eyes are brighter even than her skin, and Wendy doesn't dare disobey.

The air around Tiger Lily shimmers like the air around Peter's shadow, capturing flecks of ash and drawing them back to settle on her cheeks, on her arms. Wendy sees the force of Tiger Lily's will, holding herself together. If she stops now, everything they've been through will mean nothing.

"Hold on." Wendy turns her attention to her stitching once more.

The cave shudders again, a chunk of stalactite breaking free to crash to the ground, narrowly missing her. She thinks of Jane and Timothy, hoping they're safe, hoping they aren't afraid. Peter's lithe body arches, trying to pull away from his shadow, trying to tear the stitches free.

Tiger Lily tightens her grip. Her hands smoke where they grasp Peter's shoulders, but she doesn't let go. Wendy braces herself. She asked Jane to be brave; she must be brave as well. She pushes the needle in, concentrating on making the stitches just the way Mary taught her years ago. She ignores everything, the crumbling stone, Tiger Lily burning, all her attention on Peter.

He's still the little boy he ever was—ancient and new and burning like a fever under her touch. It seems an eternity, but finally Wendy tugs the last stitch into place. She allows her hands to shake at last, fear and adrenaline catching up with her. She almost drops her little scissors as she snips the thread, making a knot. It is done.

Her hands fall back to her sides, exhausted. And from the other part of the cavern, Jane screams.

The sound rips through Wendy like lightning. She leaps up, forgetting her weariness, forgetting Peter, forgetting everything. She charges up the slope, but as she does, the stone buckles under her, knocking her down. Her knee strikes the ground painfully, and she bites back a cry. Gravity pulls her back into the bowl where Peter still lies shivering. Wendy ignores the throbbing ache, the feeling of her knee already swelling as she pushes herself upright. She uses her hands and feet both to claw her way over fallen and sliding stone. She has to get to Jane.

As she reaches the top of the bowl, Peter moans. Wendy looks back. It's only a moment, but it almost undoes her.

"Go!" Tiger Lily shouts.

But her eyes are only for Peter, and she can't tear them away. He lies curled on his side, shuddering, his monstrous shadow flared around him. It moves when he moves, irrevocably part of him. His eyes snap open, fixing on her. All the breath leaves her body. Wendy is flying for the first time, leaving the nursery far behind. She's plunging through the dark, and everything wonderful is about to happen. Nothing bad can ever touch her. She wants to run to him. To comfort him, even now. She loathes him for it, and loathes herself even more.

"Go. Now!" Tiger Lily's words snap Wendy back to herself.

Wendy looks to her friend as Tiger Lily gathers Peter in her arms. She stands, lifting Peter with her, dragging his shadow behind him. He weighs so much more now than he did before, and Wendy can see the strain, but Tiger Lily straightens, meeting Wendy's gaze, the set of her mouth a feral thing.

It's Tiger Lily's eyes that hold Wendy though. They are embers, daring Wendy to defy her. She is beautiful and terrible, still burning, still cracking, but not breaking. And all the while, everything inside Wendy is as fragile as glass. If she speaks Tiger Lily's name, if she says anything at all, she will shatter. And her daughter needs her. Wendy turns away.

The simple motion is everything, a wound deep at the core of her, but she cannot afford pity now—not for herself, or any other kind. She runs, as much as she's able, limping through the throb in her knee. Her pulse thunders, and the sound of it is a name: *Jane, Jane, Jane*.

The cave is still trying to rip itself apart. Above the chaos comes the broken sound of sobbing. It is a sound tied to every mother's heart, and it goes right to the core of her. Her daughter, crying.

Wendy puts on a last burst of speed. Relief almost steals her legs out from under her as she sees Jane crouched on the cavern floor. But something is terribly wrong.

"You have to get up," Jane says, voice tear-choked.

Wendy's pulse stutters. Jane is covered in blood, crimson smearing her arms, her nightgown. She struggles with a weight, Timothy, trying to haul him upright. His body is rag-doll limp. Wendy's heart lurches—callous gratitude. The blood is his, not Jane's. The wound from Arthur's sword, the one that was just a play-acted thing, is now horribly real.

"Mama!" The word pierces, all heartache, as Jane catches sight of her. The expression she turns on Wendy is utterly stricken.

Wendy has never seen such raw grief. With one look, Jane

begs her to make everything better, to fix it, but there's nothing Wendy can do. The knowledge wrenches everything inside of her. She wants to fall to her knees, hold Jane and take all of her hurt away. But she can't. The cave is still coming down around them, and if she spares Jane's feelings now, they will both die.

"Mama, you have to help him." It's there, the knowledge inside her little girl. Jane is smart enough to understand the truth, but right now, it's too much for Jane to hold. And she shouldn't have to, but Wendy can't afford to be kind. Not until they're safe. Not until they're free.

"No." The word drags rough from Wendy's throat. She should say something comforting, but there is no mercy left in her, no mercy left *for* her either. Because Wendy stitched Peter's shadow back to his skin; she made Timothy's wound real.

She knows what will greet her if she touches Timothy's throat. No rabbit-racing beat of pulse. No sluggish struggle for breath. No flutter of hope against her palm. Wendy makes herself look at the baby roundness of the boy's face, and burns the image in her mind. She doesn't know him, but maybe she did, once upon a time. A child. Just a little boy, younger than her daughter, lost and so very far away from home.

"Come away, Jane." Wendy holds out her hand.

Jane clings to Timothy even harder, staring at her mother as if looking at a stranger. At least Timothy didn't die alone; at least her daughter was there to hold him tight, maybe sing him a lullaby. It doesn't ease Wendy's heart any, knowing this, and if anything it makes it weigh more heavily inside her.

"We have to help him. I promised I'd keep him safe." Jane's voice breaks, shuddering as she gasps for breath.

Wendy closes her eyes. A moment. A breath. Against her lids, she sees Tiger Lily burning. Life is unfair, that's what happens when you grow up. She'd told Peter, now she has to swallow the bitter lesson herself. She opens her eyes. She can't hate herself for what she's about to do; Jane will do plenty of hating for both of them, but only if they survive.

The ground heaves, nearly throwing Wendy from her feet. Her knee throbs, her bones feeling like they're grinding together as she takes a step to steady herself. A fissure splits the stone, cracks crazing the walls and floor. There's no more time.

Wendy grabs her daughter's arm, perhaps more roughly than she needs to. Jane screams, not terror but the sound of rage and a breaking heart. Wendy knows what it is to promise someone you won't let anything in the world hurt them and to fail. She throws Jane over her shoulder. Jane alternately beats her fists against Wendy's back and reaches for Timothy. Wendy takes the blows; there is nothing else to do.

She carries Jane from the cave. The journey through the narrow passage is over in a blink, even with the rolling ground and world trying to shake apart. Even with Jane's weight draped over her shoulder.

When she steps outside, cool night air slices Wendy's skin. The moon is still full, but now it has a bloody hue. All around it, the dark itself falters, cracks riddling the space between the stars. Jane lies limp against her, exhausted of her anger, weeping silently.

"Second star to the right," Wendy murmurs, hoping it's true in reverse, hoping that happy thoughts indeed have nothing to do with flight. "And straight on until morning."

311

There is no time now for doubt and regret. Holding her daughter as tight as she can, Wendy leaps into the wind, up into the sky, leaving Neverland behind one last time.

HOME

LONDON – ONE DAY AFTER NEVERLAND

Shadows crowd the corners of Jane's room. She's home, surrounded by all her things, but none of them feel right—the butterflies pinned in their cases, the neatly labeled rows of pressed leaves and polished stones. Empty. Lifeless. They might belong to some other girl, and she is merely here, an imposter inhabiting that girl's room. The curtains on her window, the covers on her bed, the dollhouse her grandfather gave her for her birthday when she was five—how can objects she's been surrounded by for years be at once so familiar and so strange?

She sits up, knees tucked against her chest, arms wrapped around them, and surveys the space carefully. She almost misses the sounds of boys sleeping, the tense waiting filling Peter's camp. A particular clot of shadows in the corner beside the dollhouse catches Jane's eye, and she starts. For a moment, it resolves into the shape of a boy, eyes moon-wide and trusting. Timothy.

Then the shadows are only shadows again and the momentary hope crushes her. Her chest aches with waiting tears. But she's already cried so many times already, and she's sick to death of

313

weeping. Anger chases hard on the heels of her pain, rising up and leaving her cheeks hot.

Her mother could have saved Timothy, and she refused. She left him instead of going back. She left them both in the first place. If she'd stayed rather than dragging Peter deeper into the cave, Timothy would still be alive.

The door to the hallway edges open, and Jane starts again, catching at the covers. Her mother's face peers through the gap, and Jane's first instinct is to turn away, refuse to talk to her. But at the same time, questions crowd her tongue, and there's no one besides her mother that Jane can ask.

Her mother enters, closing the door softly, and sits on the edge of Jane's bed. Her expression is drawn, tired. She looks smaller than the woman Jane saw in Neverland, the woman she imagined a figure out of one of her mother's own fairy tales.

After a moment, her mother takes Jane's hand, and Jane allows it. They sit in silence, her mother stroking the back of Jane's hand. Like the objects in her room seeming strange and familiar at once, her mother seems both close and miles away.

"Why?" It's the only question Jane can manage, out of all the choices tumbling through her mind, and her mother looks stricken the moment Jane speaks it aloud.

She drops Jane's hand, and looks up, meeting her eyes. Jane pushes, feeling for just a moment vindictive and cruel. Timothy's death is her mother's fault; her mother should know that. And if her mother accepts the blame, if she lets it hurt her, then perhaps some of the ache in Jane's own chest will ease just a little bit.

"What happened? Why did Timothy die? He wasn't hurt at all, and then you took Peter away, and…" Jane's breath hitches.

She's run out of words. If she speaks again, the tears will come, and she's done with crying. She presses her lips together, holds her mother's gaze, and waits.

"Oh, Jane." Her mother reaches as if to touch Jane's hair, but lets her hand fall.

Even in her anger, Jane regrets the missed contact. She wants to lean into her mother's hand, be petted and told everything will be okay. Lines at the corners of her mother's mouth and eyes drag her whole face down, making her look years older than Jane has ever seen her. Jane regrets her question, but she will not take the words back. After so many years of secrets, she has the right to know.

She expects her mother to resist, to put her off, or spin another pretty lie like her stories of the Clever Tailor and the Little White Bird. Instead, her mother folds her hands carefully into her lap and straightens her spine.

"I'm sorry, Jane," she says. "You deserve the truth, and I always should have given it to you."

She meets Jane's gaze. Even in the darkness, Jane sees the gravity in her mother's expression. She feels it too. Regret, not just for what has passed but what will pass. Tucked up in her bed, Jane is suddenly on the edge of a threshold. Once she passes it, there will be no going back. Her mother is prepared to treat her as an adult, and it hurts her to do so. Is this what Jane wants? She almost opens her mouth to take it back, but she closes it again, presses her lips into a determined line, waiting for her mother to speak.

And she does. She speaks of a night when she was not much older than Jane and a boy came to her window holding a shadow in his hands and asking her to sew it back on. She unfolds a tale Jane can scarcely believe, not for the fantastic idea of traveling to another world, for she's done that herself, but for what came after. How her mother was disbelieved. Locked away. Punished. All because she refused to deny Peter. When she came out of the place where she was kept, secrets were all her mother knew. Jane hears the pain in her mother's voice—the places where it grows rough and breaks. She blames herself for Jane being stolen.

It's too much. Jane is a vessel, overfull, on the point of flooding. Her head aches and she feels displaced—not the way it felt with Peter's strange, sticky-sweet tea, but as though she's been crying for hours and it's left her hollow inside. Only her eyes are dry, burning in the dark as she tries to hold onto everything her mother has told her and make sense of it.

And the words aren't even done yet. Her mother tells Jane of Peter's true shadow, of sewing it back on, and making the boy and the monster into one. She tells her of making death in Neverland real.

At last, when her mother has run out of words, she lifts a hand and places it on Jane's own. Jane doesn't pull away, she's too stunned.

"I know I'm asking too much of you, Jane, to take all of this in at once. But you've been there. You met Peter. You know." Her mother's voice is soft, and there's a weary slant to her shoulders.

Jane glances toward the window, trying to gauge the position of the moon. How long has her mother been talking? Time has been strange ever since they returned, as though a bit of Neverland's magic followed her back here. It feels as though Jane only blinked, and the cave in Neverland became her bedroom, as though no time passed at all. It feels as though they were gone for weeks, but she understands that in London, it was only just two days. It doesn't seem possible, but sometimes the world passes slower here, and sometimes faster—her mother explained that too, with a sad weary smile.

"We should count ourselves lucky, Jane. We didn't miss too much while we were gone."

The way her mother says it, Jane knows it isn't really a matter for smiling over, and she knows her mother knows that too.

"You know, I've kept this secret for so long, you're only the second person I've told," her mother says when all the other words are done.

"Papa?" Jane asks.

Her mother shakes her head, a look of regret crossing her face.

"Mary," her mother says. "Cook."

She lifts Jane's hand, places it palm to palm with her own atop the covers, then presses it again with her other hand, closing Jane's hand between her own.

"Your papa doesn't know yet. I plan to tell him very soon, but until then, I would appreciate it if you would keep my secret for a little longer. I know it isn't fair to ask."

It seems like her mother will say more, but she doesn't, letting the words hang, acknowledging the unfairness and doing nothing to right it. Jane isn't certain what her mother has told her father about where they've been. Last night—or maybe a lifetime ago—when she was meant to be sleeping, tucked into bed after the warm bath she'd so longed for while she was in Neverland, she'd heard snatches of words not meant for her ears.

"… *shouldn't have gone without telling you … so afraid.*"

"… how could she have left the house … gone so far alone? What will we tell Scotland Yard … brothers, and my father?"

"… on a little adventure. You know how curious and strong-willed she is … what we will tell them. … home. That's the important thing. Jane is home safe, and that is all that should matter."

Jane's hand tenses between her mother's, but her mother holds her hand tight, not letting her pull away just yet. Her expression is grave again, and again Jane feels it like a physical thing pressing down on her.

"I promise you, Jane, as soon as I've spoken to your father, I will never ask for your silence again. You may speak to anyone you choose to about Neverland—your father, Cook, me, even your grandfather." A look of fear flickers through her mother's eyes, but she goes on.

"You may ask me any questions you like, and I will always give you the truth. No more secrets. And you may take that truth with you out into the world, anywhere you like, but understand, Jane—it is a choice."

Her mother increases the pressure of her hands around Jane's, then lets her go. Jane's skin chills in the absence of her mother's touch. She thinks of her mother in the terrible place she described, the asylum called St. Bernadette's. She understands the choice her mother is giving her, and it's no choice at all. To tell the truth and be called a liar, or to hold back the truth and lie to everyone she knows.

And it isn't only herself she has to worry for, but her mother. Jane senses it in the look in her mother's eyes just now when she mentioned Jane's grandfather, senses it was there too in the words she overheard between her mother and her father. If she tells the truth, Jane will not only risk hurting herself, she will risk hurting her mother, too.

It isn't fair, because the world isn't fair, but perhaps that's what it means to grow up. Not just the opportunity to learn more about the world, to become a scientist as she's always dreamed, but to face disappointment, to hold secrets of her own, to choose between right and wrong, trying to do what is best with only her own instinct to go on, even knowing she might fail.

Jane doesn't want any of this weight, and she isn't certain what she'll do with it, but it's too late not to carry it at all. She has crossed the threshold, and the door is closed behind her. She cannot un-know what she knows, and she hates it. She can't bring Timothy back. She can't tell her father the truth when he asks her where she's been, not yet. She must keep secrets from her uncles, especially her Uncle Michael, because the truth would only hurt them. Worst of all, she cannot trust her mother, not fully, and yet she is the only person Jane can trust. She is the only person Jane can speak freely with, because she is the only one who will understand.

Jane wants to push her mother away, suffocated by the knowledge that has been handed to her. At the same time, she wants to throw her arms around her, and beg her to stay close. She's afraid of the shadows in her room, of seeing Timothy again, of fingers tapping on her window and calling her out into the dark.

Jane doesn't say anything at all.

After a moment, her mother stands. She smooths down the front of her skirt, and sighs. She leans forward and kisses Jane's forehead. Her lips are dry.

"It's almost morning," her mother says, and her voice is indescribably weary, sadder than Jane has ever heard it before. "Even so, you should try to sleep, if you can."

Her mother takes something from her pocket and sets it on one of the many shelves lining Jane's room. The object makes a soft click. When her mother steps back, Jane sees it's an arrowhead, like the one she used in Timothy's slingshot to shoot at Arthur. Her mother has set it beside the one Cook gave to her, but only the one her mother set down glitters strangely in the dark. Her mother's fingertips brush the knapped stone, her expression one of loss, then she turns away.

Jane watches her mother cross the room. She hesitates a moment, looking back with an expression Jane cannot read. It's almost as though she is trying to puzzle Jane out, as though she's a stranger her mother has never seen before. Jane thinks she understands. Her mother steps into the hallway, and pulls the door fully closed, stealing the light. It's the first time Jane can ever remember her not leaving the door ajar, and the room seems so much darker in her wake. Only the faint light of the city, and the mundane light of the moon and stars—never as bright as in Neverland—will keep her company until the sun rises again.

Jane climbs out of bed, kneeling and reaching into the space between the mattress and the frame. She pulls free a small stone, the one from Peter's soup, the one she nearly swallowed on her first night in Neverland—at least the first night she properly remembers. She holds it a moment in her palm. It looks like such an innocent thing. The way a monster can look like a boy, or a smile be a dangerous thing. She closes her fingers around it, letting the stone dig into her skin as she crosses to the spot her mother stood a moment before, setting the stone next to the arrowhead from Neverland.

She hasn't decided what truths or lies she'll tell to others yet, but there's one thing Jane is certain of—she will not lie to herself, and she will always remember.

LONDON – TWO DAYS AFTER NEVERLAND

Wendy sits in the window bay overlooking the street. She runs her hands over her skirt, touches her sleeves. There are no secrets hidden there now; the time for secrets is done. She rubs absently at her knee, the pain almost faded. She folds her hands into her lap, but they immediately want to fly away again. It's an effort to keep them still.

It's been two days since she returned from Neverland with Jane. Two days, and she still hasn't found the right words to speak to Ned. She'd told him that she'd found Jane lost among the trees, a half-truth, letting him assume she meant the park. She had not had to pretend to be exhausted, or terrified. She had been all of those things, her emotions catching up to her all at once—fear and grief, but also joy at having Jane home. It had left her drained, and she had pled for time.

Part of her wants to lie sick in bed like when she first returned from Neverland all those years ago. Let fever wrack her. Let her loss manifest physically. But she is a mother now; she has responsibilities, and she cannot hide from them.

Wendy had promised, if Ned would give her a little time to recover herself, she would tell him everything, which she fully intends to do. But that doesn't mean she isn't afraid. She and

Ned have always been partners, but now she sees suspicion and doubt in his eyes. And Jane—she can't quite read her daughter's expression; she only knows that it hurts to look at her in a way it never did before.

That isn't even the end of the lies and half-truths piled up against her skin, weighing her down. She must think of her brothers and her father-in-law. The story Wendy holds in her mind is that Jane crept out of the house at night, intent on having an adventure all on her own. But then she'd gotten confused and uncertain how to find her way home, and she'd been afraid of getting in trouble, so she'd hid until Wendy had found her. It makes her daughter sound flighty and foolish, two things which Jane is not, but as much as it pains her, Wendy is certain that her father-in-law especially will believe it. Girls are fanciful creatures after all, without much sense in their heads, no matter what their age.

Her brothers might have more doubt, but their own determination to forget might save her for once. It will be easier for them to swallow her lie than accept the truth.

Which only leaves Ned. At the end of the day, Wendy doesn't truly care whether or not her father-in-law or her brothers believe her. The belief and trust she wants is from Ned.

Wendy glances toward the hall. She won't have the house to herself for much longer. All the truths will have to come out of her soon.

She looks at her hands. The minor cuts and scratches she and Jane both received fleeing the cave, the ones Wendy barely felt at the time, are almost gone. It's likely they won't even leave scars. She should be relieved. Instead, there's only a kind of hollow numbness. It isn't like the hollowness she lived with for years, the sense of something missing where Peter tore her memory away. This is the ache of a thing she knows should be there and now is gone, like a trinket or a photograph meant to sit on the mantelpiece, broken beyond repair.

The last two nights, Wendy has sat at the window long after everyone else went to bed, straining to pick out the second star to the right from the sky's darkness. All the stars look the same to her now, and she's searched within herself too, reaching after the ragged fragments of Neverland. She can't feel it anymore. It isn't gone, but she can't touch it. Either it's changed, or she's changed, or both. Either way, a door has closed, and she fears no amount of picking at the lock will ever open it to her again.

Even the memories that sustained her all through her time at St. Bernadette's have begun to fracture. When she closes her eyes now, she sees Tiger Lily burning. She sees Peter with his tattered shadow trailing behind him, monster and boy rolled into one. She chose Jane, and she would never choose differently given a thousand lifetimes, but that doesn't ease the hurt.

Some part of her always believed Neverland would be there for her forever, an escape if she ever needed it. Now that way is barred to her, and she must live from here on out in one world alone.

Outside, trees stir against a clouded sky. Despite the threat of rain, Ned and Jane went for a walk. Wendy doesn't blame either of them for not wanting to be cooped up in the house with her. Ned has been patient with Jane, but Wendy knows it must be a strain on them both. She'd gently explained that Jane had been frightened, that she needs time, and that she will talk to Ned when she is ready, but the hurt in Ned's eyes as she'd said it had almost undone her.

The truth had almost come rushing out then, but she'd been a coward. What if Ned doesn't believe her? And what if he does? How will their lives change?

She watches the leaves shiver, flipping to show silver undersides to the wind. There is a storm coming. She wants to trust Ned, trust that if she gives him this secret he'll be strong enough, kind enough, to forgive her. But what if it's a bridge too far? What if it's too much to ask after he gave her his heart, placed his letters from Henry into her hands and with them all of himself, while she refused to do the same.

Wendy thinks back on that first night with Ned, their wedding. It seems a lifetime ago. They'd been strangers, but Ned had reached across the gap, taken a chance on her. She's never given anyone his secret, but is withholding her own worse?

After reading the letters, Wendy had asked Ned whether there had ever been anyone besides Henry, and he'd told her no. Awkward and blushing to even think of it, she'd told him she wouldn't mind if there was. He'd told her the same, and they'd laughed together at their nervousness, their embarrassment. That was the moment, Wendy thinks, that she'd begun to love him. Not as a husband, but as a friend. One of her best friends.

Those early days of their relationship had been a careful negotiation, but never had things turned bitter between them. There had been no jealousy. They rarely fought. Tension only ever came with his father's presence in their home, and then he was a shadow over them both.

They'd even entered into parenthood the way they had

entered into their marriage, as partners. When Jane had arrived, she'd increased the love between them. Mary had taken to Jane immediately, too, just as she'd taken to Ned. She became something like a sister to Ned, something between a sister and an aunt to Jane.

When she was young, Wendy and Ned had carefully instructed Jane to call Mary by the title Cook rather than her name, lest she slip up when Ned's father was around. It hurt Wendy's heart to do it, but Mary, for her part, had seemed amused. Alone in their home, Mary had them all in gales of side-splitting laughter with her spot-on impression of Ned's father. Together, they were happy. A family by choice.

And even so, through all the years, Wendy held Neverland close and never let a bit of it go. Not to her daughter. Not to her husband. Even now she isn't certain why. A childish thing, a desire to hold some part of herself in reserve, to control her truth after so many years of lies? Or were her motives worse? Had a tiny part of her left her daughter unguarded, bait, in hopes that Peter would return?

A sound at the parlor door draws Wendy's attention. Mary enters carrying a tray laden with tea. She sets it down and sits, and Wendy reaches automatically for the pot, pouring for both of them. It's a moment before Wendy notices the uncharacteristic straightness of Mary's posture. The weight of words hangs about her, and Wendy's stomach clenches even before Mary opens her mouth.

"This isn't a good time for this, but there won't be a good time, really," Mary says, blunt and forging onward. "A place has recently come up for sale that would be perfect for my shop. I know it isn't the best time to open up a business, but I've saved up most of the money I need, and the location is too perfect to let go. I've already spoken to Ned, and he's agreed to help me talk to the bank to get me a loan for the rest. I'm not officially giving you my notice yet. The place will take a while to get ready, but I just wanted you to know now rather than later. I like to get unpleasant conversations over as quickly as possible."

Mary keeps her gaze locked on Wendy's, her mouth twisting in a wry smile at her last words. Even now, Mary is needling her, and she knows Mary is right—unpleasant conversations are best gotten over with as quickly as possible, rather than leaving them to fester. At the same time, Wendy sees the brave face on the words, the fear behind them. She knew this day would come; it's long past time, and yet she still can't help feeling as though another part of her is being ripped away.

Wendy had been heartbroken enough when earlier this year Mary had expressed her desire to move into a small rented room of her own. She'd come to Ned and Wendy both with her plan, assuring them she could afford the rent and still set aside money to build the life she wanted for herself, everything balanced out. Mary living with them was always meant to be temporary. Wendy understood, of course she did—Mary had never had a life and space of her own, carried by her mother's marriage across the sea, locked away in an asylum. Now Wendy thinks perhaps Mary had been trying to prepare her for this moment, making her departure by degrees so it would hurt less for both of them.

"It won't change anything," Mary had told her then. "We're still family."

Wendy had struggled to believe it then. She struggles still

to believe it now. But once upon a time, she had believed she wouldn't survive leaving St. Bernadette's and not seeing Mary every single day. She had survived that, and their relationship had only grown stronger. She will survive this too, and it will be the same. Living apart from them, working apart from them, living her own life fully—it is what Mary deserves. And Wendy trusts that Mary will still choose them, they will choose each other, as they always have. The love that binds them all now will keep them together, always. "Actually," Mary says, looking down at her hands, "I've had the money for a while, but I've been a coward."

If Mary has been a coward, then Wendy has been a bigger one. She's leaned on Mary for too long, and if Mary leaned back, it was never as heavily.

"You'll be brilliant." The words come too fast, and Wendy feels tears wanting to rise. "I mean, you taught me to cook, after all. If you can do that, you can do anything."

She laughs, or tries, and the sound breaks her. She wipes her eyes.

"I'm sorry. I'm happy for you, I really am. It's what you've always wanted."

Mary sets her cup down, still untouched, and shifts closer, resting her forehead against Wendy's.

"This doesn't change us," Mary says.

"No." Wendy shakes her head slightly. There are tears in Mary's eyes too. "It doesn't."

That's what happens when you grow up. Wendy hears her own words to Peter come back to her, mockingly, and she almost laughs again, a bitter, broken sound.

"Hey." Mary's voice is soft; she nudges Wendy's forehead with her own.

The years drop away and they're back at St. Bernadette's. Everything is still in front of Wendy, and for a moment, she almost wishes she could go back. How was she to know that motherhood, that loving someone as much as she loves Jane, Mary, Ned, would be far worse than anything the asylum could ever offer?

"What if she hates me forever?" Wendy asks. It isn't where she meant to begin, but the words come out anyway.

"You're her mother," Mary answers, no answer at all.

When Wendy doesn't respond, Mary draws back, rolling her eyes.

"You keep on loving her and you keep on fighting for her, because that's what mothers do."

Wendy's skin warms, as surely as if she'd been slapped. Mary knows Jane nearly every bit as well as Wendy and Ned, maybe in some ways better. She's been there since the beginning, during those first sleepless nights as Wendy paced the floor with the new weight of Jane against her shoulder, exhausted and singing lullabies. She heated milk on the stove for them both, and whispered stories when Wendy's own voice gave out—the same stories she used to tell in St. Bernadette's, of Blood Clot Boy and the Bear Woman and the Sacred Otter.

Wendy remembers how Mary's eyes shone. Did Mary think of her own mother when she told them, or of her baby sister who had died as she was being born? If anyone knows what Wendy should do now, how to find the way through the rift she's created between herself and Jane, it's Mary.

Keep on loving her. It's that simple, and that complicated.

Love. Fight. Never back down. It's time for her to grow up, truly. It's time to fight for Jane, for Ned, for Mary, even for Michael and John. She will not give up until she's found a way to make things right, undo all the hurt she's caused in Neverland's name.

After a moment, Mary lifts a scone filled with cream and jam, holding it to Wendy's lips.

"What do you think? I've been tinkering with the recipe. I thought maybe instead of just a bakery my place could be a tea shop, too. I could put these on the menu."

Despite herself, Wendy takes a bite, not caring that crumbs and a dollop of jam fall onto her skirt. The scone is buttery, melting in her mouth, the jam sweet but not overly so.

"Perfect."

Mary sets the rest of the scone aside with a satisfied smirk.

If you had your choice in leaving, where would you go? Would you go back to Neverland? Mary's words from years ago, sitting under the tree on St. Bernadette's lawn, return to Wendy. She'd called Neverland a lie then. She thinks of Timothy's broken body, of Peter curled beneath the weight of his shadow. The door is closed to her, but if it remained open, with the truth of it laid bare, would she return? She'd claimed to want that truth, but perhaps Neverland was better off broken, better off without her interference. She'd put it back together, but too late to save the mermaids, to save Tiger Lily. She'd stitched the pieces one to the other, but that's not the same as healed, or whole.

Mary nudges Wendy's shoulder, bringing her out of her reverie. At the same moment, Wendy hears the front door open, Jane and Ned returning.

Her heart beats a complicated rhythm. Mary gives Wendy a

look as she withdraws, taking the tea things with her. It takes all of her will, but Wendy stands, brushing away a cascade of crumbs. Her chest is so tight, she can barely breathe. The whole house waits, holding its breath. It's time to grow up. Past time, really.

Wendy thinks of the first time she flew, holding Peter's hand, falling into the sky and waiting to see if the wind would catch her. It has to be the same now; she must believe that when she steps into the unknown, the love, the family, the life she's built for herself will be there to catch her. She may have lost Neverland, but she stands to gain so much more. A life without secrets. The truth laid out between her and Jane and Ned. It is the same with Ned and Jane as it is with Mary. In order to truly choose each other, there cannot be secrets. Once Ned knows who she truly is, Wendy has to believe that he will still choose her, and they will continue to love each other as they always have. The way she chose him when he gave her the secret of Henry. It will bring them closer together than they ever were.

She can do this. Wendy Darling, the girl who learned to fly, who survived, who refused to be afraid.

Wendy lifts her chin, straightens her spine, and steps into the hall where her husband and daughter are waiting. Ned and Jane look to her, expectant, wary. Wendy tries to smile. She opens her mouth to speak, the truth gathered up and heavy on her tongue, ready to step into the sky, trusting she won't fall.

Acknowledgments

This book started as a joke. Well, not a joke exactly, more like a *"ha, ha, what if I wrote..."* and I didn't tell it to anyone but myself. But I did write a flash fiction story, because of course that is the most logical place to start when writing a novel. My first thanks are due to Michele-Lee Barasso and Jonathan Laden who published the original short story "Wendy, Darling" in *Daily Science Fiction*. Without them, this novel would not exist. My second thanks are due to everyone who read that original short and responded positively, who let me know how much they loved Wendy, and that they wanted to know more about her story. Their enthusiasm helped me realize there was indeed more to Wendy's story, and that I very much wanted to tell it. My thanks, always, to A.T. Greenblatt, Stephanie Feldman, Fran Wilde, Sarah Pinsker, Siobhan Carroll, and E. Catherine Tobler for patient reading, amazing feedback, and wonderful friendship. This book would not exist without them either. Thank you to my agent, Barry Goldblatt, who believed in Wendy from the start, and my incredible editor, Sophie Robinson, who saw Wendy and truly understood her. My thanks also to Jo Harwood, Hayley Shepherd, and the entire team at Titan Books for helping to make Wendy's story shine, and making the book look absolutely beautiful. Thank you to Matt and Amy Bush for years of laughter and wonderful friendship. Thank you to my husband, Derrick, for everything, and for being the best partner in life I could have asked for. Thank you to my entire family, for believing in me, supporting me, and being enthusiastic cheerleaders even when the stuff I write isn't exactly their kind of thing. I am so lucky to have all of you in my life. Finally, thank you to J.M. Barrie for his enduring tale of a boy who refuses to grow up and all the threat and darkness that implies.

A.C. Wise is the author of two collections published by Lethe Press, a novella published by Broken Eye Books, and short stories appearing in publications such as *Uncanny, Tor.com*, and *The Best Horror of the Year Volume 10*, among other places. Her work has won the Sunburst Award for Excellence in Canadian Literature of the Fantastic, as well as twice being a finalist for the Nebula Award, twice being a finalist for the Sunburst Award, and being a finalist for the Lambda Literary Awards. In addition to her fiction, she contributes semi-regular review columns to *The Book Smugglers* and *Apex Magazine*.

@ac_wise
www.acwise.net

For more fantastic fiction, author events,
exclusive excerpts, competitions, limited editions and more

VISIT OUR WEBSITE
titanbooks.com

LIKE US ON FACEBOOK
facebook.com/titanbooks

FOLLOW US ON TWITTER AND INSTAGRAM
@TitanBooks

EMAIL US
readerfeedback@titanemail.com